TRUE CRIME

"Big, scary fun. Fill up the coffeepot and lock the doors before beginning."

—Stephen King

"Time flies when you're having fun, waiting to die, or reading *True Crime*, Andrew Klavan's nerve-plucking suspense novel."

—*The New York Times Book Review*

"One of the best novels to come down the pike in years . . . so gripping and plot-switching that you won't be able to put it down."

—*USA Today*

"The narrative plunges on at breakneck speed . . . a literate, heartfelt, and suspenseful novel of the rough friction of life. I enjoyed the hell out of it."

—*Newsweek*

BY THE SAME AUTHOR

AS ANDREW KLAVAN

The Uncanny

True Crime

Son of Man

Darling Clementine

Face of the Earth

Don't Say a Word

The Animal Hour

Corruption

AS KEITH PETERSON

The Scarred Man

Rough Justice

The Rain

There Fell a Shadow

The Trapdoor

SCREENPLAY

A Shock to the System

HUNTING

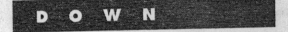

DOWN

AMANDA

A NOVEL

ANDREW KLAVAN

POCKET BOOKS

New York   London   Toronto   Sydney   Singapore

This book is a work of fiction. Names, characters, places, and incidents are products of the author's imagination or are used fictitiously. Any resemblance to actual events or locales or persons, living or dead, is entirely coincidental.

POCKET BOOKS, a division of Simon & Schuster Inc.
1230 Avenue of the Americas, New York, NY 10020

Cover design by Tony Greco

Printed in the U.S.A.

This book is for Faith

PROLOGUE

IN BETWEEN THE DEVIL AND THE DEEP BLUE SEA

1

This story begins on a summer's day in Hell.

The day was July thirteenth to be exact. And Hell was a little town called Hunnicut, Massachusetts.

Before it turned into Hell, it was actually kind of a nice little place. A fishing town. Hills of beryl forests above sunlit bays. Trim shingled houses on tree-lined lanes. A restored Main Street with quaint tourist shops and a couple of decent seafood restaurants overlooking the water.

That Friday, the weather was fine, warm but breezy. There were clouds sailing by overhead but they were cumulus clouds, not much ascended, high and fluffy and white, with great cerulean gaps between. The sun, still well aloft, shone bright and clear.

Visitors and locals alike were out strolling by the shops, pausing here and there to look in the windows. Decorative fishing nets were on display. Painted oars and scrimshaw paperweights. T-shirts that said I'D RATHER BE FISHING, or A FISHERMAN IS ALWAYS READY TO WHIP OUT HIS ROD, or I FELL FOR HUNNICUT HOOK, LINE AND SINKER! and other sentiments like that.

Atop the brick town hall, the Stars and Stripes were snapping smartly. Down in the picturesque harbor, trawlers bobbed on the curlicue waves. Sunlight glittered on the wind-dappled surface of the ocean.

It was 4:15 P.M., and life in Hunnicut was pretty much all right.

That situation remained in place for about two more minutes.

Then, at 4:17 P.M., there came a rumble, like thunder. There was no more warning than that.

People out-of-doors glanced up in mild surprise. Fishermen working their boats tilted back their heads and squinted into the sky. Everyone—a man in a canvas chair on the beach; the shopping housewives over on Main; a state trooper walking from his cruiser to the Donut Hole; the children in a playground off Hancock Street; a roofer on a housetop in the middle of a hammer blow—they all looked up at the thunder sound. It hadn't seemed to anyone as if it were going to rain.

After that, there came a half-second of stillness.

And this is what happened next:

A white-hot light spilled wide across the face of heaven—as if the sky had been obliterated by a blinding stain. An orange starburst flashed out of that white core. And with it came a roar—an agonized, hoarse—a deafening roar that made a nerve end out of your skull, that made the earth beneath you tremble.

"It sounded," said Leonard Wallingford, a banker up from Boston to visit his father, "it sounded as if God had gotten caught in a bear trap."

In the next moment, it began to rain fire. From the ether, from nowhere, lancets of liquid flame spat sizzling onto the pavements, into the trees. The people had only one more instant to stare with gaping mouths in disbelief.

And then it became unthinkable. Because the wing section hit, and it was still nearly full of fuel.

It smacked into a cornfield just east of Michaels Street. In the same split second, the earth ripped open in a seventy-foot crater and a fireball ripped out of it and up into the open air. Michaels ran through a family neighborhood of two-story clapboards. Three houses simply collapsed where they stood. Two more exploded. Their lumber splintered, the splinters flew. Pots and pans, an iron, the contents of a toolbox—they all shot off like red missiles. The body of Sharon Cosgrove, a Realtor, lifted high, high into the air and then flumped down like a doll into the burning debris where her children, Patricia and Sam, had been blown to unrecoverable bits.

The lights went out everywhere. The water stopped running. Other houses, other neighborhoods caught fire. There were fires all over town. There were people all over town who had suddenly turned into fractured things, twisted, staring, stained things lying amid piles of broken bricks and smoldering char. Other people were screaming, running, wandering dazed over lawns and down the middle of streets, past the black skeletons of automobiles and the crackling, dancing flames shooting out of windows. Black smoke—violent, rolling billows of black smoke—stormed over all of it, over the people and the flaming trees and the flaming houses, and out over the harbor, and up into the sky above the sea.

And out of the sky, and down through the smoke, poured the rain of the wreckage. Plates of silver metal fell. A jet engine dropped whole onto Hank's Fish N Tackle and demolished it. A nose cone dove into Cutter's Cove like an enormous gutted bass. Coins sprinkled down onto the grass and golden jewelry too. A retiree, Walter Bosch, was killed in his garden by a full-sized bourbon bottle, which split his skull in half and then fell to lie completely unbroken in the impatiens bed beside his corpse.

And bodies fell and parts of bodies. Flesh rained down on Hunnicut—out of the sky, into the fire—along with the liquid fire still raining down through the black smoke. There was less gore than you might have thought. Much of the humanity in the air had simply vanished. Still . . . An arm and a leg smacked wetly among the people screaming in the middle of Hancock. Emma Timmerman—her entire body still intact, still belted into her seat—landed in the yard behind Hunnicut Autobody and sat propped amid the junk there as if someone had thrown her away. A torso torn like old laundry—what was left of Bob Bowen, a high school instructor—fluttered down to dangle from the branch of a tree. The head of Jeff Aitken, a student, crashed through Sharon Kent's kitchen window. Mrs. Kent was struck dumb at the sight of the thing in her sink, its mouth open, its scalp in flames.

Over time, over the longest time it seemed, everything that was left came streaming down. Into the smoldering houses and the steaming water, into the forest, which was snickering now as it blazed. Around the bodies of the town's dead and the moaning wounded. Among the people screaming, crying. The fuselage and the workings and the furniture came down, and the supplies and the passengers—all the remains of European Airways Flight 186.

It had been a 747 on its way to London and it had just disintegrated at thirty-two thousand feet.

No one ever discovered why.

2

Amanda Dodson, who was five years old, was playing in her baby-sitter's backyard at the time. Amanda was a roundish little mixed-race girl with a quiet, thoughtful manner. Tan skin, an oval face. Big, intelligent brown eyes. Long, curly, startlingly yellow hair.

She was sitting on the bottom step of the back deck, her pudgy legs and arms poking from her light blue shorts and T-shirt. She was operating a make-believe hospital on the border of the lawn. Amanda knew about hospitals and sickness and even death because she knew about how her father had died. Right now, though, it was her furry red Elmo doll who was the patient under consideration. And his condition seemed very grave. But fortunately, Nurse Barbie was in attendance, ably assisted by a rag doll named Mathilda. And before poor Elmo could fade away completely, Dr. Amanda spread her hands over him and magically "sparkled" him back to health.

Well, a great celebration ensued: a tea party of thanksgiving. Some rocks and a milk crate and a wagon served for a table and chairs and revelers human, plastic and stuffed passed round the plastic cups and dishes that had been generously contributed by Mrs. Shipman.

She was the baby-sitter—Mrs. Shipman—a squat, cheerful widow of sixty-one. She was inside just then, in the den with the television. Knitting a pink sweater for a baby granddaughter and watching Larry Norton interview people who engage in computer sex on the Internet. She was keeping an eye on Amanda through the picture window to her left.

A mantelpiece clock chimed the quarter hour: four-fifteen. With a start, Mrs. Shipman realized she had lost track of time. She usually called Amanda in at four for a snack and an hour of cartoons. She draped her knitting over the arm of her chair and started to stand up.

That was when the first explosion went off on Michaels Street, about a quarter mile away. The force of the blast threw Mrs. Shipman out of her seat, headfirst into the TV. The screen shattered. The jagged glass ripped Mrs. Shipman's face off as if it were a rubber glove. She was still alive for a second, but then the house caved in on top of her and she was crushed to death.

The explosion shook the earth and air. Little Amanda stood. She was holding her furry red Elmo doll by its hand. She didn't understand what had happened. When the house fell down, she could only stare at it blankly.

Someone was screaming: Mrs. Jenson, the nice lady from next door who sometimes came by with cookies. Her dress was on fire and she was running across her backyard, shrieking and shrieking. She ran blindly into the washing hung on the line. She became tangled in a beach towel and fell to the ground, rolling and shrieking and burning.

Amanda stood and stared.

Mrs. Jenson's house was also on fire, she saw. So were some of the other houses on the block. And other people were running and they were shrieking too. And there was Frank Hauer—a big boy, Amanda thought, ten years old. He was lying facedown at the base of his basketball net. He was lying in a lake of red, red blood.

Amanda's face puckered. She began to cry. She clutched Elmo's hand tightly.

The old maple tree in Mrs. Jenson's yard burst into flame. Mrs. Shipman's pachysandra bed exploded as a big hunk of metal sliced down into it out of the sky. Wet earth and leaves splattered over Amanda where she stood, helpless, crying. The big piece of metal, sticking out of the ground, loomed up and up above her.

Dazed, Amanda began walking. She wanted her mother.

The very next thing she knew she was walking across Hauptman's Memorial Ballfield. She was walking stiffly on her pudgy legs, trudging over the grass between first base and the pitcher's mound. She was hugging Elmo close to her and sucking her thumb. She was sniffling tearfully. She didn't remember exactly how she had come to be there.

The ballfield bordered Mrs. Shipman's backyard to the west. There was a long stand of trees on the far side of the field. Amanda always pictured the tavern where her mother worked as being somewhere beyond those trees. The trees were the furthest thing she could see from the baby-sitter's yard or from the big den window when she was watching TV. It made sense to her that her mother was away somewhere beyond them.

In fact, the bar where her mother worked was in a completely different direction. It was off to the south-east, down by the water. The trees up ahead merely screened an old fire road—now a bike trail—and the houses and swampland on its other side.

But Amanda thought her mother was there. And so she walked on, trudging across the outfield toward the trees.

Some of the trees were on fire and some of the duff around their roots was smoldering. Smoke was pouring from the little wood. And someone inside the wood was screaming.

All the same, Amanda walked on.

She reached the rail fence that bordered the ballpark. She ducked through, clutching Elmo tightly. The smoke made her wrinkle her nose now. She coughed, her cheeks puffing up around her thumb.

The trees rose above her. They were on every side of her, big maple trees, big oaks and pines. Their branches hung down toward her from on high. The sun streamed down toward her through the leaves. Great solid columns of sunlight stood all around her, turning hazy as the smoke drifted into them.

Amanda walked on under the trees, beside the hazy columns. The smoke was making her cough more and more. The screaming was growing louder. A woman screaming in short bursts, over and over, like a car alarm. Somewhere, flames were crackling. Amanda's pink sneakers were crunching on the forest floor. She was looking down at her sneakers. She was watching them move along.

Then she stopped.

There was something on the path before her. A large shape, dark in the drifting smoke; dark and very still. Scared, Amanda stood where she was, dwarfed by the oaks and pines, by columns of sunlight hazy with smoke. She rubbed her cheek against Elmo's red fur. She nibbled on the tip of her thumb. She looked warily at the shape in the path.

Then she realized what it was. And slowly, she started toward it.

3

Just before that, before the crash, Amanda's mother,
Carol Dodson, had been tending bar at the Anchor and
Bell. It was a harbor bar. Fishermen drank there mostly.
Carol had been working the place almost three months,
ever since she'd drifted into town.

The customers liked Carol. She was pretty for one
thing. Young, twenty-three, twenty-four. And she was
tough and funny and foulmouthed like they were.
Sometimes, too, after she finished work, she would go
upstairs with one of them and have sex with him for
money. Not that she was a hooker or anything. It was
just that if you were a guy and you were about to go to
sea for two or three months and you were single or your
girlfriend was mad at you or something and you really,
really needed to get lucky in a very serious way fast and
you were drinking, say, with a friend at the Anchor and
Bell and bitching about this state of affairs, well, then,
your friend might turn to you and say, "Listen. You got
any money?" And you would say, "Yeah, sure, some."
And your friend would say, "You could try the new
girl—Carol." And you'd say, "Carol? The bartender?
She's turning tricks now?" And your friend would say,
"No, no, hell, she's a nice girl. But, you know, she's
struggling, she's got a kid. Just don't be a ginch, all
right?" So, of course, you don't want anyone to think
you're a ginch, plus maybe you're not particularly

thrilled about the idea of using a hooker either. So up you'd go to the bar and you'd start talking to Carol, just in a natural way. And just in a natural way you'd say some nice things to her like you would to any girl you wanted to sleep with. And then, later, when you were upstairs and everything was finished and you were about to leave, you might say something like, "Hey, Carol, how's it happening for you this week?" And she might say, "Aw, you know, it's always an uphill thing with the kid and all." And you would say, "Well, hey, listen, I'm flush, you know. Let me help you out a little bit here. No, really." And then you might argue back and forth a little. And finally you'd give her something.

That was how it generally worked.

Now today, this July day when the plane came down, there was a good crowd of guys in the place. Most of them were planning to ship out tomorrow or Monday. Some were sitting together at the big tables, and some were at the smaller ones with their wives or girlfriends. Still others were up at the bar, watching the Sox game playing silently on the TV above the mirror.

And then there was one guy, Joe Speakes, who was at the bar but who wasn't watching the Sox game. He was talking to Carol. She was washing glasses at the sink behind the bar and he was chatting to her over his beer.

"What's this I been hearing?" he was saying to her. "Jes Gramble says you're thinking of running out on us."

"Ah, you know." Carol shrugged, gave a half-smile. "You stay anywhere too long, you start collecting dust."

"Nah," said Joe. "You just got here. What're you, running from the FBI or something?"

"That's me," she said. "I'm The Fugitive."

"Forget it. Stick around. The fun is just beginning."

"What. You gonna miss me, Joe?" said Carol Dodson.

"Hell, yes," said Joe. "There's nothing else worth looking at around here."

Carol laughed and stepped back from the sink. She threw her hip out and made a comical palms-up gesture: *ta-daaa.*

Joe nodded his appreciation. His eyes moved up and down her.

Carol kept herself in good shape and she was proud of her figure. She had her maroon T-shirt tucked into her jeans so that it pressed close and showed off her round breasts, her narrow waist and flat belly. Her jeans were tight on the curve of her butt and the cloth was wedged up between her legs in a manner that could move a man in many deep and significant ways.

Her hair was shoulder-length, blond, curly she called it, but frizzy really down at the ends. Her face was oval like her daughter's, only white, and she had the same big, soft, intelligent eyes, only blue. She had a small sharp nose, and long, pretty lips, which she glossed almost silver. She was short and slender and looked like she would fit neatly into a man's arms.

So that's how it was. Carol stepped back and made that comical gesture. And Joe Speakes looked up and down her.

And then came that hellacious roar, that God-in-a-bear-trap roar that shook the sky. And Michaels Street exploded. And the whole bar shuddered. The booze bottles danced and rattled against the mirror.

"What the Christ?" said Joe Speakes.

"Oh shit," said Carol. She knew at once that this was trouble, no joke. Whatever the opposite of a joke was, that was this.

Joe had slipped off his stool. He was striding to the door. The other guys were right with him. A wall of thick backs was already crowding the entryway. The girls were bringing up the rear, crowding into the guys. Carol snatched up a dish towel and went after the rest of them, drying her hands.

Then they were out on Briar Street. Everyone was pouring out onto Briar Street from the bars and shops. All the drinkers, all the fishermen, all the waitresses and clerks were hurrying to the corner. And everyone at the corner was just standing there, just staring up Martin Street, to the west.

They were four miles away from the field where the wing exploded. But they could see it even from here: the fire on the horizon, the fire in the rooftops, the fire falling out the sky.

Carol saw it as she reached the corner. Standing there in the jostling, staring crowd. Still mechanically rubbing her dry hands on the wet towel.

"Oh my God," she said.

They were all saying that. "Oh my God!" "Holy shit!" "Jesus Christ."

"Fuck me," someone murmured dully. "It's raining fire."

There were other explosions then. They saw a house just come apart, just fly apart into splinters. They could hear screaming, a chorus of sobbing cries coming from all over at once. People were running everywhere like mice in a maze. Police sirens were going off and fire sirens and car alarms.

Then something wet and heavy dropped onto the sidewalk not three blocks up, splattering liquid as it hit. And a glittering sprinkle of something fell. And then one of the houses on Martin just spat its windows out in sparkling bits.

Some of the men were charging up there. Some of the women were screaming, covering their mouths with their hands.

And Carol whispered, "Amanda."

And she started running for her car.

Then she was driving, driving as fast as she could to Mrs. Shipman's house. Her car, her old puttering Rabbit, was hacking and roaring like an old hound. Its axle was shimmying whenever it crested forty. Its tires were squealing around every corner. And Carol was wrestling the wheel, battling the wheel and the road ferociously.

She had to get to Amanda.

She had to get to Amanda and she had to get through this—this hell that was rushing at her windshield, rushing at her eyes. The streets on fire. The houses burning, house after house. Bodies smoking on the lawns. The trees burning. The outlines of cars through leaping flames. The fire in the sky. The people walking like zombies. The people shrieking. People she had seen in town, faces she knew, bleeding, crushed.

She wrestled the car past all of it, all of them. There was something hard and implacable in her heart. She pushed the pedal down further to beat the Rabbit's shimmy. She was crying as she drove, but she didn't know it, she didn't care. Her jaw was clenched tight. Her eyes were fixed ahead. She had to get to Amanda.

A woman in her underwear ran out in front of the fender. She was clutching her head and her mouth was wide open. Carol cursed her and swerved the car. Her heart was hard and she cursed the woman and swerved around her. And when a gout of sizzling fire hit her windshield, she let out a high-pitch growl and switched on the wipers.

"Get off!" she shouted at it, crying.

She passed a playground. Children lay bleeding on the ground. Toddlers sat wailing up at the heavens.

Carol opened her mouth so she could cry harder, and she stepped harder on the gas, screeching away from them, around the next curve. Implacable.

She had to find Amanda.

Then she was slowing down. There was Mrs. Shipman's house just ahead of her. For one second, Carol could not believe what she was seeing.

The house was a jagged punched-in thing, lumber sticking out of it, a haze of dust around it. Carol's stomach convulsed with crying. She was sick with suspense and fear.

She was out of the car. She was running around the house. She was thinking about snacktime. This is snacktime, she was thinking. Amanda played out in the yard until four and then she came inside to watch the afternoon cartoons. That was now, wasn't it? Wasn't it snacktime now?

Dear merciful Christ in Heaven, she thought as she ran into the backyard, dear God who died suffering on the cross, please don't let it be snacktime. Don't let it be snacktime yet.

She was around the house. She saw the deck lying alop, its columns cracking. She saw the shining chunk of fuselage rising out of a hole where the pachysandra had been.

She looked down, convulsed with crying, unaware she was crying. She saw the circle of cups and plates on the ground. Mathilda the rag doll was still sitting up at her place, propped against a milk crate, her head bowed as if in mourning.

Come inside now and have your snack, Amanda.

Carol could see that that was how it had happened. Her mind was crystal clear. She could imagine it all. She was focused, alert, and felt completely aware of the explosion of grief that was beginning inside her. It was as if she were a scientific observer at a nuclear blast. She knew that in another moment the spreading cloud of grief would fill her, would overwhelm her. She would have to rip her rib cage open to let it out or just be blown apart. It would be more than life could bear.

Her mouth open, her face covered with snot and tears, she lifted her head and emitted a quiet, trembling "Oh," the sound of her devastation.

And she saw a patch of bright red on Hauptman's field.

Elmo.

Carol saw Elmo's leg trailing out from under Amanda's arm. In her light blue shirt and shorts, Amanda was hard to make out against the green grass, against the green trees. But Carol spotted Elmo's leg and then she could see her daughter.

It was like no baptism ever was. No sin ever so black was ever so washed away as that black cloud of mushrooming grief was washed away from inside her.

She saw that her daughter was moving toward the woods. She saw the smoke spilling out of the trees at her. And then she was running again.

She was running across the ballfield. She was screaming her daughter's name. "Amanda! Amanda!" She was choking on the screams, too breathless to sob.

And the child was out of earshot anyway. She had already ducked under the fence, was already at the tree line. Carol forced herself to scream her name once more. Ran on with her arms flailing, her hair flying, her flying tears.

Then Amanda began to fade from before her. She was moving into the woods. She was fading into the smoke. The smoke was growing thicker, blacker around her. It was billowing out of the trees. It was spreading, hanging in the air. It screened the child from the mother's view. The child was vanishing into it.

By the time Carol crossed the rest of the field, Amanda was out of sight. Carol ducked through the center gap of the fence. Her foot snagged on the rail. She stumbled to one knee, leapt up, kept running.

She was in the trees now, in the smoke. One arm thrown over her mouth. Coughing into her sleeve. Staring through her tears, through the smoking columns of sunlight.

She lowered her arm. "Amanda!" she shouted hoarsely. Then she started coughing, threw up her arm again. She stumbled through the smoke.

She was lost, wandering, coughing, screaming, she didn't know how long. Then a faint breeze reached her, and the smoke thinned. Carol stopped and peered into it, scanned the scene.

"Amanda!" she said hoarsely.

And some enormous creature lumbered into the haze before her.

It seemed to rise up and up, hulking, dark. Carol reared back. What was it? A bear?

It lumbered toward her stiffly. Carol clenched her fist, ready to slug it.

But it wasn't a bear. It was a man.

He came toward her through the smoke. He stepped out of the smoke and Carol could see him clearly. It was a man—and he was carrying her daughter.

Amanda lay limp in the cradle of the man's arms. Her lips were parted, her eyes closed. Her cheeks were the color of gray marble. And a thin line of blood was trickling from the corner of her mouth.

But she was alive. She was still holding Elmo. She was clasping the doll against her midsection. Elmo was rising and falling with her breath—Carol could see it. Her daughter was still alive.

She looked up at the man and the smoke blew over them both, raced past. A clearer space was made for them a moment. The man's face was black with soot, but his single eye shone white out of it. Tears were washing his cheek, showing the pink, unblemished flesh underneath.

He staggered closer. Carefully, he transferred the child from his arms to Carol's. She held Amanda close, the familiar weight of her. She pressed her cheek to Amanda's forehead and felt the fever heat. She understood everything. She was laughing and crying at once. And what she said next seemed to make no sense at all.

She said, "Oh God. Oh God. Now they'll come after her."

The media usually referred to it as the Hunnicut Disaster. Sometimes they got fancy, called it the American Lockerbie. Either way, it was a hell of a big story that summer.

The reporters covered the event like scum covers still water. They covered the victims, the survivors, the witnesses. They covered the experts, the officials, the shrinks. They covered every tear that ran down every relative's face. And then they covered each other covering it, which seemed to be the angle they liked best of all.

There were some good stories. True stories, important stories. But as the days and weeks wore on, as the cops and officials and tinkickers searched the wreckage, gathered the evidence, reconstructed the events, there was also a lot of half-baked malarkey that the press concocted to fill up the dull period of investigation. There were rumors of terrorist suspects, government cover-ups, airline irresponsibility. There was speculation about meteorites and military laser beams and uniquely spectacular incidences of wind shear. Then there were the tabloids, the supermarket papers and the strange-but-true type TV shows. It seems five or six bodies from the jet, all of them from first class, had landed remarkably intact. This was not unheard of, and scientists believed their section of the plane might have formed an independent airfoil cushioning their fall. But the tabloids figured it was UFO's intercepting the chosen. They figured it was angels wafting the corpses to earth as a sign of hope from God. One "eyewitness" on *News of the World* claimed the baby Jesus Himself had put in an appearance, worked several trademark signs and wonders, and even delivered a pithy homily or two before heading merrily on His way.

So, all in all, for those who followed the disaster in the news, there was a little something for everyone, a story for every taste.

And for one man—a man who read every story from the heartbreaking and responsible to the hilariously absurd—there was something more. The man was a vice president at Helix Pharmaceuticals. And for him, there was something about the Hunnicut crash that was more desperately urgent than anything the media reported. For him, there was something buried in the tragedy that almost defied belief. That *would have* defied belief—if it weren't for the fact that he'd been waiting for it—watching for it—for a very long time.

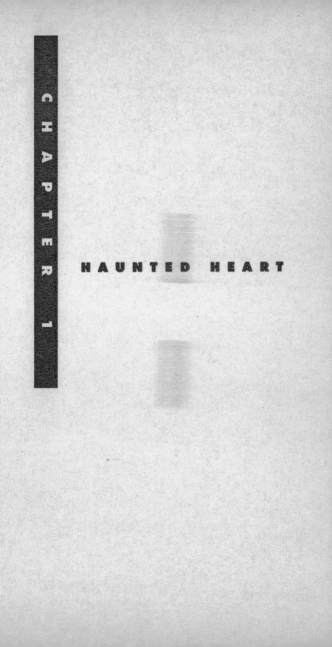

CHAPTER 1

HAUNTED HEART

1

Four months later. November, another Friday. Manhattan, New York, New York. A young saxophone player named Lonnie Blake was doing a gig at a place on Ninth Avenue.

It wasn't much of a place. There wasn't much of a crowd in the small hours. Three or four people were at the wooden bar. Four or five more were lounging at the small round tables. Almost everyone there was young but almost everyone looked sort of pale and specterly, glazed and wander-eyed as if they'd gotten lost somehow on their way to the happening thing. One doofus in the corner was actually wearing sunglasses—he was dressed in black and wearing sunglasses and bobbing his head as if stoned on the music. The supply lines of hip, in other words, were stretched a little thin in here.

The place was called Renaissance. On the walls, running around the walls, there was a mural of Florence. The owner's girlfriend had painted it, copying a picture in a book she'd found at the Strand. The mural actually hadn't been too bad when she'd finished it. But about six months ago she and the owner had a fight. She hauled for San Francisco, and now her delicate blue firmament was chipping away and the intricate white-and-red skyline was starting to blur with grime.

Against that backdrop, up on a small stage smack in

front of the fading Duomo, there was the band. A trio: keyboard, bass, saxophone. Fred Purcell, Arnie Cobb and Lonnie Blake.

Arthur Topp, meanwhile, was at the bar. He'd been sitting there for close to an hour. Nursing a scotch or three, listening to the music. Watching Lonnie.

The trio was playing standards mostly, Jurassic classics. "Night and Day," "Always," "Savoy," that kind of thing. They were snapping their fingers and saying "Yeah" a lot to make the crowd think they were really wailing. But so far, Arthur hadn't heard anything that excited him at all.

Arthur was a white man. Small and thin, forty. Bald up top but with his fringe of black hair grown long and tied into a ponytail. His pullover red shirt looked expensive and made him stand out here. And his gold watch made him stand out. He'd inherited the watch from his father. He dressed to look more prosperous than he was.

He went on scoping Lonnie with quick, dark eyes. He tapped his hand impatiently on the bar.

The saxophone player had skill. Arthur could see that, hear that. Lonnie had fast fingers, a smooth, controlled tone. His jams were flawless too; he could find his way out of the melody and back with precision. But it was pretty uninspired stuff, Arthur thought. The same old tired barroom riffs. The kind of drone you could hear anywhere.

Arthur glanced at his father's Rolex. Nearly 1 A.M. The last set was winding up. The band was preparing to stand down. Arthur felt ready to write this one off, to pay his check and bail.

But just then, just as he was turning to flag the bartender, something happened.

Here it was. Last song. "Haunted Heart." The trio was swinging into the finish. Fred Purcell, the keyboard player, nodded for Lonnie to take the break. The sax-man blew into his final solo. Only the bass kept a three-note rhythm line behind him.

Arthur Topp paused. He listened. Nothing at first. Same-old same-old. The bridge embellished with a few smeared grace notes, a couple of ornamental mordents. A chromatic fill where a rest had been to make it sound like a genuine jam.

The doofus in the sunglasses was impressed. He slapped his hand down on his table. "Man!" he said, swinging his head back and forth.

Arthur Topp stifled a yawn in his fist. Lonnie Blake was sleep-walking the baby, he thought. Same as he had been all night.

Then—then, all at once—that changed. Lonnie was floating up some fake-out scale, going through the motions, floating up and up, one note after another—and then he held there, held dully in the low reaches as if tied to an invisible tether. One note, bobbing, teth-ered and leaden, bobbing until it threatened to become a miserable drone . . .

And then—then, all at once—the tether snapped.

Suddenly—Arthur was watching him, astonished—suddenly, there was Lonnie, bent back against the painted sky, against the painted dome. The sax was uplifted, a Selmer Mark VI, a fine machine, glistening in his long fingers. And he was blowing that thing. He was wailing. His dark lips were kissing the hard black rubber of the mouthpiece. He was whispering over the reed with a sort of Miles Davis *vu* that filled the mellow blue tenor with a ghosty nothing . . .

And up on that empty breath he flew, glissing his way to a high riff of incredible Coltrane sixteenths, peaking in a seamless vibrato, a barely trembling leap from pitch to pitch.

Oh, thought Arthur Topp. *Oh, oh, oh.*

Then came another held note, but this one singing, a singing E-flat floating like a yogi in the impossible air. Then a shake, that quick trill with the lips, and then just as the note had to fall, still another shake—and then it did fall, it plummeted, *bam*, and like a rush of warm wind, the keyboard and the bass swept in under it and Lonnie *wafted* back—just wafted back—down into the melody. And the trio polished off the song.

Purcell, a gray-haired elder, looked around from his keyboard, surprised. "All right," he said.

Arthur Topp clapped and whistled. The doofus slapped the table again. A few other people let go of their drinks long enough to flop their hands together.

Purcell and Cobb, keyboard and bass, nodded, smiling slightly.

Lonnie Blake turned his back on all of them. The show was over.

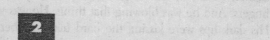

2

He was still a young man—Lonnie—not yet thirty, maybe just. Average height, slender, skin the color of milk chocolate. He had compact, angular features, almost feline features, under a dusting of very short black hair. That night, he looked sharp and formidable in a sleek gray suit, an open-necked white shirt.

He packed up his sax, came down off the stage. Paused at the coat hooks on the wall. He took down a black overcoat, slipped it on.

But he didn't go out. He came over to the bar. Set his sax case down. Leaned there, right next to Arthur Topp, his elbows on the rail.

"Bourbon and seven," he said to the bartender.

Arthur eyed the black man sidelong, drink in hand. He was nervous about this now, awkward. He'd checked up on Lonnie Blake. Heard rumors he was a tough guy, even a bad guy, a gang-banger, in his youth. Arthur knew this wasn't going to be easy.

And it meant a lot to him. If he could win the saxophonist over, if he could get him to sign on . . . well, it would be a chance, one more chance for him to prove to his father's ghost that he could be more than a middleman for weddings and bar mitzvahs, that he really did have some musical class.

He cleared his throat. "Uh, hey . . . " he said after a second or two.

Lonnie glanced at him, disinterested.

"Uh, def, uh, def jam," said Arthur Topp. "Straight up. I mean it. It don't stop. Good stuff. Really." *Excellent, Art,* he told himself. *You sound exactly like a fucking idiot.*

Lonnie Blake apparently thought so too. He gazed at Arthur a long time. It was not a friendly gaze. His eyes seemed black and depthless. Then, lifting his chin slightly, he made a sound for which there's no precise word: a short hiss of air through the nostrils. An expression of contempt.

Arthur Topp grinned stupidly. He felt sweat break out between his shoulder blades. He was grateful when the bartender slapped down a tall bourbon, when Lonnie Blake turned his attention to it and knocked back a long swig.

Still—he was nothing if not persistent—he pressed on. "No. Listen. Straight up. I know you," he said.

Lonnie came out of his drink with a breath. Shook his head slowly. "No, you don't."

Topp's laugh sounded desperate even to himself. "I know your work, I mean. Your music. Make this easy on me, how about?"

Lonnie didn't make it easy, didn't answer at all. Up went the drink again. He pulled so hard on it the ice rattled. When he set it down, he nodded at the bartender.

"Bourbon and seven," the bartender said, and set up another one fast.

"I heard this old demo," said Arthur Topp. "Someone slipped me this old demo. 'Evolutions.' Right? 'Evolutions'? Must've been two, three years old. I mean, I heard it—this is months ago now. I mean it. I've been looking for you for months."

The saxman worked his second drink, worked it hard.

"I mean, you're not around much," Arthur said to his profile.

"I'm not around at all," said Lonnie Blake after a moment. A hard edge of irritation was creeping into his voice. "I'm not around now. I just look like I'm around. Don't let it fool you."

"Okay." *Jesus*, Arthur thought. *Jesus. This is not going well.* "Okay. Okay, but, like—'Evolutions,'" he said anyway. "I mean, that was just—fat stuff, top stuff, really. The Jurassics . . . the old flavors . . . you really blew 'em.

I mean, the last time I heard 'em that fresh was . . . what? 'My Favorite Things'? I think so. Really. Straight up. I mean it."

Lonnie finally turned to him again, looked over at him as if he'd just noticed an annoying noise.

"Straight up," Arthur repeated helplessly.

"Are you queer?" Lonnie asked him.

"What?" To his own despair, Arthur let out a high-pitched giggle. "No! I mean, Jesus. I mean, queer, yeah, in more ways than I like to think about. But no. Not that way. No."

"Then what the hell do you want from me, man?" said Lonnie Blake. "I'm trying to have a drink here."

Topp perceived this as an opportunity. He cleared his throat again, steadied himself, stumbled into his routine. "My name's Arthur Topp. I represent people. Artists. I get them bookings. Musical acts. Topp Music. Tops in pop." He brought out a business card. Pressed it into Lonnie's hand. The musician looked down at it as if it were phlegm. Dropped it into his overcoat pocket as if he were wiping it off. "We're not a big organization. It's just me, in fact. But I have some good people, really, straight up. That's my . . . everything's on there, numbers, addresses. I'm in the office eight to eight, every day. Home by eight-thirty unless something's on, you know, I'm scoping talent or something. Home, office, either one, I'm working all the time. And you can always get me on the mobile. So . . . I mean, look, I'm always looking for someone. Okay? I think you could . . . I think you and I could—really do something together. Straight up. I mean it."

Well, it wasn't poetry, but at least he'd managed to spit it out. He waited as Lonnie gazed at him.

Then Lonnie faced the bar. Drained his second drink. Plonked down the glass. "Have a good one," he said. And he picked up his saxophone case.

Arthur Topp was not sure whether it was anger or desperation that did it, but now he heard himself blurt out, "Look, I know what happened. About your wife, I mean."

It stopped Lonnie anyway. The man went still. Glanced around with his feline features set, his depthless eyes hard.

"Sorry. Sorry," said Arthur Topp. "I mean, it's tragic. A tragic thing. Really. But I figured—you know—it's been more than a year, almost two years." He gestured in front of him. "Life . . . life goes on."

Lonnie Blake gave him that silent gaze. "Is that what it does?"

"Yeah. Well, I mean . . . that's not to say it isn't tragic but . . ." Arthur knew he was starting to babble. He just couldn't put on the brakes. "I mean, still . . . still a guy like you . . . I mean, I see these studio gangsters, but you, you're from the trenches, man, you're from the land of the hard . . ." The sweat was coming down his temples now. And he could feel it soaking into his shirt, the wet cotton against his armpits. And he was thinking to himself, *Shut up.* But he couldn't. "And then you . . . you get out and you go with your music, you get your wife and you got 'Evolutions' going and all that and then . . . Well, I mean, it's tragic but . . . But you don't want to trash it all, throw it . . . She wouldn't—would she?—want that?"

Finally, he stopped, clamped down on it, cut it off. And for a long, for an endless, moment, he went on sweating as Lonnie Blake went on staring at him.

Then Lonnie made that noise again. That little snort of contempt. He showed Arthur his back, started for the door.

Topp watched him go, the familiar shroud of failure settling on him. And then, without thinking, he said, "It's 'cause you can't anymore, isn't it?"

Lonnie Blake paused on his way to the door. Stood there without turning.

"I mean, play," Arthur went on. Speaking the thoughts as they dawned on him. "I mean, I was listening tonight and . . . 'Evolutions'—that's, like, over for you, isn't it?"

Lonnie Blake started walking again.

"That's the thing, right?" Arthur called after him. "You can't really play anymore since they killed her."

Lonnie pushed the door open and walked out of the bar.

The night was cold. Lonnie stood outside the bar on Ninth Avenue, his breath misting in the autumn air.

Fool, he thought. And he pushed Arthur Topp from his mind.

But not the rage. Under the bourbon, the familiar rage kept bubbling, a ceaseless low boil.

Across the street, a young man, a young black man in

a suit and tie, had opened the door of a car for his lady.
She was twenty and beautiful, her black dress slit high
up one side. Lonnie watched her lower herself into the
Grand Am, the tan skin of a fine leg flashing under the
street lamp. The sight hurt him, and his anger mixed
with something else, some sadder yearning. He had not
been with a woman in eighteen months.

You can't really play anymore since they killed her.

Lonnie turned away and started walking.

The street was quiet. The cars speeding past were
yellow cabs mostly. Under the street lamps, under the
line of painted brick tenements, under the zigzag of
their fire escapes, an occasional slouching no-one scut-
tled up the sidewalk toward the Port Authority. Lonnie
went slowly on, the sax in one hand, his other hand in
his pocket. His depthless eyes were hard, the vision
turned inward.

He went east on Thirtieth. It was a darker lane between
taller lofts. Looming brown buildings rose to either side of
him, their wide empty windows dark. The autumn wind
pressed steadily down the canyon, desolate. In the shadows away from the streetlights, trash skittered out from
under parked cars.

Lonnie's jaw worked as he walked. His lips moved a
little to the silent mutter in his mind. He was in himself
completely now. On the treadmill of his old grief, ham-
stering around the old images. The grinning white boys.
The speeding car. His murdered wife. Suzanne.

Even through the whiskey, the rage hurt him bad.
Only images of her soothed the pain and those images
hurt too. He conjured her trim, graceful figure turning
to him from the kitchen sink. Her bright, unbridled
smile and so on. The smooth brown skin of her high

cheeks and the soft recesses of her doe eyes and so on. Her hand slipping a drink into his. Her hands rubbing his shoulders. *How was your day?* she would ask.

And so on.

A low sound escaped him, a low and awful sound. He paused. He was halfway down the empty street. The husky lofts and the windy silence bore down on him from every side.

He shook his head slightly. He set his face and walked on, willing the images into shadow.

He reached his building. There was a narrow recess in a wide brown wall. A loft entry with a black wooden door that led into the building's foyer. Lonnie brought his keys out of his pocket. Stepped out of a streetlight's aura into the alcove. He peered down through the dark to fit his key in the lock. The key slipped in.

And a hand reached out behind him. It gripped his elbow hard. A woman whispered harshly to him out of the night.

"Help me," she said.

Startled, Lonnie whipped a look back over his shoulder. It was a white girl, her big urgent eyes staring up at him. Pale she was, and the breath misting before her face made her seem almost ghostly. She had short black hair.

Pretty features, but sharp and glossy and cheap. A belted black coat ended high on her thighs. Her sexy legs were in dark stockings, her feet in black high-heeled shoes.

Lonnie pegged her for a whore. This was some kind of street game, he thought. But there was real fear in her eyes, it looked like. And the small hand on his elbow was shaking so hard he could feel it right up his arm.

"There's a guy after me," she said. Her voice was shaking too. "Please. Just let me in. I swear . . . Before he sees me. Hurry. Please."

She glanced down to the corner quickly. Lonnie quickly followed the glance. He saw a car whisk past the intersection, then another. He saw the green outglow of the traffic light fading toward him into the darkness.

But there was no one coming, no sign of anyone.

The whore hissed at him, "Aw, please! Jesus!" Her grip on his arm tightened.

Lonnie hesitated another moment, figuring the angles. Then he acted on instinct: twisted the key, pushed open the door.

The whore darted past him. He slipped in after her, let the door swing shut behind.

The building's foyer was small, cramped, about the size of two elevators put together. There was one lamp up on the high ceiling. Its light was dim by the time it reached the checkered linoleum floor.

The whore leaned back trembling against one color-less wall. Lonnie stood watching her, listening to her panting breath. She raised her red plastic purse. Snapped it open. Fumbled inside.

Lonnie watched this too, expressionless. Thinking: *She pulls a knife out of there and I'll bust her fucking grill.*

She brought out a pack of Marlboro Lites. Held it

toward him. He shook his head no. She jogged a butt loose and pulled it free with her lips. Bowed over a plastic lighter, the cigarette dangling. Spark, spark, spark. She couldn't get the flame going with her shaking hands.

Lonnie took the lighter from her. Torched it, held it out. She bent to the fire, clasping his hand in both of hers. Then she tilted back until her eyes met his. She sucked the smoke so hungrily Lonnie could almost feel it go down. She sighed it out at him in a rush.

"Thanks," she said. "Sorry for the panic. Creep Alert. You know." She tried to laugh. It didn't sound much like a laugh. She held up the cigarette. "You mind?"

Lonnie gave that brief snort of his. The whore leaned back against the wall again, took another drag. Closed her eyes, communing with the smoke.

Lonnie studied her. The heels, the stockinged legs, the plastic mini-coat, the glossy makeup. She was a whore all right. But pretty under all the glop. Practically a kid too. Not much more than twenty.

She shuddered on a long breath. Opened her eyes. Her eyes were big and blue. She tried to make them sardonic, but they were pools of loneliness.

"Look," she said. "Do you mind? You can go up, really. I can stay down here. I don't care. I swear to God, man, I'm gone before daylight. Soon as there's some people on the street, I'm a misty memory. I swear."

Those eyes of hers held him, even after he looked away. *I gotta be all kinds of stupid,* he thought. Then he gave another of those snorts. Pointed a finger at her. "This place isn't mine, you hear me. It's a friend of mine's. He's letting me use it, awright? Now I let you upstairs and you steal from me, I'm gonna take that personally. You know what I'm saying?"

She came off the wall, both hands lifted. "You are so good. So good."

"You hear me now?"

"I swear to God," she said. "So help me."

"Awright then."

She smelled of violets and tobacco. In the elevator, Lonnie had to reach across her to put his key in the notch for the fourth floor. His face was close to her black hair and he caught her scent. They stood arm by arm as the box rose and he could feel the closeness of her skin.

"You're really good to do this, really," she repeated. She sucked her cigarette so hard she hissed. Nodded on the exhale. "Like, I mean, really."

Lonnie grimaced, raised his eyes to the numbers above the cage door. It was probably the police after her, he thought. About ten minutes, they'd probably be in here to arrest his ass.

The elevator stopped on the fourth floor, the top floor. Lonnie slid back the cage, unlocked the heavy metal door into his loft. He pushed the big door open and breathed in deep as the whore squeezed past him. Violets and trailing smoke.

"Hold on a minute. Don't turn on the light," she said.

He set his saxophone down. Stood and watched her in the darkness. She was a small, wandering shadow in the loft's vast spaces. She moved to his left, to the wall of high windows. She reached it. Looked out. And then she jumped back, as if she'd been burned.

"What," he said. "He out there?"

"Yeah. Yeah."

"Lemme see."

Lonnie headed quickly across the room to the windows. He felt her fingers flutter at his arm as he passed her and slowed down so he wouldn't be seen. He edged close to the sill. Looked out through the fire escape, down to the street below.

The man was on the sidewalk. He was moving slowly under a street lamp, just where they'd been standing only moments ago. He was obviously looking for someone, scanning the street, this way and that.

Lonnie had a good view of him. A tall, husky white man in an open trench coat. He lifted his eyes to study the buildings, the windows. Lonnie moved back a little behind a curtain. Peeked out and saw the man's face. It was a slab of a face with skin like gravel. Thick black eyebrows lifted ironically. Black hair in a widow's peak over a high rough forehead.

The man seemed to curse. He slid his hand into his trench coat smoothly.

Nine-one-one, Lonnie thought. A cop for certain. They'd been cracking down on the street girls a lot lately. He couldn't help but smile a little. *Well, Officer,* he thought, *seems this is the one that done got away.*

He went on watching. The man drew something out of his pocket. A two-way or a mobile phone. He spoke into it, still walking, heading out of the lamp glow toward Ninth.

A moment later, a car pulled up alongside him, long and dark. It stopped and the gravel-faced man opened the door. He slid in the passenger side. The car drove off.

"*Sayonara,* five-oh," Lonnie murmured. "It's all right, he's . . ." But the girl wasn't there. For a moment, he couldn't find her. Then he made her out in the shadows, the tip of her cigarette glowing. She was sitting hunched forward on one of the leather chairs. "He's gone," Lonnie said.

"Yeah? You sure?" Her voice sounded strange. Small and tight.

"A car picked him up. They drove away."

She touched her cheek with the heel of her palm. "Fuckers," she said. Lonnie realized she must've been crying. "Hey, you got an ashtray for this?"

Lonnie went into the kitchen, clicking on lamps as he went. He brought her a coffee cup and set it on the small table beside her. She looked up at him gratefully with damp eyes, her mascara running. Fuck the cops. He was glad he'd helped her.

"I'm making myself a drink," he said. "You want one?"

"Sure. What're you making?"

"Bourbon and seven."

"Sure."

Lonnie stood in the kitchen, glasses on the wooden counter. He poured slowly, mixing the booze and soda over ice. She'd want to hide out here till morning, he thought. He'd have to sleep with one eye open if he didn't want her to make off with the stereo.

"Nice. Nice place," she said behind him. He heard her lighter flick-flick again.

"Yeah." Lonnie watched the bourbon flow, hungry for it. "Trumpet player I know's in Europe on tour. He let me have it for six months."

"Nice."

The loft was vast. It was never well lighted. There was always darkness in the corners and the far reaches. The heat and water pipes were exposed, dodging back and forth along the ceiling in tortuous patterns, making tortuous patterns of glare and shade up there and down below. The bedroom and bathroom were walled off, but the rest of the place was just one long expanse: the living area, the open kitchen at the far end, the high windows onto the fire escape. There was not much furniture. A black leather sofa, two black leather chairs. A glass coffee table. Another table of wood by the windows with the elaborate phone-fax-answering machine the trumpet player had left behind.

They sat in the leather chairs and drank. The whore smoked, one cigarette then another. She had unbelted the plastic raincoat now. She was wearing a black dress, scooped low over her cleavage, ending high on her stockinged thighs. She raised her cigarette hand and touched the fringe of her hair, drew it aside with two fingers. Her hair was too black, Lonnie thought. Too set, too perfect. A wig, he figured. Like some little girl playing dress-up.

She was distracted at first and they sat silently. Then she tried to make conversation. "So you're, like, a musician or something, huh?"

He nodded. "Name's Lonnie Blake."

She didn't answer. Made a vague, nervous gesture, looked around her nervously. Stabbed the side of her mouth with the cigarette, taking quick, sharp pulls. "Look," she said. "The thing is: I can't go back out there. Not tonight. I mean, I know it's a lot to ask."

Lonnie lifted his shoulders slightly. He felt the bourbon warm inside him. He'd had a lot of it tonight. He was beginning to feel distant and muzzy.

"I got some money," the girl went on. "You know? I could pay you." She gave a frantic little laugh. "Give you a freebie if you want."

For a moment, Lonnie didn't understand her. His eyebrows came together, making his sharp cat features even sharper still.

The girl's cigarette waved around. She gestured at herself. "I mean, we all know what I am, right? So? I'm serious. I can do something for you. I'd be happy to, you know. Whatever."

Lonnie got it then. He shook his head no, but his eyes went down her automatically. The white upper curves of her breasts and the sleek lines of her and her stocking tops visible beneath the hem of her short dress. He was too far away to smell the scent of her, but he smelled it anyway. And he felt the sight of her flesh inside him and it changed the way he breathed.

She brushed the edge of her raincoat back to give him a better view. And when he didn't speak for another moment, she said, "You know, if you're, like, into something? If you got some kind of specialty stuff. Fantasies. Whatever. Anything that doesn't draw blood. I'm serious, man, I'd be happy to. We could have a good time just . . . just let me stay."

She brushed at her smeared cheek again. That brought him back to himself. He shifted in his chair.

"You can sleep on the couch. Stay till morning. Whatever," he said. He drained his glass. Stood up. "I'm gonna make another. You want one?"

"No. No. I'm good."

This time, he poured unsteadily, gripping the bottle, gripping the glass. Watching the brown liquor splashing over the ice with a kind of grim intensity. *Bullshit*, he thought. He wouldn't admit to himself that she'd unnerved him.

You can't really play since they killed her.

And he thought angrily: *I'm not gonna make the girl pay with her ass, I don't care what she is.* And he thought: *Crazy whore.*

"Shit, most guys'd figure they'd won the lottery," she said, as if speaking into his thoughts. "I got headgear. I always use 'em. I'm safe, really, if that's what's bugging you."

"Look, I told you you could stay." He growled it at her, more harshly than he meant to. The liquor—it was getting to him, he thought. Christ, what a night. He thumped down the bottle, snapped up the glass. "Just forget it. It's okay." He knocked back a heavy slug of bourbon, then dashed the rest of it into the sink. "I'll go get you a blanket."

He walked off quickly into the bedroom.

He yanked blankets from his closet in there, blinking hard. Yeah, the liquor, he thought. The liquor was getting to him.

She called in. "You mind if I use your bathroom?"

"Go on ahead," he called back.

When he heard the bathroom door click shut, he paused with the blankets in his hands. He took a breath, let it out, was surprised—was disturbed—to feel it tremble. *Steady there, cowboy.* He felt a kind of nauseous excitement.

If you're into something. Specialty stuff. Fantasies. Whatever.

It wasn't as if he hadn't thought of it before. Paying a girl to do the thing he wanted. Sure he had. Most guys would've figured they'd won the lottery. She had that right.

Back in the living room, he tossed the blankets on the sofa. He saw that her raincoat was lying there too. He moved away from it as if aimlessly.

He sank into one of the chairs. The leather sighed under him and he sighed. He heard the toilet flush, the water running. He touched his forehead with a couple of fingertips. His forehead was damp. *Shit*, he thought.

When he heard the door come open, he looked up and saw her. Standing and watching him, one hand resting on her purse. A ceiling lamp shone down on her, gleamed on her skin. The curve of her hip was pressed into the dress.

She'd fixed her makeup. Dried her tears. Her face seemed clearer now than it had. She was older than he'd thought at first, but still young, maybe twenty-five. Her mouth was long, glossed silver, the lips looked very soft. The big eyes were intelligent, but they were furtive and unhappy. Well, he guessed it wasn't much of a life.

She cocked her head. "You sure you don't want anything? I mean it's no big deal." He nodded, but his eyes stayed on her. She gave a little laugh. "Man! Look at you. Whatever you've got, it's bad, isn't it?"

"Look," said Lonnie Blake. "I said forget it."

"No, I'm just saying. You're all scarred up inside, I can see it. Man!"

Lonnie lowered his eyes. He found himself nodding again, not thinking, just sitting there, looking down, screwing his hands together, palm against palm. Aware of her.

"Hey, life's shit and then you die, right?" she said.

A pale little laugh escaped him.

She came forward slowly. He heard her heels snap the rhythm of her steps on the pine floor. He heard the soft whap of her purse as she tossed it on the sofa, plastic on leather.

"You know, you're making me feel bad here," she said. "After you helped me and everything." She tilted over to try to meet his eyes but he wouldn't look up at her. "Can't I do something for you here, Lonnie? I could cheer you up a little I bet."

He twisted his palms together. Not thinking. "It's been a long time," he heard himself say.

"Yeah? Well, right there, see: I could fix that."

She came closer, silently now over the worn braid rug. Closer, until she stood over him and he could smell her again, the violets and the smoke. Her hemline was at his eye level. He was breathing in that unfamiliar rhythm that the sight of her brought on.

"Isn't there something I can do?"

He looked up at her face and she smiled in spite of her unhappy eyes.

"I guess I'm not much of a Romeo," he told her.

She reached out and gently pressed her palm against his temple. "I'll bet there's something special, though. Hm? Is there? It's not like you're gonna shock me or anything." She shook her head sympathetically. "You look like you need something, Lonnie."

He let out another mirthless laugh. He looked down at his shoes. He could feel the warmth of her hand on him. "Shit," he said.

Then, with a breath, he looked up at her again. Before he'd meant to, before he'd thought about what he was doing. He looked up into those unhappy blue eyes, up at that sympathetic smile. "So like you do special things," he said. "You don't mind that."

"Go on," she told him. "Knock yourself out. What can I do for you, Lonnie?"

Lonnie gazed at her another moment, aching. He licked his dry lips.

"Make me a drink," he said hoarsely then. "Make me a drink—and ask me about my day."

5

She brought him a bourbon and seven. She stood behind him and rubbed his shoulders. He didn't even have to tell her to do that. She just did. She leaned close, brought her lips to his ear.

"What's my name?" she said softly.

Lonnie felt he had jumped off a cliff. It was surprisingly easy to just keep falling. "Suzanne," he heard himself say.

"Suzanne. That's nice. I like that." The whore went on rubbing his shoulders. "Just relax. It's okay." He felt her brush the top of his head with her lips. He felt her rest her chin on him. "So what was your day like, sweetheart? Tell me. Tell Suzanne."

Lonnie took a hard pull at the booze. Reinforcements. He rolled the cool glass against his forehead. She rubbed his shoulders. He closed his eyes. It was easy to see his dead wife, as easy as falling. He was lost in the image of her almost instantly.

"I did a gig," he whispered. He kept his eyes shut, spoke to the image. "Just a small thing. A couple of guys I did some studio work with. They ain't much, but we been playing together, you know. Just a few gigs here and there."

The whore must've caught his confessional tone. "It's all right," she told him. She rubbed his shoulders. She pressed her lips against his ear. He felt her hot breath.

She didn't smell of violets anymore. She smelled of another perfume. He still remembered that perfume. It was good to smell it again.

"I think about what they did to you," he said. "I mean it. I think about it all the time." She rubbed his shoulders. She kissed the side of his head. "It's just . . . sometimes . . . I *hear* these cats. You know what I'm saying? I put on a CD or something. Some of these cats. That Jim Carter. *Real Quietstorm.* Don Harrison. *Nouveau Swing.* They got the chops, you know. They're real. They're players." He pressed his lips together, shook his head. He opened his eyes now. Held his drink out before him in his two hands. He stared and stared at it, feeling her breath, her fingers. "I mean, I'm thinking about you all the time, baby, all the time, it's just . . . I listen to these guys sometimes and I think: I *got* those chops. You know? I'm as *good* as they are." He made a noise like steam being released from an engine. Something was welling in him now. Desire. Desire or the old rage, he wasn't sure. They were indistinguishable to him. "I been doing all this studio work, commercial work, you know, to stay alive, and that's okay. It's just sometimes—sometimes I feel like really playing, that's all. The Jurassics, you know, the way I used to. So we got this trio together, that's all. You see what I'm saying?" He stared at the drink in his hands, stared and stared.

"Yeah. I see what you're saying," the whore said, rubbing his shoulders. "You're saying: life goes on, Lonnie. Right?"

But he hardly heard her, or he heard her as if in a dream, as you hear a voice or a noise when you're dreaming. His arms were pulled in against himself now.

The ice in his glass rattled as his hands began to shake. He stared into the depths of his bourbon and his eyes were suddenly hot with self-contempt and anger and confusion.

"God!" he said.

The glass fallen to the floor—the drink spilling out of it—the ice melting on the rug—he took her on the sofa, hardly undressing. Her hem was pushed up around her waist. The straps of her bra were stripped down over her shoulders. He rose up above her, his eyes shut tight, his teeth bared. He rammed into her with long strokes, hard, and he felt his rage.

"Bitch," he said just at the end. It broke out between his clenched teeth. "Fucking whore. Cunt. Bitch."

When he came, it felt like bile spewed out of him. It felt tarry and acid. He let out a strangled cry and it flooded from him. He thought it would burn his dick off. He thought it would eat through the condom and dissolve her guts.

He rolled off her instantly. Sat on the floor. Stripped the condom off and threw it from him. "Oh shit," he said. "Shit." He sat curled up beside the sofa, his knees raised, his two hands pressed against his brow. He struck at his own forehead with the heels of both hands, rocking his head into the blows.

"Whew," said the girl to herself as she watched him. She sat up a little, pulling a bra strap back up her shoulder. "Hey, whoa, Jesus, take it easy there, Lonnie," she said. "Don't kill yourself. I mean, it's all right. You didn't hurt me or anything. You oughta see what some of these assholes get up to." She reached out tentatively, tentatively touched his shoulder. He made a noise and his body clenched, but he didn't cast her away. "I mean it, man. I mean, look: I'm still alive. That's a good night for me."

Lonnie heard this and burst out laughing. He covered his face with his hands.

The whore laughed too. "You think I'm kidding," she said.

Lonnie nodded, covering his face. He shook with laughter. "Oh man," he said then, and wiped his damp eyes.

Not half an hour later, they had sex again, in bed this time and more gently. The whore wouldn't kiss him, not on the lips. But naked under him she let him brush his mouth over her cheek, trail his fingers up her belly, paint trails of his yearning breath on her everywhere. She met his eyes as he moved inside her. He studied her with a bewilderment amounting almost to wonder. Everything while he was in her—details of the scene—a wrinkle on the bedsheet—a smear of gray dirt on the blue wall—the shape of her mouth when her lips parted—everything seemed astonishingly clear and present. He hadn't been hard like this or calm like this for ages.

Afterward she said, "I'm gonna get some sleep, okay?" and touched her lips lightly to the stubble of his jaw. She rolled away from him. He lay looking at the way her black hair rested on her white neck.

One more time, at daybreak, he was in her. On his side, curled up against her, slipping in her from behind. His eyes traveled over the curve of her spine, traced the sweet, round shape of her ass. He moved this time dreamily. He thought this time about Suzanne. Moving in the whore, he could almost taste the San Francisco mornings. The ache was terrible. The fact that he would never touch his wife like this again—never—it just seemed impossible to bear.

Finished, he pressed his brow against the girl's hair a minute, closed his eyes. He wished he could've spoken now the way he would've spoken to his wife. Suzanne was the only one he had ever spoken to like that. Given the chance, he knew he would've loved Suzanne till he died. What was he going to do now with a lifetime's worth of desire?

The whore drew away from him. Smiled at him over her shoulder, a sad, regretful smile.

"That's it, Romeo, I'm out of rubber," she said. "Plus I gotta go."

It was just dawn, an autumn dawn. The big windows in the main room were rattling with the wind. Lonnie could hear them from the bedroom. Lying on the bed alone, he could hear rain gargling in the gutters too. He could hear the whore in the bathroom, the faucet handles squeaking.

After a while, she came out. She leaned her head in the bedroom doorway. "Okay if I use your phone?"

"Yeah. Sure. Go ahead."

She moved away.

He lay where he was. The pillows held the scent of

violets. And then, for moments at a time, the scent of San Francisco returned to him, the scent of the old mornings, waking with Suzanne. Never again, he thought. The yearning was like a solid thing. It smelled of remembered weather and it weighed a ton.

Lonnie lay there and stared up at the ceiling and glimpsed a lifetime of inconsolable desire.

After a while, he heard the wind again, the rain. He heard the whore underneath them. She was talking on the phone in the other room. Her voice was a hushed murmur, but certain words reached him.

"You sure? . . . people hanging around? . . . big fucker with, like, a rough face . . . No . . . .anyone . . . ?"

Then she was quiet. When she spoke again, a gust of wind rattled the window frames, drowned out the words.

A moment later, he heard the telephone clapping back into its cradle.

Lonnie felt bad. He didn't want her to go.

She came into the bedroom doorway. She was fully dressed, had her coat on, her purse over her arm.

"All right, lover, I'm gonna sixty-six," she said. Lonnie lifted up onto one elbow. She walked over to him, sat on the bed. "You really saved my life," she told him. "Really." She forced a smile. "Hey: my hero." She leaned over and kissed his cheek.

He gave that quiet hiss of air. "Any time," he said.

She drew back. Lingered over him. Considered him sadly. She seemed about to speak again. Lonnie wanted to reach out and draw her to him. He was surprised by the strength of the urge.

She stood up.

"Maybe I could call you," he said.

She shook her head, pressed her lips together.

"Maybe in another life, you know. This one, it just ain't a happening situation."

He nodded.

She gave a mock-happy wave, waggling her fingers at him. "I'm smoke," she said.

Lonnie watched her hurry out the door. He heard the rain in the gutters. The windows banging in the wind. The rattle of the elevator cage.

When she was gone, he got out of bed slowly. Shrugged on a bathrobe. His hands in the pockets, he wandered out into the loft.

The place looked quiet and gray. The bourbon glass still lay where he'd dropped it on the rug in front of the chair. Lonnie turned away from it.

He moved to the windows. The panes were streaked with rain. The rain was blowing slantwise across them, across the view of white and brown lofts over the way and across the gray sky above them.

Lonnie stood there looking out until he saw the girl emerge below. She paused at the doorway, turning her head, glancing everywhere. Then she moved out into the sparse traffic of Saturday pedestrians hurrying toward the avenues.

He watched the black top of her head, then the back of her black raincoat. Then she was past the window frame, beyond his field of vision.

Lonnie drew a deep breath. He moved to the wooden table. He looked down at the phone-fax-answering machine. His fingers walked idly over the buttons. He felt—what was the word for it? Melancholy. Like a Berlin ballad.

His fingers found the button labeled Redial. Slowly, he pressed it down. A number—the number the girl had just called—marched across the LCD. Lonnie watched it. He picked up the pen beside the machine and wrote the number on the phone pad.

Then he tossed the pen down and turned away to look out at the rain.

CHAPTER 2

A MOUSETRAP—
NO MOUSE

1

In Jersey that day, by the Palisades, the flaming leaves were falling. The wind and the rain brought them sweeping down onto Jonathan Reese's yard. It made for a lifeless prospect: the leaves lying dark and glossy on the lawn, covering the tennis court at the bottom of the hill, sinking into the dull puddles on the plastic cover of the swimming pool. The gray sky above drained the brilliance from the maples standing on the graceful slope of ground. And the last white asters in April Markham-Reese's garden were bent into the mud by the silver downpour.

The windows in the family room—the whole rear wall of them—looked out and down over those rainy acres. The colorless bluster out-of-doors made the house seem bright and cozy inside. Reese had a fire going in the grate. All the lights were on, warm and bright. Dave Grusin was playing Mancini on the stereo.

And April was at her writing desk—her escritoire, she called it, jokingly grand. Working on her charities. The hungry children in Africa. The scholarships for inner-city youth. Planned Parenthood. The ACLU. And Michael was nearby at the Play Computer—to be distinguished from the Homework Computer in his room, Mom's Laptop in the master bedroom, and *The* Computer in Reese's study.

Reese himself was sitting on the sofa. Holding an *Economist* on his lap but not reading it. Just drinking in the scene. The wife, the son, the hearth, the bosom; the whole family thang, God love it; a still, sweet refuge in the ever-changing blah blah blah.

Well, he could joke, but it was good stuff. After two weeks away. Moscow, London. It was balm to the business-battered spirit to be here with them again. It was very good to be home.

From where he sat, Reese turned his attention to his wife. Studied the cute little ringlet of brown hair falling on her cheek as she bent over her checkbook giving away his hard-earned money. He was aware of a mild, a not unpleasant sadness. Missing his daughter Nancy, who was away at Yale. And, after a second, sensing his eyes on her, the partner of his joy and sorrow for lo these thirty years glanced up at him. And her stately bearing, her patrician face were as beautiful to him now as ever. And she knew exactly what he was thinking. She said quietly, "I'm glad we'll all be together for Thanksgiving." A display of mental telepathy which set off a flood of husbandly love in Jonathan Reese more powerful than words can rightly say.

Manfully clearing his throat to disguise the emotion, he laid his magazine aside. Stood and stretched. He was a tall man and broad-shouldered. He had full, coiffed iron-colored hair. A chiseled, almost classical face. In jeans and a bulky white sweater, he looked trim and fit. Not bad at all, he felt, for a codger of fifty-one.

Humming tunelessly along with the stereo, he moved to stand behind his thirteen-year-old son. He watched the PC monitor. The boy was currently dealing death to a series of animated demons who seemed to be rising up from the floor of a stony corridor somewhere. Transylvania maybe. Reese shook his head in amazement.

"I can remember when it took a computer the size of a house just to add two and two," he said.

"Gee, Dad," said Michael. "That's really . . . that's very . . ." The boy's head fell forward and he began to snore.

Reese laughed, whapped him. "Smart-aleck cyberpunk," he said. He threw a headlock on the kid.

Michael started laughing too. "Hey! You're gonna get me killed here!"

Reese rubbed a noogie into his hair. "I'm murdering your son," he told April.

"That's nice, dear," she said.

Reese let the boy go. Gave him a fatherly slap on the shoulder.

Then he lifted his eyes, surprised.

A car had come up the drive. He could just see it from here as it reached the garage behind the house. A Lexus sedan. Very nice. New, blue, modest but comfortable. Its headlights were on against the weather.

Then they went off. The driver's door opened. A red-haired man stepped out into the rain.

Reese held his breath. The song on the stereo ended and for a moment there was near silence in the room. The clicking of Michael's computer keys. The snicker of the fire. The wind at the windows, the rain on the pane.

Outside, the red-haired man shrugged his sleek black trench coat straight at the shoulders. Then he ducked his head against the downpour and started quickly along the path to the front door.

Watching him, Reese frowned. He still had his hands on his son's shoulders. He patted the boy gently.

He knew the red-haired man. He was named Edmund Winter and he was the new North American bureau chief for a company called Executive Decisions. What that meant, in practical terms, was that he was an extremely expensive and proficient killer-for-hire.

Watching him move quickly toward his house, Reese let out his breath at last with a silent curse.

He hated conducting business out of his home.

2

"Without making any excuses, I want to be clear," Winter said. "It's only been a few months since they brought me up here. I haven't had time to review all our personnel or carry out a full reorganization."

"This sounds suspiciously like a buildup to bad news," said Reese.

"No. No. It's good news, in fact, it's just . . . we've got a time issue on our hands. That's why I came here. I thought I ought to catch you while you were in the country. And under the circumstances, I thought it best to communicate with you face-to-face."

Reese considered this a moment. "Then you've found her, I take it."

"Yes, sir," said Winter. "I think we have."

They were upstairs in Reese's study now. A small room, modest but impressive. Hardcover business tomes on shelves. Photographs of Reese with the swordfish he caught off the Keys, the wildebeeste he shot in Tanganyika. An immense, blond wood, more or less orderly desk. An oversized computer monitor on a typing table to one side. A curtained window.

Reese sat behind the desk. Tilted back in his chair, elbow on the rest, chin on the base of his thumb, two fingers propped against his jaw. Winter was seated on the small sofa to his right. Relaxed, arm along the sofa back, legs crossed at the knee. They were both wearing expensive aftershave, and their scents mingled in the close space.

Despite his profession, Winter looked civilized enough, Reese thought. Intense, hungry, ambitious, yes. But then there was a lot of that in corporate life. He was about forty, give or take a year or two. His face was narrow, lined, ironical, edgy. There was a great deal of wit sparkling in his hazel eyes. He was no idiot clearly. At the same time, under the tailored gray suit, the white shirt, the port red tie, the gold tie clasp and so on, Reese could make out the build and carriage of an athlete, a man in prime condition. Winter, he thought, was a formidable fellow all around.

"My assessment was right," Winter said now. "She's gone underground completely now. She's operating as a prostitute full time." Reese made a noise of amusement. But Winter held up his hand. "No. Look. Don't think of it that way. This is a very smart, tough, determined individual. She's willing to do anything to protect her child."

"I can't see how her child benefits from her being a whore," said Reese.

"I'm sure she'd prefer to do something else—but if she did, we'd have had her by now." Winter ticked his reasons off on his fingers. "Prostitution is anonymous. There are no business records, no taxes, no paper trail of any kind. Even the customers have a stake in protecting her identity. With the right customers, it can be highly paid work too. And she needs the money—she can't outrun us without money—she knows that. And the equipment's portable." Reese snorted at that and Winter smiled—but he persisted. "I'm telling you. We shouldn't underestimate her. I mean, you can say: this is just a waitress, this is an uneducated woman. But she's been moving around, making it hard for us to keep track of her for years. And the minute the Hunnicut incident happened—bang—she vanished. No hesitation, no second thoughts, self-deception. She just said, yep, this is it, and she was gone. Now it's been four months. Executive Decisions has devoted substantial resources to her recovery, and yet she's kept away from us all this time. Believe me—this woman?—prostitution is nothing. If she thought she could protect her child by setting herself on fire, we'd be roasting marshmallows on her bones."

"So you're in love," said Reese.

"I'm deeply in love," answered Winter deadpan. "I've come to you for your blessing."

The two men laughed. Then Reese let out a comical groan, rubbed his eyes. "All right. All right. You've done your pitch. Now tell me what happened."

"Well. First, the good news," said Winter with a wry half smile. "She finally made a mistake. A couple of mistakes. She got arrested in St. Louis for one thing. They just threw her into the cooler for a night but I had my ops scanning the records and we picked up on it. Again, she was smart. She was gone the minute she hit the street. But"—he lifted a finger—"and this was her *big* mistake—she held on to one of her clients. Commuter. A guy going back and forth from New York. I guess she figured she could use him to start up her business in a new city. Fortunately, I'd had my guys stake him out. Him and another guy from Chicago just in case."

"That was smart," Reese allowed.

Winter nodded once. "Last night, she finally showed up. He went and met her at a small hotel near the terminal."

"And you lost her," said Reese. "I assume that's the bad news."

"The bad news," Winter answered slowly, giving Reese time to get ready for it. "The bad news is that we not only lost her, but the op was made. She spotted him."

Reese let out a long, whispered "Ah." That *was* bad news. It hit him. He pressed his hands together, held them up before his mouth as if in prayer. He needed time to think a moment before he knew how he wanted to react to that.

It was never easy for him, dealing with Winter, dealing with his company, Executive Decisions. There were inherent difficulties. E.D. was a South Africa–based firm which had begun by giving military aid and advice to corporations operating in unstable environments. For the most part, there was nothing mysterious or clandestine about them. If your manufacturing plant was under attack by rebel guerrillas in some godforsaken no-man's-land without enough government to protect a school picnic, you phoned E.D.—or contacted www.execdec.com— and they handled it for you. Reese had a friend, for instance, at Bright Young Things, the clothing people, who'd had exactly that problem at her manufacturing plant in Sierra Leone. Insurgents were hijacking shipments, sabotaging production, killing workers. So she'd hired E.D. They'd sent in some advisers, concentrated on a single village of suspected rebel sympathizers and administered what they called a short, sharp shock. They raped the women while the men were forced to watch, killed the men and children while the women watched, sold some of the women to offset expenses, and that was it, the threat to the factory was finished, the world was once again safe for khaki casuals. It was unpleasant, no question. But as peace-loving as Reese was, business, he knew, was business. And according to his friend at Bright Young Things, this had been the least expensive way to deal with the situation in terms of both money and human life.

So fine. That sort of thing worked very well as long as you were on foreign soil, in one of those hellholes of chaos and poverty that the newspapers are proud to refer to as "developing nations." If you were in Europe or America, on the other hand, matters became a bit more sensitive. Western sensibilities, laws, media being what they were, E.D. had only recently found it safe to begin operations here at all. And even now it was necessary to proceed on a local, individual and highly secretive basis.

But after some initial blunders and a couple of near-exposures, E.D. had managed to establish a network of highly trained operatives throughout the United States and Europe, many of them moonlighting law officers or others in positions of power and responsibility. And now they had brought in Winter to reorganize, fine-tune, really whip things into shape.

Winter was supposed to be the best in the business. His curriculum vitae as it had been given to Reese was, understandably, on the sketchy side. But he'd done a stint in the U.S. Marines, some mercenary work in various African and South and Central American locations. And he was said to have expertise in weaponry, martial arts, surveillance and interrogation techniques.

And he had a pleasant, professional manner to boot. For all the time he'd spent in the field, Winter handled himself like a businessman. He knew how to claim credit where credit was due. How to take responsibility for his subordinates' mistakes while managing to communicate his annoyance at their incompetence. How to acknowledge a setback while continuing to maintain an aggressive, problem-solving posture at all times.

But while this familiar behavior mitigated or at least disguised Reese's difficulties, it didn't end them. Because no matter how well Winter comported himself, his was not, at the core, a civilized profession and this was not, at bottom, a civilized operation.

Reese was vice president in charge of Business Affairs at the pharmaceutical firm Helix. And what that meant, what it had meant for several years, was that he, virtually alone, had the task of saving the company from an unprecedented disaster. The botched experimental project that had brought Helix to the very brink of a legal, financial and public relations nightmare was not his fault. But, nevertheless, the job of pulling the enormous corporation back from that brink had fallen into his hands and was now, he knew, to be the making or breaking of him.

He had come a long way. The job was almost complete. And Reese was as determined as anyone—more determined than anyone—to see it the rest of the way. He knew that Executive Decisions provided the best available means of doing that. But all the same, when you came right down to it, even a man's man like himself found it a bit intimidating to be in charge of personnel who could probably kill him with a single well-placed blow to some part of his anatomy he'd never even heard of. If nothing else, it ignited his macho, competitive instincts, which he feared would weaken his ability to make rational decisions. Right now, for instance, he found himself wishing he weren't dressed so casually, that he were wearing a suit that displayed the power of his company, his money, even his personal success. Under Winter's ironical, ambitious, hyper-energized gaze, this sweater and jeans he had on felt a little bit like a pair of pink pajamas. Which might tend to undermine his confidence—especially if he was going to have to read Winter the riot act over some idiot E.D. operative's mistake.

But in the end, this was a multimillion—potentially a billion-dollar operation. No matter how he felt, Reese had to stay in charge. He put a touch of stern displeasure into his voice.

"So your op was spotted," he said. "What does that mean? Are you telling me she's likely to relocate? That we'll be right back where we were four months ago?"

For a second, it crossed Reese's mind that Winter might simply kill him for this. But no, the red-haired man accepted the tone of rebuke gracefully. He cocked his head mildly, as if considering. "Well, in my opinion, it's not quite as bad as that," he said. "The girl saw someone following her, but she doesn't know who it was. She may be on the lookout for us but, let's face it, she's an attractive prostitute: she can't just leave town every time some creep trails her down the street. It'd never stop. On top of which, she hasn't been in town more than a month. It's doubtful she has the resources to relocate right away. So I think we have some time, a window of opportunity. Plus—we have the john, her client. Which" —he wrapped it up—"is what I'm here about."

Reese sighed, lifted his eyes to the ceiling. He could feel the tension starting to shimmer in him. He hoped he wasn't about to hear what he was pretty certain he was just about to hear.

Winter drew a breath to get ready for it. Then he said, "My op wants a priority go."

"Ach!" said Reese. He swiveled his chair to one side, presented Winter with an angry profile.

Winter continued. "We've searched the john's house, his office . . . "

"Your man bobbled the ball . . ." said Reese.

". . . tapped his phone. If he's got any record of her, we can't find it."

". . . and now I'm supposed to authorize a priority operation."

"And with all due respect," Winter pushed on. "I don't think it's exactly fair to say our operative bobbled the ball. He's a good man with full surveillance capabilities. But as I say, this is an extremely intelligent and resourceful woman . . ."

"She's a bartender. She's a prostitute, for Christ's sake."

"My man has surveilled . . . he's followed experts, believe me. Intelligence agents. International crime figures. It's a difficult business at the best of times, and this was a dark, empty street with a very sharp woman who's looking out for us. Look, to be absolutely fair here, I think we deserve full marks for tracking the woman down. She was a needle in a haystack."

"Great. Somehow that doesn't make me feel better."

"All right, sure," said Winter. "I wish the immediate outcome had been different too. But there's still time to make it good."

Reese made another angry noise, but it was mostly for show. The die was pretty much cast. He knew he didn't have any real choice in the matter. He just didn't want Winter to think he was a soft touch, that's all. He swiveled back to face him.

"What about a simple interrogation?" he asked. "You're supposed to be an expert at that . . ."

"I'm an expert at that, but this isn't some nigger in the middle of nowhere . . ."

"Whoa, whoa, whoa, excuse me, excuse me," Reese broke in sharply. "The people who work for me don't use that sort of language. Understood? It's just unnecessary." Reese could not always afford to be as idealistic as his wife but he detested racism in all its forms. "It's bad enough you're asking me to authorize murder, let's keep it on a professional level."

Once again, he waited for Winter's reaction and once again Winter was graceful and polite. "Sorry. Old habits. You're right, of course. All I'm trying to say is that we're in America now. The man we're talking about is a white, well-to-do, well-connected attorney. If we simply question him, there's no way we can absolutely guarantee his silence afterward. My people insist on airtight security—and frankly, I think that's in your company's best interests as well . . ."

"And I want his family kept out of it," said Reese, daring to level a finger at the man. "I don't want anything like last time."

"Well, that's going to be difficult on a weekend. You may be talking about a delay . . ."

"Delay then." He shook his head. "I sleep badly enough without another bloodbath on my conscience. This is an individual authorization. Understood?"

Winter seemed about to go on—to argue—but no. He remained a diplomat to the end. He lifted a hand in surrender.

"You're the boss," he said quietly. "It's your call."

3

The rain was letting up now. There was only a drizzle. Winter moved through it leisurely, down the front path back to his car.

Nice piece of property, he thought, looking the place over as he went.

In the driveway, he opened the Lexus door and paused. Over the car's roof, through the rear wall of windows that edged around the side of the house, through the tall panes still spotted with rain, he could see the Reese family gathered in the back room. They were held there in the warm yellow light as if on the other side of a gray world.

Reese was with them again. Standing behind his son. Patting the middle of his sweater.

I'm starving, Winter imagined him saying. *What do you have to do to get some lunch around here?*

Sure enough, there was another movement. The

wife—April—fluttered to her feet. With that pretty expression wives have when they're pretending to be annoyed but are really happy to be needed.

I suppose I'll just have to feed you two monsters, she would say. A real sweetie she looked like, Winter thought. He let a quirk touch the corner of his mouth. Nice house, nice family. It's the life, no question.

And he slipped in behind the Lexus's steering wheel.

He turned on the ignition first. Then he reached into his jacket pocket and switched off the TRD-2000 unit. He tugged the antenna from the unit's jack. Pulled the wristband receiver off over his right wrist. Careful not to snag his shirt, he worked the wire down slowly through his sleeve. When it came clear, he bunched the wire sloppily and dropped it in the pocket with the TRD. If Reese had tried to tape their conversation—or if a third party had been bugging them—the Tape Recorder Detector would have vibrated silently against Winter's chest. It was a handy thing to have around during sensitive meetings like this one.

Winter reached over and fiddled with the knobs and switches on the dash. A motor hummed as a monitor swiveled outward. The grid of Uniden's visual scanner and radar/laser detector slowly became visible.

All the while, Winter was considering Reese, what they had talked about, what he was going to do.

Hughes and Mortimer, he was thinking to himself. *Mortimer and Hughes.*

He put the Lexus into reverse and eased it out of Reese's long drive.

He drove back slowly along the winding country roads. He wasn't angry exactly, but on the other hand he couldn't say he was in any way pleased.

He had had to eat shit. There was no other way to look at it. He had had to eat shit, and it was one of his least favorite things to eat, right next to sushi. Out in the field—out in the street, in a bar, anywhere—if a man had spoken to him the way Reese just had he would've ripped open his rib cage and removed his entrails by hand.

But now he was Mr. Businessman. Mr. Bureau Chief. Mr. Front Office. And Reese was his client. So he had to sit there and take it.

Not that he blamed Reese either. The guy was paying good money, he deserved good service. But Hughes and Mortimer—Mortimer and Hughes—they had fucked up royally. They had lost the girl and let her spot them. It was because of them that Winter had had to eat shit. And no, that did not leave him feeling well pleased. They were going to hear about this. This was what he was here for. His brief was to streamline and modernize. To cut down on incompetence and the old blundering, inappropriate, thuggish methods. Messrs. Hughes and Mortimer—Mr. Mortimer and Mr. Hughes—were going to be extremely unhappy chappies if he had to instruct them personally on how he wanted things done.

He drove along thoughtfully, idly admiring the canopy of leaves above him, the colorful maples and oaks and tulip trees meeting overhead. They sure were brilliant, he thought, even in this dull, dripping weather. And now and then, the view beyond them would open up and there would be a rolling field, a stately home. White shingles. Black shutters. Pillared porticoes.

Nice, he thought. Nice houses. It was the life, no bout adout it. Another couple years, if things went well, if he worked his way up the ladder—who could tell? He might be like Reese. He might have it all. The house, the loving wife, the kids. The days, the loving nights, the fruitful years. Fishing the stream, mowing the lawn, raking the leaves, shoveling the snow. Faithful husband of. Loving father of. Rest in peace. So long. You're gone forever. Sorry. Bye.

Okay, maybe not. Winter laughed to himself. Maybe it just wasn't in his nature.

The Lexus turned a corner onto route 72, came out from under the overhanging trees. The road widened into four lanes here, ran on past mini-malls and gas stations to the interstate.

Winter glanced over at the Uniden detector. Nothing. No speed traps. All the same, he eased the Lexus just up to the forty-mile-an-hour limit. He joined the weekend traffic of cars not much different from his. Chauffeur Moms on their way to ball games. Do-it-yourself Dads heidi-ho-ing to the hardware store.

No, it was not his nature.

He thought of the girl. Carol Dodson. That was more in his line. He would've enjoyed going after her himself. What he'd told Reese was true: she was good. Smart and tough. To keep ahead of them this long. To keep her child away from them. To stay out of the system where they could have tracked her down in a city minute. Over these past few months, Winter had come to admire her. The way she thought, the way she acted. No hesitation, no sacrifice too hard. The way she looked was nice too. He'd seen her picture. The slim, tight figure. The round breasts, the round butt. The sharp, pert features of her face with that long mouth and those big baby blue eyes . . .

The Lexus reached the interstate. Winter slipped it down the ramp. Angled it into the southern flow of cars heading for the city, cars as nondescript as his. He tapped his steering wheel with an index finger, feeling a rhythm in him, the music of the moment.

They would have her in a day or two, he thought, all things being equal. With a priority go, it was pretty much certain. Even Mortimer and Hughes couldn't fuck up that badly. They would have her, and they would take her to the E.D. Factory. Probably have to interrogate her to find the kid. Maybe he could take over that part himself. Yeah, he thought. There was an idea. He couldn't be a desk jockey all the time. He would interrogate her himself and keep his hand in the game. Demonstrate to the troops how expertly things could be done. Set a standard of excellence.

He felt his penis shifting in his pants at the thought of it. He nodded at the windshield, nodded with the rhythm, nodded at the civilians driving past.

He thought of her salt tears on her soft cheek. His come mixing with her blood.

Now *that*, he thought—that would be in his nature. That would be completely in keeping with his personality.

CHAPTER 3

I'M FOLLOWING YOU

1

There sat Lonnie Blake the next morning, Sunday morning. All alone by the telephone. Thinking about the girl.

The rain was gone now. The day was cold and clear. A strip of blue sky, of crystal air, showed above the lofts across the way. A haze of soft southern light poured in through the windows. It spread over the wooden chair and the wooden table. It spread over Lonnie Blake, who sat there looking down at the phone.

The phone, with its built-in fax and answering machine, was a big gray job. It was about the size of a briefcase. It took up most of the tabletop. Beside it on one side was an empty coffee mug. On the other side was the message pad. On the pad was the number Lonnie had jotted down the day before, the number the girl had called before she left. Lonnie had a pen in his hand. He doodled intricate designs around the number.

Damn fool, he kept telling himself. *What the hell you thinking about? She's just some crazy whore.*

But she didn't have a whore's eyes. Her eyes were smart and soft and frightened, not dead and mocking like a whore's. *You really saved my life,* she'd said to him. *My hero.* He remembered how hard and calm he'd been inside her. He remembered the scent of violets and smoke.

He had thought about her all day yesterday, all the

lonely day. Boxing the bags at the gym in the morning. Walking the streets, haunting the record shops in the afternoon. Playing at Renaissance, drinking at the bar. Drinking alone in the loft until he could lie down. Awake through a lot of the night, he had thought about her. He had sipped his morning coffee gazing at her number.

Now his eyes moved to the phone itself. He made that noise of contempt, that sharp, quiet exhalation. He threw down the pen. *You're just being this way because she acted Suzanne, cause she pretended to be Suzanne, that's all.* But she wasn't Suzanne. And it wasn't Suzanne's hands he thought about. It was *her* hands rubbing his shoulders. It was her whisper at his ear. *So what was your day like, sweetheart?* Her long lips soft on his rough jaw. *Life goes on.* Her body under him, her breasts in his hands.

He reached out and snapped up the receiver. He punched in the number. He listened for the ring.

It rang once. A woman answered.

"Hello?"

Lonnie hesitated. He wasn't sure he had the right girl.

"Hello?" she said again.

"Yeah. Listen. This is Lonnie Blake."

A pause. Then: "Yeah?"

No. Not her. A stranger. "Yeah, I'm looking for someone," Lonnie said. "The other night, Friday night—I was with someone. Someone came to my house."

Another pause. It went on a long time. Lonnie thought about hanging up. *What the hell're you doing?* he asked himself.

"What's your name again?" said the woman.

"Lonnie Blake."

"Hold on."

And then, almost at once, she was there. "Lonnie?"

Lonnie found himself warming inside at the sound of her, smiling a little. "Hey," he said.

But her voice was fast and hard. "How'd you get this number?"

"I just . . ."

"Did someone give it to you? Tell me how you got it, Lonnie. Come on. How'd you get it?"

"You used the phone. I pressed the Redial button."

Her breath. "Aw shit. Aw, man. Is anyone else there? Please don't lie to me, okay? Just don't. Just tell me: did anyone tell you to call me here?"

"No. Hell, no. I just been thinking about you."

"Aw, man. Aw, man."

"What is it? I just . . ."

"Don't think about me, Lonnie," she said.

"I wanted to make sure you were okay."

"Lonnie . . . Don't . . . Listen to me. Are you listening?"

"Yeah. Yeah, I'm listening."

"Don't call me anymore. You hear me? Don't think about me, don't wonder if I'm okay. Don't call me. Did you write down the number?"

"Listen, I was just . . ."

"Listen to me, goddammit!" she hissed. Then more softly: "Please! I mean it. Burn it, man. Oh, burn the fucking number. All right? Just hang up the phone and burn the fucking number. Please, Lonnie."

"Look. The other night . . ."

"The other night was . . . Oh . . .!"

"Come on. I keep thinking about you. I don't even know your name. Look, I can see you're in some kind of trouble, girl. I mean, you're alone and I'm alone here . . ."

"Lonnie . . ."

Lonnie held the phone to his ear, stared out the window. Thinking about her hands on his shoulders, her whisper in his ear, her body under him. "I'll pay you," he heard himself say suddenly. He hadn't meant to. He just did. "I want to see you again. Listen, I mean it: I need to see you. I'm willing to pay."

There was silence in answer. Her low breathing. Then she said, "You're a good guy, Lonnie. Burn the number."

And she hung up on him.

The elevator started down. Lonnie watched the numbers. His hands clenched and unclenched in his overcoat pockets. He had to get out, get some air, walk around. *Breeze that bitch,* he told himself. She'd hurt him. He thought: *Forget her.*

The number-four light winked out, the number-three light winked on. He found himself remembering how scared she'd been, how her eyes had brimmed with tears. *My hero,* she'd said. Maybe she'd been scared on the phone too. *Did anyone tell you to call me?*

The elevator stopped.

Aw, man! thought Lonnie Blake. Mattie Harris. She was always doing this.

The door on the other side of the cage opened. There, sure enough, stood Mattie Harris. She pretended she was surprised to see him.

"Oh! Hi, Lonnie!"

"Hey, Mattie," Lonnie said. "Howya doing?" His hands clenched and unclenched in his overcoat.

"I was just going out for some breakfast," she said. "Or brunch or whatever. I hate cooking for one, you know." She was in her thirties. Pudgy, short. Pink-skinned, apple-cheeked. Long, straight, shiny brown hair. Shiny brown eyes. "You feel like coming in? I wouldn't mind whipping something up for the two of us."

"Wish I could," said Lonnie. He managed to sound sincere. "I gotta go . . . downtown to see this man." *And I ain't got time to shake yo' hand,* he thought.

A frantic little something flashed at the bottom of Mattie's bright eyes. But she made a comical pout. "Oh well. Then I guess I'm all by my lonesome. Off to the Sad Café."

He slid back the cage for her. He had a glimpse of her loft a moment. Art posters and wall hangings, stuffed animals and fluffy white rugs. A fluffy white cat prowling. Muffin or Mittens or some shit like that, he couldn't remember. Then the door shut. The elevator started down again.

Mattie stood by him, her head at the level of his shoulder. She was dolled up: lipstick, makeup, a perfume that smelled like lavender. She'd been waiting for him, waiting to hijack the elevator as he went by.

She chattered to him in her musical voice. Lonnie

thought about the other voice, the hard, frightened voice on the telephone. *Burn the number.* He remembered the girl's face, regretful in the morning, saying good-bye, leaving her scent on his pillow.

"I don't know," said Mattie Harris. "I try not to let it make me crazy."

Lonnie had no idea what the hell she was talking about. His hands clenched and unclenched. He thought of the girl. The blood was buzzing in his veins. *Breeze her, man,* he thought. *Forget her.* The elevator touched down.

Out on the street, he spoke to Mattie quickly. "Which way you walking?" The old city ploy. Whatever she said, he was going the other way.

Mattie Harris took it bravely. Nodded toward the east. Smiled a little. Wiggled her fingers at him. "I'll see you."

Lonnie nodded. He was sorry to hurt her feelings. "Later," he said. "Okay?" He turned away from her.

The Sunday morning streets were hopping. Eighth Avenue was hopping. Parents with shopping bags, a mother alone, a father alone. Baby strollers pushing out of the brick-lined walkways of the projects. Slim couples, childless, not quite young, boy and girl, boy and boy, taking their newspapers to the cafés.

Lonnie headed downtown. His hands working in his overcoat pockets, his eyes at gaze, his mind elsewhere. He felt he should be thinking about Suzanne. He did think about her. He thought of her sweet face in the street all bloody. Dead because he was in the city playing. Because he wasn't there to help her. He thought about that. And then, somehow, a few blocks down, he was thinking about the whore with her hands on his shoulders. Thinking about the breath of her whisper at his ear. *Life goes on.*

The skyline leveled out before him. The buildings slanted down from the Chelsea lofts and projects to the Village brownstones and shops. The blue sky grew broader above, the air clear and cold. Lonnie stared absently at the storefront windows to his left. He thought of the frightened voice on the phone. *Don't call me anymore.*

There was an Interbean just ahead of him. He slowed his pace as he approached it. In some part of his mind, he knew, he had been planning to come here.

He pushed inside.

It was one of a chain of cafés. Cappuccino and computers. Half an hour on the Internet for the price of a cup of coffee and a roll. Instructions and assistance free.

The place was made of stained wood and tile. To the right was a long glass showcase of muffins and cakes. Coffeemakers behind it that looked like Frankenstein's lab machinery. A magazine rack across from that, mostly computing stuff. Round brown tables dotted the tiled floors.

Against the left wall, there was a long brown counter with terminals ranged along it. Guys and girls worked the keyboards, watched the monitors. Their eyes reflected the white glare.

Lonnie moved to the food display. Up came a waiter, a young guy, California blond, smooth face, glittering teeth. *I want a part in a TV soap opera* was all but written on his brow. He wore the regulation Interbean T-shirt: computer on a yellow background, a steaming cup of coffee on the screen.

"What can I get you?"

"Black coffee and a corn muffin," Lonnie said. "Can I ask you something?"

"Yup." Yellow-hair moved along the counter, tipped sideways to pluck a muffin from the display.

Hands in his pockets, Lonnie followed him on the counter's other side. "Say you went on one of these computers. Say you had a phone number, okay? Could you, like, look up a person's address working back from the phone number?"

The kid popped the muffin plate up on the countertop. Turned to the machines to fill a mug with coffee. "Well, you could," he said. "But it would take you maybe—thirty . . . forty seconds."

Lonnie let a slight smile lift one corner of his mouth. "Ah, you're bragging now," he murmured. "You're bragging."

Look, he thought, *I just want to talk to you.*

Look, I need to talk to you.

Listen. Just listen to me a minute, he thought. *I can't stop thinking about you.*

He was walking again. Moving through the crisp autumn air. His arch features were working with his thoughts. His dark eyes were turned to the pavement, their focus far away. He had traversed the city like this,

his shoulders lifted against the cold, his breath visible. His hands were still in his pockets. His right hand was closed around the address he'd written down.

He had already crossed lower Fifth. Passed the polished luxury towers where they ran down to the Washington Arch. He had continued into the east, thinking about her. Thinking about her, he had walked along the stalls of silver trinkets and leather get-ups on St. Mark's.

He was heading down Second now, by open groceries and darkened restaurants. It was just edging toward lunchtime.

Look, he thought, *don't close the door. Just give me a second. All right? I just want to talk to you. Look, don't close the door.*

He clutched the address in his hand, the hand in his pocket.

I can't stop thinking about you. Know what I'm saying? Look . . . Don't go closing the door, all right? I need to see you.

He turned the corner of Fourth Street and there she was.

He wasn't prepared for it. He wasn't prepared for the impact of it.

She was way down the block, just coming off the stoop of her building. Her hair was different now. Short, curly, brown. She was wearing a reddish flannel trench coat, her legs in jeans, her feet in sneakers. For a second, he didn't recognize her at all.

Then he did—by her walk, by her profile even at that distance. He was not prepared for the painful yearning in him, for the way it hit him like a blow.

He wanted to see her face again as she whispered to him. He wanted to have that night with her to live over.

Look, don't run away, he thought. *Look, I just want to talk to you.*

But she was already hurrying away from him, hurrying for First Avenue. Her hair bouncing as she moved. Her figure receding swiftly.

Lonnie began to follow her.

I mean, look, if you're in some kind of trouble maybe I can help. Look, don't run away, he thought.

She was almost at the corner. Her head was turning back and forth. She was checking out the avenue, Lonnie realized. Looking for a threat, for a dangerous face. She was afraid, he thought. Afraid someone might be watching her, coming after her.

In a minute, she would turn around. Check her back. Take a good look behind her. And then she would see him.

Suddenly, Lonnie felt his stomach knot. He pulled up short. He felt a cold, sickly sweat begin on his forehead.

It had just occurred to him: someone *was* watching her, someone *was* coming after her.

He was.

Shit, he thought. *I'm turning into a stalker here.*

He raised his hand. He opened his mouth to call out to her. *Look, I just want to talk to you . . .*

But before he could say anything, she started running.

A bus was coming. He saw it cutting across the intersection, heading uptown. The girl hailed it as she ran but it was already slowing, pulling to the curb beyond the edge of the buildings.

And then, she was around the corner. Going after it. Gone. Out of sight.

Lonnie stood still another moment. Then he started

walking again, more slowly now. *Let her go, let her go, God bless her.* He shook his head. He ought to feel relieved. Christ, what the hell did he think he was doing here anyway? Tracking the woman down like this. Following her like some stalking crazy man. Jesus. Jesus. He kept shaking his head.

He walked on, glancing up at her brownstone as he passed it. The punch of that first sight of her was still with him. The punch of yearning. He could feel the sore spot every time he breathed.

When he got to the corner, the bus was still in view. It had pulled to the curb two blocks away, taking on passengers. Then a groaning roar. A plume of black exhaust in the gray air. The bus pulled out into the traffic. Lonnie watched it, his shoulders slumped.

He turned around to hail a cab. There were plenty on the street, yellow blurs streaking uptown fast. Two went by him—the drivers pretended not to see him because he was black. The third one pulled over. Lonnie climbed heavily inside.

The driver was a small brown guy in a huge purple turban. He spoke over his shoulder. "Where?"

Home, he thought. *Out of here. Breeze the bitch. That's the end of it.*

"See that bus up there?" he said.

"The bus?" said the turban. "I see it, yes."

"Just follow after it," Lonnie said.

He sat back against the seat as the cab started off.

4

The bus stopped at Fifty-second. The girl dropped down out of the center doors. Three steps across the sidewalk and she was gone again, into a restaurant.

Lonnie had the cab pull up on the far side of the street.

The day seemed colder here. The soaring apartment buildings lining the side streets seemed to squeeze the wind between them. The wind blew in off the river with a fresh bite, almost wintry.

Lonnie moved to stand beside a liquor store in lengthening shade. He watched the restaurant across the street. Ed Whittaker's, it was called. The name was written in large script on its long window. The window was dark. Cars whisking past were reflected there on the pane. From where he was, Lonnie could only make out the shapes of the people sitting inside.

He stood there, unmoving, undecided. There was an evil taste in his mouth. He was sick about what he was doing. Going after her like this, watching her like this. How had this happened to him? Just thinking about it made him queasy.

Second after second, he stood there, trying to resist the urge to cross the street, trying to make up his mind to walk away.

But he didn't walk away. He stood where he was. He watched the restaurant a long time. He didn't even know what he was looking for, what he wanted. He only knew that the touch of her skin still haunted his fingers, that the rage had left him when he was with her and he'd been calm for long minutes in the dark between her legs.

He moved to the corner. He crossed the street. He approached the restaurant.

As he came closer to the window, the glass became less opaque. He could see through. He turned his back on it, pretended he was waiting for someone on the sidewalk. In that way, he hovered there, just outside the restaurant, stealing glances into the place from time to time.

It was a steak house, he saw. Very fancy, very fashionable. Dark wood, white tablecloths. Black and white photos of the city on the wall.

There was a big crowd, a brunch crowd judging by the mimosa glasses, by the baskets of sweet rolls on the tables and the remnants of eggs Benedict. There were four or five people standing on line near the front door, waiting for the maîtresse d' to find their names in her big book.

But the girl was already seated. She was at a table on the right, a little ways into the room. There was a man seated across from her.

Lonnie could see a bit of her face, but mostly she had her back to him. He could see the man clearly. The man was turned his way.

He was a thin, elegant, eccentric figure. White man with long black hair flowing over his shoulders, framing a narrow face. He had a white suit on. He was wearing an eye patch over his left eye.

The girl was leaning toward him, gesturing at him,

talking, her elbows on the white tablecloth. She hadn't even taken off her coat.

The man listened to her quietly. He had one hand by his face, the index finger resting against his cheek. The other hand was hidden under the table. There was a platter in front of him holding a bun, half eaten. He nodded once or twice as the girl talked.

Lonnie watched, hanging back from the window, pretending to wait for someone, only sometimes glancing through the glass. He had his hands in his pockets, his arms pressed tight to his side. He was trembling a little—with the cold and with the sickening sense of what he was doing. He saw the man with the eye patch speak briefly. His arm moved—the arm under the table. It was a subtle motion, but Lonnie spotted it. The man was advancing his hand toward the girl.

Lonnie watched. His stomach clutched. He felt angry as the man's hand slid forward under the table. Well, what did he expect? he asked himself. She was a whore. This is what she did for a living.

When he looked again, Lonnie saw that she had also dropped her hand under the table. She seemed to be moving her hand toward his.

He wasn't sure whether their hands met or not. They were both hidden by the edge of the tablecloth. But a second later, he saw the girl sit back. He saw she was holding a white envelope. Quickly, she slipped the envelope into her purse.

Then she was standing up, pushing her chair back, backing away. Gesturing the whole time, talking the whole time. The man in the eye patch watched her. He went on nodding quietly.

Lonnie saw her turn to leave. She would be coming

out now, any minute. She would be looking around, checking the street.

Lonnie turned and walked away from the restaurant. He walked to the corner, keeping his back to the restaurant door. He couldn't let her see him. Following her, stalking her like this. He felt ashamed. He felt sick of himself. And he felt sick with desire.

He turned the corner. Leaned against the wall. Just beside the restaurant's Dumpster, he pressed his back into the white wall and stayed there, taking deep heavy breaths, staring at nothing. There was sweat at his temples. He was nauseated. How had this happened to him? How had he found himself coming here, doing this?

Then there she was. She was walking past him. Right past him to the corner. She stopped at the light there, her back to him. She waited to cross the busy avenue.

Lonnie straightened. Looked at her, stared at her. She turned nervously and he saw her profile. He stared at her mouth, the mouth that had brushed his cheek, that had whispered in his ear. She bit her lips. Her eyes scanned the street, but he could tell she was distracted, thinking about something else. She would have spotted him—she would have spotted him before this—if she had not been so preoccupied.

The light changed. She stepped off the curb, away from him.

"Wait," Lonnie called out.

Even over the noise of traffic, he heard her gasp. She spun round. She saw him. Her big blue eyes went wide.

"Look," said Lonnie, stepping toward her. Holding up his hand. "Look—don't run away. I just want to talk to you."

5

"Oh God. Oh God." She stared at him. She shook her head. Her expression was a mixture of fear and helplessness and fury. "What're you doing here? What're you doing?"

She backed away from him into the traffic. Her eyes were desperate and afraid. A horn dopplered as a car swerved to miss her.

"Hey, be careful," Lonnie said to her. "Listen . . ."

She stopped. She looked around her at the oncoming cars, realizing where she was. And then she came toward him. Running her fingers through her hair, clutching her hair. "What're you . . . What're you, following me?"

He watched her approach, his hands in his pockets. "I need to talk to you," he said.

She stood under him, stared up at him. Her eyes were damp. "Need . . . ? You don't even know me. And you were watching me? Just now? Were you watching me just now in the restaurant?"

"I'm . . . sorry."

"Were you?"

"I need to see you."

"Oh God." She let out a terrible laugh. "Oh God, Lonnie. This is . . . God."

She turned half away from him, turned back, desperate. Sunday pedestrians moved past them on the sidewalk. A silver-haired grande dame with her Lhasa apso. A well-to-do dad with a bagload of bagels. They glanced at her as they went by. They glanced darkly at Lonnie.

She came closer to him. Her eyes were swimming. "I mean, are you crazy? Jesus. Don't you listen to people? I told you . . . You saw me in the restaurant? Oh God."

"I just . . ." But he had no answer. He could barely meet her stare. "I just needed to talk to you," he said again. "I can't stop thinking about you. I had to see you again."

She shook her head at him. Her blue eyes glistened. She stared at him with a kind of miserable wonder. "I can't believe this."

A young man walking past eyed them. The girl noticed this, noticed she was drawing attention. She moved off the avenue. Past Lonnie, to where the Dumpster was.

He moved with her, into the teeth of the cold river wind. He tried to think of something he could say to her. He thought: *Fool, fool, fool.* How had he let this happen?

They stood together beside the wall. She came close to him. He looked down at her. She looked different—a gamine—with her short, curly hair. But the face was still the same. He remembered how her face had looked when she was under him. He felt the yearning for her again.

"Don't," she said. "Don't look at me like that. Okay? Jesus. I can't believe this . . ." She reached up and touched his lapel. It was a gentle gesture, almost affectionate. "*Listen* to me. Okay? Please. It was pretend, Lonnie."

Embarrassed, he averted his eyes. Looked off over her head, down between the dignified brick high-rises to where the river water glittered. "I know that."

"Whoever she is, I'm not her. I can't be her."

"That's not what it's about."

"Yes, it is. Yes, it is. And you have to understand. You have to get it, Lonnie. I need you to get it. You don't want to be in my life. I swear it to God. You don't want to be in my solar system."

"Look, if you're in some kind of trouble . . ."

"*Jesus!*" The frustration flashed across her face. "Jesus, Lonnie! Don't you listen?"

"I want to help you."

"Well, I'm sorry. You play the saxophone. That's just not very helpful to me right now, okay?"

He drew his hand from his pocket. It seemed to move to her of its own accord. He reached out to touch her face. But she put her own hand in the way to block him and his palm touched hers. His fingers closed over hers. She looked up at him a long moment.

"I need you to get this," she said. "I need you to walk away. Look . . . It's like: I'm a damsel in distress. Okay? I'm a helpless damsel in distress here, Lonnie. And you gotta rescue me. And the only way you can rescue me is by leaving—me—alone."

He smiled bitterly at this. The breeze brought her scent to him. The violets were still there beneath the smell of soap, the trace of cigarettes mingled with the chill weather. She gripped his hand in hers, gave it a single, urgent shake.

"Please," she said. "Please."

And then she was gone.

He didn't watch her leaving. He looked at the river. He felt her hand slip away. He sensed her, moving from him. Moving for the corner, moving out of his life.

Before he could stop himself, he swung around.

"She was my wife," he said. "She was murdered. They murdered her."

"I'm sorry." The girl swiveled to face him, but kept walking, backing toward the corner. "I'm really sorry, man." She raised her arms from her sides. "I mean it."

Then she turned her back to him and hurried on.

And suddenly, Lonnie was going after her. He didn't think. He hardly even knew what he was doing. He was suddenly just behind her as she reached the corner. Her shining hair was just beneath him, the scent of her just beyond him.

He didn't mean to grab her hard but he did. His hand clamped on her elbow.

She whipped round violently but couldn't pull free. "Get off me . . ."

"I don't have anyone," said Lonnie as she struggled. "They murdered her. I don't have *anyone!*"

"*Get off me, you dumb black bastard!*" She wrenched her arm from his grasp. Backed away from him, running a trembling hand up through her hair. "Christ, what does it take? You know? What does it fucking take?"

Then she hurried away from him, almost ran away from him across the street.

Lonnie stayed where he was, though people glanced at him, though other men stopped and peered balefully from him to the running white girl. He stayed where he was and he watched her go, breathless.

Slowly, his hands slipped back into his overcoat pockets.

6

One note and another, no matter how close, have an infinite distance between them, and that's where the blues happen. The same can be said of people, of one person and another. That's why the blues get played.

That night, Lonnie played the blues, sitting in his loft alone, sitting in the leather chair, pressing the tip of the hard rubber mouthpiece of the Selmer Mark VI into his tongue, speaking to it in a minutely subtle language of breath, milking the breath from the horn again as music  with the slow pressure of his fingers on the stops, agonizingly precise. He played the same old songs, the songs he loved. He made them blue in the infinite distances.

I can't forget you . . . I can't let you go . . .

His wife, as it happens, had never known much about music. The best she could do was bang out a tune on the upright for the kids she taught at school.

The wheels on the bus go round and round . . . round and round . . . round and round . . .

Beat that thing, he would tease her whenever he heard her hammering away. *That's a bad thing. You beat that thing, baby.* Until Suzanne would lean forward over the keys, helpless with laughter.

They had lived in San Francisco. She had taught elementary school down on the peninsula. He was starting to do well, a local player with a good word on him. They had an apartment that looked out on trees and through the trees to a sliver of the bay. They had friends who talked about music and books. Dear hearts and gentle people. Teachers and musicians and grad students, black and white and yellow. Lonnie liked to see them gathered in his living room. He liked to sit and listen to them talking and laughing. And he would think about his other friends, his old friends from the neighborhood.

He liked to drive out to San Mateo, to the school where Suzanne taught. It was a good school, mostly middle-class kids, mostly white. Lonnie liked to drive Suzanne over sometimes and pick her up in the afternoon. He liked to show up early and watch her in her classroom through the window on the door. He liked to see the clean-cut faces beaming up at her. He liked the way the children eagerly raised their hands. He liked to watch them and think about where he had come from and the schools he'd been in and the children he'd known.

His friends. His homeboys. His old friends.

His old friends had called him Pump-Pump because he was good with a shotgun. Because he had once blasted his way out of an ambush of Nineties—a rival gang—and the shotgun had bucked in his hands, dull and thunderous. Pump-pump. *Boom-boom.* He had heard the Nineties screaming in the night beneath the sound. Afterward, his old friends, his homeboys, had clasped hands with him and chanted, *Can't stop, won't stop.*

He'd been fourteen years old at the time. At fifteen, a gentleman by the name of Big Dick had placed a .38 against Lonnie's forehead and pulled the trigger. The gun had misfired and Lonnie, annoyed, had taken the weapon away and beat Big Dick into a coma with it.

So he'd had to run. From L.A. to Oakland. Where he lay low at his grandmother's place. Lay in her attic bedroom and blew on his horn and waited till the coast was clear and he could head south again.

Only problem was, lying there, playing, he realized something: he *never* wanted to go back there. He hated that place. He hated his life. His friends. His horsehead mother. He hated the thing he was turning into. He couldn't even play the neighborhood music anymore, the gangsta and the g-funk. He started digging up some of his grandmother's records. Actual records. Actual wax or vinyl or whatever the hell that old shit was. Louis Armstrong. Duke Ellington. Cannonball Adderley. The Jurassics . . .

And tonight, in the loft in Manhattan, he played those songs he'd come to love. He played them blue. Sitting alone with the lights out, slouching in his chair. Eking out cadences almost like speech, almost like crying, ghosting grace notes almost unheard and slurring others to a wail of high and mournful drama. His saxophone—which mostly tootled and blustered these days through studio gigs and sideman throwaways—seemed to stretch now in his fingers like a cat and waken.

Just to be with you again for an hour . . .

He hadn't played like this since the night they'd murdered her.

She had had a late meeting that night. He had had a gig. He was playing at The Loft, one of the city's best clubs. He could remember to this day how he was wailing through the breaks, how the crowd was rocking, how sweet it was.

Just to be with you again for a single day . . .

Suzanne had stopped at a mini-mall on the way

home to buy milk for her morning coffee. Five white teenagers, drunk on beer, had surrounded her in the parking lot. He'd been playing at The Loft. They had circled around her. They had reached for her and grabbed and jived her. They had called her nigger and spun her from one merciless grin to another.

What wouldn't I give . . . What wouldn't I do . . .

He saw that scene in his mind every day. Their grinning white faces. He tasted her terror on his tongue like some kind of bitter wine.

She had broken away from them. She had run blindly into the street. The Cadillac that struck her down was going sixty. There was no chance for it to stop. Lonnie had been wailing at The Loft, tilted back with his sax upraised and wailing.

She had died lying there in the street in a spreading pool of her own blood.

Just to be with you again, my love . . .

He couldn't face his friends after that. Those dear hearts and gentle people, black and white and yellow. They all somehow seemed part of the life that had killed her. They became mixed up with the punks who'd chased her from the lot, as if those taunting white faces were now superimposed on theirs. He went back to L.A. for a while but he still hated the place. And the old connections from the neighborhood were alien to him, were gone.

He was alone. He had connections but no friends. Admirers but no companions. He went to St. Louis for a few months. Chicago. New Orleans. He picked up sideman stuff, studio work, commercials. He couldn't play in the old way, couldn't lean back and wail.

And now he sat here. New York, New York. Eighteen

months after Suzanne had died. He sat on the leather chair and blew into the sax and milked out music and made it blue. And he thought about the whore who had pretended for him. The music drifted up from him like smoke, and images played through his mind like music. The songs were the old songs but the images were of the girl. He played the San Francisco weather he remembered but he smelled the violets and the smoke. He played his wife's smile as she turned to him in the kitchen and he saw the girl's face as she turned away from him on the street.

I need you to get this, she'd told him. *I need you to walk away.*

He couldn't walk away. He knew that as he sat there. He had to see her again. He had to. Tomorrow . . . tomorrow, he would find her. Somehow, tomorrow, he would convince her to talk to him.

But tonight he played the blues.

CHAPTER 4

JACK—YOU DEAD

1

A comfortable car on a cold night on a lonely road. To John Harrigan, this was a little cup of bliss. The heat on low, the blue light of the dashboard glowing. The CD player just whispering a James Taylor ballad. This was Currier and Ives stuff to him, hot chocolate at Grandma's after a sleigh ride, chicken soup and *Leave It to Beaver* reruns during the flu season—the cozy safety of home. Outside you had your slightly spooky forest furtively ducking back beyond the edge of the headlights' glow. You had your slightly nippy air, your brooding woodland silence. But in here, inside the Maxima, this sleek blue sedan like a floating island in the sea of night . . . Well, a shrink might've said it was womblike but that wouldn't do it justice. You don't get that Sony quality sound *in utero*. You don't get that humalong J.T. whisper. *That's why I'm here* . . . To Harrigan, it was coziness personified.

He took this route home every night. He looked forward to this stretch of it especially, the last leg of the drive over the winding backwoods Westchester road. One hour from New York City, ten minutes from the interstate, but for Harry, the forest here was especially full of mystery and the car felt all the cozier because of that. Another ten minutes, and he would be in Armonk, at his house. Monica would be upstairs going over the boards of her next ad campaign. Their three children would be asleep in their beds. Harrigan would reheat whatever his wife had left for him, drink a beer with it and catch up on the sports pages. Read a brief until he dozed off. It would be fine, it would be restful. But it wouldn't have that special haven-like quality, that familiar homey comfort that he got here, in the woods, in his car, in his Maxima . . .

Or with Diana. He felt a measure of the same cozy warmth when he was with her.

He wasn't exactly happy about visiting a prostitute. He was still a good-looking guy, after all. Only forty-five, six feet tall, lanky, muscular. Boyishly handsome despite his salt-and-pepper hair. He was successful too. Head of the Legal Department for Skylight Developers. A fairly important Magee in behind-the-scenes city politics. And he loved his wife. He adored his kids. Whenever he even considered the possibility that they would find out about his trysts with Diana, it made him physically ill. He tried to be strict with himself about it. He only allowed himself to see her once a month, usually when his wife was on the rag. Sometimes he went twice in December when Christmas made him yearn especially for that old feeling of home, but that was really all. Still, he wished he could give her up entirely. It wasn't something he was proud of.

But she did things with him. Fantasy stuff. Things he could never tell his wife about. Things he hadn't even told his therapist about the two or three times he went. In bed with her, with Diana, he was like a child playing games. And it brought him back to those good days, as if he were lying on the living room floor again doing jig-saws while his mother sewed and watched TV and waited for his father to come home.

He gazed through the windshield dreamily. The road wound toward him out of the dark. Patches of dense forest were lifted out of nothing by the headlights and then sank away. The CD player played and he thought of Diana. He thought of what they had done together this Friday night just past. He began to rehearse it again in his mind . . .

He was just getting to the part where she commanded him to put on the tutu when the red light of a police flasher splashed across his rear window. A siren whooped once and fell silent.

Harrigan pulled over to the side of the road.

He waited there, confused but clear of conscience. He'd been speeding a little, sure, but the last car that had actually traveled this road at the twenty-five-mile-an-hour limit had probably been drawn by horses. No one was going to stop him for speeding here. He squinted into his rearview where the cruiser's headlights glared at him, where the red flasher whirled lazily.

A figure came strolling slowly out of the headlights' beam. Harrigan busied himself turning off the CD player, buzzing down the window. He wondered if maybe one of his brake lights was out or something.

The trooper came up beside the car. He leaned down to look in the window. He was a pale, pimply boy in a khaki highway patrol uniform. God, he looked young, Harrigan thought. When did they start hiring children?

The trooper smiled. Touched the bill of his cap. "Could I ask you to step out of the car, please, sir?"

"Did I do something wrong, Officer?" Harrigan asked. But he'd already loosed his seat belt, popped his door. He'd already started to climb out into the chill of the night.

Harrigan heard—he dimly registered—a harsh double rasp—a deadly sound. Everything inside him let go. His limbs, his muscles, his bladder—they all gave way together. He was distantly aware of the wheeling world as it seemed to fall upward into the sky.

Then he was sprawled stupid on the pavement, wedged between the door and the car. He was staring, openmouthed, drooling. He was blinking, groaning, trying to say something—he had no idea what it was.

Red and black, red and black, the patrol car's spinning flasher passed over him.

He became vaguely conscious that a second figure was standing there. Standing above him, looking calmly down. The patrol car's headlights picked him out of the dark. Harrigan could see him as through a spinning haze.

It was a tall, thick man with a blocky face and skin like gravel. He was not in uniform. He was wearing a trench coat. He smiled down at Harrigan. A brief, pleasant, disinterested smile of greeting.

Then someone—the trooper—had Harrigan under the armpits.

"Uuuuh," Harrigan said. He could feel the groan in his throat, but his brain could make nothing of it. He wanted to say something but he couldn't think what it was.

He was being dragged around to the back of the car now. He could see his shoes in front of him, heels moving along the pavement, toes swaying. He wished he could coordinate his arms to cover himself. He was embarrassed by his wet pants.

There was a sound. A *thunk*. The trunk was opening. Now the other man, the gravel-faced man, was at his feet. He had him by the ankles.

"Upsy," said the gravel-faced man.

Harrigan felt himself go up in the air, felt himself go down again. He was inside the trunk of his own car. There was an instant when he saw the lid above him. There was something, something he had to say quickly.

Then the trunk lid closed over him. Darkness. The smell of his own urine.

Harrigan's mind was beginning to clear a little. He understood now what it was he wanted to say.

He wanted to say that this was the most terrifying thing that had ever happened to him in his entire life.

He heard the engine start. The Maxima began to move.

Mortimer was feeling anxious also. There was just too much pressure in this operation. Everything about it was so fancy, so high-tech. The state cruiser. The stun gun. The backup cars. This was Winter's doing. Winter wanted everything to run like some kind of James Bond international military operation. *But this is America, for Christ's sake,* Mortimer thought. What the hell was wrong with a Chevy and a sap?

He drove Harrigan's Maxima around the bend. It wasn't far. There was a dirt turnoff just up ahead. He guided the Maxima onto it. The car's suspension was so good the body undulated smoothly over the path's ruts and gullies.

Good ride, Mortimer thought. *Maybe I should get myself one of these.*

He was trying to take his mind off his nerves.

He drove about half a mile into the woods. There, he came to a building site. An acre of ground had been cleared for a new house. The house's insulated frame was already standing amid scrub and piles of lumber. Mortimer brought the Maxima to a stop here. Killed the lights, then the engine. He popped the trunk with the handle under the seat. Opened the door and slid out from behind the wheel. It was a crisp, cool November night. Mortimer took a good whiff of it as he walked around to the back of the car. Fresh air, he thought. The country. Made you grow big and strong. He could hardly wait to get the hell out of here.

He glanced once around the building site, around the silent circle of the woods. He shifted his big shoulders in his trench coat. Then, with one gloved finger, he lifted the Maxima's trunk lid the rest of the way.

He shone his flashlight down on the dazed Harrigan. Harrigan weakly held up his hands to fend off the beam. With his hands waving in front of him like that and his eyes staring and his mouth opening and closing silently, the head of the Legal Department of Skylight Developers looked to Mortimer for all the world like a newborn baby, like his new niece Carla when he leaned in over her crib.

The effects of the stun gun seemed to be wearing off. Which was good. The lawyer was clear headed enough to be afraid.

Mortimer switched the flashlight off. Slipped it in his pocket. It was dark except for a sliver of moon but

Harrigan's white eyes still seemed to glow. Mortimer leaned his big, square head down toward the other man. He caught a mingled smell of piss and coppery fear. That was good too. He let a pleasant smile crease his pitted skin.

"All right, concentrate now, Mr. Harrigan," he said. "This is very simple. You answer my questions or I hurt you. Yes?"

"Uuuuh," said Harrigan. "Who are . . . ?"

"On Friday night, you were with a prostitute," Mortimer went on in his gruff, quiet, side-of-the-mouth voice.

"A pros . . . ?" Harrigan started to say. But Mortimer reached into the trunk swiftly. Clutched him by the throat. "Don't fuck with me, okay, I'm not in the mood!"

The lawyer gagged, his tongue showing. His eyes went wider still.

Shit, Mortimer thought. He let him go, withdrew his hand. Took a deep breath to calm himself. Nerves. That was no good. He couldn't let the pressure get to him. He knew he had screwed up. He knew he had let the girl get away from him. He knew that Winter was pissed off and he understood full well that this was not a good thing. But he had to stay cool, show this gink he was in control here. Take his time. Get it right.

He held up a single finger in warning. Controlled his voice. Spoke softly. "Let's not make this unpleasant. Okay?" Harrigan nodded eagerly. "Now you were with a prostitute at the Caldecott Hotel and I want to know her name."

"Diana," Harrigan cried out at once. His voice was trembling. "Don't tell my wife," he whispered. "Please don't tell my wife."

Mortimer nodded. This was better. This was going to be all right. He gave the man a friendly chuckle. Bonded with him a little bit. "No, no, no," he said amiably. "This isn't about your wife, this isn't gonna be public in any way. Okay. So her name is Diana. Right? And you don't know her last name?"

"I swear to God. I swear . . ."

"No, no, hey, I believe you." Mortimer heaved a sigh. Turned a little and propped his butt on the edge of the trunk. "But what I need to know here is how you get in touch with her."

Harrigan swallowed hard. "Voice mail."

"Voice mail."

"I leave a message for her. Then she calls my beeper, sets up a time."

"Sheesh. High security, huh." That explained why her number wasn't in Harrigan's records, why her calls hadn't been on his wire. Hookers these days, Mortimer thought. With all the crackdowns and technology and whatnot. It was like dealing with Mata Hari half the time. But still, he thought, this was good. They were almost there. "So you got a number?"

Harrigan rattled the number off instantly.

"And you leave a message for Diana."

"She just has an ID code. Four six seven."

"You wouldn't lie to me, right? Cause I know where you live. There's Monica and the three kids to think about here."

"Oh God," said Harrigan. "Please. I swear."

"No, no. I'm just saying."

"It's the truth, so help me."

"Good enough. I trust you."

And he thought about it for a minute, perched on the

trunk there, and it was good enough. It might take an hour or two, but they ought to be able to track her down with this. With any luck, they'd be at her place by midnight.

Mortimer nodded. "Okay. That's it. Let's get you out of there."

Mist coiled up from Harrigan's mouth as he let out a rasping breath. It sounded as if he'd been holding it all this time. Mortimer bent down and took him by the shoulder, helping him sit up in the trunk. Harrigan groped at him for support.

"You swear my wife won't find out," the lawyer said.

"Absolutely," said Mortimer.

With his free hand, he drew out a straight razor and sliced open Harrigan's throat. At the same time, he released the man and stepped backward, neatly avoiding the first gout of blood.

There you go, he thought with satisfaction. *A* razor, *right? Silent but deadly. With some things, Winter, the old ways are still the best.*

The attorney's body, still spewing blood, was still convulsing violently. Mortimer had to push the kicking legs aside before he could slam the trunk shut. There was thumping inside for a few more moments after that. Then it stopped.

3

Now a second car pulled up the drive. A black Grand Marquis, solemn and substantial. Mortimer shook his head. *Look at this,* he thought. *It's like a movie.* Pulling off his gloves, he moved toward the car.

A muscular giant in a sweatsuit got out of the passenger seat: Don Bland, his name was. Don Bland smiled briefly around his chewing gum as Mortimer approached him. Mortimer raised a wave as they passed each other. Then he slipped into the Marquis and took Don Bland's place beside the driver.

He shut the door. Looked out through the windshield. Big Don Bland was lowering himself behind the wheel of the Maxima. Mortimer shook his head again.

"Look at this," he said aloud.

"What," said the driver. The driver was Hughes, a bulky fellow with a jolly face and a rich brown beard. "What'm I looking at?"

"This. All these cars. People getting in and out. I feel like I'm in a fucking gangster movie."

Hughes laughed. "Hey. You know Winter. This is a precision military operation we're running here."

"I feel like Robert DeNiro already."

"You look a little like DeNiro, I ever tell you that?"

"Oh yeah? You find me attractive?"

Hughes made a kissing noise in the dark. Mortimer snorted.

The Maxima was now leaving the scene, disappearing down the dirt path to the road. Car and body never to be seen again.

"All right. Let's go," Mortimer said.

Hughes hit the gas, turned the wheel. The Marquis began a wide circle over the dirt, rumbling back to the path.

"So how'd we make out?" Hughes asked.

"Oh, man," said Mortimer. "This broad. More aggravation. I'm telling you. The vagina was a very good invention. The brain was a very good invention. But putting these two things together in one body—that's a mistake. It's like pistachio fudge ripple. It just doesn't work."

The Marquis headed into the dark of the woods, the headlights picking out the rutted lane ahead. Hughes glanced at Mortimer.

"You're not telling me she got away?"

"If she got away, would I be here?"

"No shit."

"If you think I'm calling Winter to tell him we staged a priority op and she got away . . ."

"Don't even talk about it."

"I won't even think about it."

"Don't even think about it. Jesus."

The car bounced down into the street. The Maxima with the body of John Harrigan in the trunk was already out of sight.

Mortimer blew out a long stream of air. "It's just we gotta run some checks, some phone stuff. She had a . . . you know, a security routine she used. Voice mail and shit."

"Voice mail!" Hughes said, shaking his head. "Why

do you think they call it voice mail? I mean, what's 'mail' about it?"

"I don't know. Could you keep your mind on what we're doing here, please?"

"I'm just wondering. What makes it mail?"

"I don't know. Maybe . . . I don't know."

"Anyway, what's she got voice mail for?" said Hughes. "What is she, like a CIA agent or something?"

Mortimer shrugged his heavy shoulders. "She's a mother. She's protecting her kid. It's an instinct."

"Instinct," Hughes muttered into his beard. "I'll give her some fucking instinct. I'm getting tired of this already."

"It's like a bear or something."

"I'll give her some fucking bear. I'll give her more fucking bear than she can bear." Hughes burst out laughing. "You hear me? More bear than she can bear."

Mortimer nodded in the dark of the car. He didn't laugh. He wasn't in the mood for Hughes.

"How do you figure animals recognize each other?" Hughes asked. "Their kids, I mean. How does a bear know it's her kid?"

"Who's gonna call Winter?" said Mortimer. "You or me?"

Hughes groaned. "Woof."

"Never mind," said Mortimer. "It's no big thing. He'll run the check. We'll have her by midnight."

"Great. So you call him," said Hughes.

But Mortimer had already reached into his trench coat. He drew out his mobile. Summoned Winter's number. He held the unit to his ear, gazing out the window. In the white glow of the headlights, the empty road twisted between the lowering autumn trees.

"It's nice up here," said Mortimer as he waited for the phone to ring.

"Yeah," said Hughes. "I like driving on these roads at night. You know, when it's all dark outside and you're all warm inside the car. It feels like . . . I don't know what. Like something."

"Yeah," murmured Mortimer, waiting, gazing. "I don't know what either."

All the monitors in Winter's Central Park West apartment were glowing. There were a lot of them—computers everywhere on glass tables and Formica pedestals—and every one of them was on. You could see the bright screens reflected on the picture window. They almost blotted out the view of the park fifteen stories below.

The room's other lights were off so the machines provided the only illumination. In their strange, colorless, alternating light, Winter's creased and handsome features looked to be carved out of some weird metal or stone. His flesh seemed to have no color. The flaming red of his hair seemed to have drained away. He barely looked animate.

He was sitting in a butterfly chair of leather and chrome. He was tapping the telephone handset against his fingernails. It made a soft noise: click, click, click, click.

Hughes and Mortimer, he was thinking. *Mortimer and Hughes.*

His eyes moved, his hazel eyes, reflecting the monitor light. They moved from one screen to another. He saw the readout from the remote GPS that was tracking Hughes and Mortimer. It showed the Grand Marquis as a blinking set of coordinates moving steadily south toward the city. Another monitor flashed semi-encrypted messages from various Executive Decisions locations around the world. A third, worked by one of their researchers in Washington, was playing a slow roll of information on the passengers of European Airways Flight 186, especially those whose bodies had not been found.

Now Winter's eyes flicked up to what he called the Billboard. This was a long, nearly flat pane of glass. It was hung on a wide wall over the dark fireplace. There was a mantelpiece on which lay several books—*The Seven Habits of Highly Effective People, The Great Game of Business, Swim with the Sharks Without Being Eaten Alive*—and the Billboard was just above that, just where another man might have hung a picture of a church in a meadow or a pleasantly pastel abstract.

The Billboard was a plasma-gas display in which electrical charges lit colored crystals to produce a picture which was perfect in every detail. The PGD was hooked to a computer into which important documents from several Executive Decisions operations had been scanned. Right now, Winter had it keyed exclusively to the Dodson case. Articles, photographs and other materials appeared and disappeared on the display in leisurely rotation as Winter watched from his chair.

Headlines went by. AMERICA'S LOCKERBIE: ONE VICTIM'S

STORY. MIRACLE AT HUNNICUT. HUNT FOR SURVIVORS CON-
TINUES. INVESTIGATORS LOOK FOR A CAUSE IN HUNNICUT
CRASH. A Safety Board investigation report rolled up, vanished; a European Airlines passenger list did the same. All
the while, simultaneously, snapshots, passport photos and
newspaper art faded in on other portions of the screen,
stayed for a few moments, then faded out again.

Winter watched—and after a short time, there she
was. It was the best picture of her, Winter thought. His
favorite. A photograph of Carol Dodson standing
behind the bar at the Anchor and Bell. Laughing, her
body tilted to one side, one hand holding a bar towel,
the other waving comically at the camera. You could see
her from the thighs up. You could see the curve of her
hips dipping up into her waist, flaring up to where her
breasts rounded her T-shirt.

Winter gazed steadily at that picture, tapping the
phone against his fingernails. One corner of his mouth
lifted in a smile as the computer light played over his
face. He tapped the telephone against his fingernails.
Click, click. *Mortimer and Hughes.*

They were good enough men really, he thought. Not
his kind of men—old-fashioned—not the kind he pre-
ferred to use, but good, solid, well trained. They would
have her by the end of the evening, that was the important thing. The priority op had been an unnecessary
annoyance, but it had paid off as Mortimer promised.
They would have her by around midnight, assuming
Reese's delay hadn't given her time to escape. The Helix
VP's qualms about killing Harrigan's family had held
them up only a day. Winter doubted whether even she,
even Carol, was sharp enough, resourceful enough to
take the plunge, to relocate that quickly.

He studied her picture, smiling. *Are you?* he thought. *Well, maybe, baby. I doubt it, but maybe you are.* In some part of him, he was almost rooting for her. She had been so smart, so tough, so determined. She'd stayed ahead of them so long. He'd be almost sorry to see it end.

A discreet little blip came from one of the machines. A terminal on a glass pedestal across the room. Winter's eyes shifted to it. The information he was waiting for flashed up on the screen. The security people had completed their check on Carol Dodson's voice mail service. While she had arranged a complex system for paying her bills through a post box, she had called in for her messages from home several times. The researchers had run the calls down to her address on East Fourth Street. The address was being relayed to Hughes and Mortimer right now.

When Winter turned back to the Billboard, her picture had faded, had blended into a photo of the sailor who'd fathered her child. And still, Winter went on thinking about her, about her face, about her big, vulnerable blue eyes and her long lips laughing.

She was beautiful, he thought, on top of everything else. He'd be sorry when she was gone.

But then it would be nice to get his hands on her for as long as it lasted. He'd really become kind of fond of her after all this time.

CHAPTER 5

ROUND MIDNIGHT

1

Lonnie had tried all day to stay away from her. He was no stalker. And no damn fool to go chasing after a woman who didn't want him.

He had a studio gig through most of the morning, playing backup on a demo for some rich man's daughter. That kept him busy till after lunch. Then he went out to eat, went to the movies. Didn't come home until quarter to nine.

By half past, he was sitting in his leather chair with the Duke on the stereo and a bourbon in his hand. Twenty minutes later, he was at the phone table, sipping another drink. Sometimes he stared out the window, sometimes he gazed at the numbers on the phone. Sometimes he doodled feverishly on the pad. He drew a picture of the girl, and a picture of the man she'd met in the restaurant, the man with the eye patch and the long hair. His hand raced over the page. His body pulsed inside with a strange urgency.

"Damn!" he said finally. He angrily threw down the pen. He was on his feet, crossing the room. He grabbed his overcoat and headed out.

They had Monday jazz at the Velvet Village. He went down there. It was a new club but made up to look venerable. Posters of Miles and the Monk and Corea were slapped up haphazardly on the wall overlapping as if they'd been collecting up there for years. Likewise, the big semi-circular bar in the back was made of scuffed, unpainted, cigarette-burned wood, though it had been installed barely four months ago. Up front, the small round tables had been specially selected to look cheap and worn, and each had an old-fashioned teardrop candleholder on it.

Only the crowd looked fresh. All around the bar, all around the tables. Kids from the university mostly, some of them working hard at grunge, some of them pierced full of holes or bulging with implanted metal, but all of them young and sweet and dewy despite their best efforts. All of them watching the band with bright eyes. Bobbing and nodding and swaying to the music.

Lonnie stationed himself at the far curve of the bar. Wearing a light gray suit, an off-white collarless shirt buttoned to the top. Pressed up against the wall by the crowd, he nursed his third bourbon and seven, and then his fourth. He barely felt it. Inside, he was still pulsing with the same strange urgency.

He lifted and lowered his glass mechanically. His deep eyes were dark. The catlike angles of his face were tense. A sheen of sweat made his brown skin bright and beads of sweat gathered at his temples and rolled down, leaving trails from his sideburns to his jaw. He had never felt anything like this urge before. It was a fever.

He tried to focus on the music. The band was modern. Mighty Men of Valor, a quartet. They weren't much, Lonnie thought. Too loud, too chaotic. Showing off their chops with speedball riffs. More ambition in it than soul.

He managed to listen for an hour or so, then he'd had enough. The band. The pulse inside him. He would finish this drink, he thought, and go home.

He lifted the glass to his lips and drank quickly.

He knew damn well he wasn't going home.

2

Just then, on Fourth Street, the Grand Marquis was sliding into an open space at the curb. Mortimer glanced at the brownstone across the way. Nodded to himself. *This is it. Finally. This is where she lives.*

A fire hydrant blocked his door and he groaned as he unfolded his big body up through the narrow gap. Hughes also gave a grunt, squeezing his chubby frame out from behind the wheel.

There was traffic whisking by on the avenues that flanked the block, but the street itself was empty and silent. The two men paused for a moment to smooth themselves down. *Cool as cool*, thought Mortimer, *almost there.*

They crossed the street toward the brownstone side by side.

Frost formed in front of Hughes's lush beard. He spoke Mortimer's thought. "Finally. Right? This ought to get us off Winter's shit list anyway."

Mortimer made a noncommittal noise. He didn't

want to jinx it. "I'm just glad he's letting us handle it alone," he said.

"Yeah. Too many cooks."

"I keep thinking he's gonna have reinforcements parachute in here any second."

They stepped up onto the sidewalk.

"Why do you think your breath does that?" said Hughes. "Why do you think it makes smoke like that?"

"Condensation," said Mortimer. "I don't know."

They reached the brownstone stoop. Hughes danced up the steps first, his big form sprightly in his green pea jacket. As he moved to the door, he pulled a palm-sized rectangular black box from his coat pocket. Mortimer rose heavily just behind him.

"What's this now?" he said.

Hughes read the white words on the box's front. "The Spymaster ESK-Three Hundred."

"The Spymaster."

"Winter issued it to me."

"Oh, he *issued* it to you."

"Yeah. It's an electronic skeleton key. Works on anything."

Mortimer shook his head.

They reached the front door, brown wood with a big pane of glass in the top half. Hughes fiddled with the black box, pressed a slide on the side of it.

"Boys with toys," said Mortimer.

"I know. Winter loves this stuff. It's state of the art."

"What now?"

"It's gotta heat up. It's got this special plastic, you melt it, then it goes in the keyhole and hardens, opens the door."

Mortimer nodded. He drove his elbow through the

door's glass pane. It was already cracked and a neat little wedge of glass fell from the corner and shattered on the floor inside.

"Hot yet?" Mortimer said. He reached through the hole, turned the knob and opened the door. "Maybe you could stick that up your ass, open your brains with it."

Hughes shrugged and put the ESK-300 back in his pocket. "You're an enemy of progress," he said. But Mortimer had already gone inside.

Hughes followed him.

The cool, cool, cool of the evening was a relief to Lonnie Blake. He could feel the sweat drying on his skin as he left the Velvet Village behind. It was good to get away from that throbbing music too, good to be out in the night city with its sounds of whispering traffic, thrumming tunnels, fizzing lights.

He walked along with his shoulders hunched, with his hands in his pockets. He was still telling himself that he was going to hail a cab.

But, of course, he didn't hail a cab. He wasn't even walking toward home. He was walking east, the other way. Across lower Fifth, past the Washington Arch.

Back toward Fourth Street. Back toward her.

4

The brownstone's lobby was nearly dark. A single bulb on the high ceiling let down a gray pall. There was a linoleum floor tiled black and white, some of the tiles uprooted. There was a bicycle with one wheel missing chained by the super's door beneath the stairs.

Mortimer began to climb the stairs, lifting out of the gray light into the darkness above. Hughes hopped along behind him.

"Third floor, right?" he said.

"Three E," said Mortimer.

On the second floor, the lights were out. Someone's stereo played reggae softly. Aside from that, the place was quiet. They rounded the stairway's bend. They continued up.

The third floor was lighted. Here, they could see the chipped green walls, the somber, chipped black doors. They went down the hall to 3E. They stood at the door shoulder to shoulder.

They could hear noises coming from inside. Music; some kind of sprightly piano jazz. A woman's voice, sharp but soft, becoming audible as it rose to a hissing whisper, then falling away. There was a man too, moaning.

Mortimer lifted his chin at Hughes. Under his lush beard, Hughes's cheeks reddened with suppressed laughter.

"Working girl," he chuckled softly.

Mortimer smiled tensely. Then he pointed at the door. "Police lock," he whispered.

Hughes held up a finger. "Have no fear, Spymaster is here."

Mortimer rolled his eyes. "Spymaster."

"It's all warmed up and everything."

Mortimer watched, shaking his head, as Hughes pressed the box to the keyhole. Then Hughes touched a red button. There was hardly a sound, only a shuddering whisper as the softened polymer rod entered the slot. Air and increased heat made the rod expand to fit the tumblers. Then it cooled, hardened. The whole process took about forty-five seconds. Hughes went through it twice, on the police lock and then the latch.

"See this?" he whispered. "Better living through technology."

Mortimer tilted his head to the door listening. There was no change. The music, the voice, the groaning went on.

Hughes turned the device, and the door opened almost silently. Mortimer pursed his lips, grudgingly impressed. The two men went in.

They entered a broad living room. This was where the stereo was playing, but there was no one in sight. There were three doors leading off from it, one of them into a bathroom.

Mortimer and Hughes moved steadily and quietly. Mortimer scanned the place as he moved. It was shabby, but dolled up to hide the wear and tear. Gilt mirrors and museum posters hung on the fraying white walls. A half-finished drink sat on the cheap wooden cabinet beside the plush sofa. Magazines—*Playboy, Penthouse, Sports Illustrated*—lay fanned on the scarred coffee table.

Hughes moved to the bathroom. Scoped it. Shook his head. Empty.

Mortimer moved to another door on his left. It was open. He looked in. A bedroom. Dark, but clearly empty too.

Both men looked at the third door. It was standing ajar and light spilled out of it. The woman's voice, the groaning, were coming from there.

Mortimer raised his eyebrows at Hughes. Hughes nodded. He had unbuttoned his coat now and his hand went in under his armpit. It came out with a gun, a Cougar nine millimeter modified for an integral suppressor. With its subsonic ammo, the thing hardly made a sound, just a sort of *phfft* like some kind of dart gun. Mortimer left his revolver in the holster at the small of his back. He put his hand in his pocket. His fingers curled around the straight razor.

The two men moved together to the other door. When they reached it, Mortimer shifted round so he could see through the opening.

The girl was in there.

Her back was to him. She was wearing the wig she'd worn the other night, the short black hair with the movie-star cut. She was wearing a leather teddy. Her fishnet stockings showed off her legs but Mortimer thought they weren't very good: too much cellulite up near the ass. He could see she was holding a leather thong, smacking it against her palm. He could hear her hissing like a snake, hissing out a string of curses: "You worm. You scum.

"You're going to learn your lesson," Mortimer heard her say.

He shifted again. He could see her john.

The guy was on the bed, naked. He had a hard-on. He was held to the iron bedstead with leather handcuffs. He was facing the door and Mortimer could see he was gagged—he had one of those tubular contraptions stuck in his mouth.

Mortimer made a face. Incredible, the things people get up to.

He pushed the door open. He and Hughes stepped into the room.

The john saw them right away. His eyes went wide. His dick shriveled. He tried to sit up but was held back by the cuffs. He started kicking his legs and jutting his head and grunting. "*Ur! Ur! Ur!*" Trying to alert the girl. But of course, he couldn't talk. He had that crazy plastic thing in his mouth. And she thought it was part of the game. So she kept hissing at him. "Worm. Scum." And he kept saying, "*Ur! Ur!*" Bucking up and down on the bed, trying to tell her.

Well, it was pretty funny. What with the tension and everything, Hughes turned purple, trying not to laugh. Even Mortimer had to press his lips together.

They stepped up behind the girl. The man on the bed bucked and twisted in his bonds.

"*Ur! Ur!*" he said through his gag.

"You're going to get what's coming to you," the girl snarled at him.

Hughes cracked up. He let fly a high-pitched giggle. Mortimer snorted with laughter.

The girl heard that all right. She came spinning around.

Hughes pointed his gun at her. She turned right into the muzzle of it. Gasped.

Mortimer stopped laughing. "Shit!" he said. He felt a real rush of despair go through him. A real premonition of disaster.

It was the wrong goddamned girl.

5

Around St. Mark's Place, Lonnie considered turning back. The smell of trash on the midnight streets. A drunk who sat weeping on the sidewalk chin to chest. A weary sense of his own lonesome desire. He hesitated on the corner. What was he looking for? What did he hope to find?

Glaring balefully at the WALK sign across the street, he stood with his hands deep in his pockets. White wisps of his shallow breath drifted up from between his lips.

Then he was moving again. He made no conscious decision but he thought of her face, the girl's face, and he went on. Crossing the street. Turning toward Fourth.

Well, hell, he thought, he was almost there anyway.

6

Mortimer, meanwhile, fighting panic, grabbed the hooker by the throat. "Shut the fuck up," he said.

The naked john handcuffed to the bed struggled and tried to scream through the tube. "*Ur! Ur! Ur!*"

Hughes stood over him. "What is this thing in his mouth?" he asked.

Mortimer grit his teeth. "It's a piss gag. Shoot him."

"A piss gag?" said Hughes, and shot the john. *Pfft*, went the Cougar and the man's head spattered. Hughes pulled a grimace. "A piss gag. Feh."

The hooker made a terrified noise and Mortimer clutched her throat tighter, almost lifting her off the floor. He pointed a finger at her. "Shut up, I told you. I told you, right?"

In his mounting fear of disaster, Mortimer hated this bitch. Ugly she was, nowhere near as pretty as the other. Her skin was all pitted and swarthy. She had a hooked nose and graying teeth. She was thirty-five at least, and looked fifty. He was furious at her. She gagged in his tightening grip.

"The other one," he said through his teeth. "Where is she?"

"Gone," the hooker choked out. "She's gone. She left this morning."

"Left?" said Hughes beside them in a voice suddenly small.

"She took everything, packed everything."

"She left?" said Hughes.

And Mortimer knew just how he felt. This was bad. He could feel how bad it was. It was very bad. It had been one thing to blow a tail—that happened to everyone. It was another thing to let an amateur spot you—it was an empty street, the girl was sharp. But to call for a priority op and then come up with nothing—to leave bodies behind and get nowhere—that stank of incompetence. That was the mark of a guy playing catch-up with his own mistakes. Winter wouldn't stand for that. He and Hughes had to come up with something here or they were forehead-deep in shit.

"Jesus," groaned Hughes. He was clearly thinking along the same lines. He moved away from where the john's naked corpse lay crowned in a halo of blood and brains. He moved toward Mortimer and the hooker. "Jesus. Can you believe this shit?"

"Shut up," Mortimer told him. "Where'd she go?" he asked the hooker.

"She left, like, town?" said Hughes.

"*Just shut up!* Go check the other room again."

"Jesus," said Hughes, shaking his head. He started for the door.

Now Mortimer and the hooker stared at each other, linked by Mortimer's arm, by the big hand squeezing the hooker's throat. His gravelly face was contorted in his fear and anger. Her eyes were wide and wet as she struggled to breathe. Moisture flecked with mascara pooled in the bags beneath them. Mortimer tried to control the fear that made him hate every sleazy inch of her, that made him want to kill her right then and there.

"Where did she go?" he asked slowly.

He felt her shake her head in his grip. He felt her quickening pulse in his fingers. "I don't know. I swear. She didn't tell me."

Mortimer let her go. Then he punched her. She stumbled backward, bumped into a lamp table. She and the lamp fell over. The light snapped out. The hooker sat sprawled, her face bloody. One of her high-heeled shoes had come off.

Mortimer moved to stand over her. She looked up at him—but now she was insolent. Her eyes narrowed. She sneered. Mortimer hated her.

"Where'd she go?" he said down at her.

"Fuck you," said the hooker. "You're gonna kill me anyway."

Hughes came back in the room behind him. "Gone," he said. He was breathless now. "No clothes. Nothing. The place is empty. She's left."

The hooker smirked up at Mortimer. Mortimer drew out the straight razor. He flipped it open. When the hooker saw the blade, her smirk failed her. She swallowed.

"I'm gonna cut you," said Mortimer.

She swallowed again. "You can cut me all you want," she said. "I still won't know."

"You'll know. You've gotta know. I'll fucking cut you till you do."

"Fuck you," she said again. Her voice was quivering now. "You're gonna kill me anyway. Right?"

"Shut up."

"Right? Fucking right? You're gonna kill me anyway?"

"I'm gonna hurt you, bitch."

"Hey, you know what?" she said.

And she started screaming.

She had a loud, high, curdling shriek. Like a girl in a horror film. They could've heard her in the boroughs. She screamed and screamed.

Mortimer lunged down to grab her, but she started crawling away from him. She crawled under the lamp table, and knocked it over. It blocked his path. She went on screaming and screaming as she crawled across the floor.

"Jesus Christ, shut her up!" said Hughes.

"C'mere, goddammit," growled Mortimer, chasing her.

She crawled behind a chair, out of reach.

"For Christ's sake," said Hughes.

The hooker went on screaming.

Enraged, Mortimer hurled the chair out of his way. The girl took a breath and screamed louder.

"Shut her . . ." said Hughes.

"You bitch!"

Mortimer went at her. She kicked him in the ankle with her other heel.

"Ow!" screamed Mortimer, stumbling, reeling to one side.

The hooker screamed and screamed. She was backed into the corner, sitting up against the wall. Mortimer spun to go after her again.

Then her body bucked. Her chest puffed open. Rich scarlet appeared above the neckline of the leather teddy. She slumped in the corner, staring, dead. It was very quiet after all that screaming.

Mortimer stared down at her. He didn't understand what had happened. Then he turned and stared at Hughes.

Hughes was still pointing the gun at her. He'd shot her, for Christ's sake. He'd shot the hooker dead. Mortimer hadn't even heard the *pfft* under all the noise.

"What did you do?" said Mortimer.

"What do you mean what did I do? I shot her. She was screaming."

"We don't have anything now."

Hughes raised his hands and shoulders at him. "She didn't know anything. She was screaming."

"Yeah, but . . . " Clutching the razor, Mortimer rubbed the heel of his thumb over his lips. "Jesus."

"The whole house could've heard her. The cops are probably on their way."

"Jesus Christ," said Mortimer.

"We gotta get out of here," said Hughes.

"Yeah, I know but . . . what do we do?" said Mortimer. "I mean, Christ, we lost her. The girl. She's gone. We lost her. I mean, Winter . . . I mean, what're we gonna do now?"

7

The noise of the city being what it is, the hooker's screams didn't carry much past the corner. Lonnie never heard them. They had already stopped by the time he came within sight of the brownstone.

Lonnie paused on the sidewalk beneath the stoop.

He looked up at the door. He looked down the street toward the river. He stood with his hands in his pockets and shook his head.

What had he expected? To bump into her again? Here on the street, after midnight? Or maybe to get a glimpse of her through a window. Or maybe just to be in the air she breathed.

He made that habitual noise of his, that snort of contempt. It was self-contempt this time.

Either you are the dumbest-ass black man that ever lived, he thought, *or you are going home.*

He was going home. He had a full night of rage and remorse and sexual obsession ahead of him. He wanted to get an early start.

He turned back toward Second. The brownstone door opened.

"You the cops?" said a man.

Lonnie glanced at him. A short fat guy bulging out of a sweatsuit. Balding, swarthy, maybe Jewish, maybe Italian. He held the brownstone door open, called down the stairs.

"About the girl screaming," he said. "Cause I'll tell you one thing, man: *I'm* not going up there."

Lonnie's hands came out of his pockets. "What floor?"

"The girls," said the man. "Up on three. God knows who they got up there half the time."

Lonnie ran toward him. The man in the sweatsuit jumped back, holding the door wide. Lonnie ran over the threshold. Bounded up the stairs.

She's dead, he thought. He thought of the girl's pretty face staring up from the floor. *I let her chase me away and I wasn't there to help her and now she's dead.*

"Hey, be careful, there could still be people up there," said the man behind him.

Lonnie wasn't careful. He didn't slow down. He took the stairs two at a time. In a moment, he was in the dark of the second floor. He could hear latches clicking. He could feel eyes peering out through chain locks at him. He didn't stop. He went up the next flight. His gut was twisting like a screw. *She's dead.*

Breathless, he reached the third-floor landing.

8

Mortimer and Hughes watched him.

They had just left the apartment moments ago. They were just settling into the front seat of the Grand Marquis. Hughes had not started the ignition yet, had not turned on the lights. Mortimer was slumped in the seat next to him, staring out the window like a crash test dummy. He was devastated at this turn of events. He was thinking about what he'd say to Winter. He was trying to imagine some kind of explanation scene that wouldn't end with him being dead.

I don't know what it is, he was thinking. *I must be in some kind of slump or something.*

He could already hear police sirens in the distance.

"I told you," said Hughes. "Here they come. We gotta go, go, go."

That was when Lonnie showed up.

Mortimer gazed out at him dully. Lonnie was standing on the sidewalk under the stoop. Just hanging around looking uncomfortable and suspicious.

"Who's this jo-jo?" Mortimer murmured, too depressed to really care.

Hughes turned on the engine, turned on the lights.

"No, wait a minute," Mortimer said.

"Oh, good idea," said Hughes. "Wait a minute. Why? You think the police may need a hand?" He put the car into reverse.

Mortimer watched the black man hovering on the sidewalk in front of the stoop.

A *john*, he thought. *He must be a john.* His mind raced desperately. Maybe he knows something.

Some guy was looking out from the brownstone doorway now. The super probably. For a moment, Mortimer wondered if he had spotted him and Hughes as they'd left the building. But no, they'd been watching. No one had had the guts even to peek into the hall. The super must've come out later, after he figured the coast was clear.

Now the super was talking to the black guy. And now—hold on here—now the black guy was running into the building like Superman to the rescue.

"Wait. This could be something," said Mortimer, trying to convince himself.

The sirens were louder now, very loud. Hughes backed the Marquis up, spun the wheel. Put her into drive.

"No, I mean it, wait a minute," Mortimer said.

"Wait shit," said Hughes. "I'm getting out of here."

Mortimer opened the door.

"Hey!" said Hughes.

"You go ahead," said Mortimer. "I'll call you."

9

Upstairs, Lonnie moved down the third-floor hallway. The door to 3E was not quite shut. He approached it cautiously, his heart beating hard. Piano music filtered out to him in the hall.

Harry Connick Jr., he thought vaguely. *Decent hands.* He reached the door.

The music stopped. The hallway was quiet except for the muted voice of a television pitchwoman coming through the walls. Lonnie was half aware that someone was behind him. Another apartment door had been pulled ajar, another set of frightened eyes was peering out. He didn't turn to look.

He pushed open the door to 3E.

The empty living room was before him. The lights on, the green panels of the stereo glowing. The unfinished drink on the cabinet. The magazines on the coffee table. Lonnie saw the half-open doors across the room. There were more lights on in the room to his right. He could see the edge of something in there. A bed probably.

He stepped into the apartment.

He edged forward slowly, his hands lifted in self-defense. He sensed the place was empty, but his eyes moved quickly, watching for an ambush. The floorboards creaked beneath his shoes. He headed for the lighted room, set all his concentration on the room.

He didn't hear the footsteps coming up the stairs behind him.

And he didn't see the corpses until he reached the doorway. There was a second, just before that, when he caught a whiff of something wicked. The smell of shit, the thick, metallic aroma of blood. A hot danger signal flashed through him. His step began to slow.

And then he spied the body on the bed. A dangling arm. The spray of red on the white wall.

"Oh man . . ." he said aloud. He thought of the girl's face, her damp eyes grateful. *Dead*.

He pushed into the room and he saw it all.

He saw the naked body ending in the bloody mess that had been its head. He turned and, as he was turning, he saw his murdered wife and then the girl whom he'd come to find—he imagined he saw them and then, having fully turned, he saw in fact the woman—a stranger—who was sitting there alone, her wig askew, her chin on her gory chest, her eyes staring at the single shoe still half on her foot.

He stood and stared at her until he understood what he was looking at, the carnage.

But by that time, the barrel of a pistol had been pressed into the back of his head.

10

Lonnie's heart gave a great painful thump. The breath flowed out of him like water.

A hard voice spoke in his ear. "Fuck with me, jo-jo. Go ahead. I want you to fuck with me."

Lonnie looked over at the dead man on the bed. He looked down at the dead woman in the corner. The dead woman stared at her feet.

Shit, Lonnie thought. He sighed. He put his hands up. "I'm not fucking with you," he said.

"Put 'em behind your head."

Lonnie did. He couldn't believe this. How many kinds of idiot had he been? Well, all that was over. Suddenly, all his urges and pulses and obsessions were gone. The fever of his desire was gone. The haze and passion and compulsion of the last few days—it had vanished utterly. Suddenly, the world was very clear to him. And what was clearest of all was the cold sting of the handcuffs snapping around one wrist and then, as his arms were forced down, the cold sting again as his wrists were cuffed together.

Typical, Lonnie said to himself. *You came to your senses just in time to have your stupid ass arrested.*

He was turned around.

And there they were, large as life and twice as ugly. Two uniformed New York City patrolmen. One was sandy-haired and the size of a small building. The other was black-haired and thick around and stupid-looking. Stupid had holstered his gun. But the sandy-haired building cat—oh, he liked his gun. He kept his gun way drawn and leveled and just about three inches from Lonnie's nose.

Lonnie stared down the barrel hard into the building's squinty eyes. He didn't like cops to begin with—and he was pissed off at himself for having sleepwalked into this shit. He was feeling just irritable enough to get himself into some *real* trouble.

"You have the right to remain silent," the building said.

Lonnie snorted. "How about the right to have that gun taken out of my face?"

"You're fucking with me, jo."

"Yeah, you picked up on that, huh."

The building looked like an unhappy building, like a building that was about to fall on Lonnie Blake. But before it had the chance, another man walked into the room.

Lonnie's eyes were locked with the building's and he wasn't going to break away first. When the building turned to look at the new guy, Lonnie looked too.

Lonnie looked—and he laughed once bitterly at his own incredible stupidity. He recognized the man at once. It was the five-oh who had been following the whore the night she'd come to his loft. It was the big block-headed gravel-faced cop who had been looking for her on the street.

The gravel-faced man went into his pocket, brought out his wallet, flashed his shield. Yup, he was a cop all right. Lonnie had pegged him from the start.

"I'm Detective Mortimer," the gravel-faced man said quietly. His flinty gaze was fastened on Lonnie. "And who, pray tell, are you?"

CHAPTER 6

BIRTH OF THE BLUES

Earlier that same day, Howard Roth had lost the battle to save Western Civilization. Vandals, Visigoths and other assorted barbarians had poured across the landscape like ants at a picnic. It was the sack of Rome revisited, what Gibbon had called "the triumph of barbarism and religion." It was even worse than that—because the barbarism was represented by the hideous personage of Althea Feldman and the religion was that humorless amalgam of leftism and feminism which, being in retreat everywhere from the forces of goodwill, common sense and humanity, had taken up seemingly permanent residence in Morburne College, Vermont.

Still, Roth had fought the good fight. He was Horatius on the bridge. He had bearded the Feldman-creature in her den—if you can beard a woman—if woman is what she was. He had stood before her desk jabbing two outstretched fingers at her with an unlit cigarette clamped between. The cigarette, of course, represented his defiance of the college's fascistic health edicts. Roth was in agreement with Milton's Satan in this: an excess of power must be opposed even when it's in the right.

"Every thought these students think," he told her, "everything *you* think—everything you say—the *language* you say it in—not to mention the freedom to say it: it all *comes* from places, Althea. It comes from England and France and Rome and Greece."

"Oh yes," she drawled in her nasal twang. "Where the white urmales invented fire."

"Yes!" Roth cried. "That's right! Tough luck! If Homer hadn't lived you would never have even thought to say *that*. And if you don't teach these kids—teach them what made them who they are, every one of them—so they can like it, or lump it, or change it or hate it—then you're just indoctrinating them with your own . . . opinions." *Imbecilic, half-baked, indefensible opinions,* he almost added. But he was not entirely without diplomacy.

Diplomacy or no, however, it didn't matter in the end. She sat there behind her desk, Althea, her pale froggy face flaccid, her dull eyes blinking soullessly through her enormous square glasses.

"I'm sorry but I just don't think Homer is really relevant to these kids, Howard," she said. "All these myths you love to tell them. All that glorification of war, the romance of rape. I'm sorry. I just don't think they're important to us anymore."

This was when Roth, staring down at her with a kind of mute wonder, knew that his bid to reinstall Western Civilization as a breadth requirement course had failed. He had known it would fail all along, and yet even so he could have wept for it. If Socrates had realized it would come to this—that the glory that was Greece would ultimately lead to this cultural black hole—this dead end— this . . . this . . . Althea Feldman . . .

Well, maybe Socrates had known. He had drunk hemlock, after all.

Storming from her office, Roth knew even then that

his anger was a thin cover over bottomless despair. He couldn't even console himself with the idea that he would live to fight another day. Just now, that seemed unlikely in the extreme.

Dejected, he left the Administration Building and set out across the campus. Winter came early up here in the North. The trees around the grassy quad were already bare. The sky above the venerable brick castles and clapboard barracks was white and the air smelled of snow.

Roth put up his collar as he walked. His cigarette was bobbing, clamped between his lips now. He brought out his lighter, held the flame to it.

The very first drag set off a rumbling cough. He plucked the cigarette out, held his fist to his mouth. Two students he recognized passed him on the path and he lifted his chin to them but went on coughing. A productive cough, that's what the doctor called it. Very productive. An artist, a Picasso of a cough. *Yes, right now I'm in my Phlegm Period,* Roth thought. He brought out a tissue and spat into it, glanced at the gob with resentment and fear.

It was in the phlegm that the doctor had found what he referred to as "renegade cells."

His cough subsiding, Roth reached the edge of the quad. He dashed his cigarette angrily to the sidewalk. Renegade cells, he thought. Saboteurs in the body politic. Communist cells probably. Recognizable by their black berets and shifty looks. The X ray had been inconclusive, but the CAT scan had turned up "a troubling shadow." Now they wanted to run some sort of tube down his throat and into his lungs and by that highly unpleasant means perform a biopsy to confirm what Roth in his heart of hearts already knew: he was fifty-seven years old. Fifty-eight would be a gift. Fifty-nine was pretty much out of the question.

What a waste, he thought irritably. *All of it. Everything. What a stupid, terrible waste.*

He moved along the sidewalk more slowly now, tired. Across the street was the town's main stretch. Quaint brick shops and clapboard restaurants, the old stone Ethan Allen hotel. Roth looked at none of it, staring into the middle distance, abstracted. The absentminded professor. Well, he had always been that. He'd heard that when people are dying the details of the world become very clear and sharp and beautiful to them. So far, he hadn't noticed it to speak of. He was just as distant and fuzzy-headed as always, just a lot more depressed at the same time. But then he had managed to put the biopsy off for two days, delaying the inevitable certainty. Maybe the side benefits of mortality would come later, when the test results were finally in.

He went on, a rumpled, shambling figure, bent and small. His face was gaunt, his eyes baggy, his nose beaked. His head was bald but for a fringe of flyaway silver hair. Once he had considered himself a rather elegant figure: a waspish intellectual, a slightly haughty citizen of the world of ideas. Now when he looked in the mirror, he saw an old Jewish man—a figure he secretly despised.

He left the campus and town center behind him. He pressed on up Maple Street. This was a tree-lined lane of increasingly modest houses pressed shoulder to shoulder on small lawns. His own house was down a few blocks, a dreary two-story looking sad and neglected under the white sky and naked branches.

Roth neared it, wheezing quietly. Thinking: What a

waste. The entire enterprise. Everything he had ever loved was now rejected by the world. Everything he had hoped to pass on had melted into air.

All these myths you love to tell them. I just don't think they're important to us anymore.

He climbed the porch stairs slowly. Clutching the banister, breathing hard. *Look at me. Christ. I barely made it.* He shuffled across the porch to the rocker.

He plonked himself into the chair and started it going. *Out of the cradle, endlessly rocking . . .* He looked over the railing at the comforting old view of lawns and houses much like his. He wondered if he should call either of his ex-wives or his two children, tell them the news. His daughter was a born-again Christian and might have to at least pretend to care. But she hadn't spoken to him in three years. And his son was in rehab with troubles of his own. And his ex-wives were—well, they were ex-wives. It was too depressing to think about.

He spent a few more minutes in this reverie—then he began to notice the soft, musical chatter coming from Geena MacAlary's yard next door.

He glanced over there. A child was sitting on the pale winter grass. Yes, he vaguely remembered Geena had said something about a cousin coming to visit. Something about the child's mother being ill.

The girl must have been four or five, he figured. Blond-haired but tan-skinned, as if one of her parents was black or half-black. She was bundled up against the cold, wearing a hooded pink jacket and some kind of thickly padded red pants. Holding a tea party it looked like, the wintry weather be damned. Sitting before a small half circle of dolls and stuffed animals. Babbling some little lecture to them, the frost puffing out before her.

Roth somehow found just the sight of the child extremely moving. Here on the porch with thoughts of death so near—with death itself so near. *Out of the cradle, endlessly rocking* . . . He watched the girl, entranced, touched by every gesture of her small gloved hands, fascinated by the piping timbre of her voice.

"Now, Barbie, drink all your milk because it's very, very good for you."

Roth felt a lump in his throat. His lips pressed together and he frowned. The child passed a paper cup to Barbie, and then another one to the other one next to her, the red furry one from TV, what was his name? He couldn't remember.

Then all at once, the girl looked up and caught him staring at her. He smiled at her. She studied him a long moment with big, solemn brown eyes.

Ah God! thought Roth. *None of it ever mattered but the love, and I squandered it all.*

"Hello," the little girl said to him. "My name is Amanda."

"Well, hello!" said Roth. He had to clear the renegade phlegm from his throat to get just the right happy, hearty man-to-child tone. "It's nice to meet you, Amanda. My name is Howard."

The girl answered nothing. She continued her solemn study of him. He found the steady, childish gaze a little unnerving.

So he cleared his throat again and said, "It's kind of cold for a picnic, isn't it?"

But the girl merely took hold of her stuffed animal and cradled it close to her. She spoke with infinite gravity. "This is Elmo."

Oh, Clarence, let me live again! I want to live again! Roth cried in his heart. The kid was just that incredibly cute. In fact, looking at her from this vantage point in the great stage show of life—the hook round his neck, one foot on the banana peel—it seemed suddenly crystal clear to him that he had gotten everything, all his priorities, wrong. He should've dedicated all the energies of his existence to the loving care of just such an adorable little person as this. Her trivial tempers, moods, illnesses and crises should have been all in all to him, more to him, yea, than Western Civilization itself. Fatherhood—family—love—that had been the ticket all along!

Of course he knew that if he'd been cured of his cancer tomorrow he would have reverted instantly to the insensitive, argumentative, self-obsessed fellow he by nature was. But how marvelous that a simple CAT scan had suddenly rendered an entirely different set of values clearly superior to his own. He almost felt he loved the child seated there on the grass before him.

Well, it had been an emotional couple of days.

"Hello, Elmo," he said hoarsely. "How are you?"

"He's fine," said Amanda.

She sniffled a little. Her tan cheeks were flushed. She squinched herself together in her makeshift snowsuit.

She *was* cold, obviously. Geena MacAlary had been a nurse for a while and had raised three children of her own. Roth figured she knew what she was doing. Still he said, "Are you sure you shouldn't go inside?"

"We have to have tea out here," piped the girl, "so Mommy will see us when she comes."

"Ah," said Roth—in his sensitized state even he understood the deep poignancy of this remark. "Where is your mommy then?"

"Far away in a dark place," said Amanda mysteriously. "She has to come all the way up to get here so she can take me with her. That's why she's gone for such a long time. And she can't ever look back or they'll take her down to the dark place again."

All during his brief exchange with the child, Roth had gone on rocking gently in his old wooden porch chair. But now he stopped, shifted his chair toward her, leaned forward in it with a small grunt of interest.

"Really. She can't look back?" he said. "Why not? Why can't she?"

The child answered in the same chanting, lecturing tone with which she'd spoken to her dolls. "Because you're not allowed to see the dark place," she said.

Roth nodded slowly, hovering there in the rocker. It wasn't really in his nature to involve himself very deeply in the concerns or opinions of a child—or of anyone else for that matter. But she had touched an intellectual chord in him. With his chair tilted forward, he rested his elbows on his knees, his hands clasped between his legs. The child hugged Elmo to her, but watched him with those big, serious brown eyes.

"You know," he said, "I know a story like that. About a man who wasn't supposed to look back." And then—

uncharacteristically—the child's feelings occurred to him and he added, "But it's a sad story—it's not about your mother."

"How does it go?" said the child at once.

"It really is sad. Are you sure you want to hear it?"

"Ye-es," drawled the child.

Roth sat back in the chair and set it rocking again. He gathered his thoughts for a moment, conscious all the while of her grave gaze on him.

And then he told her the story of Orpheus and Eurydice.

He spoke in an increasingly weak, increasingly rough voice. He had to fight down the cough that threatened to go back into production from time to time. He simplified for her as he went along. Edited out the really wicked parts.

But he told her about Orpheus, son of a muse and Apollo; a musician so great that when he played his lyre, the animals of the woods came to listen, and the trees bowed down and even the rocks sighed. Orpheus married a forest nymph named Eurydice and he loved her passionately. But one day, Eurydice was attacked by evil men who wanted her for their own. She ran for her life, terrified—so terrified that she didn't watch her step. Her heel came down on a poisonous snake. It bit her, and she was carried off by Hades to his everlasting country of the dead.

"I know Hades," Amanda broke in solemnly. "He's blue."

Roth acceded to this with the best grace he could muster and went on.

Orpheus was so sad—he loved Eurydice so much— that he decided to do something no one had ever done before: he decided to go living into the land of the dead and bring her back with him. Now the only way into the dark country was across the great River Styx and the only way across the river was in the boat piloted by a black-cowled, empty-eyed figure named Charon. Charon would not take living passengers—they had to pay him in a coin only given to the dead. But Orpheus played his lyre for him, and the music was so beautiful that Charon let him come aboard and they sailed across the river.

But then, on the far side, at the very gates of Death, a dog named Cerberus stood guard. He was a giant dog with three heads, each head with a mouth full of fangs, each mouth frothing and growling. Again, Orpheus played his lyre, and each of Cerberus's heads slowly sank down to rest neck-over-neck on the creature's folded paws as he listened. And Orpheus passed on.

At last, he came to the throne of Hades himself. And Orpheus played his lyre. And the music so moved even the King of Death that Hades agreed to let Eurydice go—on one condition. Orpheus must lead her home along the cliffs of Hell—and *he could not look back* at her until they had reached the land of the living.

"Because he wasn't supposed to see her when she was dead," said Amanda, nodding.

Roth paused. He considered her remark. He had always wondered about this part of the story: where had Hades come up with this *fakakta* condition of his. Don't look back. What sense did it make? He still wasn't sure. But somehow, what the child said rang true to him. He was moved by that. He smiled at her as he went on:

Orpheus began to ascend toward the sunlight, holding Eurydice by the hand as she followed behind. But as he came closer and closer to the top, Orpheus began to wonder if maybe Hades had tricked him, if maybe it was really a monster who kept its hand in his, who was only waiting for the right moment to drag him back to Hell. With every step he became more and more convinced the monster was about to attack him, to destroy him.

Finally, he couldn't stand the suspense any longer. Just as he was about to break out into the living light of day, Orpheus looked back.

There was Eurydice. He saw her for one moment— all her beauty, all he loved—one moment only. He had broken his agreement with Hades. And in the next instant, Eurydice vanished before his anguished eyes and she was carried back to the country of the dead forever.

In all the days, all the years after that, Orpheus was so sad that the music he played on his lyre was heartbreaking. The creatures of the forest listened and groaned in misery, the trees withered at the sound and even the stones shed tears. Even after he was dead, Orpheus's body went on singing with such wondrous and terrible grief that the poets took up his song. And they've been singing it ever since to all the world.

"And that," said Roth, rocking, smiling, looking up and out beyond the porch, through the naked branches of the trees and into the white sky, "that was the birth of the blues."

When he lowered his eyes again, the child was just sitting there, just holding her Elmo doll and staring up at him with those grave brown eyes. For a moment, Roth was worried. Was the story too sad for her, too harsh? He'd bowdlerized it as much as he felt he could. He'd left out the part about Orpheus being torn to pieces and so on. But still—what did he know about children these days?—maybe he'd said something horrible, something that would damage her little psyche for life.

Then Amanda tilted up her flushed cheeks and murmured in a voice that seemed hushed with awe. "That's a *good* story!"

That voice, that hush, that awe—Roth's feeling for the child rose up in him, overwhelmed him. He pressed his lips together. He nodded. His eyes swam with tears.

Oh, children, he wailed inwardly, *children are God's answer to History.*

"Do you know any more stories like that?" she asked him.

Roth lifted a knuckle to the corner of his eye.

"All of them, kid," he said gruffly. "I know them all."

CHAPTER 7

HIT THE ROAD, JACK

It was 4 A.M. Tuesday morning when Detective Mortimer came into the interrogation room. It was a cramped gray room crowded with a single long metal table, two uncomfortable plastic chairs. There was a heavy door that had one of those one-way mirrors in it. For the last hour or so, Lonnie had been waiting in here alone.

Mortimer had questioned Lonnie at the murder scene and one of the patrolmen had questioned him there too. Then they'd brought him here to the precinct house on Fifth Street and a detective named Grimaldi had questioned him as had a guy from the DA's office. Then they'd left him alone in here and then it had gotten to be four in the morning.

And all this time, Lonnie had been going over and over in his head how he'd helped this whore on the street one fine evening and wound up sleeping with her and thinking about her and following her around and finally found himself in a room full of corpses being questioned by the police. Of course, he hadn't told the police any of this because . . . well, because fuck them. He was sure in his heart that the girl hadn't killed anyone and if the cops wanted help finding her they could get it somewhere else. Which meant now he was lying to protect her. Which didn't strike him as such a smart idea either. So he went over and over that in his head too.

And so just about now—about four o'clock Tuesday morning—Lonnie was tired and angry and more than a little confused and generally ready to breakfast on someone's heart.

And that's when Mortimer came in. His gravelly face twisted into an immensely unappealing smirk.

"Hey, Lonnie. You remember me from our last episode, right?" he said. "I'm Detective Mortimer."

"Yeah, I remember you," Lonnie said wearily. "The ugly one. Say, are you people gonna charge me here or can I go home to bed?"

Detective Mortimer laughed a bogus coplike laugh. He turned the free plastic chair around backward and straddled it. He winked at Lonnie. It was the kind of wink you wanted to wash off. Then he looked Lonnie straight in the eye and spoke to him man-to-slimy-piece-of-Negro-criminal-garbage.

"Let me ask you something, Lonnie," he said. "If you were me, would you believe your story?"

"Let me ask you something," Lonnie said. "How come I'm *Lonnie* and you're *Detective* Mortimer?"

"Well, because I'm a police officer and you're a lying scumbag," Mortimer explained. "Does that clear it up for you?"

"Oh man! Listen to that shit. You know, I don't think you like me."

"Breaks your heart, doesn't it?"

"In twain, baby. And you know what? I want a lawyer."

"I want a Mercedes. Life is full of disappointments, what can I say."

Lonnie laughed once and shook his head. "You folks never change, do you?"

Mortimer sat back in his turned-around chair a little.

"That's right," he said. "You know all about us folks. Don't you, Pump-Pump?"

Lonnie couldn't help himself. Hearing his old gangster nickname took him by surprise and the surprise showed. He looked at Mortimer sharply.

Mortimer grinned. "That was your banger handle, wasn't it? I mean, you were a stone blue gangster, weren't you . . . *baby?*"

I was a stone fifteen-year-old child with a horse-sloppy mother, Lonnie thought. *And three years later, I had a music scholarship to UC, so fuck you.*

"Is that what I was?" he said aloud. "Well, I guess you know."

"Hey. Hey. You know what I know, Lonnie?" Mortimer had shown off his hard ass, now he'd play conciliatory. "I know I got me a run-away hooker, all right? I got two people dead in her apartment. And I got you in her apartment with the two dead people. Now to these old eyes, that means you're either some kind of suspect or some kind of witness. If you're a suspect, no sweat, just let me know so I can start beating a confession out of you. But I don't think you are a suspect. I think you're a witness—and I think you can help me find that girl."

Lonnie threw up one hand. "I already told you, man. I ran up there because the super said there was some girls screaming. Ask him!"

"I did ask him. And I believe you, Lonnie. And I also believe you came there in the first place because you wanted to see Carol Dodson."

Lonnie shook his head. "I told you that too. I met her once. In a bar, Renaissance, where I was working. She gave me her address and said we should party. I didn't know she was a professional. I didn't even know that was her name."

"Yeah. Now here," Mortimer said. "Here's where we get to the lying scumbag part." Once again, the big block of a head pressed forward. The sharp widow's peak pointed straight at Lonnie and the rough skin dimpled as his mouth twisted in a smirk. It wasn't a pretty sight. "Because I was after Carol Dodson on a vice rap Friday night," the cop went on. "I was chasing her down the street and, lo and behold, she disappeared. She vanished right from in front of me, Lonnie. Right on the street where you live. On the very block where you live."

This time, Lonnie managed to show the man nothing. The look he gave him was slow and empty. He still remembered the fine art of looking at a cop that way. All the same, he felt the pulse of blood going crazy in him. This was the first time Mortimer had mentioned that night. Lonnie hoped he hadn't made the connection. But if he had, why had he waited so long to spring it on him?

"Now I think she came to you, Lonnie," Mortimer went on. "I think she ran away from me and came to your home for help and you let her in. And that tells me you were more than just a casual acquaintance in a bar, Lonnie. That tells me you knew her. You knew her well enough to risk getting in trouble with the police."

Lonnie had a strong impulse to say, No. No, I didn't know her, she just came. But he kept his mouth shut.

The big cop shook his big head at him. Laughed. "Man oh man, she really got her hooks into you, didn't she? Christ, what the fuck she do for you? Something special? There something special she did just the way you like it, Lonnie?"

Lonnie felt the truth rise in his eyes—*she pretended to be my dead wife*—but his gaze stayed steady.

"It sure must've been something," Mortimer went on. "I mean, some Susan B. lies down for you and suddenly you're lying to protect a murder suspect? You're lying to protect some five-and-dime whore who left town without bothering to clean up the two corpses in her fucking apartment? Come on. You're too smart for that. I mean, you're opening yourself to a charge of accessory here, Lonnie. That's a piss poor career move, I want to tell you. So if there's something you have to say to me, you had better say it now and you had better say it fast."

Lonnie didn't answer. He kept his gaze locked on Mortimer's. He kept his face blank and his deep eyes empty. But in fact, he couldn't help thinking about it.

Maybe the cop was right. Maybe he was getting himself into all sorts of shit over a lying hooker he didn't even know. Maybe she was a murderer. And maybe he was still lost in some kind of crazy dream or something where this whore had become all tangled up in his mind with his wife. And when he thought about his wife and how sweet she was and how straight-up and how there was a kind of peace and goodness inside her; and when he thought about this scared, frantic, fucked-up call girl . . . well, maybe he just ought to tell this cop everything he knew and get the hell out of here.

Mortimer must've sensed his indecision. He leaned in further, his small eyes bright. "I'll take a hint, Lonnie," he said, and Lonnie thought there was almost a tone of desperation to it. And Mortimer said: "Something. Anything. Cause you're going down here otherwise, my friend, I'm telling you. Just give me one thing that'll help me find the girl and you are out of here and on your way home, I swear it."

Lonnie's lips parted. Suddenly he was thinking about the man in the restaurant, the man with long hair and an eye patch whom the girl—Carol Dodson—met at Ed Whittaker's. A man like that, a description like that, the cops could probably find him. Hell, they probably already had a file on him. That would do it. He could tell them about that. Fucking five-ohs could hunt down their crazy bitch and he could go on home and forget about it. Everything good, what's the problem?

Mortimer studied him and he studied Mortimer a long time. A long time.

Then Lonnie said, "I just got one question."

"Yeah. Go ahead," said Mortimer eagerly.

"Does your mama know what you do for a living?"

Mortimer sat back in his chair and laughed. It sounded real this time. A genuine laugh. His eyes seemed almost to sparkle with the laughter.

"All right, Lonnie. Get out of here. Go on home," he said.

Lonnie stared at him. "Say what?"

"You heard me. Go on. We'll talk again later."

For a moment, Lonnie was too dumbfounded to move. He just sat there. He just stared.

And Mortimer laughed again. And Mortimer waved at him. And Mortimer said, "Go on. Go home. Get out of here. You be a free man."

2

"El Penis," Mortimer muttered as the Grand Marquis glided across town.

From behind the steering wheel, Hughes glanced over at him. "El Penis? What is that? Is that some kind of cop talk? What?"

Mortimer's jaw worked as he gazed out through the windshield, as he watched the streetlights paling under the mellow blue of the pre-dawn city. "L.P.N.S.," he said. "Lying Piece of Nigger Shit."

"El Penis!" Hughes laughed: "I get it. El Penis. That's pretty good."

Mortimer didn't answer. His jaw worked.

"So you're pretty sure he knows something, huh?" said Hughes.

"Oh yeah," Mortimer growled. "He knows something. He almost spit it out right there but he got clever on me at the last second."

"Well, it's better this way. At his place."

Mortimer nodded grimly.

"I hope it's something good," said Hughes. "I told Winter we just about had her. I told him we were one step away. He's not too happy about the whole thing."

Mortimer gave a bitter harumph. His stomach felt like a lava pit. He didn't need to be reminded of Winter. The guy was never far from his thoughts as it was.

The Marquis stopped now just at Sixth, idling under

a red light as the thickening morning traffic passed before them left to right. Steam poured up through a manhole into the chilly sunrise.

"Where do you figure that steam comes from?" Hughes said quietly. "How come it's always coming up out of the street like that?"

Mortimer looked around at him slowly. "Fuck is it with you? Why can't you keep your fucking mind on things?"

"I'm just wondering. It relaxes me to think of something else."

"Well, stop relaxing. What the fuck are you relaxing about? If we don't have that bitch in hand by lunchtime, let me tell you something: we are well and truly fucked. We are two men fucked beyond all reasonable expectation of becoming unfucked. So stop relaxing."

Hughes shrugged. The light gleamed green. The car started rolling again.

" 'It relaxes me,' " Mortimer muttered. "Christ."

After a moment, Hughes said mildly: "At least you're NYPD."

Mortimer grunted.

"No, I'm serious. What if you weren't a cop? What if they'd taken this Lonnie Blake guy in and we had *no* way to get to him? Then where would we be?"

"I thought I'd never get him out of there as it was," Mortimer allowed. "Grimaldi had nothing on him, but he just wouldn't let go. *I got an instinct about this guy. I got an instinct.* He wouldn't shut up about it. Instinct shit."

"Guess he'll be pretty pissed off when they find Blake's body. He'll say, *I told you I had an instinct.*"

Hughes's cheeks flushed with pleasure when Mortimer

actually laughed a little at that. "Yeah, well," Mortimer said. "Better him pissed off than Winter."

"See?" said Hughes. "So it's not so bad. You gotta look at the sunny side sometimes. All we do, we go to this Blake guy's house, we find out where the girl went, we kill him, we're on our way again."

"Your mouth to God's ears."

"Amen, brother. About time things started going right for us in this stupid op."

They parked around the corner from Lonnie Blake's apartment and walked the rest of the way there. Mortimer, gigantic in his trench coat, glanced down at the short, chubby, bearded Hughes in his green pea jacket. Lo and behold, Hughes had his little black box out. The Spymaster. He was pushing the slide on it, heating it up.

"This again," said Mortimer.

"What," said Hughes. "It's a miracle machine. It opens anything."

"Climb up the fire escape, we go right in the window."

"Yeah, yeah, yeah. You can't always live in the fucking past. Y'know?"

In the event, they opted for the wonders of modernity. Hughes held the Electronic Skeleton Key to the outer door and shot the heated polymer through the keyhole. They were in the lobby in under a minute. In under another minute, they had the elevator working and were heading up to Lonnie's place. They stood shoulder to shoulder, watching the vator's lights. The L went out. Number two was broken. Number three went on. And then they were on the fourth floor.

Once again, they waited while the Spymaster ESK-300 worked its magic.

"You do have a warrant, right?" said Hughes.

Mortimer snorted. "Stop fucking around."

Hughes, red with mirth, turned the key. Mortimer pressed the lobby button so the vator would go down again. Both men stepped out into the loft.

They were pretty sure the place was empty. They had followed Lonnie to a coffee shop, waited to make sure he would stay to eat. All the same, Hughes pulled out his silenced Cougar nine and walked cautiously through the rooms.

Mortimer, meanwhile, wandered into the john and took a leak. There was a can of Old Spice shaving cream sitting beside the sink. He considered this thoughtfully as he pissed. After a while, he picked the can up and slipped it into his trench coat pocket. He smirked to himself.

They met up again in the main room. By that time, Mortimer was standing at the windows, next to the telephone table. Hughes entered, slipping the Cougar back into its holster.

"Nobody home," he said. "You see him?"

Mortimer peered through the fire escape, scanned the street. "Not yet."

"We got time," said Hughes. He settled his big bulk into the leather sofa. Snatched a magazine from a lamp stand nearby. He leafed through the magazine.

At the window, Mortimer glanced down. He noticed the pad on the telephone table.

"Wait a minute," he said.

He picked up the pad.

"Jesus," he said. "Look at this."

Hughes lifted his eyes.

Mortimer wagged the pad gently in the air. He smiled broadly for the first time that day.

"Paydirt," he said.

3

Sitting at the window counter of Designer Java, Lonnie was working on his second Styro of Kenyan blend. He held the cup to his lips without drinking. A corn muffin sat on the little plate in front of him, less eaten than worried to powder and crumbs.

The day was not yet bright. The window still reflected him. He gazed out through the reflection at the avenue stirring in the cold, clear dawn.

He was tired to the sinew. He was angry to the core. He didn't like being a fool, and he didn't like cops pushing him around and he wished the fuck he knew why they'd let him go and whether this girl, this Carol Dodson, had been worth covering for, and why this cop, this Mortimer cat, had looked so desperate at him, and why he waited so long to mention the night the girl had first come to him and why the whole thing just felt all sorts of *wrong* to him somehow.

He held the cup to his lips and thought about it. He watched the city waking up beyond the window. The rumbling traffic rose like a river as the morning rose. The men in suits appeared on the sidewalks and the working women passed with their purposeful strides. It might have been a city on television for all it touched him, for all he cared about it or the people in it. A city of strangers. The capital of a world of strangers. All of them running around fucking each other and killing each other, lying to each other and hating each other and dying in each other's arms. What had he helped the girl in the first place for anyway? He had no truck with her. He had no truck with any of them. They could all go to Hell for all he cared. This was their Hell, this city. This world of lonesome cities. They made it Hell.

The day grew brighter. His reflection grew dim on the pane. He looked through the image of himself at the rising traffic, at the people passing. The day grew brighter still. His reflection faded. Finally, he vanished before his own eyes. There was only the city beyond.

He knocked back his Styro, drained the coffee grounds. He stood. He headed out. He headed home.

"Euphonium," said Hughes, meanwhile.

He was still sitting on the leather sofa. He was leafing through the magazine again. The magazine was called *Wind Instrument*.

"Who the hell ever heard of a euphonium?" he said.

Mortimer was at the window, looking down through the fire escape at the street below.

"Here he comes," he said.

"I mean, what kind of word is that?"

"He's at the building. Let's go."

"You ask me, it's a fucking tuba." Hughes laid the

magazine aside, shaking his head. "I don't know," he said with a sigh.

He lumbered to his feet, drew out the Cougar. He checked the slide port as he wandered over to the elevator door.

"Euphonium," he muttered. "Ya ya ya."

Mortimer lumbered slowly around to the far side of the elevator door. Hughes stood on the other side so that Lonnie would walk out between them.

They could hear the elevator door open in the lobby below. They heard a *chunk* and then a hum as the machine started up toward them.

Mortimer lifted his chin at Hughes. Hughes sighed again and nodded, raising the gun beside his face.

They waited for Lonnie Blake.

Lonnie was exhausted. By the time he'd reached his block, he'd barely been lifting his shoes. The early pedestrians went buzzing by him at Manhattan's waking pace and he slogged along, weary, until he reached his building. He leaned heavily against the door as he unlocked it. He nearly fell inside as the door swung in.

The elevator was waiting for him. He stepped inside, turned the key in the notch for four. He propped himself against the wall and closed his eyes as the box began to ascend.

Why had they let him go? he wondered. Why had the police just let him walk free like that?

But he was too tired to think about it anymore. He was sick of thinking about it. He was sick of the whole thing. He listened to the soothing hum of the machine.

The elevator stopped. Lonnie opened his eyes. He pulled back the cage. He fumbled for his key.

But then the outer door swung open as if on its own. Startled, Lonnie looked up.

Jesus Christ, he thought, *it's not even seven o'clock.*

All the same, there she was: Mattie Harris, his downstairs neighbor. She had hijacked him again as he passed her floor.

"Hi, Lonnie," she said brightly. "I was hoping it might be you."

She was wearing a blue silk bathrobe. It was soft on her pudgy form. It was open up top to show the line of her generous cleavage and the frilled edge of her bra. And though she was dressed as if she'd just awoken, her hair was in place. It was brushed to a shine. And even from where he stood, Lonnie caught the whiff of lavender.

"Mattie?" he said. It was all he could think of.

She smiled at him, a wincing, apologetic smile. "Sorree. I need a favor."

Lonnie gaped at her stupidly. He had a sense he'd been doing that for some time. "Now?" he said finally.

"It's just: one of the lights in my bathroom ceiling's gone out?" Her voice rose as if this were a question. "I'm not tall enough to reach it and I can't see to put my makeup on. You know, I was afraid I'd go to work looking like one of those crazy ladies with the painted-on mouths? I didn't hear you come in last night so when I heard the elevator, I thought . . ."

Lonnie gaped at her stupidly some more. "You want me to change a lightbulb."

Mattie blushed. "Sorry. Helpless Female Alert." She made a Helpless Female gesture.

After a while—a long while—Lonnie blinked. Then he lifted his chin. Then he sighed.

"Okay," he said.

He stepped out of the elevator.

6

"She wants him to change a lightbulb," said Hughes. He had his ear pressed to the elevator door.

"Oh, for fuck's sake," said Mortimer. "It's six-thirty in the fucking morning here."

Hughes shrugged. "She's doing the helpless female thing. Sounds like she likes him."

"Great. That's just great. That's just what we need. Now he'll probably fuck her."

"Just hold on," said Hughes. "Let's see what happens."

"If he fucks her, we're going down there. I mean it. We're killing them both. That's it. I've had it up to here. Jesus. What do they think this is?"

"Just take it easy."

"Nothing is going right on this op. I swear it to God."

7

Lonnie followed Mattie's trailing scent across one end of her loft. He was aware—dimly aware—of the place around him. The density of its plant life and decorations. The warm, homey fuzz that seemed to grow on the furniture and the rugs and the walls. As he turned a corner, the tendrils of a spider plant brushed against his face. He felt a distinct urge to rip the thing down and stomp its hanging ceramic pot to splinters.

"So," Mattie said. "You look like you've had a long night." She managed to make it sound casual.

He managed not to strangle her. "Yeah," he said. "I have."

"I guess you're living the wild musician's life, huh."

"I guess that must be it . . . shit!"

Mattie's snowball of a cat had raced out in front of him. He nearly tripped over it.

"Careful, Muffin," Mattie sang out.

"Yeah," said Lonnie through his teeth. "Careful, Muffin." *Before I mount your fucking head on a stick.*

They reached the bathroom door. Mattie stood aside and pointed the way.

"I tried, I just couldn't get to it," she said. "I guess I gotta get a new stepladder."

With another long sigh, Lonnie looked in. The bathroom's main light—a dangling bulb with a pink shade around it—was fine, was on, was gleaming merrily off the porcelain of the sink, off the makeup cases on the counter, off the toothbrush mug with the cartoon character Cathy on it. But there was a stepladder in the middle of the floor, right by the sink. And, raising his eyes, Lonnie saw another light, recessed into the high ceiling far, far above. And that light—he had to admit it—had well and truly blown.

Lonnie shook his head. Damn thing had probably been out for ages, he thought. She'd probably been saving it so she could pull this stuff, get him in here. Spying on him like some kind of suspicious wife cause he'd been out all night. Shit, what the hell did it take to get rid of this woman?

Suddenly—and against his will—he thought of Carol Dodson tearing her arm out of his grip. Backing away from him on First Avenue.

What does it take? You know? I mean, what does it fucking take?

He sighed yet again. "All right," he said aloud. He thumped sullenly up the stepladder.

It was a reach, even for him. He had to stretch his arms all the way up, his head tilted back painfully. He unscrewed the recessed light cover—the metal rim, the round glass plate beneath. He slipped them into his overcoat pocket to free his hands to unscrew the bulb.

"Awright, gimme the fresh light," he said, reaching down to her.

"I'm really sorry about this, Lonnie," Mattie said pitiably. She stretched up to hand the new bulb to him.

Yeah, yeah, yeah, he thought. He was putting the new light in now.

"I could make it up to you," she said. "I could make you breakfast if you want?"

He glanced down at her. Her broad face turned up to him, hopeful. *Yeah, well,* he thought after a moment. *I guess I know the name of that tune.*

"I can't, Mattie," he told her more or less gently. "I'm beat. I mean it. Another time. Okay?" He put the glass plate over the light, started to twist in the metal seal. "Just as soon as I finish with this"—and with each word, he twisted the seal sharply—"I. Am. Going. Straight. Home."

"All right, hang on to your shorts," said Hughes. "He's coming."

"He better be fucking coming."

Hughes listened at the elevator door. "She says thank you. Is he sure he doesn't want to stay for some coffee?"

"If he stays for coffee, we kill them both," said Mortimer.

"Hey, be a human being here. She's a nice girl. She likes him."

"Yeah, if we don't get the Dodson slash soon . . ."

"I know, I know. Hold on."

Mortimer fell silent. Hughes listened. He heard the rattle of the elevator cage opening downstairs.

"Here we go," said Hughes.

"About fucking time," said Mortimer.

The elevator door closed between Lonnie and Mattie Harris's wistful, still-hopeful face. *City of strangers,* he thought. He leaned against the wall. Now on top of everything else, he felt vaguely guilty. Maybe he should've stayed for the damned coffee too.

The elevator began to rise. The light on four—his light—came on. The elevator stopped. Lonnie slid the cage back. He turned his key in the door, pushed it open. He stepped out into his loft.

The gun barrel jammed hard into his temple.

"Talk and you die, blink and you die, breathe and you fucking die," hissed a voice in his ear.

Then—like a nightmare—Detective Mortimer's enormous gravelly face swam before him, bright with malice. He saw it for an instant only. Then he was grabbed. Muscled to the floor. In his shock, he had no strength to resist.

He went down hard. His back slammed into the wood. The breath went out of him.

Mortimer was on top of him, sitting on his chest, knees pinning his arms. One big hand clutched his throat. The square, rough face bore down, its grin bore down.

Lonnie gagged as the cop throttled him. His eyes rolled back. He saw another man, a fat, bearded man, standing above him. Laughing down at him, loosely waving a gun at his face.

"Now we're going to take up where we left off,"
Mortimer said. His hot breath washed over Lonnie's
face.

"What the fuck . . . ?" Lonnie choked out.

"Ssh," said Mortimer. "Ssh." He squeezed his throat
tighter until Lonnie could only let out a soft wheeze.
"You gonna be a tough guy, Pump-Pump? What do you
think? You a tough guy?" He glanced up at the fat man,
grinning. "Pump-Pump used to be a tough guy," he said.
"Used to be a gangsta. Used to be a stone blue G."

The fat man's cheeks turned a jolly shade of red
beneath his beard. "Hit him," he said, laughing. "Hit
him in the euphonium."

Mortimer sat back on top of Lonnie. His grip on
Lonnie's throat eased a little.

"Get the fuck off me," Lonnie said hoarsely. Rage
and fear were flowing through him like liquid fire.

Mortimer did not get off him. With his free hand, the
big cop drew a canister out of his trench coat pocket.
Lonnie stared at it, frightened. But it was just shaving
cream. His own red canister of Old Spice.

"Let me clarify this situation for you, Pump-Pump,"
Mortimer said. "The policeman is not your friend."

He sprayed the cream into Lonnie's face. Lonnie
grunted, struggling under the grip on his throat. The
white lather sputtered down onto him.

Mortimer tossed the can aside. As Lonnie twisted,
writhed, gasped, the cop jammed a rough hand down
on him, smeared the cream all over his mouth and jaw.

Lonnie spit out the sour foam. Through blurred
eyes, he saw Mortimer pull something from inside his
coat. A flip of the wrist, and the blade gleamed. A
straight razor.

"You been up all night, jo-jo," Mortimer said. "You need a shave."

Lonnie stared at the razor, breathing hard. The terror and the rage were a single thing inside him now. He felt the fire of them fill him. He felt they would punch through him in his helplessness, erupt like a volcano.

Mortimer forced Lonnie's head to one side. Above them, the fat man laughed a snuffling laugh. Mortimer set the razor to Lonnie's throat, just at the jawline. Lonnie felt the cold of the steel. He stopped struggling, afraid to move.

The cop's eyes shone blackly in his pitted face. "If you lie," he said, "I'll know."

He started to shave him. The blade scraped over Lonnie's stubble. Lonnie couldn't speak for the fire of feeling in him. He grunted as he felt the sharp edge sting his skin.

"Tell me about the girl," said Mortimer in his ear. "Tell me about the girl and Freddy Chubb."

"What?" Lonnie gasped.

He felt the blade press down hard against him.

"Uh-oh," said Mortimer. "That's not the right answer."

"That's not the right answer, Lonnie," said the fat man, laughing.

"No, no," Lonnie said quickly. His mind seized at the possibility that this might all be a mistake. "So help me. So help me. I don't know any Chubb."

"The closer you shave," Mortimer whispered hoarsely, "the more you need Noxzema." The blade started moving again, scraping away the lather smeared over Lonnie's face. "Oh, you are going to need a shitload of Noxzema, Lonnie."

"I don't know any Chubb! I'm telling you. Christ!"

"You drew a picture of him, Pump-Pump. Huh? On the pad by the phone. Remember? You drew a picture of the man with the long hair and the eye patch. You telling me that's not Freddy Chubb? You gonna try and tell me that, Lonnie?"

It was a moment before Lonnie could grasp what Mortimer was saying. Then he remembered. Sitting by the phone. Doodling on the pad. Drawing a picture of the man in the restaurant. The man who had passed the girl the envelope. Freddy Chubb.

"Oh," said Mortimer—a long hot breath over Lonnie's face. "You'll tell. I'm gonna peel your face off strip by strip. I'm gonna skin you like an apple, Pump-Pump. You'll tell."

Lonnie lay pinned to the floor, the razor digging into him. The terrible fiery pressure of fury and fear kept building inside.

"Let it all come out, Pump-Pump," Mortimer said. "Save yourself a world of pain."

Lonnie would have killed him if he could have, if he'd had the chance. Instead, he said:

"Cut me." A single tear of rage fell from his eye. "Cut me and go fuck yourself."

Mortimer cut him. He dug the blade in and with a long, slow sweep ripped an inch-long strip of flesh off Lonnie's jawline. Lonnie's roar of pain was choked off by the hand clamping hard on his throat. The pain rose through every pore of his face like molten sweat. He convulsed in the big cop's grip, his stomach churning with terror and rage and the pain now too, his eyes burning with tears.

Mortimer grinned, breathing harshly. He casually wiped the skin and blood off the razor onto Lonnie's forehead. For another moment, he considered the man trembling underneath him.

"I can see this is gonna be a long conversation," he said then.

He stood up.

The cop's weight lifted off him. Lonnie groaned, coughing bile. He rolled over onto his side, curling his knees up to his chest. He lay there trembling. Through blurred eyes he saw his own blood running onto the floorboards.

Mortimer paced over him, nodding. Snorting through his nostrils like a bull. Too much adrenaline, too much release. He had to work it off, cool down.

Hughes was excited too, was nodding too. "So see?" he said. "Chubb? This is good, right? Winter'll like this. We can bring him this, right?"

Mortimer nodded some more in answer. His eyes were bright and dreamy. He settled down, came to rest. Stood so that Lonnie lay—curled up and trembling—at his feet.

"Pick him up," said Mortimer. "We'll do the rest in the can. I can work better in there. We can gag him and everything."

Hughes nodded. He shifted his gun hand to hold the Cougar secure against his ribs. He bent down, reached out, grabbed a handful of Lonnie's overcoat.

"Come on, tuba-boy, on your feet," he said.

But this was the thing: when Lonnie Blake had changed Mattie Harris's lightbulb, he had stashed the various pieces of the fixture in his overcoat pocket. Then, when he was done, he had taken the pieces out again and put them all back in the ceiling.

All except for the dead lightbulb. There was no reason to put that back.

It was still in his pocket.

That is, it *had* been in his pocket. When he rolled over onto his side, he had felt the shape of it in there. He had just managed to avoid rolling on top of it and crushing it to bits. Instead, while Mortimer was pacing around over him, while Hughes was yammering in his excitement, Lonnie had quietly removed the dead light-bulb from his overcoat.

Now it was in his hand.

So anyway, Hughes leaned down, grabbed Lonnie's coat and tried to haul him to his feet.

And Lonnie jammed the lightbulb into Hughes's right eye.

The bulb imploded with a perky little *pop*. It broke into approximately a million pieces of glass each as fine as a grain of sand and all of them sparkling. Hughes, of course, couldn't see them sparkling because—well, because they were in his eye, and also because he was too busy clutching his face and letting out a series of wild shrieks something like the cries of a raven.

In order to do this more efficiently, he had dropped his Cougar nine.

Lonnie grabbed the gun and scrambled to his feet.

Lonnie himself was a pretty scary sight at this point. Covered in shaving cream and blood, dripping blood, his eyes like lanterns in his rage-twisted face. He was waving the gun at the startled Mortimer. A deep, stran-gled growl was dribbling out between his bared teeth. He was trying to shoot Mortimer. He wanted to shoot him. He'd thought he was going to shoot him when he grabbed the gun.

But as it turned out, he couldn't do it. Not in cold blood like that, not even now.

He found this turn of events very frustrating. "Errrrrgh," he remarked, or words to that effect. The sound came from too deep in his throat to be made out clearly.

Hughes had now fallen hard to his knees, clutching his face, keening. In another moment, he tumbled to his side. He curled up in a ball, sobbing and crying with the agony.

As for Mortimer, he took all this in and thought, *That's it. I'm disgusted. I am frankly disgusted.* What was it with this op anyway? Was it him? Was God pissed off at him or something? Everything he touched turned to shit all of a sudden. Every fucking thing went complicated on him. He had half a mind to just walk away from this and keep on walking.

But there was no walking away from Winter. And— hope springing eternal—there was still a chance he might come out of this with something. He could see Blake didn't have the stones to actually shoot him anyway.

So with a sigh, he shook his head and said, "All right, you made your point, put the gun down."

"Errrrrgh!" Lonnie repeated. He waved the gun wildly in the air. He gestured wildly with his free hand as if trying to draw a picture of his rage.

Mortimer rolled his eyes. "What're you gonna do, genius, shoot a cop?" he said. "Put the fucking gun down before you get hurt." But Lonnie didn't. And Mortimer, already annoyed, said, "Goddammit."

He reached behind him for the holster in his back. He brought out his service revolver.

"Now put it down," he said.

Lonnie killed him.

The Cougar was so quiet, its recoil so slight—and

Lonnie was so crazy with rage at this point—that he didn't even know he'd pulled the trigger at first. He was still standing there, still waving the gun, still growling madly, when Mortimer looked down in surprise. Lonnie followed his gaze and saw the red-black hole in the big cop's trench coat, saw the bloodstain spreading around it.

Mortimer raised his face to Lonnie in dumb dismay. Lonnie met his eyes. There was confusion in both their glances. Both understood they were in the presence of a monumental irony.

Then Mortimer's attention seemed to turn inward. He collapsed to one knee, pitched over onto his side.

"Uh . . ." said Lonnie.

Staring, he stepped toward the fallen man. It occurred to him he ought to be careful. He pointed the gun at him.

Mortimer rolled over onto his back. Blood spread in a puddle underneath him from what must have been a large exit wound. Lonnie stared down at the man. The cop's attention still seemed to be turned inward.

Then, as Lonnie watched, a line of shadow seemed to rise up slantwise over Mortimer's features. When it had passed, whatever had been Mortimer was gone from the eyes. The face was meat. The cop was dead.

Lonnie's breath ran out of him. "Oh . . ."

Behind him, Hughes sent up a low wail of pain. Startled, Lonnie spun around, crying, "Don't move! All right?" He spun from Hughes back to Mortimer, pointing the gun at one, then the other. "Don't anybody move! Just leave me alone! You hear me? Everybody just leave me alone!"

Hughes made another noise. Lonnie pointed the gun at him.

"I mean it!" Lonnie screamed at him. "I mean it! I'll shoot you too, man! I'll shoot everybody!"

He had no idea what he was saying.

He began backing away from them, from the moaning, twisting Hughes, from the dead Mortimer. Waving the gun between them, at one, then the other. Screaming at them:

"Leave me alone! Everybody! Just . . . just leave me alone!"

He bumped into the windowsill. Looked around. Outside, through the fire escape, above the lofts across the street, it was a full bright blue day. On the sidewalk, people were hurrying past. In the street, cars were riding to the corner. Ordinary life in morning gear. Everything good, everything normal. Lonnie gaped at it.

He hadn't just killed a cop, had he?

He glanced back at the room.

"Oh Jesus Lord," he said.

His mouth hung open as he stared at what he'd done. Absently, he raised his hand to his face. Wiped the foam and the blood away; the tears now too.

"Oh Lord, Lord, Lord."

He'd killed a cop, all right. Blinded another. He was already a suspect in a double murder and he had already told lies to the police and now . . .

"Oh Jesus."

He couldn't think. He had to think. They would come for him. They would take him away. He needed time to think.

Trembling, he seized the window with his free hand, forced it open. The cool air washed in over him, and the cough and sputter of traffic washed in.

He thought he heard a noise behind him. He swung

around, waved his gun at the dead Mortimer, at the sobbing Hughes. Neither noticed him.

"I'm not sorry!" he said. "You hear me? I'm not sorry!"

No one answered. He swallowed hard.

"Not sorry," he murmured.

He slipped the gun into his pocket. Wiped his face again with his sleeve, ignoring the pain of his slashed jaw. Quickly, he ducked under the window. Climbed out onto the fire escape. He glanced back once more at the two men in the room.

Then he left them and scrambled down the stairs to the street below.

CHAPTER 8

A WHOLE MESS
O' TROUBLE

1

A cab pulled up in front of St. Luke's Hospital that evening. A passenger was in the back, a man.

Just as the cab arrived, Jennifer Hughes came out through the glass doors with her eight-year-old and five-year-old sons in tow. She spotted the cab with relief. It was almost rush hour and she hadn't known how she was ever going to get back to Grand Central.

The cab's passenger stepped out of the backseat. He held the door for Jennifer. She was an attractive, slightly harried-looking brunette in her thirties. She smiled up at the man.

"Come on, kids, into the cab," she said.

The man smiled back at her. He winked at the five-year-old, Larry, as the boy climbed into the backseat.

The man was handsome, stylishly dressed, forty or so. Judging by the Cerutti coat, and the haircut and the smell of his cologne, Jennifer thought he must be very successful. An executive or something. He had bright red hair, which she found attractive. He was carrying a rolled-up newspaper in one hand.

"Thank you," she said to him.

She climbed in after the kids.

The man shut the door and saluted them with his newspaper through the window. The cab drove away and the red-haired man went into the hospital.

It was Edmund Winter, of course. He was here to pay a visit to Jennifer's husband: Hughes.

Hughes was in a room on the third floor. A private room. It had its own bathroom, a bed, a chest of drawers. A small window overlooking the roofs and water towers of lower Manhattan. It was covered by Executive Decisions' generous corporate health plan.

Hughes was lying on the bed, lying on top of the sheets, wearing a green bathrobe over his pajamas. Gauze bandages slanted across the top of his head, covering the socket that had once contained his right eye. An IV needle was in his wrist, carrying antibiotics from the bag on its pole into his arm.

Hughes lay there, his free hand resting on his middle. The hand with the needle in it was by his side. He stared up at the ceiling, his mouth working under his beard.

The visit from his wife and his two boys had been nice, but now they were gone and Hughes could not deny he was depressed. He was depressed about losing his eye. He was depressed about losing his partner, Mortimer. And the idea of confronting Winter was like an iron pall lying over him. He didn't even want to think about it. He liked to consider himself an optimistic, happy-go-lucky sort of guy, but it was very hard to see the sunny side of this particular situation.

The door to the room was open and, with a start, Hughes suddenly realized that Winter was standing there at the threshold. The iron pall of dread seemed to sink into him, become part of him.

Oh God, he thought. *Not yet. Jesus.*

The red-haired man smiled easily as he stepped into the room. He saluted Hughes with the rolled-up newspaper he carried.

"Winter." Hughes hurried to slide himself up into a sitting position. The IV bag flapped against its pole as he moved.

"How you feeling, Hughes? How's the eye?" Winter said.

"S'okay, s'okay," Hughes said quickly. "Doctor says it's not serious. That's funny, right? You lose an eye, it's not serious."

"Well, I'm glad to hear it."

Winter tossed the paper down on the bed. Hughes nearly jumped, as if it might explode. The paper fell open. The *New York Post*. A front-page photograph of Lonnie Blake with an inset shot of poor old Mortimer.

SAX AND DEATH
COP SHOT AS MUSICIAN ESCAPES MURDER INQUIRY

"Sorry I didn't bring you flowers," Winter said. He moved to stand at the foot of the bed.

Hughes swallowed hard. Licked his lips. Stared at the paper. He felt very naked, very helpless in his bathrobe and pajamas. Tied to the IV bag. *He won't just shoot me,* he told himself. *Not here. Not with everybody around.*

But he was aware of Winter's reputation and in fact he was none too sure.

"Yeah," Hughes said. He looked up at Winter, tried to laugh. "Flowers. Right. Hey, Christ, Winter, I'm sorry, I don't know what to tell you. It got fucked up. You know? Shit happens."

Winter smoothly waved it away. "Hey, I know that. I should never have sent you guys up against a jazz musician. Those guys are dangerous."

Hughes tried to laugh again but all that came out was

an empty wheeze. He wondered if it was time to start pleading yet. *Listen, I've got a wife and kids . . .*

But he restrained himself. Instead, he said, "It wasn't, like, a useless thing or anything. You know? I mean, we were in there working for you, Winter. We got some stuff, we did, we got some good stuff."

Winter frowned thoughtfully. "Okay. Let's hear it."

"Well, Blake? You know? The sax guy? He saw the girl with Chubby Chubb, with Freddy Chubb." Winter did seem interested in that. Hughes seized on this hopefully, went on eagerly, "So see? It must've been Chubb who came out of the crash. Right? All this time, we've been wondering, trying to figure out who it was. Now we know, right? Huh? Right? And then that would make sense because, then, maybe she's got him financing her. See? That's what I was thinking. See what I mean?"

Winter stood easily at the end of the bed, his hands folded in front of him. He considered it. He considered it, it seemed to Hughes, for a long, terrifying time.

"Did Blake identify him?" he asked then. "Did Blake say positively it was Freddy Chubb?"

"Uh . . . Well . . . no," Hughes admitted. "Not positively. But he drew a picture."

"A picture."

"On a pad. A whatchamacallit."

"A pad?"

"A pad, yeah, but on it. A drawing. A sort of . . ."

"A doodle," said Winter.

"A doodle, yeah."

"He doodled a picture of Freddy Chubb."

"Yeah."

Winter laughed once. Hughes couldn't tell if it was a hey-you're-some-kind-of-all-right-my-friend laugh or more of a you're-gonna-look-funny-with-your-intestines-wrapped-around-your-throat laugh.

All Winter said was, "And so did Blake doodle a picture of where Chubb was? Or where the girl was? Or anything like that?"

"Uh . . ." said Hughes. "See, we were, see, that's just what we were getting to, we were getting to that and . . ."

Winter lifted one hand in a silencing gesture. A nurse had just entered the room. She was a fat black woman, waddling on squeaky shoes. She was carrying a clipboard and a fresh IV bag.

"Afternoon, gentlemen," she said as she entered.

She went about her business briskly, checking the chart, checking her clipboard, changing the nearly empty bag on the pole for the fresh one she'd brought with her.

During all this, Winter remained silent. He stood at the end of the bed with his hands folded in front of him and smiled down at Hughes. Obviously, they couldn't very well continue their conversation with the nurse in the room. All the same, Hughes found that the silence and the smile and the waiting all combined to bring his fear to the boil. *He won't just shoot me,* he kept thinking. But he was beginning to think that maybe Winter would. And Hughes, in point of fact, didn't want to die. He wanted to live to see his sons grow up. He had some land in Florida; he wanted to build a retirement house on it. Jennifer—his wife—how would she get on without him? Hughes felt cold sweat breaking out on his forehead.

"Afternoon, gentlemen," said the nurse again. She waddled out of the room, her shoes squeaking. Hughes wanted to beg her not to leave him alone.

"Listen," Hughes broke out the moment she was

gone, "it was Mortimer's play. Okay? I mean, he made the plan. I'm going along. I gotta go along, right? I mean, I can do good things for you, Winter, ask anyone. I mean, listen, let me be honest with you: you're making me really nervous just standing there like that." He was sweating hard now. "Just tell me, all right? Just tell me. Am I dead? Am I dead here or what?"

Winter gave another short laugh. He raised his eyes heavenward. "Well, let me see," he said. "We're on what we might call a secret mission, right? And so far we got a whore shot dead while screaming bloody murder, we got her john, a respectable insurance salesman, with his head blown off. We got this Blake guy now on the run with every cop in the tristate looking for him."

"It was Mortimer's play, I'm telling you."

"Yeah, okay, I believe that. But Mortimer was a cop killed during an investigation. As for Lonnie Blake, the police'll probably kill him too, maybe even nail him for the double downtown. But you—who are you?—you're a question mark. That's how the police will see it. You understand what I'm saying?"

Hughes's hopes nose-dived. He felt like bursting into tears. "Please, Winter," he said. "I could do good work for you. I know it. Ask anyone. What about Chubb? I found out about Chubb, didn't I?"

"Yeah, Chubb was good. I can work with Chubb." Winter considered, made a face. "Nah. Sorry, Hughes. You're a dead guy."

"Aw, come on, Winter," Hughes whined. "I got a wife and kids."

"Oh no, don't worry about that," Winter told him. "We took care of them too."

"What?" Hughes cried out. And he was about to sit up

straight. But now a sort of ripple passed over the air between him and Winter, just like the ripple you see in lake water. For a moment, Hughes didn't know what it was.

Then, wide-eyed, he turned to look at the IV bag.

The IV bag! Jesus, he thought.

Then he was dead.

The day, as days will do, wore on. The sun sank into the Palisades. Its reddening glow rode in across the Hudson and painted the blank-faced windows of the city skyline a brilliant orange. Amid the shadows of the sycamores in Central Park, the last light lay in deep yellow patches. Then it faded away. The yellow patches and the shadow blended together. Chill autumn night came down indigo.

There, in the park, the streetlights along the paths switched on, haloed circles of white one after another. Men and women walked home; in pairs; alone. Their figures became hazy in the dark.

After a while, a lot of the park was empty. There were still joggers around the reservoir, some kids blowing smoke and music out over the lake, plenty of late workers on the paths near the southern border. But away from these centers of activity, north of them, on the west side, under the trees, there was not much moving. Wind and the night birds and the leaves blowing over the grass, that's pretty much all.

And yet, here and there, under one tree or another, some tattered bum or two had set up camp. Blanket rolls were hidden at intervals under the low bushes. Vaguely human forms stirred under piles of rags.

Two black boys, neither yet fourteen, were prowling among these castaways. Passing with bobbing, rhythmic walks, with sharp eyes, with predatory smiles. One boy was called Junebug, the other was generally referred to as Mickey D. They were looking for Dead Presidents: enough dollar bills for a snack of scoobie and eats on the deserted ball field.

They found a likely vic, a man curled within a cluster of black maples north of the rec house. Homeless. Drunk probably. All alone, by the looks of it. And wearing a coat that might have bankrolled the evening's entertainment by itself.

"Target zero," said Mickey D.

"Yayo Central," said Junebug. He slipped on a set of spiked brass knuckles. "Hey, nigga, what you sleeping for?" he called to the drunk.

"Wake your ass up, nigga," said Mickey D. "The fun is just beginning."

They were standing over the bum now. Junebug kicked him lightly at the base of the spine. "Little man, he's had a busy day."

"Now, nigga, wake your ass up. We gonna . . ."

The homeless man rolled over. He pointed the barrel of a Cougar nine millimeter handgun at Junebug's testicles.

"Whoa!" said Mickey D. "Nigga's strapped."

"That's Mister Nigga to you," said Lonnie Blake. "Now get the fuck outta here."

Crazy how familiar the gun felt in his hands. After all these years. Crazy how familiar the fear felt percolating away in his belly. The whole damn situation seemed pretty natural to him, as if it had been in the cards from the beginning. Shit, maybe it had. Anyone looking at his fifteen-year-old gang banger self might have guessed he'd end up wanted for killing a cop. So what was it? It was like he'd gone to bed and woken up fifteen years later with his destiny all fulfilled. And what was the point of everything in between, right? The school, the music, Suzanne?

Dreaming, Pump-Pump. You were only dreaming.

The two punks had run off now. Lonnie slipped the gun back into his overcoat pocket. He stood up. Shivered, cold. Bitter. Mad. The wound on his jaw was beginning to throb. Throb. More like it was covering Billy Cobham's drum solo intro to "Stratus." Must've been infected pretty good by now. And his throat ached from when Mortimer had throttled him and his back hurt and his joints were stiff. And he could feel every cop in the city dreaming the same dream about killing him dead.

He glanced at his watch. Looked through the night, through the trees, toward the lights of the west side. He had a plan anyway. Such as it was. That was another thing: the way he'd come up with a plan just like that.

The way he'd started thinking like a criminal again, like a fugitive, almost as soon as he'd hit the street. He'd been panicked then. Shit, he'd been half crazy with fear and rage, not to mention remorse at having killed someone. But soon enough, his brain had started clicking away. He'd started trying to think what the cops were thinking, trying to outthink the cops. That had come back to him too.

But it had been easier in those first hours. He'd had a head start. Word hadn't gotten out yet. No one knew they were after him. He had time then to get to a cash machine, get himself a handful of dollar bills. He could walk into a liquor store and pick up a bottle of juice. Join a group of winos. Disappear into their numbers. He was thinking straight enough even then to stay away from the usual traps: hotel rooms with nosy desk clerks; buses and trains that could be sealed and searched; stolen cars that might be reported.

So he'd made it this far. And now night had fallen and that was a plus. But by now too, his picture must've been on every TV show and in every paper. Every cop must've had a copy of it—probably tattooed onto the handle of his gun. And with his jaw festering, and his beard growing in patches around where Mortimer had shaved him and with his clothes dirty from sleeping on the ground, well, Lonnie might just as well have been wearing a sign that said ARREST MY BLACK ASS, MR. PO-LICE PLEASE. He was a neon nigger now.

Probably a dead one too. Almost surely a dead one.

But then he'd hummed that tune in his youth also and he remembered how it went.

And so his mind felt more or less clear. And he was thinking about what had happened, about what had to happen now. And though he had no friends who were likely to help him, and though he had no story any sane man would believe, and though he had no chance any sane man would give odds on—he did have a plan.

So he started moving.

"No Hootchie Cootchie," Arthur Topp was saying into the phone. "I promise. Straight up. Really. It's a Hootchie Cootchie free zone. I know. I know it's a wedding. But these are . . . no, no, no. These are cultured people. Well, then they're hip people. Exactly. Hip, young, cultured people. Exactly. There could be many influential musical opinion makers on hand. Really. Straight up. Plus the money is not bad. All right, maybe. I know you're an artist. Maybe one *hora*. Look, I don't . . . Wait, my other phone is ringing. No, my girl has gone home. I'll talk to you later. Take the gig. Straight up. I mean it," said Arthur Topp, and hung up.

He sat for a moment. Tilted back in his chair, his feet propped on the desk. The office was silent around him. Silent because, of course, the other phone was not really ringing. There was no other phone really. Other phones cost money. Girls—secretaries—cost money too so there wasn't one of them either. There was just a swivel chair and a gunmetal table. A computer. A file cabinet.

A wall full of autographed photos. A window over the warehouse facades of lower Broadway. Arthur Topp.

He glanced at his father's gold watch. It was almost eight. Five in California. Time to close up shop, go home. Start making calls from there.

He swung his legs down with a weary groan. Tossed a sandwich wrapper in the wastebasket. Grabbed his coat from the coat stand. Shucked it on over the red polo shirt. Headed for the door.

And the phone rang. What else was new? Arthur rolled his eyes and immediately swung back around to get it. He had never let a ringing phone go unanswered in his life.

"Topp Music, tops in pop," he said.

The voice over the phone was gruff and deep but not impolite. "Arthur Topp, please."

"Speaking."

"My name is Detective Grimaldi of the ninth precinct," the voice said.

A policeman. Okay. That was interesting. Naturally Arthur Topp immediately remembered the wannabe singer he had wangled into bed in Miami last year. He had known in his heart she wasn't any sixteen. The sweat was already beginning to break out on his forehead when Grimaldi said:

"I'm calling about a man named Lonnie Blake."

Right. Lonnie Blake. Arthur had heard the news. The double murder. The cop killing. So now his mind started coming up with all kinds of paranoid scenarios in which he became a suspect . . .

"Ye-ah?" he said cautiously.

"You know who I'm talking about?"

"Yeah, sure. I met him. Once."

"On Friday night in a bar called Renaissance."

Arthur cleared his throat. "That's correct," he said formally, as if he were already a witness on the stand.

"And were you with anyone else? Or did you see anyone else talking to Mr. Blake? A woman? Anyone?"

"No. No one. Why?"

"But you and Mr. Blake did have an extended conversation?"

"Well—I guess."

There was a pause. A sound of lowered voices conferring. Arthur tried to hear what they were saying, couldn't.

Then Grimaldi was back on the line. "Mr. Topp, I know it's late, but would it be possible for me and a colleague to drop by and talk to you this evening?"

"Uh . . . yeah. Sure," said Arthur Topp. "I was just heading home . . ."

"That's still on West Sixty-ninth?"

They knew his address? "Uh . . . yeah."

"Well, we'd be happy to meet you there if it's more convenient."

Arthur consulted the watch again. "I usually get home by eight-thirty . . ."

"Why don't we say nine o'clock?" said Grimaldi.

So that's what they said.

Nine o'clock.

5

It made him nervous at first, but by the time he climbed out of the subway on Seventy-second, Arthur was almost looking forward to his interview with the cops. The prospect of talking to a real-life detective about a murder wasn't exactly tranquilizing, but it did have a welcome edge of excitement to it. Danger. A sense of being connected to the news of the day. It would make a story he could tell his colleagues at lunch tomorrow anyway.

He walked home the rest of the way as usual. Reached the corner of Columbus and West Sixty-ninth around eight twenty-five, exactly as usual.

The block was a quiet, charming stretch of brownstones between the fashionable Columbus Avenue and Central Park. There were antique streetlights shining down through well-tended gingko trees. There was stoop after Dutch-style stoop fading into the backdrop of the park wall and the tangled autumn darkness beyond. Arthur had had an apartment here for almost twenty years now. It was the best investment of his father's money he'd ever made.

It was quiet as he headed for the place. Just a young woman walking her yap-dog on the opposite sidewalk. The thunk of a door, a cab pulling away from the line of parked cars. Arthur wasn't paying attention. He was deep in a fantasy about how his evidence would help the police put Lonnie Blake in jail.

So it wasn't until he'd climbed his stoop and stepped inside that something began to bother him. Something. Maybe just the atmosphere in the brownstone's lobby at the foot of the stairs. The stairs were dim with only a few shaded lanterns on the wall lighting the way. The maroon carpeting and flocked wallpaper absorbed even what little light there was. Probably it was only nerves, but Arthur felt there was something—something brooding in the shadows around him. He climbed the steps slowly, cautiously, scanning the way above, looking behind him, around him, as if he expected some phantom to suddenly call his name in a hollow tone.

But there was nothing. He reached the third floor. Went down the hall to his door. He was hurrying by then. Nervous. Fumbling for his keys, fumbling to get his keys into the door's three locks.

But he did pause to look behind him once. He checked over his shoulder as the key slid home for the last time.

He would've sworn there was no one there.

He unlocked the door. Pushed it open. Reached in to flick on the light.

He caught a smell—rank, rancid, thick, dark. But by then it was too late.

Something barreled into him from behind. Shoved him through the open door into his apartment.

Arthur Topp's small body hit the sofa, his thigh banging hard against its arm. Terrified, he heard the door shut behind him. He felt his stomach bunch inside him like a fist. He was trembling as he turned around.

Lonnie Blake stood there, wild-eyed, wounded,

unshaved. Insane, it looked like. Leveling a gun barrel
directly at Arthur's face.

Arthur thrust his quivering hands high into the air.

"So, uh, I take it the music career didn't work out,"
he said.

"Close the windows—the shutters," Lonnie Blake said.

"Right. Right, right, right," said Arthur Topp.

He backed away, watching the pistol closely as if it
wouldn't go off as long as he kept his eyes on it.

"I don't want to be racist or anything," he babbled.
"But big black guy pointing a gun at me—it makes me
nervous, Lonnie, straight up. Hey, maybe it's just the
gun, I don't know."

"Just close the goddamn shutters."

"Right."

He bumped up against the window seat. Turned
around, reluctantly tearing his gaze from the pistol. The
whole time he was closing the shutters, he felt the bullet
in that black bore itching for his spine.

But at the same time, his mind was racing. Nine
o'clock, Grimaldi had said. Just thirty minutes and the
cavalry would arrive in the person of two NYPD detec-
tives. Was that a good thing or a bad thing? Would it be
a rescue or a wild shoot-out in which innocent talent

agents were sacrificed right and left for the greater good? Should he try to stall Blake till they arrived or just tell him they were coming and hope it scared him off?

He set the clasp on the last shutter. He turned around slowly.

"Eat," said Lonnie, gesturing with the gun. "I need something to eat. Water too. I need food and water."

Hands in the air, Arthur nodded his head toward the kitchenette. "In there."

Lonnie stepped back. Waved the gun. "Get it."

"Right."

The apartment was not large. Just two rooms and the kitchenette. A maplewood counter divided the kitchenette from the living room. Arthur had to edge close to Lonnie to get around the counter. Moving cautiously, always watching that gun. The stink of the fugitive nearly made him gag.

But he reached the kitchenette. Opened the refrigerator. Looked in. Felt the gun still trained on the side of his head.

"All right. Let's see," he said, gulping air. "What've I got here? Some Brie, some nonfat vegetable chips, they're very nice . . ."

"Just give me anything," Lonnie said. "Gimme some water."

"Sparkling or still?"

"Just gimme some goddamned water!"

"Okay, okay, okay," said Arthur. "Jesus. Just take it easy, all right?"

He dumped some chips on a plate with a wedge of Brie. Brought out of a bottle of Evian, began to set it on the counter.

Lonnie had hurried around to the other side. He

snatched the bottle out of Topp's hand. He sat on one of the bar stools. But he paused before he drank. Regarded Arthur suspiciously. Arthur held his breath.

"Come out from there," Lonnie said. "Sit down over there on the couch."

Arthur obeyed at once, trying to radiate amiability and compliance. All the same, the gun followed him as he came back around the counter. As he moved to the sofa, his eyes flicked up at the clock on the wall next to the print of a Hirschfeld Sinatra. Only twenty-six minutes now before the cops arrived.

When Arthur sat down Lonnie tipped the bottle up. The water glubbed as it rushed into his mouth, as it dribbled over his chin. All the while, he kept his eyes shifted toward Arthur. All the while, the gun was trained on Arthur's chest.

Arthur attempted to smile pleasantly, his eyes shifting now and then to the clock.

Lonnie gasped out of the drink. Set the bottle down hard. Grabbed a handful of chips, shoveled them into his mouth. For a long moment, there was nothing but chewing and crunching and the fugitive's baleful glare.

Then Lonnie said, "All right. I need your help."

"My help?"

"That's right."

"I don't mean to be negative, Lonnie. But I think the career moment has passed. Really."

The sax man gave his patented contemptuous snort. "I don't mean that. You heard the news?"

Arthur saw no point in lying. "Yeah. I heard."

"I found a paper in the park," said Lonnie—he almost sounded sad about it. "I don't expect you to believe me, but that's not the way it happened."

"O-kay," said Arthur carefully.

"I didn't kill those two people. And the cop and the other guy, the one the paper said was a private eye? They did this to me." He laid a finger along the swelling infection on his jaw.

Arthur felt a chill in his balls just looking at it. "Wooh, that looks nasty," he said.

"Something was wrong with the whole thing," Lonnie went on. "They had me right there in the cop house, you know? They could've done anything they wanted. But they let me go, waited till I got home. It was like . . . it was like they didn't want the other cops to know what they were up to. See what I'm saying?"

"Sure," said Arthur Topp, stealing another glance at the clock. Twenty-three minutes now. Oh come, Grimaldi, come. "Sure, I see what you're saying."

"And I know what happens to cop killers in slam. I'm not giving myself up until I show people what happened. So you're gonna help me with that."

"Me?" Arthur burst out. He couldn't help himself. "I'm a booking agent. Why me?"

"Just your tough luck, man. You gave me your card. Told me your schedule. Your address was near the park so I could get to it without being spotted. Plus, the cops won't know I know you. They'll check the people I usually see. But we only met that one time so they won't think to look here . . ."

"But they do know!" Arthur Topp blurted it out. If that was why Lonnie Blake had come here, maybe the truth would make him go away. "They called me before I left the office tonight. They're coming here in, like, twenty minutes."

Lonnie snorted again. "Yeah, right. Whatever."

"I'm serious. Detective Grimaldi . . ."

The gun stiffened in Lonnie's hand. Arthur shut up. "Don't fuck with me, man. I know he was in the paper. I'm not a fool. They ain't gonna come here."

Arthur Topp swallowed hard. *Okay*, he thought.

"You got a computer?" said Lonnie Blake.

"A laptop," whispered Arthur.

"And you can connect to the Internet and all that?"

"Yeah. But . . ."

"Get it," said Lonnie Blake.

Arthur got it. He set it up on the oval dining table. Lonnie watched him, polishing off the water, tearing into the Brie, holding the Brie in one hand, Arthur noticed, and ripping into it with his teeth as if it were a wedge of pizza.

By the time Arthur had the laptop up and running, it was eighteen minutes before nine o'clock. He tapped onto AOL, conscious all the while of the gun trained on him. The dial tone sounded, the beeps of the numbers, the modem signal. "Welcome," said a woman's voice, fuzzy through the laptop's speakers. He was online.

Lonnie moved to look over his shoulder. The fugitive's dark and crawly smell surrounded him.

"You know," said Arthur meekly. "I was serious about the cops."

Lonnie ignored him. "You got one of those search things. I saw it at the coffee shop, one of those . . ."

"A search engine. Sure."

Arthur called up Alta Vista. The smell, the presence, of Blake pressing in behind him made him queasy. He glanced at the clock. Sixteen to.

"All right," said Lonnie Blake at his ear. "Look up Carol Dodson."

Arthur keyed in the name. Waited.

"Eight hits," he said. "A family tree. A list of the faculty at University of Virginia."

"No, no, that ain't her, man. Okay, okay," said Lonnie. "Now try Chubb. Freddy Chubb. Frederick Chubb."

"Frederick Chubb," said Arthur. He tapped it in. Glanced at the clock while the computer searched. Fourteen minutes.

"Yeah," said Lonnie.

Arthur looked at the screen. Close to a thousand hits.

"What do you want?" he said.

"His address. His phone number. Something."

"Well, I don't know . . . You gotta find a different engine for that. I'm not sure."

"Shit. The guy at the coffee shop did it."

"Well, that's his job. You want a bar mitzvah gig, you come to me."

"Well, get me a picture, something with a picture, so I'm sure it's him."

Arthur went down the list. Found an article reprinted from *The New York Times.* He clicked it. Up came the article. A picture too. A thin-faced man wearing an eye patch.

The hiss of Lonnie's voice in his ear was electric. "Yeah. That's him! See that? That's why those fuckheads did me that way. Because I saw him. They were looking for him."

Arthur's eyes scanned the screen quickly. "This guy? You saw him? When?"

"Sunday. Yeah. Just this last Sunday. He was at a restaurant."

Arthur was silent a moment. He couldn't see Lonnie

just then but he sensed him pacing behind him. He
sensed the gun too, felt it, imagined it pointing at the
back of his skull. He spoke with everything he had of
tact and gentleness.

"Well," he said, "okay. Okay. Only . . . the trouble
with that—Lonnie—the trouble with that is: it says here
that this man—this Freddy Chubb—is dead."

He could feel Lonnie's pacing cease. "Say what?"

"See," said Arthur, swallowing. "See, right here. He
went down in that plane that crashed in Massachusetts."

"But that was like . . ."

"Four whole months ago," said Arthur Topp.

Agents of the Federal Bureau of Investigation have turned
their attention to one of the passengers of European
Airways Flight 186 as they continue to examine whether
the 747 jet's disintegration last month over the town of
Hunnicut, Massachusetts, may have been due to criminal
causes. According to FBI sources, investigators believe
that a plot against a 47-year-old suspected smuggler,
Frederick "Chubby" Chubb, may have led to the explosion that brought the jet down.

Although Chubb's body is among dozens which may
never be recovered or identified, he was believed to have
been flying in the aircraft's first-class compartment at the

time of the crash. He is believed to have booked his passage under the name Frank Chester, one of several aliases Mr. Chubb used during his alleged criminal operations, investigators said.

According to the investigators, Mr. Chubb—a somewhat elegant figure with his piratical eye patch and refined manners—had been long suspected of running an international billion-dollar smuggling operation which involved counterfeit computer programs, CD's and videos. Investigators believe that Chubb's recent expansion of his operations into Asian markets may have earned him the enmity of those already operating in the area . . .

Arthur now ventured a glance over his shoulder. He saw Lonnie Blake standing transfixed, openmouthed. He looked at the clock. Only ten minutes now.

"Lonnie . . ." he said.

"That's not right," said Lonnie Blake. "That's the man. I saw that man."

"Everybody on the whole plane died, Lonnie."

"Then he wasn't on the plane. I saw that man, goddammit."

And now, for the first time, Lonnie turned his back on Arthur Topp. For the first time, he lowered the gun, lowered it to his side. His head hung down in thought or dejection, he walked across the room to the shuttered windows.

And Arthur, watching him, suddenly thought, *He's telling the truth.* And though he laughed the thought away—*Yeah, like, right, an insane gunman telling the truth*—it stuck with him.

"Damn!" said Lonnie Blake.

"What now?" said Arthur Topp.

Lonnie looked around as if surprised Arthur was still there. "What's that?"

"Is there something else you want me to do here?"

Lonnie turned. Sank down on the window seat. Shook his head. "Nah, hell. I thought if I could find this Chubb guy, I might find the girl, find out what was happening . . . Damn."

"Lonnie," Arthur heard himself say. "It's almost nine o'clock, man."

"What?"

"Really. Straight up. I mean it. The cops are on their way."

Lonnie gazed at him. It seemed to take a moment for the words to sink in. Then he gave that little snort of his. "Shit. You're serious, aren't you?"

"Straight up. I swear," said Arthur Topp.

Lonnie raised his eyes to the clock. Seven to nine. "Nine o'clock," he said.

"You better go," said Arthur Topp.

Lonnie shook his head. "I guess I'm rusty at this criminal business. I'm not as good a fugitive as I thought."

Arthur lifted his hands. "It's not too late to reconsider a career in the field of entertainment."

Lonnie seemed to think for another minute. "I need some stuff. Food. Water."

"You know, there really is no time."

"Any clothes you got that might fit me. A razor . . ."

"Okay. Okay. You might think about taking some of my deodorant . . ."

Lonnie smiled. "Some of that, yeah. And some tools. Anything you got. A wrench. A screwdriver. A wire coat hanger."

"A wire coat hanger?"

"Just get it."

Arthur's eyes moved to the gun. "All that stuff's in the other room."

Lonnie nodded. "Go ahead."

Arthur Topp stood unsteadily. He walked to the bedroom doorway. He paused there. Once he stepped across the threshold, he would be out of range of the gun. He stepped across it. Lonnie stayed where he was. Once again, the thought came to Arthur: *He's telling the truth. I mean, come on, this is an innocent man.*

Again, he laughed the thought off, but he found himself rushing to gather the things Lonnie needed. Grabbing his Knicks gym bag, tossing in an oversized sweater, some elastic shorts. The coat hanger. Hurrying into the bathroom for razors, deodorant, his unused spare toothbrush. Some antiseptic cream for that thing on his jaw—he thought of that himself. And then he came back out into the living room—of his own free will back out to where Lonnie sat with the gun—to get the water, the chips, some bread, the tools in the kitchenette cabinets: a screwdriver, a box cutter, a wrench. Hurrying the whole time because . . . well, because he *wanted* Lonnie to get out of there before the cops showed up. He actually *wanted* Lonnie Blake to get away.

Jesus. Must be that Stockholm thing, he thought.

It was two minutes to nine o'clock when he was done. For all he knew, Grimaldi and Co. might be downstairs already, might be coming up the stoop. For all he knew, the buzzer was going to go off any second.

Lonnie went to the door. Arthur handed him the gym bag. He could almost feel the second hand moving on the clock face now.

"Thanks," Lonnie said.

"Hey. You got the gun," said Arthur Topp.

Lonnie smiled, looked down at the weapon. "Sorry, man. I never would've shot you." He dropped it back into his pocket. "If you could give me a few minutes' head start before you tell them I was here . . ."

"Okay," said Arthur without thinking. "Sure. You better go, though."

Lonnie opened the door. Stepped out into the hall.

"I'm not gonna tell them," said Arthur Topp suddenly. "That you were here? I'm not gonna tell them at all."

Lonnie glanced back. Nodded his thanks.

"And if you make it through this, I get exclusive representation."

Lonnie laughed. He started to move away.

Arthur Topp watched him another second. Then he called after him, "What're you gonna do now?"

"I'll think of something," said Lonnie Blake.

8

What he thought of was this:

The steak house Ed Whittaker's stopped serving around midnight on weekdays and was generally shut up tight by 2 A.M. Lonnie found this out around eleven o'clock with a call from a phone near the park.

At two-fifteen, he made his return to the restaurant

where he'd seen Carol Dodson meet with the allegedly late Frederick "Chubby" Chubb.

It was a long trip. The streets of Manhattan are never empty and never dark. Quiet as the city was at that hour, there were cars, cabs, a few pedestrians. Cops cruising crosstown on the side streets, up and downtown on the avenues. Not enough shadows, too many eyes.

Lonnie walked with his head hung, his hands in his pockets, Topp's Knicks bag slung over his wrist. He kept the collar of his coat turned up around his throbbing jaw as if for protection from the biting wind. He forced himself not to look when a car passed him. When pedestrians came in his direction, he would give them a casual glance—he found it kept them from staring. He tried to avoid long stretches on the well-lighted avenues. He hung close to the lee of buildings.

He walked on.

Once, as he was hurrying south beneath the skyscrapers on Madison, a crumpled page of the *New York Post* blew between his feet. For a second, his own face stared up at him. He remembered Mortimer's face likewise staring, the baffled look in his eyes before the soul rose out of him. He remembered the feel of his own finger on the trigger.

Fuck him. He earned it.

He kicked the paper aside. Walked on.

He reached First Avenue coming from the west, crossed it to Ed Whittaker's. The corner seemed abnormally bright to him, its street lamp casting a wide net of light over the sidewalk, the buildings, him. He told himself he'd done this sort of thing before. There was nothing to it. All the same, he felt the pulse of tension shudder in him as if a hummingbird were caught in his chest. A big hummingbird. A great fucking humongous monster of a hummingbird.

He hurried out of the light. Down the side street, past the Dumpster where he'd stood before, the last time he'd seen Carol. He'd figured there'd be a door nearby, where they brought the kitchen garbage out. There was. It was metal with a handle and a lock underneath.

Lonnie drew a deep breath. It trembled on the exhale. He scanned the street, squinting into the biting wind that came off the East River. There was a doorman outside a building down the way, but even as Lonnie watched him, he turned and went in. There was no one else. Only a steady stream of cars on the avenue. Lonnie hoped the Dumpster would block him from their view.

He removed the gun from his overcoat pocket. Pointed it at the lock. He tried to hold his breath but couldn't. A choked sound of tension broke through his teeth as he squeezed the trigger.

Easy pickins, he thought. *No sweat.*

Then the gun snapped in his hand. There was a loud, whining ricochet. Lonnie said, "Shit!" and gritted his teeth like a boy who's just sent a baseball through a church window. A moment later, he actually thought he heard the bullet strike brick somewhere behind him.

"Shit, shit, shit!" he said.

This stuff had seemed simpler somehow in his youth.

He looked down at the door. The lock hardly seemed dented, just scarred and a bit askew. He tried the handle, glancing back over his shoulder as he did. He saw the doorman down the street hurrying to push outside again to check out the noise.

To his surprise—to his intense excitement—the handle went down. The door swung open. Lonnie slipped through it, shoved it closed behind him.

Awright! he thought.

But the hummingbird hummed louder.

He was in a small alley at the restaurant's back. He had to stop here a second, lean against the wall, get steady. He tossed the Knicks bag to the pavement. Wiped his mouth with the back of his gun hand.

He looked up.

There was the kitchen door, just a few steps away from him. A wooden door with a large glass panel in the top half of it. All right. Lonnie pushed off the wall. Crossed the alley. Reached the door. He struck at the glass with the gun butt. It shattered.

The alarm started screaming.

It was a loud, hammering bell. He knew it was coming but he wasn't ready for the way it seemed to play on his spine. He pinned himself against the door, stuck his arm through the broken window. Jagged teeth of glass snagged and tore at his coat. Grunting, he felt for the lock inside. Found it.

A deadbolt. It needed a key.

"Damn!"

He drew the gun and fired again. The sound was barely audible under the hammering bell. The door splintered at the jamb. Lonnie kicked it and it flew open.

He was in. The alarm screamed and went on screaming. It was as if the hummingbird inside him had broken loose and now the whole atmosphere was shuddering too. He looked through the dark, every way at once. The kitchen to his right. A shadowy hallway before him.

He plunged down the hall, stumbling in his rush, ricocheting off the walls. He threw his arms out to either side to steady himself. Felt his hands knocking pictures askew, touching glass frames, and the brass plaque on the men's room door.

The ringing of the bell filled him, surrounded him. A battalion of police could've been on its way, sirens blaring. He wouldn't have known, he wouldn't have heard. He heard nothing but the ringing of the bell.

Then he broke out into the dining room. More bells, louder. And the blinking of a red alarm light above the storefront window. And through the window, the startling flash of traffic, passing headlights.

The pounding of his heart was loud. His rasping breath was loud. And beyond these, and beyond the screaming bells, he thought he heard them now: sirens. Very faint, but urgent, insistent. He tried to tell himself: it's just an alarm at a restaurant. At most, a single cruiser would drop by to check it out. In his mind, he heard dozens of police cars racing to the scene.

Lonnie stood at the rear entrance to the room, right beside the bar. His mouth hung open as he drew breath. His eyes were wide and staring. He saw the silhouettes of tables, the chairs overturned on top of them. He saw the little podium near the front door where the maîtresse d' had stood to welcome her customers.

He humped it across the room. To the podium. He reached underneath to the lower shelf.

He felt the thing at once, grabbed it: an outsize leather-bound volume.

The reservation book.

He pulled it out.

He turned and headed for the exit at full speed.

CHAPTER 9

THE TOUCH OF YOUR HAND IS LIKE HEAVEN

1

In the morning, after a sleepless night, Howard Roth climbed wheezing down the stairs. He made himself a mug of coffee in the old house's old kitchen. He carried it into the study, breathing in the steam, hoping to clear his cancerous lungs enough to enjoy his first cigarette of the day.

He was wearing the baggy gray cardigan his second wife—Wendy—had bought him. He was wearing the wire-rimmed reading glasses Wendy had liked. She said they—the cardigan, the glasses—made him look "professorial." She said that because she thought being a professor was a cozy, homey sort of thing to be. She wanted her husband to wander around the place, bemused, muttering thoughtfully, searching everywhere for the pipe he was already holding in his hand. She never quite comprehended his own image of himself as a Bare-Torsoed Warrior of Ideas, a Ferocious Sword-Wielding Defender of the Classical Faith, Conan the Intellectual. She knew he could be irritable at times—she discovered he could be vicious as the marriage wore on, wore out. But she never really understood the depth of his rage, the acid heat of his frustration. For "this is the bitterest pain among men," Herodotus said, "to have much knowledge but no power."

Welcome to Academia.

Roth's study was a small room in the front of the house. Crowded with shelves crowded with books. There were windows on the wall to his right and over the desk before him. Pleasant views of the lawn, the street, the MacAlary hedges. The desk itself was large, but cluttered with papers and magazines and volumes over every inch. The computer dominated the center of it. He switched the machine on before sitting down on the high-backed leather swivel chair which was his greatest luxury.

Yes, Wendy had hardly known him, he thought, reaching into the cardigan's pocket for his Kents. But then he had only married her for her youth and her large breasts and her low IQ. To be fair, he'd thought he'd loved her cheerfulness at the time and her kindness and sweetness. But, in fact, as he soon discovered, he'd despised these traits in her. He thought they were the height of insipidity.

He shoveled the Kent between his lips. *Ah, who can find a virtuous woman?* he thought. *For her price is far above wholesale.* He lit up and was gratified to find he could still take a deep, satisfying drag without coughing up an excess of malignant bile.

Wendy was on his mind this morning because he was planning to write her a letter. A note to tell her of his illness ostensibly. But more than that. His valedictory address, so to speak. His farewell to her and to their daughter and to the things of this world.

He'd composed much of the letter in his head as he'd lain through the endless hours of darkness. He'd composed the *tone* of it anyway. It was going to be a fine letter. Clear, simple, majestic—eminently publishable should it ever come to that—written in lines of almost classical elegance, in prose that suggested even more than it proclaimed. It was going to be a letter both wise and grave and yet gently ironical; melancholy too and yet sweetly so; it would be all-forgiving and yet tinged with just enough paternalistic rebuke to induce a lifetime of guilt in anyone who'd happened to, say, divorce him before his earthly race was run.

With these guidelines to inspire him, Roth found himself an hour later staring at a blank screen, tears coursing steadily down his narrow cheeks. The waste, he kept thinking. The failure, the waste. The hundred books he'd planned, the two he'd written, the one he'd published— ridiculed, remaindered. A million deep phrases which had turned banal when they touched the air. All Greece and Rome had been in his head and yet he couldn't speak the things he knew. A million mythologies, which he understood as no man had. A million . . .

Well, he could've gone on like this another ninety minutes easily, but he had slowly become aware that someone was watching him. And, hastily swiping the tears from his face with both hands, he turned to find the little girl, Amanda, staring at him from the study doorway.

She stood just beyond the threshold in the shadows of the front hall. A little Jamesian ghosty of a thing, clutching her Elmo doll, gazing at him eerily.

"Hello," croaked Roth, sniffling. Scanning the chaos of his desk for a Kleenex. Seizing one. Blowing his nose. "Amanda, right? Come in. Come on in."

"I knocked but you didn't answer," she said. "I could see you through the window. You didn't lock your door."

"I never do. I'm not sure it has a lock."

"I knocked," she said again.

"No, that's all right. I was working. Come on in. Sit down."

The child hesitated, studying him. Then she came forward slowly. Crossing into the room and into the light of the room.

Roth waved his hand in the gray air. "Sorry for all the smoke. Just push those books aside and sit down."

There was an extra chair. Scarred, armless; wood with a cushioned seat. A Jowett and a Bloom lay on it, open, upside down, one atop the other. The child didn't push the books aside, but she was small enough to fit on the edge. She perched there, watching Roth solemnly.

"Aunt Geena says you shouldn't smoke or you'll get sick and die," she said.

"Does she? Well, well. Aunt Geena. What a wit. Does she know you're here?"

"Yes. I said I was coming over."

Roth nodded. The child was silent and for a moment or two he couldn't think of anything to say.

"So, uh, how's Elmo?" he asked after a while.

"Fine."

"Would you like something? Milk and cookies? I don't have any milk actually. Coffee and cookies? A scotch?"

"No."

"I was joking."

"Oh."

"I don't have any cookies either."

"I'm full," she said. "I had breakfast."

"Ah."

"I had eggs and blueberry muffins."

"Mm, those are good."

"Are you sad?"

"Sad? Oh! No, no, no. Just . . . allergic, that's all. I have allergies."

Having spent little time on the chores of fatherhood, Roth was still sentimental about children. He thought they knew something. He thought Amanda could see through him, see through his lie, that her steady, serious stare could bore into his soul in some mystical childlike way, bore straight to the very depths of him. Averting his eyes, he had a vague urge to confess to her, to tell her everything and rely upon her baby wisdom to guide him.

Fortunately for everyone, the girl's mind had already wandered on to matters of far more pressing importance to her.

"You said you would tell me more stories," she said. "Like the one about Orpees."

"Hm?" He had been sinking into his own self-pitying thoughts again and was annoyed at the interruption. In fact, now that he thought about it, he was a bit annoyed at having her here altogether. She had barged in on him while he was trying to work—just as he was about to break through his block, to begin his brilliant letter. So it seemed to him now at any rate, now that she was making demands on him.

"You said you would tell me . . ." the girl repeated.

"Oh. Oh yes." Automatically, Roth reached into his cardigan pocket for his Kents again. His irritation threatened to grow. The effort of telling a story to the girl seemed too much for him somehow. He stalled, trying to think of a way out of it. "So you like those stories, huh."

"Yes."

"What about Elmo? Does he like them too?"

"Elmo's stuffed."

Cigarette between his lips, lighter raised to it, Roth laughed, and then gave a series of wheezing coughs. "Now be careful," he finally managed to say. "Be careful, because around here we're multicultural. Just because a fellow's stuffed doesn't mean we shouldn't listen to his opinion."

"Well, that's stupid," said the child.

"Tell me about it. I wish you were on the tenure committee." Roth lit up—and this time the first drag got him, sent him into a deep paroxysm of hacking that threatened to be productive all over the place.

The child sat quietly and watched him. "Are you sick?" she said after a while.

He waved the cigarette at her but was coughing too hard to answer. When he could, he stood from his chair but only remained beside it, gripping the back of it for support, still bent over, still coughing. "No, no," he squeezed out. He cleared his throat into a Kleenex. "I'm fine. I'm fine."

Fighting down another fit, he carried his cigarette over to one of the bookshelves. "Here. Here, look. I'll show you something." He brought down an oversized volume. Handed it to the child. "Try this."

Amanda set Elmo down beside her chair and carefully set the big book on her lap. Opened, the wide wings of it dwarfed her.

"See that?" said Roth. Standing above her. Gesturing vaguely with the smoking butt. "Those are pictures, paintings. That one's a statue. They're from all the stories. See? They're, like, illustrations people made long ago. Back when they could still paint."

The girl turned a page. "People can still paint."

"No," said Roth. "No, they can't."

"I can paint."

"Can you? Well, good for you. Start a trend."

The girl held the book balanced on her little knees. Pointed at a picture. "What's this one about?"

"Let's see." It was upside down to Roth. He crooked his head to look at it. "Oh, that, that's Icarus. He and his father Daedalus were imprisoned in a labyrinth—in a maze—by the king of Minos."

"Why?"

"Well, Daedalus was very clever at building things, and the king wanted to keep him around basically. But Daedalus wanted to leave. So he built wings for himself and his son Icarus. And he attached them to their backs with wax and they flew off over the sea. And Daedalus told Icarus, Be careful, don't go too near the sun, because you know what wax does when it gets too hot."

"No-o."

"Like when a candle has fire on it?"

"It melts."

"It melts. Exactly. But Icarus didn't listen—and you can see there how it turned out."

"He fell into the water."

"That's right. Right out of the sky. Splash."

"Is he drowned?"

"Yep. Yep, he sure is. It was a definite case of 'Bye-bye, Icarus.' "

Amanda nodded. "That's a good story too," she said, and turned the page.

Roth smiled down at her with one corner of his mouth. He was not annoyed anymore. In fact, he found the child's offhanded approval absurdly gratifying.

"Who's this lady?" she asked him now.

"Hm. Let's see. Who is that?" Roth came around so he could read the caption over her shoulder. "Ah, that—that's Europa."

"What did she do?"

"Well. Well, I'll tell you." A note of glee entered his voice here. He began to work out how to tell the story to her—composing, bowdlerizing, seeking out effects in his mind, all with a measure of excitement, anticipation. It was one of his favorite fables, this: the rape of Europa. It had a world of meaning for him. He saw the founding of the West in it. The carrying off of the past into new nations, the mingling of bloodlines in violence and passion, the mysterious, enduring connection to the wellsprings of Greece and, through Greece, to civilizations more ancient still.

"Europa was a princess . . ." he began.

But that was as far as he got. Because now Roth's cigarette ash had grown long, the reed itself burning down to its filter. He stepped away from the girl to reach the ashtray on his desk and, as he did, he took a final drag of the thing.

The smoke seemed to catch in his throat like a fish bone. The coughing fit that shook him started out harsh and grew swiftly in violence. Roth had time to reach out half blindly and extinguish the cigarette, but then he was doubled over, wracked and hacking. He felt like someone was in his lungs with a shovel trying to chuck hot gravel up his gullet and never quite making the grade. He braced one hand on the desk, tried to wave the other at the girl in apology. Coughed and coughed.

And then his mouth was wet, spilling over. A wet gob that seemed the size of his fist had burst up into his mouth. Roth seized a Kleenex. Hawked into it. Hawked again. Brought it away.

It was stained full scarlet.

Roth stared at the tissue. The world accordioned in and out around him and his stomach fell. *I know the color of that blood* went through his mind. And he finished the quotation aloud, weakly, "It is my death warrant. I must die."

Even that small effort at speech set him off again. He coughed so hard his head swam, his vision grew dim. A darkening veil seemed to be falling over his eyes. And then he heard a thump and he turned and looked down through tears.

The child, Amanda, was sprawled at his feet. She lay on her back on the study floor. The book she'd been looking at lay beside her. Her little arm was flung out over it. A thin line of blood spilled from the corner of her mouth.

The blood trickled down across her chin, as Roth stared, terrified.

3

The next few minutes spun past him in breathless panic.

He was on his knees beside the girl. Touching her face, her shoulder.

"Amanda!"

Her tan cheeks had turned yellowish. Her skin was cold as ice. She was breathing, but faintly. She didn't budge.

"Amanda!"

Roth was on his feet next. Around his desk. Stretched clumsily to the window. Forcing it open. As the cool air came in on him, he shouted out through it, out at the hedge.

"Geena! Geena, come quick!"

No answer. Roth rushed back to the girl, knelt, and lifted her into his arms.

He was outside, down the stairs, running with his burden, crossing the space between his front lawn and Geena MacAlary's when Geena's screen door banged and she was running down her own porch stairs to meet him.

"Oh my God, what happened?"

In a few steps, they came together. Geena's hands fluttered toward the girl, but Roth held on to her.

"Amanda?" Geena cried.

"I'll take her in. Call a doctor."

"What happened?"

"I don't know. I was sick, I was coughing. And suddenly, she just collapsed, maybe I scared her, I don't know."

He continued running to Geena's porch—but then glanced back to discover she wasn't with him.

She seemed to have frozen on the lawn. Was standing there, staring after him. She was a sweet-faced woman in her fifties. Disproportionately large breasts in a still-slender frame. A tan V-necked sweater, a plaid, pleated skirt. A tint of red in her silvering hair. She was a straightforward, down-to-earth woman, Roth had always thought, sharp with longtime-mother smarts. He'd always admired her, feared her slightly.

But now she stood there pale and staring. Open-mouthed and stupid-eyed.

"Come on!" Roth said, and turned away and hurried up the stairs.

Inside, Geena caught up, was with him again. She fretted at his shoulder as he laid the child on the sofa in the living room. Amanda let out a soft moan.

"Thank God," said Roth. "She's breathing better now."

There were two pink spots rising to the tan surface of the girl's cheeks.

Roth wiped his sweaty palms on his pants legs. "It was really shallow before. It scared the shit out of me."

Geena sat down on the edge of the sofa. She put her hand on Amanda's brow.

"I'll call an ambulance," said Roth, turning to look for a phone.

"No," said Geena quietly. She stroked Amanda gently, pursed her lips to make a comfort noise.

"What—have you got a pediatrician or something?"

Geena shook her head. "It'll be all right."

"No, Geena, listen . . ." Roth said. "We've gotta . . . I mean, don't you have to call someone?"

She went on shaking her head, touching Amanda, pursing her lips. And then she said, "This happens, Howard. It's all right. She has a . . . a form of epilepsy. Sometimes this happens." She glanced up at him with troubled hazel eyes. "The worst is over now, all right? You did the right thing. She'll be fine."

Roth stood there, held her gaze. Tried to plumb the meaning of it without success. "Well, don't you want . . . ? I mean, is there some medicine? Can I do anything? I mean, she was just sitting there, Geena, I swear it. One minute she was fine . . ."

"Ssh. I know," said Geena, comforting Roth and the girl at the same time. "It's all right. There's nothing for you to do. Go on home, Howard. Go ahead. Let me take care of her. I'll let you know that everything's all right."

Roth lifted his hands from his sides, dropped them back again. "Yeah? I mean . . . you're sure?"

"Mm-hm. I'm sure. Really."

"Okay. I guess." He hesitated. "You'll come by, though," he said. "I mean, you'll let me know."

She nodded. "Don't worry. I'll come by later. It's all right, Howard. Really."

Still dazed, still high on panic, Roth backed away from her. "All right, I'll . . . You're sure . . . ? I can't . . . ? I mean, listen, Geena, if there's anything . . . ?"

But Geena had turned back to the child. "It's all right," she kept saying, as if to both of them.

"She was just sitting there . . ." Roth said again. "She was looking at a book."

"I know."

Roth continued to back away, watching the two of them on the sofa, the woman sitting over the girl, stroking the girl's forehead. Finally, with nothing more to say, he turned and headed for the door.

It wasn't until a few moments after that, when he was out on the front lawn in the wintry day, that Roth finally paused, that he finally stood, baffled, with one hand held tentatively against his chest. He drew in a long stream of frosty air. A long, steady stream.

He hadn't realized till now: he wasn't coughing anymore. He had shouted for help. He had lifted the child. He had run with her from one house to another. And he was only slightly out of breath. He wasn't coughing. That rasping sensation in his throat was gone, that burning sensation in his chest as well.

Roth blinked and lifted his eyes. Blue morning shone pale through the latticework of naked branches. A starling on the rooftop sang. He turned to look at it, to look at the house, at the doorway through which he'd just come.

He took another breath, another deep breath. And the air flowed into him clear as a crystal stream.

CHAPTER 10

MY HEART AND

I HAVE DECIDED

TO END IT ALL

1

Freighted with care, meanwhile, Vincent "The Nutcracker" Giordano wandered through the hedgerow maze on his Long Island compound. He did this whenever he wanted to think things over. And there was a good deal on The Nutcracker's mind.

They called Giordano the Last of the Sicilians—they being many of the same federal investigators who had put the Rest of the Sicilians behind bars. But the source notwithstanding, Vincent was very proud of this sobriquet. *The Last of the Sicilians.* It made him feel like a Man of Respect, like one of the great figures from the Old Days when the family businesses were run with dignity and honor. Vincent knew there had been such Old Days because he had seen *The Godfather* some twenty-six times. The film was, in fact, his primary source of historical information, not to mention the fountainhead of his personal style.

And apparently it had served him well. While other old-style mobsters had fallen to the law, or to the new immigrants or to the disloyalty of their followers or their own indiscretions, The Nutcracker had stuck to his cinematic model and thus could not only render a passable imitation of Marlon Brando from time to time but also maintained control over a sizable East Coast criminal empire.

It was the business of this empire that occupied his thoughts now as he wandered round the hawthorn corridors toward the center of the maze. It was drugs, to be precise. The movement—as The Nutcracker phrased it to himself—of large quantities of illegal substances from one group of semi-civilized colored people in the jungles of South America to another group of semi-civilized colored people in the jungles of America's slums. There were many difficult stages to this process and many middlemen, many places along the way where the transfer could go awry. Powder could be unduly cut, profits could be secretly skimmed, minions could be unkindly shaken down and so forth. And you had to react to these things, deal with them, guard against them insofar as possible. And at the same time you had to acknowledge that a certain amount of cutting and skimming and shaking down was bound to occur, human nature being what it is. So it was a subtle thing, a delicate thing: when to acknowledge, when to react; when to turn a blind eye and when to gouge one out and stuff it into an ear. The Nutcracker had to think very hard about these and other weighty matters on a daily basis.

Which is why he loved to come here, to his compound, to this maze, to this place where he could find solitude and a measure of peace.

Like everything else about him, Giordano's Long Island estate was fashioned after his semi-fictional notions of the past. The grounds centered on a sprawling neo-classical mansion. With its Ionic columns two stories tall, its raking cornice above its sculpted frieze, the house was considered the height of elegance by many of The Nutcracker's closest and most strangely nicknamed associates. *The New York Times*, on the other hand, in a less than flattering article, had once referred to the place as Giordano's "armed fortress on the North Shore."

The *Times*, it must be admitted, had a point.

A wall ran around all fifteen acres of the place, a white brick wall some ten feet high. It was topped with rolls of razor wire and the razor wire was electrified. There was only one gate, and this was locked electronically and guarded by an armed "soldier" in a booth of bulletproof glass. Other soldiers patrolled the inner perimeter, pacing back and forth at a distance of some twenty-five yards, each within sight of the next, and all carrying what law enforcement officers have been known to refer to as "spray-and-pray weapons": automatic guns that discharge enough rounds per minute on so many various trajectories that even an invading army would be riddled to pieces before the shooter was obliged to take aim.

There were more guards at the house, by the garage, by the stables. There were light-activated alarm systems in every building and some featured self-sealing steel window plates and doors. Vincent himself was generally accompanied by two armed companions, one large, one larger. The smaller one looked like a gorilla imitating a bulldozer; the bigger one looked like a bulldozer imitating a gorilla. Right this very minute, in an effort to protect their employer's privacy, the duo was stationed at the hedge maze entrance, one on either side of the opening. Their hands, clasped before them, were ever ready. Their eyes, behind their sunglasses, were ever vigilant.

The privileged, spoon-fed reporters sitting safe within their offices at *The New York Times* might have considered these security measures excessive. But it was precisely because of these precautions that The Nutcracker could wander to the center of his hawthorn maze in relative tranquillity of heart. Because of them he could soothe his troubled mind with considerations of the quiet and the greenery. Because of them he could pause to rediscover the Roman urns and headless Venuses placed piquant in this niche or that; could appreciate the fresh November morning and the blue November sky; and could come now to the center of his labyrinth where a marble bench stood surrounded by statuary in an open square.

And it was precisely because he had surrounded himself with such extensive and elaborate systems of self-protection that Vincent "The Nutcracker" Giordano was absolutely appalled to find that Edmund Winter, uninvited, was already sitting on the bench when he arrived.

How the fuck . . . ? Giordano asked himself.

But no answer was immediately forthcoming. This never happened in the movies.

"Hey-ho! Morning, Vincent," said the red-haired man pleasantly. He lifted a finger and any shout that might have issued from the mob boss's throat quickly died there.

Because now there was movement in the hawthorn shadows and two more men stepped into plain view. Giordano knew these men by reputation. Ferdinand was a wiry brown-skinned fellow with a face that looked like a Halloween skull. Dewey was enormous, neckless, a slab of a man. In fact, Giordano sometimes liked to watch television shows that professed to explicate "ancient mysteries" and sometimes he would see a slab the size of Dewey in those shows and he would ask himself, "How the fuck did those ancient dickheads move a slab that size?"

So Giordano did not want to make an enemy of Dewey. Ferdinand either for that matter, who was said to have once been a professional torturer somewhere in South America. And Winter especially, who was said to have committed acts of violence Giordano hadn't even dreamed of.

So instead of shouting, Giordano changed tactics and decided to sweat, which he did profusely.

Winter stood up, meanwhile. He smiled amiably. His crisp black suit, his silk red tie, his gold tie pin, his delicate cologne all seemed startling and out of place in this arcadian setting. In fact, considering the impossibility of his being there at all, his corporate elegance made him appear terribly *present* somehow, terribly real.

"Wonderful to see you again, Vincent," he said. "Truly."

Giordano swallowed. Then he resumed sweating. "Yeah," he said.

Hands in his trouser pockets, Winter ambled toward him. Stood within inches of him, eyes on his eyes. Vincent was a short, squat man, dressed today in blue running pants and an aqua polo shirt. Winter's authoritative air—not to mention his cologne—seemed to overwhelm him where he stood.

Nonetheless, The Nutcracker was no pushover. He mustered his fortitude. "All I have to do is snap my fingers . . ." he began hoarsely.

"And Dewey will stuff them so far down your throat you'll be able to scratch your ass with them," answered Winter, smiling. "Now shut up and listen, you dago toad. I know that Chubby Chubb's alive."

"Eyy . . ."

Winter held up his finger again. Giordano shut up and sweat.

"I know he's alive," Winter said, "and that you're running his old operation. Which tells me that you bought him out, made him liquid. Which tells me you can help me find him."

The Nutcracker sent Winter a look of arrogant defiance, marred only by the steady rivulets of moisture pouring down his flabby face. "Maybe you never heard of *omertà*—the code of silence," he said gruffly.

Winter laughed. "Vincent! Vincent! You're a charming Old World figure and I love you for it. But I represent an American-based multinational corporation." He reached out and patted the mobster's wet cheek, two sharp slaps. "Don't make me hurt you."

Lonnie played. He was onstage under a single spot. The audience was all around him, invisible in the dark. He felt them rather than saw them. Suzanne, Carol Dodson, even he, Lonnie himself, was out there listening while he played. There were hundreds of hidden faces beyond the edges of the light but all of them somehow belonged to those few people he had loved, the living and the dead. He bent back on the stage and lifted his sax and played for them all and the sound was like starlight, celestial. He strove to name the melody and couldn't and understood it was so beautiful that this had to be a dream. And still he played and the notes rose up sparkling from the sax's bell and sprinkled down over the hearts of those who heard it like balm. The living and the dead, it soothed them all. It soothed him, Lonnie, as it rose and rose, as it sounded clearer and louder—and then suddenly discordant—and then suddenly it was a car horn screaming by on the highway beyond his window, and Lonnie sat up in the motel bed and all the evil of his life flooded back in on him.

Lonnie groaned, his heart beating hard. He moved to the bed's edge. Sat there, his feet on the floor, his face in his hands. Beyond the curtains over his window, the cars on the highway kept screaming by. He was in Jersey somewhere, he remembered. It was almost noon. He hadn't hit the bed till after dawn.

Naked, he padded into the bathroom. Leaned into the small mirror over the sink. Examined his face. Not bad, he thought. He'd shaved in a gas station men's room before coming here, so the stubble was even again. The ointment Arthur Topp had given him had taken the edge off the cut on his jaw. It was still inflamed, still infected, but the throbbing was gone; it was just a raw sting now.

Only his eyes were awful. Only the expression in his eyes. In them, he saw the distance from his dream to this shabby, threadbare cubicle. It was a vast distance. It was harrowing.

He took his time washing up. The toilet, the sink, the shower—they all still felt like luxuries to him. And then too, there was the phone in the other room, waiting for him on the table by his bed. He thought of it all the while. What if his one lead should fail him? What if there was nowhere to go from here?

The raid on the restaurant had been a long shot to begin with but he'd had reason to hope it might pay off. A place like Ed Whittaker's, exclusive, crowded. You'd need a reservation for Sunday brunch and they were almost sure to ask you for a confirmation number too. Plus, Lonnie had read the article on Arthur Topp's computer. He had a strong hunch that this smuggler he was looking for, this Frederick Chubb guy, was arrogant, flamboyant. The kind of man who dared you to catch him if you could. What other kind of man would fly under the alias Frank Chester, a name so tauntingly similar to his own?

That'd been Lonnie's reasoning in any case. And sure enough when he ran out of Ed Whittaker's, he had the reservation book in his hand and in the book he found the name F. Childs. And there was a cell phone number scribbled in the space beside it.

He hardly dared hope that Childs was Chubb, that the number would actually connect him. And yet he couldn't dare but believe that he was, that it actually would. And the possibility—even the slim possibility— that he might really be able to clear his name before he turned himself in to the police, that he might actually find Chubb, that he might actually . . .

find the girl, see the girl again . . .

No, that was over. It was past that now. He just had to find Chubb, see if Chubb could make some sense of the murders in the girl's apartment, give him *some* information, at least, that might show he had killed the cops in self-defense. It was the only way he could think of that might get him out of this mess.

Anyway, the first wave of publicity must've passed, he'd figured. The ordinary man on the street would soon forget his face. The time was ripe to take the chance and try to get the hell out of town.

He'd stolen the license plates first, from a decaying Mustang on Ninety-fourth Street. Its parking spot was good all day. Lonnie thought he might get twenty-four hours of grace before anyone even noticed the plates were gone. He got the car farther north. A hoopty old Dodge he found in the Heights. It was a dangerous neighborhood to complain in. Maybe the owner would think twice before he reported the theft to the police.

Using Topp's screwdriver, wrench and wire coat hanger, it took him five minutes to switch the plates and forty-five seconds to jump the car.

All the same, the sky had been growing lighter by the time he rolled over the GW Bridge and into Jersey.

Now he was here, in the motel, rested, more or less, put together—more or less. It was time to face this thing. It was time to find out just how far he was going to go.

He came out of the bathroom, got dressed. Pulled on the old white sweater Topp had given him. He stood with the room still dark, the curtains still drawn. He looked at the phone a long moment. He licked his lips.

Right.

He went to the table. Picked up the phone. Punched in the number from the reservation book.

The phone rang once. Twice. Then the ringing stopped.

Lonnie waited, listened.

Nothing. Not even the sound of breathing. No sound at all on the other end.

Lonnie spoke into the silence.

"Mr. Chubb," he said, "my name is Lonnie Blake."

No answer. Nothing. Lonnie felt his palm grow damp against the handset.

"I know you don't want to talk to me, Mr. Chubb, but you've got to. I know you weren't really on that plane that crashed. I know you didn't die. All I want . . ."

But then the silence on the line came to an abrupt end. There was a loud burst of sound in Lonnie's ear.

Someone was laughing.

"Hello?" said Lonnie Blake.

The laughter went on another second or so. And then a voice said, "I'm sorry, Mr. Blake."

Lonnie held his breath. His throat felt dry.

"It's just funny, that's all," the voice continued. "You've got everything exactly wrong."

"Sorry?"

"I *was* on that plane. I *did* die."

"Say . . . say what?"

"And as for my not wanting to talk to you—why, you're exactly the man I've been looking for. You're exactly the man I want to see."

But Winter now was also on his way.

At noon, he was in Manhattan, in the twenty-third-floor men's room which exclusively served the Park Avenue office of Skite, Wylie and Pratt, Attorneys-at-Law.

Jeremy Skite discovered Winter's presence there as he stood at the urinal with his honorable member in his hands. It was then that Dewey came up behind him and pushed the lawyer's face into the tile wall.

There was a soft clattering noise as Skite's teeth sprinkled to the floor. Then Skite himself was lying among them, his face bloodied, his pants wet, his organ exposed.

Winter stood over him, smiled down. There was also a gigantic slab of a man and a wiry brown man with a face like a skull. The wiry brown man was holding what seemed to be a cigarette lighter in his hand.

"Giordano sent me," Winter said. "He told me you could help me find Frederick Chubb."

Skite the attorney shook his head. "Ca. Hew kew meh . . ." he said through his broken mouth.

"Pardon?" said Winter. He glanced at the slab beside him. "What did you have to knock his teeth out for?"

"Sorry," said Dewey. "He lifted his chin."

"Kew meh. . .Hew kew meh!" the lawyer insisted.

Ferdinand, the skull-faced one, cleared his throat. "He's saying Chubb will kill him."

"Oh!" Winter laughed pleasantly. Leaned down toward the lawyer. "He'll kill you? Is that what you're saying?"

Skite nodded. "Peese. Hew kew meh Ah sswah."

"Yes. He probably will," Winter conceded. "But then, Ferdinand will burn your penis off."

Ferdinand bared his teeth and pressed a button on the cigarette lighter. Only it wasn't a cigarette lighter. It was a Lensmaster C-14 Laser. The beam from it shot upward four and a half feet where it struck the ceiling. The plaster up there charred, cracked and burst away from around a dime-sized burn hole. Then the beam vanished.

"Apsboowy, Apsboowy!" said Skite, quickly covering himself with his hands.

"Apsboowy?" said Winter.

"Apsboowy i Wockland Counee."

"Oh," Winter laughed. "Oh, oh. Hapsburg. In Rockland County. Okay. I know it. What's the address?"

Skite curled up onto his side, his hands between his legs. His blood and tears spilled down onto his teeth. "Portee Bweckenwidge Wo."

"Forty Breckenridge Road," said Winter. "Thank you very much. And of course, if he's not there, we'll be forced to come back."

But he didn't press the point. The way the lawyer lay convulsed with sobs convinced him that he was no longer listening

—and that he hadn't dared to lie.

Winter stepped over the man and started for the door. Ferdinand and Dewey fell in behind him.

Hapsburg, Winter thought. It was about a hundred miles away. He ought to get there just about two o'clock in the afternoon.

4

Lonnie Blake got there around one-twenty-five.

Hapsburg was a pleasant little village, situated not ten miles from the Hudson River. Its small Main Street was lined with quaint white clapboards. Wooded hills, still decked with fall pastels, rose to every side of it.

Lonnie stopped the Dodge at a light in the center of town. To his right was a row of stores. Books 'n Things, Wholly Doughnuts!, Century 21. He sat looking through the windshield at the storefronts, at the sidewalk shoppers reflected in the storefront glass. Mothers still young, still beautiful, walked chatting with their toddlers, or pushed their babies in strollers by each other's side. One older woman, silver-haired, stately, greeted an ancient man who seemed to shuffle along contentedly to no purpose. A dome-bellied Realtor in his shirtsleeves hurried back to his office from the doughnut shop, rollicking with supreme confidence, commenting on the weather to one and all.

Lonnie ached at the serenity of the scene. He had had days like this. He had imagined a life like this. He and Suzanne had imagined it together.

Yeah. Well. Tough shit, cuz. It be that way sometimes.

Without thinking, he found himself searching the little crowd for another black face. There was none. Which made him feel like a man's shadow on a movie screen: just as welcome, just as noticeable. And so when a state trooper pulled up at the curb nearby him, his heart seized. How could the cop miss him? He was as good as busted.

Luckily, just as the trooper unfolded from his cruiser, the light turned green. Lonnie, hissing in relief, eased his foot down bit by bit so that the car moved gently away.

Sayonara, Main Street, he thought.

And on he went.

Breckenridge Road led him up into the hills. The leaves were growing sparse now but there were still swaths of orange and red, patches of yellow. The trees grew denser as the road wound up. The houses grew larger and were set farther back from the road. He could see them—their white walls, their brown walls— through the thinning leaf cover.

The place he wanted was near the top of the grade. Its driveway wound on even further up the hillside. By the time Lonnie reached the house itself, he could see—through the car window, through the breaks between the trees—a spectacular view of the town below, the hills beyond, the sparkle from the river where it ran through a valley of mist.

The house was modern. Fresh brown wood in slanting planes. An enormous window, darkened on the outside, looking on to that sweet southeastern vista. There was a circular gravel drive before the double garage. No car was visible.

Lonnie parked close to the front door. He stepped out into the cool of the day.

It was quiet. After the car, after the city. You could hear the breeze in the high branches. You could hear the whisper of traffic on the streets below. But other than that, the woods around were still. Not even a bird was singing.

Lonnie cast a slow glance around him. No one nearby, no one in sight. Quiet enough to make him edgy. He slipped his hand into his overcoat pocket, curled his fingers around the grip of his gun. He stepped toward the front door cautiously. Ready for a fight, muscles pulled tense as a bow.

A footstep crunched on the gravel behind him. He whirled around, whipped out his gun.

Frederick Chubb laughed. "Really, Mr. Blake," he said, "if I'd meant to kill you, you'd be a long time dead by now."

"As things stand, I'd say I have about half an hour to live."

They were on an indoor balcony now, an open deck above the living room. They sat before the enormous window. The rolling hills and the river valley spread beneath them.

The long thin man sat relaxed in a canvas chair. He was wearing khaki slacks and a khaki safari shirt. Elaborate sandals over bare feet. His long black hair was tied back. The strap of his eye patch was at a jaunty slant. His single eye was green and bright. His hand moved in the air with graceful gestures. Overall, the smuggler gave an impression of elegant sophistication.

Lonnie sat across from him, swigging water from a plastic bottle. He didn't give a shit how elegant Chubb was or how sophisticated. He just wanted to know why he'd walked into a bloodbath. Why a cop had tried to shave his face off. He wanted to know how the hell he had suddenly become a killer being hunted by the law.

"I've received a phone call of warning. A man named Edmund Winter is on his way here," Frederick Chubb went on. "His plan is to torture and kill me. If he finds you here, he'll torture and kill you too."

Lonnie shook his head slowly. "No. He won't."

"That's right." Chubb smiled. "You're the man who killed Mortimer. You're a hard case, right?"

"I just don't like being fucked with," Lonnie said. He could still feel Mortimer's hands on him. He could still feel the anger and the fear inside him. "I've been fucked with enough."

"Well, let me explain something to you, Mr. Blake. Winter is no Mortimer. Winter is to Mortimer . . . Well . . . You've heard of Plato? Mortimer is the killer in fact. Winter is the killer in God's mind. If he finds you here, take my word for it, he'll fuck with you all right. He'll fuck with you until you're dead."

Lonnie gave his small snort of contempt. "Right now I got a lot of people with guns after me, Mr. Chubb. Most of them got badges too. Winter's gonna have to wait in line. Meanwhile, I want to know what the hell it's all about."

Chubb's lips tightened a little. He was a man who liked to be listened to with respect. A grocer's son from Nyack, he had come a long way in the world. He had worked hard on his elegant, sophisticated persona. He wanted it to be taken seriously.

He calmed himself with an elegant, sophisticated sip of coffee. "All right," he said then. "I'll tell you. Winter is the North American bureau chief of an organization called Executive Decisions. It's a private fighting force that hires itself to companies and countries around the world for military and covert actions. Recently, they've been trying to expand their operations into the U.S., recruiting personnel from security, law enforcement, the military. Moonlighters . . ."

"Like Mortimer and Hughes," Lonnie said.

"That's right."

"They were working for this Executive Decisions, not NYPD."

"Well, Mortimer, at least, was working for both—but, yes, you get the general idea. An international paramilitary is setting up house in the United States. But see, the primitive methods that pass muster in other countries are no good here. Winter, on the other hand, is used to working with corporations. He has an acceptable manner, good business sense. He's worked his way up through the ranks to the front office. So E.D. has brought him over here to work out the rough edges of the new setup. This operation you've become involved in is one of those rough edges. In fact, partly because of you, it's about as rough as they come. In fact, it's now become so rough that Winter has decided to handle it himself."

"Yeah? So what are we talking about here?"

"E.D. has been hired to hunt down a girl."

In spite of himself, Lonnie felt a sharp emotional hitch. He sat forward in his chair. "Carol Dodson."

But Chubb shook his head. "Her five-year-old daughter. Amanda."

Lonnie sat back. He tilted his water bottle to his lips, covering his surprise. A daughter. He had not imagined Carol Dodson with a daughter. He had not imagined her any way but the way she had been that night when he held her and she whispered to him and he felt his wife was still somehow alive in her. Those images raced through his mind now again.

And meanwhile Chubb set his coffee cup down and said quietly, "The thing I'm about to tell you you will not believe. But you've got to. And quickly. Because we really don't have much time."

They really didn't. Just about then, Winter turned onto Hapsburg's Main Street.

He was still driving his blue Lexus. His two golems were with him. Ferdinand in the passenger seat, mirrored glasses on his skull-face now. Dewey slab-like in back, mirrored glasses on the part of him that was probably his head. All three of the men were silent.

The Lexus stopped at the light. Winter glanced through the windshield. He saw much the same Main Street scene that Lonnie had. The mamas with their babes, the old codgers, the small-town businessmen striding behind their own bellies.

He smiled to himself.

He was thinking about Carol Dodson. He was thinking about the things he was going to do to her before he let her die. He was thinking about the taste of tears on her soft skin.

And it was good. Good to be out in the field again. Good to be active and in control. And these folks out there through the windshield, these Main Street folks, they had no idea how good it was. How real it made things, how sharp and clear. How rich it made the whiff of life.

Part of him was almost glad

—glad that Mortimer and Hughes had screwed it up

—glad that he'd been forced to take the op in hand. After his transaction with Giordano that morning, after the bagatelle in the men's room with Jeremy Skite, with Frederick Chubb's interrogation and Carol Dodson's rape and torture still to look forward to, Winter was a-feeling mighty like a man with wires in his body instead of veins, with electricity coursing through him instead of blood.

These folks on Main Street. They did not know. They had no idea how good it was.

The light changed. Winter gave a deep sigh of contentment.

He eased his foot down on the pedal and headed for Breckenridge Road.

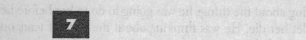

7

"Four months ago, I was murdered," said Frederick Chubb. He spoke quickly, urgently, but quietly too, clearly.

And Lonnie looked at him deadpan and thought, *Say what?*

"A competitor—a man named Abubakar—placed a bomb on my jet and blew it out of the sky."

"The crash in Mass," Lonnie said.

"That's right. It wasn't much of a bomb, but it did the trick. Most of the people on board never even hit the ground. Some came down in pieces. But, for reasons that aren't entirely clear, a few bodies—a few people in first class—fell almost entirely intact."

"Yeah. Okay. So what?"

The tone of Chubb's voice didn't change. It was still urgent, still quiet, still cool.

"My body fell intact," he said. "It fell intact—and a few moments later, I stood up and I was fine."

Lonnie let out a single laugh. "Ah-hah."

"Oh, yes. I was fine, Mr. Blake. No burns. No internal injuries. No damage at all. Does that strike you as a believable scenario?"

"I don't know, man." Lonnie lifted his shoulder. "These things happen, I guess. How the hell should I know?"

"What if I were to tell you I was dead, Mr. Blake?"

"What?"

"That I fell from that plane and I was dead—and that then I was alive again."

"Oh, come on, for Christ's sake," Lonnie broke out. "I killed a cop, man. I got the whole world after me. You're gonna sit there and testify to the resurrection . . . ?"

But Chubb seemed not to hear him. His single eye gleamed distantly. He shook his head as if in wonder. "I stood up," he repeated. "I stood up and I looked around me. Stunned, I was. Amazed. The woods—I saw the woods were on fire, burning. And then I saw, there, at my feet, a child was lying, a little child. Carol Dodson's daughter, Amanda. She was unconscious. Bleeding from the mouth. And right then, right then I knew she had done it."

"Done *what?*" said Lonnie.

Again, Chubb ignored him. "Without knowing what I was doing or why, I picked her up in my arms and carried her away from the smoke and flames. And then, finally, I found Carol, her mother, searching for her . . ."

"What is this?" Lonnie sneered at him. "What are you trying . . . ?"

"*Listen to me.*" Chubb's long fingers curled into a fist. "Listen. I don't know myself what happened, not all of it. Only what Carol would tell me. There were some experiments . . . a pharmaceutical firm . . . I don't pretend to understand. All I know—all I know is that I was dead. I was dead and that child—that child *did something to me.* She *did something* and I was alive again."

Fuck me, he's a nutcase, Lonnie thought. *I waste my time, I risk my life to come here and he's raving out of his fucking mind.*

Chubb made a noise in his throat. Tried to bring a

measure of calm back into his voice again. "Look. It doesn't matter. How or what or why. It doesn't matter. It doesn't even matter if you believe me. The point is: I was the man they meant to kill and I alone of all the passengers on that plane survived. *Survived*, you understand." He shook his head. "That can't just be coincidence. It can't be . . ." He had to steady himself again before he could continue. "I vowed from that moment on that my life was going to be different, was going to be . . . *better*. Somehow. When Carol told me, blurted out, that someone was after her, I vowed—I told her—right there, as we were standing there, I told her . . . anything . . . *anything* I could do to help her I would do. All my resources, all my contacts, anything she could use to protect her, to protect her daughter. At first, there was nothing. She didn't trust me. She thought she could make it on her own. But now . . ."

Lonnie watched the man. He saw a quick grimace of suffering tighten Chubb's features and he knew, at least, that that—the suffering—was real.

"Now she's finally come to me," Chubb said, "and I've tried to help her."

After a strained moment, Lonnie sighed. "Yeah? So?"

Chubb drew a long breath. "So instead, I've sent her into a death trap," he said. "And you're the only one who can get her out."

8

Winter found the house he was looking for.

He parked the Lexus on Breckenridge Road, a few yards from the head of the driveway. As Ferdinand and Dewey unloaded themselves into the afternoon, Winter cracked open the glove compartment and drew out one of his contraptions: a pair of goggles attached to a thick headset. He climbed out of the car and handed the thing to Ferdinand.

The brown-faced, skull-faced man sniffed and removed his mirrored glasses, slipped them into his coat pocket. He pulled the goggles on.

Then all three men started for the house.

They walked on the drive, carelessly letting the gravel crunch beneath their shoes. The trees rustled gently all around them. A wedge of geese flew over their heads honking in the blue sky.

Winter glanced at Ferdinand as they walked. Ferdinand scanned the area with his goggles, shook his head.

The three men kept walking.

It was another minute before they came within sight of the house. There was a bend in the drive and then they caught a glimpse of the brown wood walls through the sparse yellow leaves. Winter slowed to a stop and the men behind him stopped.

Winter's eyes moved over the woods, over the house in the trees. He saw no sign of security. But then Chubb was like that. He never surrounded himself with guards, never took the usual precautions, never—even now—made much of an attempt to hide from anyone. He simply had a way of slipping through your fingers at the last minute.

But Winter did not think Chubb would slip through his fingers. He had troopers watching for him on every road out of town, for one thing. For another, he didn't think Chubb wanted to slip back into a life of pursuit and evasion. He thought Chubb would stay, would try to negotiate, would ultimately sell him Carol Dodson's whereabouts for some cash and some peace of mind.

Paused where he was, Winter glanced at Ferdinand again. Ferdinand again scanned the area with his goggle-machine. It was a FLIR—forward-looking infrared—thermal-imager. It detected heat from objects, especially life-forms. When he trained it on the house now, fuzzy red images formed against the dark background.

"There are two of them," he said softly. "Inside. Upstairs."

Winter cocked an eyebrow at him. "No one else? No one in the woods?"

Ferdinand stripped off the goggles. He shook his head. "Two in the house. That's all."

Winter nodded. Ferdinand and Dewey reached into their jackets. Each drew out a Walther P99.

"Let's take 'em," Winter said.

The two thugs vanished into the forest.

Winter continued up the drive alone.

Chubb went on speaking. The quick, cool tone again. "When I met Carol at the restaurant I'd had no time to make arrangements for her. My organization is gone now, most of my contacts are gone. I only have this house, one or two other places. A lot of cash. I have to improvise and it can't always be done on the spur of the moment. When she told me her pursuers were getting close, I gave her what money I could. And then I told her I'd arrange to have a lot more—and false-name credit cards and passports and other papers—left for her anywhere she chose. She gave me one of the keys to a bank deposit box and I promised to have the material dropped there."

He paused for a deep breath but then pushed on quickly, speaking on the exhale. "Arrangements to transport her and Amanda out of the country were more difficult. I told her to call me after she picked up the papers and I'd let her know where to meet her pickup. Do you understand what I'm saying to you?"

Lonnie's head was swimming. "Not really. No," he said.

Chubb's long face registered his frustration. "In a few minutes, Winter will be here. In about two hours, Carol's going to call to find out what she needs to know. When she calls, it'll be Winter who answers. He'll have her traced in seconds and he'll be on her trail again.

What's more, he'll have my phone records, computer transactions and so on. I've covered my tracks as best I can but . . . basically, if someone doesn't get to Carol and warn her before she makes that phone call, he's got her."

Lonnie gazed at the one-eyed man a long, long while. He couldn't take all this in, couldn't figure it out, couldn't think at all. He could only imagine this man, this Winter—the killer in God's mind—moving closer and closer to Carol Dodson.

He shook the image off. "Why don't you have one of your people warn her?"

"That's what I'm telling you. I don't *have* any people anymore. The people I can get work for cash and they're not always trustworthy."

"Then warn her yourself."

"Winter's onto me. He's got state troopers working for him everywhere. He'd have me before I got ten miles. Even so, I would have tried it. I was going to try it. Then you called."

Lonnie made a curt noise. He already knew he wasn't going to like what came next.

"After Mortimer was shot," Chubb said, "Carol risked a call and told me about you. She thought I should know. She said you might even be smart enough to come after me. I prayed you would. It's pretty obvious to me that you were just an act of desperation on Mortimer's part. I figure it'll be obvious to Winter too. In which case, he'll probably let the cops take care of you. He won't be expecting you to climb right back into the frying pan."

Lonnie stood up. "Yeah, well, he's got that right. I followed this woman once already, man. She's bad for my health."

It was as if Chubb hadn't heard him. He reached into

his pocket, pulled out a key chain with a pair of keys on it. Tossed it to Lonnie. Lonnie caught it automatically.

"There's a car in the garage," Chubb said. "A BMW. The plates are clean. Winter hasn't got them. She'll be at the First National Bank in Tyler, Putnam County, by three o'clock when it closes. You can just make it."

"Hey, I'm telling you . . . This is nothing to me. All I want is some information—not this crazy shit—something real, something I can take to the police . . ."

"It's no good. You've got to find her, Blake. Tell her I've arranged for a chopper to meet her on Meridian Mountain in New Hampshire. It'll be at the old Meridian Lodge at dawn on Friday. Got that? The lodge used to be one of my places, one of my transfer points. It's abandoned now, but it still has a field the chopper can land in. Help her, Blake. She'll take you with her. You'll be out of the country. She'll have enough money to arrange papers for you. You understand what I'm saying? You'll be away. You'll be out of this. You'll be free."

"Free." Lonnie tossed the keys back at Chubb. They hit the smuggler on the shoulder, slid down onto his thigh. "I'll be a fugitive the rest of my life. I'm not running away from anyone, man. I'm gonna prove these people came after me. Whoever these Executive mothers are, whatever they're after, I'm gonna bring them down."

Chubb swept the keys up angrily. "If you don't help her, Blake, she'll die," he said. And once again, he flung the keys across the deck.

Once again, Lonnie caught them. Held them. Stared at Chubb, his jaw working.

"She'll die, Mr. Blake," Chubb said again.

And slowly, Lonnie's hand closed, the keys digging into his flesh.

10

Winter knocked on the door.

He stood on the welcome mat and waited in plain sight. Despite the autumn chill, he was not wearing an overcoat. Just the black Cerutti, the red tie. His shirt—tailor-made by Jeraboam's of Savile Row—was white and featured a napoleon: a hidden snap-away front that would allow him to reach in easily underneath his arm. Underneath his arm, he was wearing a super-light Kramer holster. In the holster was a custom-made nine-millimeter semi-auto based on an H&K stock. Even with the compact holosight—which cast a 3-D grid over any target—the weapon was less than seven inches long and weighed only slightly more than thirty ounces. Powerful as it was, the setup made it virtually undetectable.

But Winter was not really expecting to use the gun. He was approaching Chubb openly, as a negotiator, and he thought he'd be received the same way. He had no doubt he could reach some amicable arrangement with Chubb before he tortured him—to make sure he wasn't lying about Carol Dodson's whereabouts—and killed him—for the purposes of security.

So he stood calmly on the welcome mat and waited. Conscious of the two Walthers covering him from the woods. Letting his hand rest lightly on his tie, near the spot where the false front of his shirt could be snapped away.

There were footsteps inside. Then the door opened.

Winter put his tongue in his cheek, closed one eye comically. But he kept his hand near the napoleon.

A woman stood in the doorway. Pretty; in her thirties; short black hair, pug nose, bright smile.

She was holding a baby on her hip.

"Hi," she sang out. "Sorry. We were upstairs having a change. Can I help you?"

Winter winked at the baby. Smiled at the woman. "Yes, hi," he said. "I'm here to see Forrest Childs?"

The woman's brown eyes narrowed. "Forrest . . . Oh, Mr. Childs! That's up at the top of the hill. Number fourteen."

"Fourteen!" Winter's hand left his shirt. He made a little tossing motion with it. "Fourteen, not forty. That explains everything," he said. "The man who gave me this address had no teeth. It was a little hard to understand what he was saying."

"Oh!" The woman gave a surprised little laugh. "Well . . . it's fourteen. Right up near the top."

Winter reached out and stroked the baby's cheek with one finger. "Thanks a lot," he said. "Sorry to bother you."

He was halfway up the drive before his two companions came out of the woods and joined him. They holstered their Walthers as they came.

Winter glanced at Dewey. "What did you have to knock his teeth out for?"

"Sorry," said the slab.

The three walked back to the car.

11

Up the hill, in Chubb's house, for a last long second, Lonnie's gaze stayed locked on the smuggler's single green eye.

If you don't help her, she'll die, he thought.

Damn, he thought.

He looked away. "All right," he muttered. "I'll do what I can. What about you? You just gonna sit here? Wait for Winter to come and torture you? Shit, he'll make you tell him the same stuff you just told me."

Out of the corner of his eye, he saw Chubb move. When he looked again, the smuggler was holding a small revolver in his hand. A snubnosed .38.

Lonnie gave a snort. "Oh great. This guy's as good as you say he is, I think he's gonna come prepared for *that* action."

Chubb frowned. He would be taken seriously in this, at least. "I wasn't planning to use it on *him*."

"Oh." Lonnie lifted his chin. "What? You mean you're gonna cap yourself. To protect her?"

"To protect the child. It's what I swore I would do if given half a chance." The expression on Lonnie's face seemed to amuse Chubb. He smiled now. "It's not as if I'm afraid of it, Blake. Remember: I've been there before."

"Oh yeah, right," said Lonnie dryly. "I forgot. You're the Lazarus man."

"That's right," said Chubb mildly. And his gaze grew

distant again. "Sometimes I even think I remember it, remember what it was like."

Lonnie snorted. "What? You mean, being dead? You remember being dead?"

"It's just a feeling I have sometimes but . . . It's a very specific sense . . . that there was a moment, you know . . . a moment of—*E pluribus unum*. Do you understand?" Lonnie didn't answer. He stood gazing at the man. Chubb smiled. "Read your nickels, Mr. Blake," he said. "*E pluribus unum*. It means 'Out of the many—one.' Sometimes at night . . . when I think back on what happened after the plane blew . . . well . . . I imagine I'm sitting at this big table, this long table. And there are . . . the worst people I can think of. Not, you know, your nasty aunt Ethel but . . . worse than that. The great villains, I mean. Stalin, Hitler. And the best people too. Jesus. Whoever. Take your pick. And I think, you know, that . . . that maybe for a moment, after the plane went down, after I fell, maybe I was there, maybe I sat down with those people at that table—this long table with food on it and drinks. And we all sat down and we all suddenly understood each other. We understood that we were part of something together—all of us—the evil and the good and the in-between—we were all part of something big and—and perfect somehow . . . That it was all right. You see? All of it. It was beautiful, every part. And we sat there at the table, the evil and the good, and we shared out the bread of love one with another. And it was all right. All of it. *E pluribus unum*."

Chubb smiled again, to himself now. He shrugged. "I guess I just wanted to tell that to someone before I . . . before this was over. Now I strongly suggest you get going while there's time."

But for another moment, Lonnie still stood, still stared, his mind far away. He was thinking about the boys who had surrounded Suzanne. The boys who had shouted *nigger* at her and grabbed her and chased her out into the road where she died. He thought of their grinning white faces, their taunting smiles. And he thought of sitting down with them at the long table and sharing out the bread of love.

He put his hand in his overcoat pocket. His fingers curled around the Beretta Cougar.

"I'm not sure I like that death of yours, Mr. Chubb," he told him.

Chubb laughed quietly this time. "It's death, Mr. Blake," he said. "No one asked you to like it."

The Lexus moved slowly up Breckenridge Road. Number fourteen was near the top.

Once again, they parked on the street beside the mouth of the drive. They approached the place in much the same way as before. As before, they paused within sight of the house and Ferdinand scanned it with the thermal imager.

Through the lenses, he saw Chubb's moving image, red on the dark background.

"There's only him," he said. "Just one."

Then, even as he spoke, he saw a sudden flash of scarlet. Winter, standing beside him, heard the shot.

"Goddammit," he said.

He started running toward the house. The front of his shirt was open, flapping. The modified Heckler and Koch was in his hand. Skull-face and the Slab were right behind him.

They found Chubb on the balcony, still in his chair. His head flung back, his mouth open as if he were snoring. There was a ragged crater near the crown of his head. There was gore splattered on the window behind him.

Rivulets of blood ran down the glass. They cast moving shadows on the dead man's face like rain.

FANCY MEETING
YOU HERE

The town came out of the forest suddenly. There was a graveyard, a church, a lake and then the town.

Not much of a town either. A few buildings of brick and concrete. A town hall, a post office, a courthouse and police station combined. A hardware store, a sporting goods store and a TV repair and video rental shop clustered nearby. A couple of loungers outside the firehouse: guys with plaid shirts and red-and-black checkered jackets; potbellies, cigarettes and sluggish conversation.

Lonnie cruised by slowly, cruised slowly round the corner onto Route 311. There were some weary-looking clapboard houses here. A barbershop. A restaurant. The offices of a weekly newspaper. And then the strip mall: a long parking lot bordered by a Stop-n-Shop, a Rexall's and—there it was—the First National Bank.

Lonnie could see right away why Carol had chosen the place. There was a gas station beside it, then a few more houses on the road beyond. But after that, the pavement rose sharply and the forest closed in fast. The town sank back into the forest as quickly as it rose.

Lonnie glanced at the clock on the dashboard. Two-twenty-seven in bright green digits. Still early.

He drove past the parking lot. Pulled into the gas station.

He filled the Beamer's tank. He bought a wrapped

sandwich at the shop inside. His scarred black face felt like a wanted poster pinned to his head. Any minute he expected someone to spot him and start screaming.

There was an enormous woman behind the shop's counter. In her uniform blouse with its broad stripes of red and white she looked like some kind of gargantuan peppermint. Lonnie kept his eyes lowered as he paid her.

"Have a good one," she muttered—but she hardly looked at him. By the time she spoke, she'd already turned away.

Lonnie went into the men's room. Pissed. Washed his hands, his face. Looked into the mirror, into his own eyes. His hunted, haunted eyes.

"Man oh man," he said aloud to the reflection, "I wouldn't want to be you."

He left the shop quickly, quickly returned to his car.

He drove back to the mall. Parked at a distance from the bank. Shut the car down. Sat there.

He ate his sandwich and watched the bank. The bank was a brick box at the far end of the lot. There was a thick glass drive-through window on one side. As Lonnie watched, one car then another pulled up for cash. The cars drove on again, parked again nearer the supermarket.

Lonnie ate his sandwich and watched the bank. Two or three people walked into the bank building. They stopped in the foyer to use the cash machine. Then they came out again.

The minutes turned slowly over. The sense that he was noticeable, sitting there, even suspicious—a black man casing a bank—began to press in on him. This was a small town deep in the woods. Not many strangers passing. No other blacks that he could see. He began to feel hot in his overcoat.

It was two-forty. Two-forty-five. A pale middle-aged woman entered the bank. A blustery man in a windbreaker. A housewife type with her long red hair pinned up. The blustery man used the cash machine and came out again.

Where the hell was Carol? What was keeping her?

Lonnie finished the sandwich. He felt as if the world were drawing in on every side of him. As if he were at the center of a narrowing beam of light, light narrowing to a glaring pinpoint that would attract all eyes his way. An old woman pushed a shopping cart past the front fender. A heavy-browed mother with two screaming boys went by. A waddling fat man in a plaid shirt . . . As each passed the car, Lonnie felt himself clench inside, felt himself wait for it—the shout, the jabbing finger— *There he is!*

Nothing. No one noticed him. It was two-fifty.

Where the hell was she?

Lonnie made a sort of drumming noise between his teeth. *Ch ch-ch-ch ch-ch-ch.* He wagged his head back and forth. The car was growing colder, but he wiped sweat from above his mouth.

Two-fifty-five. Another five minutes and the bank would close. Had he missed her? Where the hell was she?

"Damn it," he said.

He got out of the car.

The back of his neck prickled as he walked across the lot. The scar on his chin, the color of his face, just the fear radiating off him—he felt like a walking alarm bell. He was glad to reach the bank's glass door. To pull it back, step into the foyer.

The pale woman was still there, standing at the cash machine. She glanced over her shoulder as he came in. She smiled at him.

Lonnie smiled back. He went past her, through the glass foyer, through the inner door, into the bank.

The main room was small, rectangular. Two thirds of the way between Lonnie and the far wall was the counter, a chest-high counter running from one end of the place to the other, from the drive-through window on the left to the open vault door on the right. There were three people behind the counter, two female tellers and a heavyset man in a suit. To Lonnie's right were a couple of desks. A woman was sitting at one of them tapping at a computer keyboard.

Lonnie stopped in his tracks. He held his breath. Everyone in the room had looked up when he came in. Everyone was watching him. It was a small bank. He was the only customer in sight.

This was a mistake, he thought.

But running away would be even worse, even more suspicious. Casually as he could, he walked over to a narrow ledge on the wall to his left. There were pens there and deposit and withdrawal slips. He took a pen from its holder, a deposit slip. Dawdling, playing for time. Sweating under what he felt were the steady stares of everyone in the room. He hardly knew what the hell he was doing.

A minute passed or maybe it was a day. Two more customers came in, both men. One, in slacks and a corduroy jacket, walked over to the counter to talk to a teller. The other, also in slacks, also in a corduroy jacket, walked over to the bankers' desks and sat down across from the woman there.

Lonnie glanced at the men.

Cops, he thought.

But he shook the thought off. He couldn't start pan- icking now. He went back to mulling over his deposit slip.

"Sir?"

Lonnie looked up quickly to find one of the tellers blinking at him from behind her large glasses.

Excuse me, sir, but how did a Negro fugitive such as yourself come to be in our lovely white bank?

"Say what?" said Lonnie.

"I said, 'May I help you, sir?' " the woman repeated.

Lonnie licked his lips. Managed a brief smile. "Uh, I was . . . Actually I was just waiting for someone," he told her. He abandoned the withdrawal slip on the ledge. He backed away from it. "I was supposed to meet her here. But I don't . . ."

And still, he felt the stares, the silent stares. The frightened eyes of the women, the belligerent eyes of the heavyset man. Only the two customers in corduroy seemed oblivious to him.

"Well . . ." said Lonnie. "I guess, uh . . ."

He was about to turn and hurry away when the red- haired housewife he'd seen before came out of the open vault. He glanced at her.

It was Carol Dodson.

2

It was a good disguise. Not just the hair—copious, flowing bright red hair that drew your gaze—but her complexion, the shape of her eyes, the shape of her mouth had all changed. It was small stuff, subtle stuff, just makeup effects, but it altered the look of her completely.

Only her little start of surprise when she saw him gave her away. That—and the jolt of warmth and longing he felt, the surprising power of his urge to help her.

She was just coming out of the vault. She was folding the edges of a small manila package, trying to stuff the package down into her purse. She glanced up—very cool, very casual.

And that's when they spotted each other.

Lonnie felt his breath catch. He saw the hitch in her movements, saw her lips part.

Then she continued stuffing the package into her purse. Smiled her thanks up at the heavyset man.

And Lonnie, likewise, finished his sentence to the woman behind the counter. "Well, she's not here. I guess I'll see if she's over the way."

The teller smiled at him. Tightly, he thought, nervously, but he didn't have time to pay attention to her now. He was walking back to the foyer door. Carol was walking directly behind him. He put his hand on the door. Pushed it open, held it open for her.

She gave him a nod of thanks, their eyes meeting. She moved level with him.

"Chubb sent me," he murmured to her.

She stopped cold. Right there in front of him, right before the open door. He thought she was startled by what he'd said. Then he realized she was staring at something outside.

He followed her wide gaze. Looked out through the foyer, into the parking lot.

The police had arrived in force.

There were three cruisers out there suddenly, a fourth already pulling in. The cars were lined up end to end to form a barricade. Under that cover, officers scrambled for position, bent double, pistols drawn. Townies, county deputies. Some riflemen with their weapons already propped on the cruisers' hoods and trunks.

The bank was under siege.

As Lonnie, in that single instant, scanned the scene, he spotted the giant peppermint woman from the gas station. She was gesturing wildly at the bank while an officer tried to calm her down, tried to push her enormous bulk out of harm's way.

She had recognized him. She had called the law. Lonnie understood it all.

It was over. They had him.

He stared. Carol stared. Neither moved from where they stood at the foyer door.

A voice, startling, sounded from behind them.

"Just step away from the door, Mr. Blake. We don't want any trouble."

Lonnie and Carol both looked around.

The two customers in the corduroy coats of course.

Plainclothesmen. Of course. One by the bankers' desks, one by the tellers' counter. Both had drawn their service revolvers.

Both were pointing them at Lonnie Blake.

Lonnie looked from one plainclothesman to the other, from one gun barrel to the other. He glanced outside again at the battery of rifles.

He had only felt like this once before: when he had identified his wife's body. When he had seen her stretched out on that long white table—so cool, so cold, so fair—and realized that all hope was gone, that every option had collapsed, every appeal was exhausted, every avenue closed.

Then, as now, he had felt a wild, blinding, animal rage before the incontrovertible fact of his own helplessness.

Lonnie looked at the policemen around him and he thought nothing would feel better than to pull out the Cougar and just start shooting.

"Just step away, Blake," the plainclothesman by the desk said more urgently. "We don't want anyone to get hurt."

Lonnie took a deep breath . . .

And then Carol threw herself backward against him.

"Don't shoot!" she screamed. "He'll kill me! He means it!"

For a single frozen second, Lonnie gawped stupidly down at the red hair piled on top of her head. He had let go of the foyer door. It was swinging shut.

Then he got it. He wrapped an arm around Carol's neck. Pulled out the Cougar and jammed the muzzle to her temple.

"I'm serious, man!" he shouted. "Put your guns down! I'll blow her away!"

"Jesus," said the plainclothesman by the desks. "Hold your fire. He's hot a gostage."

"A hostage!" Carol shouted.

"A hostage!" shouted the plainclothesman. He had his two-way in his hand. "He's got a hostage!"

Lonnie swung from one cop to the other, clutching Carol, swinging her body back and forth while she let out a shriek.

"Don't anyone think about it, man!" Lonnie screamed. "Don't anyone think about anything! Just hold your fire and no one gets hurt!"

"Oh please! Please!" Carol cried.

"Now I am walking out of here, man," said Lonnie. "You tell those boys outside they better keep their trigger fingers soft as their dicks. One mistake and she dies, you hear me?"

The plainclothesman by the desk made a calming gesture at him. "Easy. Take it easy," he said.

"You tell 'em, man!" Lonnie said. "I'm going out there. You tell 'em."

He shouldered the foyer door, pushed it open, muscled himself and Carol through.

The corduroy copper at the counter feinted toward him.

"Don't you do it!" Lonnie yelled over his shoulder.

Carol threw in another shriek for good measure.

The cop held back. The other cop, the one at the desks, had his two-way to his mouth, was calling to the barricade.

Swinging Carol this way and that, Lonnie pushed his way out into the foyer. The door swung shut behind them.

They were alone in the glass box—trapped there between the guns in the bank and the guns in the lot outside.

Lonnie leaned back against the wall, gasping for breath. Holding Carol in front of him all the while, his arm around her throat.

"Not so tight," she gurgled. "I'm strangling."

"Man oh man, are we ever gonna die," he said.

"No, we're not. I can't die. I have a child."

"Well, forget it then. I'll give myself up. They won't shoot you."

"Yeah, right. They'll just haul me in for the killings in Manhattan. Once the cops've got me, Winter and his guys'll have me in a second."

"Shit," Lonnie said.

"Stop strangling me, damn it!"

He loosened his grip on her neck.

The sound of their frantic breathing filled the little space. The tiled green walls, the staring mechanical countenance of the cash machine, the glass doors on either side seemed to Lonnie to yaw this way and that as his eyes roved round in a desperate search for away out.

"Jesus," he said.

"Listen . . ." Carol began.

"Blake!" Lonnie stiffened as an amplified voice

pierced the foyer. "This is Undersheriff Lester Jackson!"

"Christ, with the bullhorns now," Carol muttered. "These clowns watch too many movies."

"Yeah, well, it sounds like this is the scene where they start shooting."

"Just listen to me . . ." she said.

"Let the girl go!" boomed the undersheriff.

A crazed laugh burst out of Lonnie. " 'Let the girl go.' I'll bet he's always wanted to say that." The sweat poured off him.

"Just listen, listen. We're going out," said Carol. "Right now, before they have time to think. Where's your car?"

"Too far. Behind the barricade."

"All right. We'll take mine. It's just to the right of the door. We're in it, we're gone."

"Put down your weapon and come out before someone gets hurt!" said the amplified undersheriff.

"What're you driving?" said Lonnie.

"A yellow Bug," she said.

He laughed wildly. "Great. Those yellow ones are fast."

Carol snorted and burst out laughing too, stifling it in the arm he held around her throat.

"It's all right . . ." she said, laughing.

Lonnie tried to answer but only started laughing again. He hid his face in her hair so the cops wouldn't see.

"I've got a plan," she said.

This made Lonnie laugh until the tears came.

"No, no, really, it's a good one," she laughed.

"Come out with your hands up, Blake," said the undersheriff.

Lonnie snorted loudly, trying to stop the laughter.

" 'Come out with your hands up,' " he said. "Can you believe this cat?"

"Come on," said Carol. "Before he starts doing his Al Pacino impression."

Lonnie took a breath. "All right," he said. "All right. We gotta be serious now."

She giggled into his arm.

"Come on!" he said.

"All right," she said. "I'm okay. I'm serious."

"We'll be the comedy team of Dead and Buried."

"Let's just do it."

Lonnie nodded. He pulled her closer to him. His face was pressed into her hair. He caught the scent of violets and tobacco.

"Okay," he said. "This is it."

And he dragged her out of the bank.

"Don't anybody move! Don't get smart! I'll kill her, man, I mean it!"

♦The bullhorn had fallen silent. Everyone in the mall lot had fallen silent. As the fugitive and his hostage edged out of the building, they were a single point of movement and noise in a vast tense motionless quiet. Carol's slender form kicked and writhed. Lonnie wrestled with her, holding the gun against her head.

"You just stand there, motherfuckers! Just put your guns up! Just take your fingers off the fucking triggers! Just stand there!"

He dragged her sideways, away from the doors, out of the firing range of the plainclothesmen behind him. She let out small, breathless shrieks of anguish as they moved along. They were very convincing.

"Fuck up and she dies, man, you hear me?" Lonnie screamed. The fear in his voice was convincing too. Well, it was real. Any minute he expected to hear the crack of sudden death.

They sidled along the wall of the bank. The policemen watched. The crowds, pushed back to the supermarket across the lot, watched. Some, like children, held their fingers to their open mouths.

Lonnie's mind raced, worked, as they moved, trying to keep track of the logistics. It wasn't easy, this hostage business. If he took his eyes off the bank door, the plainclothesmen might follow him out and open fire. If he turned wholly away from the riflemen—*pow*—they would take him down.

He pressed himself hard against the side of the bank, moved with Carol through the hedge-and-wood-chip border between the building and the pavement. The rifles propped on the cruisers followed their progress. The eyes of the policemen followed them. The eyes of the people by the supermarket followed them too.

And all around, the chilly air was still. No cars were passing on the street or moving in the lot. No birds were singing in the nearby trees. There seemed to be no sound at all beyond Lonnie's gruff shouts and Carol's little cries.

He inched along, dragging Carol with him. There

was a line of parked cars in front of him now. Carol's yellow Volks was five cars down.

It was seventies vintage. They were definitely going to die.

"Don't anybody get smart, man, don't anybody do a thing, not one fucking thing!" Lonnie screamed.

He negotiated Carol's kicking, twisting form along the bank wall, over the wood chips, toward the yellow Volks.

"You got the keys?" he muttered.

"Yeah," she said breathlessly. "Right-hand coat pocket."

They reached the car. Moved around to the side of it. Its humped little body gave them some scant protection from the rifles in front of the bank. But there were more cops to the other side of them. This was going to have to be fast.

He pulled the keys out of her pocket. Crouched down between the Volks and a Buick, drawing her down with him. He had to let her go then. Transfer the gun to his left hand. He had to pray the cops didn't find a clear shot between the cars before he got the door opened.

He tried to get the key in the lock. His hand was shaking too badly.

"Damn!" he said.

"Hurry up," she whispered.

The key went in. The door was open. He put his hand on the back of Carol's neck and pretended to force her inside. He followed after while she was still climbing across the stick shift to the passenger seat. Her feet kicked at him.

He shut the door. Stuck the key in the ignition. Carol was twisting around, sitting up now beside him. He handed her the gun.

"Here, hold yourself hostage a minute," he said.

His heart was beating jig-time. It seemed to swell like a balloon every time it beat. He turned the key over hard.

Putt-putt-putt went the little engine.

"Mm, listen to her roar," said Lonnie softly.

Carol exploded with laughter. She bowed her head, covered her face with her hand. "Shut up, shut up, they'll see me laughing," she said.

He shoved the stick into reverse. He felt the eyes of the police all around him. He felt their guns trained on him.

" 'I've hot a gostage,' " he muttered.

Carol bent over, laughing hard.

Lonnie pressed his foot down on the gas.

Putt-putt-putt went the little yellow car's engine.

"Shit," said Lonnie Blake.

"Just go! Go!" said Carol.

Lonnie backed out of the parking space, swung the Volks around. Shifted. Floored the gas. And sputtered past the police barricades, past the trailing guns. Waiting for the crack of the rifle. The shattering glass. The second of searing pain.

Then the Volks bounced over the curb, out of the lot, and they were on the street again.

"Up the hill," said Carol breathlessly.

Lonnie laughed bitterly as the little bug began to strain up the grade. He shifted back down into first gear. The car edged up to thirty miles per hour. He glanced out the window, back at the mall.

The cops were scrambling for their cruisers. The red beacons were whirling. The cries of the sirens began winding up over the little town and into the lofty sky.

"Here they come," said Lonnie.

"Just go, man, will you," Carol said.

"I'm trying, baby."

The Volks whined as the hill grew steeper. They neared the top. Lonnie flipped the stick into second. The car sprung forward, up over the crest. The mall disappeared behind them. They started rolling downhill, gathering speed.

"Yeah," Lonnie murmured. "Yeah, yeah, yeah."

He goosed the car through its gears. They accelerated to forty, then to fifty. Ahead of him, he saw the last of the town vanish. The forest closed in on either side, brown wood crowding the macadam, tangled boughs and vines fading back and back into deep mysterious distances.

And the air grew thick with sirens and the sirens grew louder. Lonnie glanced at the rearview mirror. The first red beacon was rising over the crest of the hill.

"Okay, here they are," he said. "What's the plan?"

"Just stay ahead of them," said Carol.

He laughed. "That's the plan?"

"Just to that next turn down there."

The lead cruiser leapt the crest. Its front tires came down hard.

Lonnie tore his gaze from the rearview. Looked ahead, through the windshield.

The hill plunged through the lowering woods. The road curled away at the bottom out of sight.

He tried to push the gas pedal through the floor. They were almost going sixty.

But the cop cars were gaining. A line of three was visible in the rearview now. Their sirens were growing louder every second.

And the curve below was coming nearer. Lonnie watched it racing toward the windshield.

"I think I can, I think I can," he said.

Carol laughed. "Shut up! Just drive."

Lonnie glanced in the rearview. The headlights of the lead cruiser glared at him like two great eyes, growing larger.

"Oh, Lordy," Lonnie said.

And then the cruiser slipped out of sight behind as the Volkswagen rounded the curve.

Lonnie glanced at Carol. Her stare was riveted forward. Her face was set. Her hands were out in front of her, clutching the edge of the dashboard, white.

He faced the windshield. Saw where the road forked up ahead. Another two-lane went off to the left.

"Which way?" he said.

"Left."

If there had been oncoming traffic, they'd have been cut in half. Lonnie wrenched the wheel and the Volks slid across the two-lane and down the left fork.

They buzzed over a small rise in the pavement, then down the other side, out of sight of the main road behind them. It would gain them a second or two, Lonnie thought. When the cops reached the fork, they wouldn't know which way to go.

For a second or two. No more than that.

Sure enough. The sirens behind them dimmed a moment, but a moment later grew steadily louder again. The Volkswagen was shuttling through the forest shadows at little more than sixty. The cops were gaining again.

Then Carol said, "There! Go in there!"

Lonnie looked. He saw the garbage.

It was just off the shoulder, maybe ten, fifteen yards into the woods. One of those illegal dumps that seem to grow up everywhere by America's forest roads. There was the shell of an old Chevrolet, a busted chest of drawers piled atop busted chairs. Car parts, tires, plastic bags full of God knows what. A great pile of the stuff.

Lonnie understood. He twisted the Volkswagen's wheel. The little car rumbled off the road. It went bumping over a worn forest path, straight for the trash.

Another moment and they were in it. The car rocked hard from side to side. Sticks cracked under the tires. A bag burst. Pebbles flew. Lonnie wrestled the wheel around hard. The Volkswagen circled behind the big carcass of the Chevy.

"Kill the engine," she said.

He turned the key. The engine died.

"Now wait," she said.

They waited. Their panting breath was loud in the little car. The sirens were loud and growing louder. They sat there and Lonnie felt the suspense like insects crawling under his skin. The Chevy's skeleton only partially obscured the Volks from the road. A sharp-eyed cop would spot the yellow paintwork in a city minute.

They waited. The sirens grew louder still. Lonnie looked at Carol. She looked at him. He wondered if his eyes seemed as enormous as hers, as frightened.

For one more second, the sirens screamed louder until Lonnie thought he would burst with waiting.

Then the first cruiser raced past, its shrill cry skirling down. He saw it through the dead Chevy's windows.

Then another passed with a whisk of air. And then a third.

Then a lull. They waited.

"They split up to cover the fork," said Carol. "Let's go."

"Go where?"

"Come on."

She pushed the Volkswagen's door open. He did the same on his side. She tumbled out into the woods and so did he. She ran and he ran after her. A moment or two and he'd overtaken her, had seized her hand, was pulling her along behind him.

"There," she panted. "Up ahead, up that hill. Before they figure it out."

They charged up a narrow path, over a small ridge. The sirens were in the high branches of the trees all around them. Lonnie grunted as his legs stretched for the ridge top. Carol fought for purchase on the dust and stones as he practically lifted her behind him.

They were over, out of sight of the road, half running, half tumbling down the other side into a valley of trees.

Lonnie skidded over the yellow leaves. He came up hard against the trunk of a white birch. Gasping for breath, Carol slid around in front of him.

"Come on," she managed to say. "They'll be back any minute."

She pushed off the tree, stumbled away again. In a moment, he was stumbling right beside her. He stopped when she stopped and followed her eyes as she scanned the woods.

To him, it looked like nothing, like a thorny wild. He was a city boy, his whole life long. He'd never really been in a forest before. All he saw was a mesh of vines and branches, a vast stretch of tangled emptiness. All he heard were the leaves blowing over the ground, the branches chattering, the whispering wind.

And the sirens, of course. They hadn't lost the sirens.

Carol said, "Okay."

She took his hand and led him on.

There was another rise. Another tumble down a slope over slippery leaves. A great rock loomed out of the earth to Lonnie's left. Carol tugged him past it, whispering, "Come, come, come."

Then she stopped. Lonnie stopped beside her. He looked—stared. At first, he wasn't sure what he was seeing.

There was a gap in the earth before him. A gaping black hole right there in the rocky ground. Lonnie had never seen anything like it. It looked unreal to him. Surreal. Like a tear in the very fabric of things. There was the forest all around and then this black hole, like a doorway into nothing, and everything seemed to be falling into it: the ground funneled down to it and the trees leaned toward it with their roots half torn from the dirt and hunched up like great spider legs and even the living limestone slabs that formed its massive border seemed about to cave in and vanish through the enormous gateway and into blackness.

I mean, what the fuck is that? he thought.

The two stood only another moment. The wind rose. The trees above them swayed, cracking. Leaves swirled out of the air and pattered to the forest floor. A siren grew louder, grew nearer. It peaked, then stopped ominously.

Lonnie glanced back over his shoulder. Swallowed hard. Had the police spotted the Volks? He could no longer see the garbage dump.

"All right," said Carol. "We better hurry."

She moved toward the hole. As she got closer, the ground dipped fast beneath her. She had to lower herself onto it. Pick her way down over the rocks.

She glanced up. Lonnie was still standing there, watching her.

"You coming?" she said.

In there? he thought. "Oh," he said. "Yeah. Sure."

He started climbing down after her, the limestone cold on his fingers.

Soon, he was beside her. Right at the border of the hole. It didn't get any brighter in there. It was lightless, bottomless as far as he could see.

"Listen," he finally couldn't help asking. "What the hell is this? Where're we going?"

"It's a sinkhole," she said—as if any idiot would know. "Haven't you ever seen a sinkhole?"

"Oh!" he said, climbing. "A sinkhole! Right. I guess I didn't recognize it there for a minute." *I mean, what the fuck . . . ?*

Carol went on down over the sinkhole's edge. She reached for purchase on the rocks around, found it expertly. Her face was hidden by a fall of red hair as she looked down at her feet. But Lonnie could see her breath rising up in little puffs and plumes of frost.

"So this is, like, some kind of cave or something," he said.

"Yeah." She was panting from the climb. "That's it."

"Well, then, aren't we gonna get cornered in here?"

"Hell, no. It goes on for miles. Has four different

exits. The cops won't know which way we went. They'll never find us."

"Will anyone?"

Carol laughed. Then she vanished. Her voice trailed up from the gaping dark.

"Hurry up, man. You gotta stay with me. You won't make it through here alone."

"Yeah, tell me about it," Lonnie muttered.

And then he followed her into utter blackness.

CHAPTER 12

THE WHOLE DARNED WORLD TURNED UPSIDE DOWN

1

Roth sat perched on the examination table. Stripped to his underwear. Dazed with an almost religious wonder. Not to mention half an hour of intravenous Demerol only now beginning to wear off.

So? he thought. *What's the prognosis? I'll tell you what's the prognosis. Paradise. Immortality. Death shall have no dominion.*

Yeah, he could just see the doctor saying that. *I see by your chart, Professor, that the Lord God will swallow up death in victory and wipe away tears from off all faces.* He could just imagine the headline in the *Journal of American Medicine: Death Shall Be No More. Cranky Jew in Gadkes Heralds Coming of Child Messiah.*

Roth pinched the bridge of his nose between thumb and forefinger. He could barely keep from laughing. Laughing? How could he keep from singing? He was cured! He knew it! He was fucking cured!

The doctor—a boy who barely looked old enough to collect the pencil tops from cereal boxes—was standing just outside the door. He'd been returning to the examination room and had paused out in the hall to chat with one of the nurses. His hand was on the knob and the door was slightly ajar. Because the whole world needed to see a flabby-titted old man in his Fruit of the Looms.

Roth snorted laughter, but a wave of nausea, a druggy

haze of it, washed over him. He closed his eyes and swayed where he sat.

Finally—after a nice, pleasant talk with Lovely Nurse Nelle with the door half open—finally, Dr. Dentons deigned to return to his naked patient. Carrying his Official Authoritative Clipboard no less. Which he probably got as a prize for selling magazine subscriptions.

"You can get dressed now, Professor Roth," he said cheerily.

"Thanks. Don't think I don't appreciate it."

He moved slowly, lowered himself slowly off the table. Shuffled unsteadily to where his clothes hung on a hat rack in the corner.

The doctor went on speaking behind him.

"We won't have the biopsy back for about a week, so right now we don't know anything for sure. The X rays were inconclusive before but . . . I mean, they seem perfectly clear to me. You sound clear. The cough's gone, right? There's no sputum. There's not much point doing another MRI until the lab work comes back. The way things stand . . ."

Roth, buttoning his shirt, turned around in time to see the doctor shrug. He wasn't sure whether it was the aftereffects of the Demerol or a burgeoning sense of man's puniness before the miraculous works of the Almighty but, in either case, his eyes suddenly misted over.

Didn't this munchkin understand? There wasn't any *need* to see the lab work. There wasn't any need for Roth to have come here at all. He already knew everything he needed to know.

He had been sick. He had been mortally ill. And then a little girl had . . . done something . . . touched him. She'd touched him, and now he was well. I mean, wake up and read the headlines, Doc: MIRACLE TOT IN END OF DEATH SHOCKER!

Roth bit his lip, fighting back the tears.

Mr. Medicine, embarrassed, examined his zippy I'm-a-Doctor clipboard. "I'm sure this hasn't been easy for you," he muttered.

Roth gave a laugh, shook his head, pulled on his trousers. "Tell me something," he said hoarsely. Pulling the pants closed. Buttoning up. "Have you ever wondered whether everything you've ever believed, everything you've ever been taught, everything you hold most true— your values, all those facts you know, every single thing— whether it was all just wrong? Just simply wrong?"

The young doctor thought about it. Shook his head. "Not really. No."

Roth smiled with one corner of his mouth. Yanked up his zipper. "You ought to try it sometime," he said.

He walked back from the Medical Center. Worried about any lingering dizziness from the drugs, he had left his car, his old Citroën, at home. A nurse had asked him if someone—a friend or family member—would come to pick him up. He'd lied, said yes, embarrassed to say there was no one.

There was no one. He walked back alone.

He shambled slowly over the sidewalk toward the campus. Pausing frequently. Leaning on lampposts, trees. He took deep breaths. The cold air braced him. The Lord-have-mercy hallelujah wonder of it all—that braced him too.

As he neared the quad, he stopped awhile. Pressed his shoulder into the oddly feminine curve of a gruff old maple. Looked out over the way, past the crisscrossing traffic. Watched the campus. The ivied brick. The long white wooden barracks. The little elms and birches. The neatly trimmed grass. The students walking on the pathways.

The students. Young. God. They were unimaginably young.

Roth contemplated them from afar. Children. Little children. New ones every year, and every year the same. Once the predictability of their thoughts and emotions had made him cynical. He had smirked at their confidence, their conviction that they were original, incorruptible, fresh and wise. Only the great Roth understood that they were merely a few more droplets in the ceaseless human sea . . .

But now—now how marvelous they suddenly appeared to him as well. Even their silliness, their still-adolescent attitudes—the lazy, sullen, lordliness of their ignorance—for the first time, it all struck him as touching, as dear.

All these years, he had fought to teach them. He had fought to bring them to the well of the classical world so they could drink from the tradition that had formed them. He had fought against the leftist and feminist cant that was being drummed into their heads: the Great

Ideas of the Moment that were tomorrow's silence and ash. He had fought to bring them what was steadfast in the whisper of the mighty dead.

He had fought to bring them Western civilization.

And he had lost.

All these myths you love to tell them. I just don't think they're important to us anymore.

It was true. He was irrelevant. The battle for the hearts and minds of the young was over. The field belonged to ignorance and ideology: to Althea Feldman.

And it had seemed there had been nothing for him to look forward to but bitterness and rage.

And now—all at once—they were gone. The rage, the bitterness. The tumor in his lungs was gone and they were gone. Gone completely. And the children looked beautiful. And the day was fine. And *shine, perishing republic,* he inwardly sang.

> *While this America settles into the*
> *mould of its vulgarity . . .*
> *   life is good, be it*
> *stubbornly long or suddenly*
> *A mortal splendor: meteors are not*
> *needed less than mountains:*
> *   shine,*
> *perishing republic.*

Roth finally understood. All was as it should be. Existence was a rose of bliss.

He smiled. Pushed off the feminine maple. Moved on.

Unfortunately, by the time he reached his house, the last effects of the drugs had pretty much worn off and the rose of bliss was beginning to develop a canker of care. He stood on his leaf-strewn lawn before his porch steps, under the hanging empty branches of his trees. And he was tired. And he felt as if lead were running in his veins instead of blood. And he needed a cigarette. God, he needed a cigarette.

He clung desperately to his religious joy but nonetheless felt it slipping inch by inch away. Doubt was seeping in, steadily poisoning his ecstasy.

It couldn't be real. What he thought had happened to him. It couldn't have happened to him. Not really. There were so many other possible explanations.

What if the tumor had been imaginary to begin with? What if it wasn't gone at all and the biopsy came back positive? What if this sure and certain sense that he had been somehow healed was simply an illusion?

And then, on the other hand ... what if it *was* all true? What about that? What the hell did *that* mean? What *could* it mean?

He needed to know what the hell this was all about.

I'm an intellectual, damn it, he thought. *I'm not just going to stand here and be happy!*

He turned away from his own porch and lifted his eyes to the house next door. Geena MacAlary's house.

Where Amanda was.

He headed for it.

3

He stood at the door, peeked in through the sidelight. He could make out Geena's silhouette in the darkness within. She was sitting on the sofa. Elbow on the arm, chin on her fist. The classic pose of Contemplation.

Roth knocked gently. Saw her turn her face toward him.

"It's open, Howard," she called. "Come in."

Roth entered, closed the door. Stood at the edge of the rug. The lights in the living room were off but the windows admitted the afternoon sun. There was a sort of border of reddening radiance on one side of the place giving way to a central shadow.

Geena remained in that shadow. Roth peered at her but her features were difficult to make out.

The silence between them went on an unnatural moment. Then Roth said, "Is she . . . is she all right?"

"I don't know." Geena swallowed hard. "I mean, she's better but . . . I don't know."

"Can I see her?"

She nodded. "She's upstairs. She's looking at the book you brought for her. The myths."

Roth didn't answer. Heavily, wearily, he started to move past her to the stairs.

"Howard . . ."

Geena caught his hand as he neared the sofa. He stood and looked down at her. Now he could see her clearly, her sweet features set in a tired frown, her intelligent eyes frantic.

She searched his face and the two of them understood each other: he knew.

She drew her hand away. She covered her eyes with it. Roth patted her on the shoulder softly. Then he walked on to the stairs.

He found the child sitting up in bed. The book of mythology was held open on her middle. It hid her from him almost completely. When Roth came to the doorway he could only see the dome of her head above the book jacket, the arc of yellow hair.

He knocked on the open door. Amanda let the book fall flat and looked up at him. It pained Roth to see the sickly, ashen pallor beneath the tan surface of her skin.

"Hello," she said to him. "Thank you for the book."

He found he was almost misty again just at the sight of her. A lump rose in his throat. Who was this child who had touched him? *What* was she?

"Hi there," he said gruffly. And added, "You're welcome."

He swung a chair from its desk to the bedside. Swung it backward. Straddled it. This was not a child's room, he noticed, glancing around. It looked as if it had been a study or a den—a sewing room probably, judging by the little white table with its lathe-turned legs. The place had only been hastily rearranged for its new purpose. The Hollywood bed, Sesame Street sheets and coverlet. A *Beauty and the Beast* coat hanger on the wall against the dull grown-up diamond-pattern wallpaper.

A small chest of drawers had been brought into service as a bedside table. There was a reading light on it, the bulb supported by a juggling clown. A pink clock with a smiling pony on the face. A stack of picture books. A palm-sized dollhouse which somehow Roth knew was called Polly Pocket. There was also a photograph. A picture of a woman in a Winnie-the-Pooh frame. Hands in the pockets of her windbreaker. Legs akimbo in jeans. She was standing out in a field somewhere, out in the blustery weather. Her frizzy hair was windblown. Her smile was bright. From the shape of her face and eyes Roth guessed she was Amanda's mother. He wondered where she was. He found himself thinking: *Arise . . . and flee into Egypt . . . for Herod will seek the young child to destroy him.*

And again, he had to fight down tears.

He cleared his throat. "So," he said. "Geena tells me you're feeling better."

"Okay," she said. "Will you tell me some more stories?"

"Uh . . . Yeah . . . Sure . . ."

"I want to hear the one about Dem . . . Dem . . ."

"Demeter?"

"Yes. And her daughter."

"I . . . uh . . . sure," Roth said again.

She gazed up at him with her solemn brown eyes, waiting.

Roth shifted in his seat. Her gaze seemed to go right through him, see right into him. *Thank you for the book. Tell me more stories.* What did it all mean? he wondered. Was there something she was trying to tell him?

"Listen," he said finally. "I'd love to tell you more stories. That'd be great but . . . I have to ask you something first."

"Okay," she said.

"Well . . ." He gave a nervous laugh. Scratched his

fringe of white hair. "Did you . . . ? Did you do something to me, Amanda?" He laughed awkwardly again but there was no comedy in his heart. "Did you . . . When I was coughing. Is there something you did?"

Amanda broke the connection between them, looked away.

"Amanda?" said Roth.

"I'm not supposed to tell you."

Roth opened his mouth, gave a long slow nod. "Ah-ha." And what did *that* mean? She wasn't supposed to tell him. Because . . . why? Because Mom didn't want the publicity? Because it was a top government secret? Because her Father in Heaven wanted to keep things quiet until He broke the seventh seal? What?

He pressed her. "But you saw me coughing, right? You knew I was sick and . . . ?"

Amanda frowned down at her book, at the picture of Orpheus leading Eurydice by the hand. She touched the photo of the marble figures. "You said you were going to die," she said.

"I did?" Roth couldn't remember.

The child nodded gravely. "When you were coughing. You said you were going to die."

"Uh-huh. So . . ."

She lifted her eyes to him. "So I sparkled you."

"You sparkled . . . ?" In a rush, Roth understood. His hands rose to the sides of his head. He stared at her in wonder. "You sparkled me." He laughed as the tears sprang to his eyes again. "Merciful God," he whispered. It was true.

"Are you all better now?" Amanda asked him.

He could barely speak. He nodded, pressing his lips together. "Yes," he finally managed to say in a broken voice. "I'm all better."

After a long moment, he lowered his hands again. He looked down at her. She looked back deadpan. Roth made more vague gestures as he sought for words. There were so many questions he wanted to ask. He hardly knew where to begin.

"So . . . Is this . . . ? I mean, is there . . . ? Is there something . . . something this is about . . . ? Is there something you want to tell me?"

A second's silence. The child gazed at him solemnly. Then, drawing out the word, she said, "No-o."

Roth grimaced with effort. Maybe he wasn't saying this right. "What I mean is . . . is there . . . something you want to, you're trying to tell me or . . . people or . . . Like a message, I mean. Is there a message you want to tell us? Or something . . . ?"

"I don't know," said Amanda singsong. "Like what?"

"Well . . . A message. You know. Is there something you want to . . . to teach us or . . . or say to us or . . . teach the world? You know."

The child considered this very deeply. Then slowly, she said, "I don't think so. I'm only five."

At which point, Roth heard how silly he sounded and simply cracked up. He pinched the bridge of his nose and squeezed his eyes shut as tears spilled out over his fingers. He sat straddling the chair and shook like Jell-O, laughing silently.

"What's so funny?" said Amanda, smiling along.

"Everything apparently," said Roth at last.

4

Geena stood waiting for him at the bottom of the stairs. Roth came down to her, still flicking tears from the corners of his eyes. As he reached the last step, she took hold of his hand again. Her fingertips were cool against his palm.

"So apparently I've been sparkled," he said hoarsely.

"Howard, listen . . ." Geena's voice was soft. "Have you told anyone? Your doctor . . . ?"

"No, no, no. Of course not."

"Not anyone? It's important, Howard. You may be in danger. We could all be in danger."

"Yeah, I know," he said. "Amanda told me. The bad men want to steal her. Look—you don't have to tell me anything if you don't want to . . ."

"No. No," she said with a forlorn little laugh. "You already know enough to get us killed."

"Yeah, well, I'd like to avoid that if I can. Hell, if I can, I'd like to help you." He puffed his cheeks, pushed out a breath. "But it would clear my head a little if you would tell me . . . I mean, what the hell is it, Geena? Am I imagining it, is it some kind of gift from God, is it magic . . . ?"

"No," she said—said sadly. "No. It's just . . . it's just really . . . a terrible, terrible mistake."

A moment's silence. Then she led him into the shadows, over to the sofa. They sat down together. She folded her hands on her lap. Her features were dim in the dark.

"It's hard to know where to begin," she said. "I don't know that much, not all the details. What I do know I found out because . . . Well, there was a girl. A woman I went to nursing school with. Marie, her name was. After school she went to work for a pharmaceutical firm called Helix."

"Sure," said Roth. "I've heard of them."

Geena nodded. Thought a moment, sitting still in the shadows.

"Have you ever heard of T.T.?" she asked him then. "The Therapeutic Touch?"

He snorted. "What, you mean, like, nurses touching people to help them heal. Yeah. Sure. I heard something on NPR about it. I thought it was all supposed to be bullshit."

"Well . . . it's like any talent," Geena said. "Most of the people who claim to have it don't. And even those few who do, well, it's not as if they understand anything about it. They sit around and talk about 'energy realignment' and 'transferred intentionality,' and a lot of New Age nonsense like that."

"Yeah? But . . . ?"

"But," she went on, sighing. "But all the same, some people do seem to have a gift, a slight gift of some sort anyway . . . And so apparently, about seven or eight years ago, some researchers at Helix decided to see if they could locate the source of it. It was just this—small, sideline project, you know. They must have a thousand of them going on all the time. The idea of this one was to gather some people who claimed to be healers, cut away all the woo-woo energy stuff, and focus on the immune system. Cytokines, especially."

Roth gave a little shrug.

"Cytokines," Geena repeated. "They're proteins that carry information between cells. You hear about some of them sometimes in the news—like interleukin-2 or interferon?—because they can stimulate healing and boost up the immune system, some of them, by sending messages between cells in different parts of the body. And the idea was . . ."

"I get it. Maybe they could somehow send messages from one body to another."

"Exactly. Exactly," she murmured, as if to herself. Then: "Anyway . . . Helix located a small number of patients who seemed to possess the power of Therapeutic Touch and injected them with a drug that was supposed to stimulate the thymus gland to produce a kind of super-cytokine. If nothing else they thought it might ultimately be used as a vaccine of some kind. But the thing is . . . the thing is . . . when they injected these people . . ."

"They didn't tell them."

"The subjects thought they were just part of a study on healing powers. They thought the shot was one of a series of vaccines given to protect them from the diseases they might encounter during the study."

"Jesus," said Roth. "Helix Pharmaceuticals. Touching Your Life Through Immoral Chicanery."

"Right."

"But the drug worked obviously."

"No! No!" said Geena. "It was a disaster. Within two years of the test, every one of the subjects was dead. Some kind of autoimmune reaction, a monster version of myasthenia gravis. It was awful. The people were just . . . devoured—devoured from within. And the worst part was, since the victims didn't know each other and weren't aware they had anything in common, no one had any idea what was happening."

"No one but the good people at Helix anyway."

"Right," said Geena MacAlary out of the shadows. "Helix realized they had to cover their tracks, erase the records of the tests and so on or risk bankruptcy, lawsuits, even jail. But at the same time, secretly, they continued to do follow-up work. Because the drug was known to have effects at the genetic level and a few of the subjects—three of them—had had children in the period between the test and their deaths. And as it turned out, those children . . ."

"Oh God. Oh man!" Roth sat blank-faced. "Man oh man oh man." He was beyond trying to sort out his emotions now. Fear, disgust, wrath at what these Helix turnip-heads had done—and amazement at the same time, wonder, *elation*—because it had really happened. He'd been *healed*. Each new discovery convinced him afresh that it was true.

Geena went on. "It quickly became apparent that at least two of these children had significant healing ability. Which caused a problem for Helix because if anyone started looking into it and connected the company with the tests that had killed the parents . . . well, it would've been worse than bankruptcy, it would've been jail for a lot of very important people. They knew they had to prevent these children being discovered by the public, but they were unsure how to proceed. The Research Department wanted to kidnap the kids and run experiments on them to see if new drugs could be developed from them. The Legal Department just wanted to kill them—you know, erase any evidence that

the tests had ever taken place. But then Business Affairs
. . . Business Affairs came up with the bright idea of kid-
napping the children, doing a few tests—and then selling the kids' abilities to people overseas."

Roth didn't get it. "Selling . . . ?"

"You know. Some rich person who's sick, who's willing to pay millions—tens of millions—for an instant
cure. And it was a perfect plan because, listen to this,
Howard. As it turned out, the children's ability was fatal
to them."

"I don't get it. Fatal. What do you mean?"

"After they used their Therapeutic Touch a few times,
the same autoimmune reaction set in that had killed
their parents. For Helix, it was perfect. Research got their
tests, Business made a profit, and Legal got rid of the evidence—after performing a number of cures for cash, the
children got sick and died."

"Jesus," said Roth. "They died?"

He saw Geena's silhouette nod. "Those first two of
them did anyway. They were the two who were born to
stable people with fixed addresses. So it was easy for
Helix to trace them, keep track of their development.
They got them right away, the minute the healing ability
showed itself. They stole them, used them, sold them.
Killed them basically."

"And the third child was Amanda," said Roth.

"She was harder for them to find. She's the illegiti-
mate child of a sailor named Tom Wilson and a woman
named Carol Dodson. It was Wilson who was given the
drug. And he met Carol afterward. And she was . . . and
she wasn't anyone really, that's the point. Just a high
school dropout. A waitress, barmaid; kind of a lost soul."

"Uh-huh. I get it, I get it."

"So she was already hard to keep track of and then . . . Then the follow-up on Wilson's case was done by my old school friend."

"Ah," said Roth. "Enter Marie."

"That's right. Marie was one of a very small group of people who knew what was going on. I can't make any excuses for what she did, but at least when she found out what was happening to the children, she rediscovered her conscience. She was too late to help the first two kids. But she managed to sabotage the company's records so they couldn't find the Wilson-Dodson child, Amanda. Then Marie went to Carol Dodson herself and warned her what might happen. Carol didn't believe it at first, but then the healings started. A neighbor's fever, a child's cold. Amanda is very . . . generous. She always wants to make people feel better. And she has the power far more strongly than the other two. It was unmistakable from the start. So Carol knew—Marie convinced her—that the minute word got out, Helix would find a way to hunt her down." Geena studied her hands in her lap. "Fortunately, she's a very resourceful lady, Carol. Very tough, very independent—and very scared too. She didn't tell anyone. Didn't trust anyone. Didn't ask for anyone's help. She just took to the road. Never stayed in one place very long. Wandered around, earned whatever money she could, mostly off the books. Did whatever she had to to stay alive and keep her head down, keep out of Helix's radar. It might have worked too. Except one of the towns she passed through was Hunnicut, Massachusetts."

"Oh yeah. Yeah. Where the jet crashed."

"Right. And, of course, Amanda 'sparkled' someone. And there was a witness—some hysterical woman who thought she saw the baby Jesus performing a miracle, bringing someone back to life. That's what she told the tabloids anyway. And they printed it—and that was enough to put Helix on Carol's trail."

Roth gave a small, mirthless laugh. He was beginning to get the big picture. "Wouldn't it have been simpler if someone had just called the cops on these bastards?"

Geena drew breath. "Marie did. Marie went to the cops. She was afraid to at first. She thought they wouldn't believe her and . . . and she felt Helix was too well connected, that any official complaint would get back to them. So at the beginning of it, she came to me instead. She said our acquaintance was old and tenuous enough that she thought Helix wouldn't find me. She asked me if, in an emergency, I would give the child a place to stay. I only half believed her, but of course I said yes. And she passed my name on to Carol."

"Who showed up after Hunnicut."

"Yes. She said she was going to try to put together enough money to get Amanda out of the country and then come back for her."

"Great. And what about Marie? You said she went to the police."

"Yes. After she came to me. She went to a policeman friend she had in San Francisco. Three days later, her body was found in the waters off the Golden Gate."

"Uy." In the tumult of his feelings, Roth let the small groan escape him. He got to his feet. Paced. Rubbed a hand over his bald pate. He stood still finally, stared absently into the shadows.

"All right. So let's see," he said. "What we got here, we got major bad guys coming after us. The cops can't be trusted. Our only ally is this high school dropout barmaid running around doing God knows what. The child won't stop using this power she's got and if she uses it often enough she'll die horribly. Am I missing the good news here?"

"The good news . . ." Geena sighed. "Well, there is some."

"Please."

"Possibly—okay? Possibly . . . According to Marie—the Helix researchers believe that Amanda's ability will wear off. The reason the drug worked on the children and not the adults was because the thymus gland does most of its important work in childhood. It stops growing around puberty—and the researchers predict that when that happens the healing ability will disappear."

"Puberty." Roth snorted. "She should live so long."

"Well, yeah. That's it. If we can keep her alive for another six or seven years, she could become normal. In which case, Helix will have no use for her and no reason to be afraid of her."

"Wonderful. Six or seven years."

Now Geena stood too. Came to him, stood near him. "Howard, you have to promise me . . ."

"What."

"If you tell anyone . . . *anyone* . . ."

"Ach. Please. I'm a curmudgeon, not a shithead. I just want to know if there's anything I can do to help."

In answer, Geena gave a little sniff. And then, to Roth's surprise, she tilted toward him and pressed her face to his chest.

So Roth put his arms around her. Her hair was soft and clean-smelling under his nose. The press of her large breasts against him was rich with comfort. It had been a long time since he'd held a woman.

"I'm sorry," she said. She pushed away from him. Smiled miserably through tears.

Roth smiled back. He had never found her particularly pretty. A sweet face is how he'd always put it to himself. But now the darkness softened all her features and he saw just how sweet a face it was. Soft, kind, gentle.

Everything looks beautiful to me today, he thought.

He reached out and laid his palm against her damp cheek. "Tell me what you want, Geena," he said.

Her slender shoulders rose and fell. "I just don't want her to die, that's all."

"Die?" he said. "What, are you kidding? Who's gonna kill her? Some ruthless multinational corporation? She's got a classics professor and a retired housewife on her side."

Geena laughed.

Roth said, "The bastards don't stand a chance."

5

Roth trudged wearily back to his house. Cutting a meandering pattern across the lawns. Barely lifting his feet to walk so that he made a *chk-chk-chk* sound among the fallen leaves. He was muttering to himself. Chuckling sometimes. Looking around at the trees, the sky, the rooftops. Shaking his head. Chuckling some more. An absentminded professor pondering an arcane joke.

Geena watched him from her window. He was a good man at heart, she thought. He just wasn't very good at life, poor soul. Still, he was a decent neighbor and she had always liked him. And when she asked herself now if he could be trusted, she felt pretty certain that he could.

She watched a moment more as he dragged himself wearily up his porch steps. As he opened his door. As he pushed into his house. She was sorry when he had gone inside, when he was out of sight. She felt alone then and she felt the full weight of her responsibility.

But her decision was already made.

She moved away from the window. She moved across the shadowy center of the room. To the fringe of light. To the table. The telephone.

She picked the phone up. Hesitated. But no. The child was ill, the secret was out. The mother had to be told.

Geena punched in the contact number. She stood in the half-light, waiting for the distant ring.

CHAPTER 13

STARDUST

1

Cold, sterile stone, invisible. A chilled, cumbersome humidity in the air. Something always slick and slippery beneath his fingers, green to the touch. Lonnie had never known such blackness. They went down and down.

He felt for handholds. Every time he touched the stone, he was afraid there might be something there. Something alive, slithering beneath his fingers. Bats or spiders or some shit like that. Gigantic worms with fangs. Well, how the hell was he supposed to know? The only sinkholes he'd seen in Oakland had liquor licenses. This was not his sort of scene at all.

Now and then, Carol would call to him. "You have a foothold to your right." Or, "It's wet here, be careful." He was thankful simply for the sound of her voice. And now and then she would flick on a flashlight, a small yellow box she must've carried in her purse or pocket. Its wan beam would trace a path for him over the expressionless rock. Lonnie's heart would practically leap with gratitude then. Light. God, the light.

When the light went off, the instantaneous shroud of darkness was suffocating.

Down and down. A world of stone and absolute shadow. Lonnie had never been claustrophobic before, but this was dreadful; dreadful. They were beneath the earth, he kept thinking. They were *down here*, man. There was no way out. Just dead rock on every side and nothing else. No light. No air. No earth. No color, no living sound. A circus could be going on right above them. A carnival. Carousels and Ferris wheels. Children could be chasing each other through the green grass. Couples could be holding hands. A girl in a flowered dress could be standing there, lifting her face up to the sun. And Lonnie could reach up for her, dying down here, dying, and she would never know. He could cry to her for help, he could claw himself bloody against the rocks. He could breathe his last and rot to bleaching bone. And that girl, that girl in the flowered dress, she would bask in the light and shake out her hair and wander off dreaming of love and be none the wiser.

Shit.

As he thought these things, an unfamiliar feeling was growing in him. Panic, that's what it was. He was a hard-assed dude but that was sure enough panic beginning to scrabble at his chest, a frantic creature trapped inside him. *I gotta get outta here*, he thought, sweating in the chill air.

But they went down farther and farther still.

"Hey. Hey, Carol. They got any animals or things or, like, bats down here?" he finally asked her. He tried to sound casual about it. He tried not to sound like some kind of pussy.

"Pussy," she said.

"Hey. This is not exactly my neighborhood, you know what I'm saying."

"Yeah," she said. "This is *my* neighborhood, okay? I grew up here. I know every inch of this place."

"Yeah?" That made him feel a little better.

"Yeah. I wouldn't worry. You might see a bat. That's it. Most living creatures hate these places."

"Well, you can add me to the list."

Carol chuckled breathlessly. The sound faded away beneath him. Down and down.

The worst of it came after an hour or so—it felt like an hour; it might have been less—or more—he'd lost all track of time. For yards, the passage through which they'd been moving had been getting narrower and narrower. Lonnie could no longer stand up straight in it. He was bent over, his hand touching the slick stone wall close on either side.

And then Carol said, "Okay. This is the tight part."

"The tight part?" She turned on the flashlight and Lonnie said, "Oh man!"

The beam illuminated an almost solid wall, green and smooth as a backyard pond. The ceiling above this wall was so low that Lonnie was forced down to one knee as he approached it. But that was not the worst thing. There was water flowing on the floor here and gritty mud, which soaked through his pants leg and grimed and scraped and chilled him.

But that was not the worst thing either.

The worst thing was the crevice. The one that Carol was pointing to.

"No way," Lonnie said.

"Just like being born, sweetie."

"Yeah, but after being born, you're alive. I mean, like, that's the whole *point* of being born. Nobody just does it for fun."

"It's this or the cops behind us, take your pick," she said.

He didn't answer. She handed him the flashlight.

Then she went into the crack in the wall.

Lonnie's stomach rolled just watching her do it. The rock seemed to swallow her. Her legs waggled behind her as if she were struggling to break free. Then her legs were engulfed as well. And then her sneakers pulled so close to the rock he could only see the soles. And then—like the last bit of spaghetti being slurped in—those also disappeared. The crevice stood empty. Waiting for him.

"Hurry up," it said in Carol's breathless voice. "The faster you do it, the better it is."

Well, Lonnie could believe that all right. Already, the sounds of her movement were fading. He was alone here with the thin flashlight beam and nothing around or behind him but darkness and stone.

He took a breath, approached the gap. It was no good. He was a lot bigger than Carol. He couldn't even begin to figure out a way to corkscrew his body into the thing. When he did—when he got his head through—there was just no squeezing his shoulders past the edge. He backed off. He couldn't hear Carol at all now.

"You still there?" he called.

She didn't answer.

"Man, I am getting to be sorry I tried to help this woman," he said.

Quickly now—desperate to catch up to her—he stripped off his overcoat. He wrapped it into a bulky parcel, careful that his gun was held inside. He stuffed the parcel into the crevice. Then he went after it. This time, his shoulders just barely made it through. His torso. His legs.

He was in the tunnel.

He dragged himself along, pushing his coat ahead

of him. The gap didn't get any wider. There was just enough room for his body—and no room at all for the panic that now swung screeching and grabbing like a gibbon in his upper frame. His arms were stretched out, were stuck in that position. He could hardly bend his legs. If he hadn't had the flashlight picking out little patches of hard green nothingness here and there, he felt he would've gone crazy right then and there.

"Carol?"

Nothing. Just his own breath racketing off the walls. His own slow progress, the sound of him dragging along the damp floor. The walls pressed close against him, clamped around him. Once, tired from the slithering exertion, he stopped to rest. That was the worst. Lying there, unable even to turn his head. The tunnel became a coffin around him. The dark beyond his flashlight threatened to bury him alive.

He wriggled on frantically, grunting, panting.

"Lonnie?"

Her voice. Oh yeah. Yeah, yeah, yeah. A human voice. It was like water in the desert to him.

"Carol?"

"Keep coming. A little more. You're almost there."

Almost there. He pushed the coat ahead of him. Fought his way after it. And then he felt the coat moving on its own. Carol pulling it. He felt her hand touch his.

"Thank you, Jesus."

He spilled out into an open chamber. She was there, helping him find his footing. She squeezed his shoulder.

"You're all right," she said.

"Whoa! Nothing to it. No sweat. Whoa, mama!"

She took the light from his trembling fingers. Held it

while he caught his breath. He was shaking so much it was hard to put his coat back on.

"Whoa!" he kept repeating. "Whoa, mama! Whoa!"

And now—her face white in the outglow of the flash—Carol smiled at him. Tilted her head.

"Come here," she said.

He followed her across the chamber's sloping floor. When he was beside her, she turned off the light.

"Look up."

He looked. Saw nothing at first, the cave's utter nothing. Then shifted his gaze. Was there a glow? Yes. A gray glow.

"Come over here," she said.

He followed the sound of her. Moved to look from another angle.

And he saw . . . oh, light. The light of the world. A little silver dollar of it far, far above.

"Look at that. Look at that," Lonnie heard himself murmur.

Color. There was color in the light. There was warm air coming to him redolent of life and you could make out brown and blue and yellow. The brown of tree bark it was, the blue of sky, the yellow of autumn leaves. Oh, he thought. Oh, oh, oh. Brown and blue and yellow. How could he have seen such wonders every day and never known the meaning of the word *hallelujah*?

"Cool, huh?" said Carol.

"Yeah," said Lonnie, laughing. "Cool."

"Let's go," she said.

They started climbing.

2

She led him through the forest a long way. The sun was going down by the time they stopped to rest. The dark drops fast in the woods and even though they could see the dusk horizon still bright beyond the tree line, here the air was deep blue and they had to peer hard through gloaming to find their way.

They came over a rise. Something—a structure—a hulking silhouette—loomed blackly beneath them. They were almost on top of it before Lonnie could see it was some sort of tower—a chimney—of gray stone.

Carol stopped, panting. Lonnie stopped. Looked around him.

There were more of these things. Black towers, roofless black cubicles of stone, sudden black pits lined with stones interwoven, fragments of a wall. As if a primitive village had been abandoned here. It was eerie. Ghostly, with the trees swaying in the deepening dark, their wood cracking, the leaves whispering down.

Carol moved through the indigo twilight to where a small stream trickled over pebbles. She knelt and drank from her cupped hands. Lonnie knelt beside her and drank. The water was gritty but cool.

After a few moments, Carol rose, moved away from him. She dropped to the ground beneath a pillar of stones. She leaned back against the pillar, her knees raised, her hands draped over them.

Lonnie stood, too, but remained where he was. He panned his gaze over the mysterious shapes around them. At every sound the trees made or the leaves made or animals made scrambling for cover in the underbrush, he turned suddenly, searching the dusk.

"What the hell is this place?" he said finally.

"When I was a kid, we called it Auburn," she told him. "There was some kind of town here once. In colonial days, I think. I don't know. I don't know what happened to it. The story used to be that everyone died in some kind of plague or something. It was supposed to be haunted. You know. We used to dare each other to come out and spend the night, that kind of thing. There's even a graveyard just out there, beyond the buildings. It's pretty spooky."

She pointed to the graveyard with her chin. Lonnie, following the gesture, made out the black shapes of headstones amid the trees. She was right. It was pretty spooky. Dead folks out there in the night, the stones all grown over, all hidden in the woods, the leaves falling on them. He shuddered, turned away.

Carol gave a wry smile. "Look at you. You were such a tough guy in the city. Don't you like the forest?"

"Hey, are you kidding?" he said. "They got bears out here—werewolves, shit like that."

She laughed. "Yeah. Well. The thing is, there's at least a couple of miles of forest in every direction. The cops won't try searching for us with the dark coming on. By morning we'll be gone."

"Oh yeah? You got another plan, huh."

"Soon as the fuss dies down, I'll go buy us another car. No one'll recognize me without this."

She reached up and pulled off the red wig. Set it on

the ground beside her. Patted her short curls back into place. It was so dark now that he couldn't see the color of them. But he remembered their honey brown well enough.

"What're you looking at?" she said.

Lonnie gave that little snort of his. "Pretty girl, that's all."

She shook the curls out. Paused. Glanced up at him through the gloaming.

"What the hell are you doing here, Lonnie?" she said. "Why did you come after me?"

He moved toward her. Stood over her. "Chubb said you were in trouble. Said if you called his place they'd trace you—that Winter guy. Executive Decisions, whatever. Chubb wanted me to come tell you where he's arranged a pickup for you."

"And you just did. With the cops after you. Just like that."

He gave a sort of shrug. Shifted around beside her. Lowered himself down to sit in the leaves beside her, his back against the stone tower like hers.

He eased his legs out before him. He felt her eyes on the side of his face. Smelled her sweat and the scent of her on the chill air.

"Haven't I caused you enough trouble?" she asked him.

Lonnie laughed a little. "Just about. Just about enough, yeah."

"And you still want to help me."

He took a breath. Turned to her. Met her eyes, the spark of her eyes in the twilight. "I don't know who this Winter is, who these Executive Decision people are. But they're gonna have to come through me."

"Because . . . I had sex with you? Because I pretended to be your dead wife?"

He looked away from her. Looked out across the forest ghost town. He didn't know how to answer. Man, she was a hard little creature, this Carol. Out here scrabbling, fighting, running. Challenging him with her flinty eyes. Hard and ferocious.

She was nothing like his wife. His dead wife.

They sat in silence. The dark closed in on them like hands closing. The stone walls and broken houses and chimney towers and gravestones sank deeper into silhouette, became more abstract, became shapes among the other shapes: tortuous branches spreading above and coiled vines hanging; hunched roots grasping at the earth and smooth rocks slanting out of it. The twilight wind arose and soughed and the brook gabbled and now and then there came the sudden crunch of an animal scuttling over the leaves.

"They killed her, huh," Carol said finally.

Lonnie nodded. "Yeah." He had been thinking about it as they sat there. "Bunch of guys. White guys. Called her names. Chased her. She ran out in the street. A car . . ."

"Oh." She let it out in a long slow sigh. "That's tough."

"Yes it is."

"I was you, that'd pretty much make me hate every white man on earth."

Lonnie gave another short laugh. "Yeah, that's it." He leaned his head back against the stone. Gazed up through the black branches above. The stars were coming out. "Nah, shit," he said. "I've seen ugly in all colors. I don't care about any of that. I'm just out here, man. I'm just me."

"You mean, like, you hate *everybody* on earth."

"Now you got it."

They both laughed, their heads tilting together. Then they were quiet.

Then she said, "So how come I'm the exception?"

He faced her. They were very close.

"How come you gotta know?" he said.

He kissed her. She hadn't let him the first time and she pulled away now too. But then he drew her back, his hand on her cheek. She let him press his lips to hers. She pressed hers to his softly. His tongue went warm into her mouth. Her fingertips were gentle against his face. They kissed a long time.

Finally, she drew back again. She looked at him, looked him over. Without saying anything, she shifted on the ground. Lowered herself a little. Put her head tentatively against his chest. He put his arm around her. They sat like that. After a moment or two, he felt her begin to tremble. She was weeping.

Lonnie held her. She rocked her body against him. Now and then a sob broke from her. The air grew colder. The dark grew full. The wind that had risen at twilight subsided. The million forest noises combined into a single stillness into which she wept.

"I don't give a fuck about anything," she cried angrily into his coat. "You know? Except my baby. I don't give a fuck about any fucking body anywhere. Except my little girl. That's all."

Lonnie nodded, holding her. "I understand. It's okay."

She yanked back away from him. Glared at him through the dark. "You don't understand. You can't understand."

"I understand," he told her. "You don't give a fuck about anybody."

"That's right. Except my little girl."

"I get you."

"You hear me?"

"I hear you. It's okay."

She sniffed once. "All right," she said. She began to settle back against him. "I don't care what I have to do," she said more quietly. "I'll fuck anyone I have to. I don't care. It's just my body, it's not me. I don't care about any of them." He put his arm around her. She put her head on his chest again. "I just get the money and it doesn't matter. I don't give a fuck. I'm gonna get her away from these bastards no matter what it takes."

Lonnie kissed her hair.

"I don't care about anything else but that."

"I know," he said.

She sniffed again. "And I don't let *anyone* kiss me. You understand? Nobody fucking kisses me. Ever. I don't care."

"I thought it was just your body."

"Shut up."

He smiled. "It's okay, Carol."

He put both arms around her now and held her against him. She made a terrible noise and began to cry hard again.

"I just get scared, Lonnie," she said. "I'm just so . . . out here. You know?"

"I know. We're all out here, baby."

"I get so fucking scared."

He held her. He kissed her hair and gazed over her into the dark. The hulking stone shapes of the dead village, the graves all but invisible in the night beyond, the murmuring leaves, the branches creaking. He began to sing to her under his breath, a tuneless jazz lullaby at first, softly at first, and then even softer, half a whisper, the old music just sort of rising out of him. He could hear it as he sang it, he could hear it in his head, the way the saxophone would play it full volume with a texture like honey and the slow notes shattering like stardust into countless hurried notes that skittered swiftly through a tune still slow. Like stardust.

> And now the purple dusk of twilight time
> Steals across the meadows of my heart.
> High up in the sky, the little stars climb,
> Always reminding me that we're apart.

He sang to her and he thought: *I would've sung it to you if I'd been there, baby.* That was the burden of his song, the burden of his heart. *I would've held you and sung it to you just like this.*

He would've too. He would've held her in his arms and crooned it to her for her comfort while she died. He would've stood outside the gates of eternity and sung it to her through the golden bars forever. He would've sung so sweetly, he would've played her such sweet melodies, they would've opened up the doors of death itself and let him be with her again.

> You wander down the lane and far away
> Leaving me a song that will not die. . .

He would've held her in his arms and lifted her and brought her home to the years she should have had and the children she should have had and the life she *would* have had if he had been there to protect her.

If he had only been there.

Ah, but that was long ago.
Now my consolation is in the stardust of a song.

He tilted back his head, leaned his head against the stone chimney, sang into the murmuring forest, stretching the notes and bending them, bending one sound down into another until it reached that borderland between them which they sometimes call blue.

"Nice," Carol murmured against him. She had stopped crying now. "That's nice."

She held on to him. He sang to her. A blue lullaby. "Stardust." The music surrounded them and seemed to deepen the stillness of the woods, to leave the forest wholly silent until it seemed as if the ghosts of this dead village and its standing stones, its graves, its ruined houses, the trees and vines and brush that had grown over them, the animals among them, and the sky above had all paused in their various motions and in their one vast synchronized rotation from dark to dark—had paused and gathered round them and were listening, as she was listening pressed against him, to the sweet and living and mournful sound he made.

CHAPTER 14

A TELEPHONE

THAT RINGS

1

It became midnight. There were still some lights on in the Black Tower then. Someone heading home along Madison Avenue might have looked up and seen them through one window or another, their glow dimmed to a yellow-brown by the tinted glass, the building's interior hazy. If he'd craned his neck, he would have seen the light in the penthouse on the thirty-third floor. But with the height, and the darkened glass and the venetian blinds, he couldn't have seen what was happening inside.

Winter was in there, and his employer, Jonathan Reese. They were sitting at opposite ends of a large oval conference table. The light that burned there hung just above the table's center. It was the only light on anywhere on thirty-three. The rest of the offices were deserted.

Reese, just then, was in the process of drawing out a pause, milking the silence for all it was worth before he continued speaking. He was taking a perverse sort of pleasure in this final confrontation.

The power was all on his side this time. He was dressed for battle, his pinstripe as sleek as Winter's navy blue, his tie pin as golden, his cologne as rich. And, while Winter, the assassin, had mastered a sort of studied smoothness of manner, Reese felt fully aware of the fact that his own breeding came to him naturally. It was his birthright, and his civility was honed to a razor edge.

On top of which, he was here to hand the man his walking papers. So for all Winter's martial, not to say savage, talents, Reese felt fully master of the situation.

"We want to part company without any personal hard feelings," he said finally. He gave a pursed smile through steepled fingers. "We understand that you came late to the operation. Executive Decisions' American bureau was just opening, it wasn't up to your own high standards yet. I mean it, Winter. We understand all that and we wouldn't hesitate to recommend you or to use your services again." He tapped his fingertips together twice as he said this. It was a lie—they both knew it was a lie—and it made Reese feel mighty indeed to tell it, and to be disbelieved with impunity. It was odd, he thought. Whenever he fired people, he always wound up feeling a kind of contempt for them. As if they wouldn't have been in this position if they'd only played their cards right. As he went on, he sounded a little condescending even to himself. "The problem is: this project has just become too . . . what's the word? *Fraught*— fraught with risks of various kinds. It's expensive for one thing. And considering the uncertainties and time constraints, we're not entirely sure we'll be able to show a profit over the long run. Plus the unfortunate . . ." He made a show of searching for the kindest way to put it. ". . . delays and . . . unforeseen events make us feel concerned about the issues of secrecy, containment, security, that sort of thing. Basically, we want to quit while we're ahead. We're casting no aspersions on you or your organization. We're just terminating the entire operation, that's all."

He was at the end. He fell silent. He would give Winter the dubious dignity of a response and then bring this meeting quickly to a close. Already, part of his mind was moving on to the trip home. A few days off at the house with April and his son. He was looking forward to it.

He watched Winter over his steepled fingers and waited for his reply.

The red-haired man nodded. Smiled blandly into Reese's eyes. "I understand," he said without expression. "I've already spoken to your board."

Reese's lips parted. He was shocked. The board? It took him completely by surprise. It set off all kinds of alarms. Was his independence being challenged? Was his authority being questioned? He tried to maintain his appearance of control and superiority. He gave a curt nod, a noncommittal "Uh-huh."

But Winter obviously knew he'd hit home. "We've agreed to continue our relationship solely on a contingency basis," he went on smoothly. "E.D. will sever all communications with your firm unless and until the target is recovered."

Another blow. Reese couldn't deny it, could only just hide it. An arrangement had been made behind his back! His hands came slowly away from his face. He tried to keep the rising indignation from entering his voice. Tried instead to sound dark, dangerous, threatening. "I wasn't consulted about this," he said.

"No," said Winter with a casual—possibly even mocking—gesture of one hand. "It's as you said: issues of secrecy, containment, security, that sort of thing. That's why they wanted me to have this meeting with you."

Reese narrowed his eyes. "I don't understand."

"Well, they asked me if before I left I wouldn't mind killing you."

"What?"

"Which, of course, I wouldn't," said Winter. He drew a good old-fashioned .38 revolver from his jacket pocket. "But it would help if you'd hold still for a minute," he added. "They want it to look like suicide."

Winter had this in common with the late Jonathan Reese: he felt a faint contempt for the people he destroyed. Maybe it was the contempt of all survivors for the dead. He felt that if they'd wanted to avoid their fates they should have been smarter or stronger or quicker or simply somewhere else.

So as he rode down the Black Tower in the elevator after the termination of his meeting, he reflected that it was hypocrisy that had killed Reese really. Well, of course, *he* had killed Reese really, but it was hypocrisy that had brought the situation about. Reese, so to speak, had sneered at the hunter while eating the meat. He had wanted the big money, the big house, the security, the privileged family life. But he thought himself superior to the ugly side of the business that provided him with these things. He felt superior, that is to say, to Edmund Winter.

Winter buttoned his Hugo Boss overcoat, smoothed down the front of it. *No, no, no, no, my friend,* he thought. As long as there's dirty work to be done, it's the man who does it who ultimately holds the power. Enjoy the comforts of civilization, yes, but stay in touch with your inner savage. That was the lesson to be learned here today . . .

By the time he left the elevator, however, by the time he crossed the lobby with a smile at the night watchman, stepped out onto the avenue and into the chill of the first minutes of morning, he had lost this train of thought. He had put Reese out of his mind completely.

He was thinking about Carol Dodson again. He felt certain that the hunt was finally drawing to a close.

Chubby Chubb's suicide had delayed him, there was no question about that. But even with his hard, professional eye, Winter couldn't blame himself. It was the incompetence of Mortimer and Hughes that had made it necessary even to find Chubb in the first place. And— Chubb being a shrewd and careful old bird with excellent connections—it was hardly to be expected that he would let himself be taken alive for Winter's brand of questioning. His death was a predictable contingency.

Now, anyway, they had the smuggler's papers, his phone records and so on. They were beginning to establish the pattern of his calls over the last few days. They were beginning to uncover his current connections and work out the possible links to his old smuggling operations.

Winter was already fairly certain that Chubb had been arranging Carol's escape somehow. Getting cash for her, papers. Probably sending her to one of his former rendezvous points in the East—one of the islands off Massachusetts or Maine, the old Meridian Lodge in New Hampshire or the abandoned camp near Lake

Placid, New York. A generous act on his part; a change
of personality for the former criminal. But then maybe
resurrection'll do that to you. Who can say?

Winter could picture just how it had happened.
Chubb—delighted at not being dead—had probably
given Carol a contact number and offered his help. But
Carol had been smart, trusted no one, operated on her
own—until she felt her pursuers were simply closing in
too fast. Then, in her hour of need, she had turned to the
man her daughter had touched at the plane crash site . . .

Heading to the corner, Winter shook his head in
admiration. That Carol. God, he'd come to like that
woman. For every trick he pulled, she pulled another.
For every inch he tightened the cordon, she took
another risk in her efforts to break free. She was like
. . . like some sort of noble beast—a deer, a lioness—
twisting and turning in a brave, doomed effort to avoid
the implacable hunter.

Yeah, he thought. He liked that. *The implacable
hunter. Little old me.*

But no self-satisfaction, he counseled himself, no
arrogance—and no mistakes. The end was not a sure
thing by any means. Reconstructing Chubb's plans
would probably give them Carol's current destination.
But if she actually had cash, a false identity, a lift out of
the country . . . well, that would magnify their difficulties
at least a thousandfold. Once she could move through
the entire world anonymously, she would be a very sharp
needle in a very big haystack. Finding her would be a
lengthy and expensive proposition. Helix had already
withdrawn its backing and the E.D. head office would
neither approve nor support a contingent operation of
that magnitude.

Not that that would stop Winter, of course. He was going to find this babe eventually, one way or the other, for profit or just as a matter of honor. Besides, with her intelligence, her courage, her maternal ferocity—she had captured his imagination. He had very specific plans for her once he caught her and he wasn't going to be cheated out of his simple pleasures.

So as it turned out, Winter experienced a sense of disappointment when his big break finally came. Because, ironically enough, his people didn't locate Carol Dodson at all.

They found her child. They found Amanda.

Winter had now walked around the Black Tower and left Madison heading for the parking garage on Fifty-third. His mind was running over fresh approaches, checking any angles he might have missed. And he hit on Lonnie Blake. He had heard about the crazy spear-chucker's disastrous attempt to rob an upstate bank. He wondered if he should divert a little of his overextended manpower to track the fuckhead down and kill him before he caused some kind of unforeseen trouble. Sort of a support-your-local-incompetent-police-type operation.

But then it occurred to him to wonder: maybe Blake's escape was not entirely unconnected to Carol Dodson's. It seemed unlikely Mortimer and Hughes could've been right about anything but, on the other hand, what if just for argument's sake . . .

But before he got any further, the cellular vibrated inside the pocket of his overcoat.

He glanced around. There was an attendant smoking idly in front of the garage and a bouncer shifting his shoulders outside the gay bar across the way, but for the most part the street was empty. He pulled out the phone.

The caller was using a scrambler. His voice—her voice maybe—sounded nasal and mechanical, but the words were clear.

"We've intercepted and traced a call to the target's voice mail. A woman named Geena MacAlary in Morburne, Vermont."

"Yeah?" said Winter. He lifted his arm high as he held the phone, protecting himself from the cold wind off the East River. He turned his back to it, faced the west.

The operative went on. "The voice print on the caller indicated a very high level of distress and it seems possible her message was a coded warning. The content was: 'Hi, it's me, stop. Why don't you come up and visit, question. Bernadette and I would love to see you as soon as you can make it, stop. Okay, question. Bye, stop.' End of message."

"Bernadette," said Winter with something like a laugh. "As in Lourdes."

"Yes, affirmative. And a preliminary check on MacAlary shows she went to the same nursing school as Marie Davenport."

"The Helix RN," said Winter.

"Affirmative," said the toneless voice.

It was then that Winter experienced his disappointment. Standing there with the phone to his ear. Gazing to the west through the mist of his own breath. He nodded to himself. This was it; they had her. They already knew it was Marie Davenport who had alerted Carol. So Carol had sent Amanda off to MacAlary. It made sense. It was right. It was over.

And Winter felt disappointed because now he could get the child without ever catching up to Carol Dodson at all.

"Our nearest operative," said the remodulated voice on the phone, "is a New Hampshire state trooper named Ike Lewis but I thought . . ."

"No, no, no, you're right," said Winter. "No more fuck-ups. I'm handling this personally. With the jet I can be there in a couple hours. Get Ferdinand and Dewey to meet me at Newark and have the New Hampshire man join us at the nearest airstrip to Morburne."

"You got it."

He killed the call. Pocketed the phone. Shrugged off his disappointment and headed for the garage.

All right then, he thought. He would get the kid first. Carol Dodson was sure to follow.

On to Vermont.

About the same time, Geena MacAlary received a phone call too. It dragged her out of a deep sleep. She found herself sitting upright on the living room sofa in the dark. All the lights in the house around her were off. She wasn't sure for a moment where she was.

Then the phone chirruped sharply again and she jumped. Rolled to her feet. Hurried to the sound.

Stumbled over the leg of a chair and then—as she disentangled herself—barked her shin against a low table.

"Ow! Sugar!" she said. She grabbed the phone.

"It's me," said a soft voice.

Carol! Geena let a sigh of gratitude rush out of her.

"How is she?"

"Fine," said Geena quickly. "Well, she's better. She was really sick at first. I almost had to call a doctor. But it's like you said. She's improving. God, I'm so sorry. I told her and told her. She was only out of my sight for a few minutes . . ."

"No, no, I know. It's hard. She likes to do it. She likes to make people feel better."

"She's asleep upstairs now anyway." Geena paused. She swallowed. "Are you coming?"

"I'm on my way."

Geena sagged with relief.

"Figure three A.M.," Carol said. "You know that McDonald's right off the interstate? That's twenty-four hours, right?"

"Yes. I think so."

"Okay. Three A.M. Bring her there. That way I can just pick her up and keep going."

"Okay," Geena said. She hated the high, frightened trembling of her own voice. She shook as she waited through a long pause.

Then Carol said, "Geena? Listen. I think they're close. Okay?"

"Oh God." It broke from Geena in spite of herself.

"No, no, it's all right. They don't know about you but . . . I had to leave New York in a big hurry so just . . . be careful. You know? Especially when you leave for McDonald's. Keep an eye out. Be careful."

"I will."

"And if I don't make it . . ."

"Don't say that."

"Get out," said Carol. "Wait for me and if I don't make it by three or so, then get out and get her out. All right?"

"Just make it," said Geena.

"I will," said Carol. "I'm on my way."

Geena hung up. The quiet that followed filled the house. It made her shiver and hug herself, her frightened eyes darting this way and that. All around her was the dark. She felt it pressing in on her, alive with menace. She felt it everywhere in the house.

And it was dark, she knew, in all the wide world beyond.

In that darkness, Lonnie watched for the moon.

"Just sit there," Carol had told him. "Just keep looking out in that direction. About forty minutes, an hour, the moon'll come up. A half-moon. Should be around midnight. Okay? Most of the leaves are gone, you should be able to see it no problem. Just move around a little to make sure, okay? And when it comes up? Just head straight for it. Maybe twenty minutes, you'll come to the road. I'll be there. I'll be waiting for you."

Then she'd kissed him. Then she'd left him there.

He'd sat against the chimney tower. He'd watched her, flicking her flashlight on and off. Trailing through the dark where the beam had gone. Disappearing into the night woods, her footsteps on the damp leaves fading and fading until Lonnie couldn't hear them anymore.

Then he was alone.

He sat against the chimney tower, hugging himself, shivering with cold. Alone in that godforsaken ghost town in the moaning woods. With the ruins and the graves hulking blackly amid the rustling trees. With the sounds of living creatures snickering in the duff of the forest floor. With sudden movements at the edges of his vision that were gone when he faced them head-on.

Fool! he thought. He'd been raised in the trenches, on some nightmare streets. He was being chased by the police, by professional killers. He was a grown man. It was bullshit to sit here worrying about werewolves and vampires.

He kept telling himself that.

But he sure was glad to see that old devil moon.

At first, he didn't know what it was. He was watching for it, waiting for it, and, all the same, he didn't recognize its glimmer on the horizon beyond the trees. It seemed a bright light coming toward him. He scrambled to his feet. A car? he thought. A chopper? The cops? The light expanded and grew brighter in what seemed to him a queerly silent and unnatural way.

A UFO. Just his luck.

Then he saw the arc of the disk. The moon. Just head straight for it, like she'd told him.

She'd made it sound easy.

So for the next fifteen minutes or months or whatever

it was, Lonnie stumbled wildly toward the rising moon. Roots grabbed at his feet like fingers. Branches scratched at his face like claws. The cold of the night dissolved into a clammy heat around him. His breath came short, his heart pounded. His overcoat hung on him like lead.

And damn it, it wasn't easy. It was hard—incredibly hard. It was hard just to find a fucking path to the horizon. Rocks, trees, sudden dips in the earth, sudden streams that wet him to the ankles all seemed to hurl themselves beneath him as he blundered through the night. Once he fell—a blind tumble that seemed to go on forever, that left plenty of time for panic before he thumped down onto the stony earth. The jar went through him. He felt it in his bones. Then he was up again, aching. Limping forward. Feeling his way.

The half-moon—and its dark half, a pocket of gray night—bounced and hid and flashed from out of the branches before him. It seemed to have shot from the horizon, to be climbing the sky on some invisible jet of energy. Was he supposed to keep after it, he wondered, or head for the place where it had risen? Was he going in the right direction even now or had he lost it?

He wondered that and he wondered: What if she wasn't there? Carol. What if she'd deserted him? What if she thought she'd be less conspicuous without a black fugitive with her? What if she thought she'd have a better chance of evading Winter and the police on her own?

Groping, gasping, stumbling, he didn't see the road at once in that tangled darkness. He sensed it first. He sensed a sort of flat emptiness at the top of the short, steep rise just ahead of him. He hardly dared hope.

Sweat streamed down his face, his breath whistled as he climbed that ground. He slid on the leaves beneath his shoes, had to grab at roots to pull himself up the grade.

Then he was there, standing on the ridge. And an empty two-lane lay in the moonlight just beyond the trees.

Dragging his feet, Lonnie staggered to it. He stepped gratefully over the border onto the pavement.

Instantly, her headlights flashed.

Another moment and he'd collapsed onto the seat beside her. She was pulling their new car—a rusted old Chevy—from the shoulder.

They were on the road, heading for Vermont.

CHAPTER 15

MOONLIGHT IN VERMONT

1

The moon was sailing toward its crest when the Learjet 31A touched down at Rutland State. Even as the whine of its twin engines subsided, a green Mondeo was racing up to it over the runway's grassy verge. The vehicles ran parallel for several yards, glinting under the runway lights.

The small jet rolled to a stop. The Mondeo stopped alongside it. The car's driver was at the jet's opening door in a moment, was receiving two hefty cases, hauling them back to the Ford's open trunk. As the driver loaded the cases, the jet's passengers quickly disembarked. Three men in black overcoats: the brown-faced, skull-faced man named Ferdinand; Dewey, the neckless slab; and the red-haired man, Edmund Winter. They were all in the car before the driver shut the trunk.

The driver lowered himself behind the wheel. Nodded a nervous greeting to the red-haired man.

"Ike Lewis?" Winter said.

"Yes, sir."

"Let's go."

But the car had already begun bumping over the verge toward the road.

The driver—Ike Lewis—was a youngish fellow. Thirty, not much over. He had crew-cut blond hair and pale features pocked with red acne. His eyes were bright and hazel. They gave him the quick, fixed, startled look of a sociopath. Winter found this encouraging.

And he—Lewis—handled the car well too. Beating the lights, moving swiftly but unobtrusively through the empty city streets.

"You made good time," he said after a while. "You run into any weather?" Making conversation with the new boss.

Winter shook his head. "We had a little trouble rousting a co-pilot. How quickly you figure we can get to Morburne?"

"This time of night? We should be outside Geena MacAlary's house in thirty, thirty-five minutes tops," Lewis said.

Winter nodded. He glanced at his Rolex.

It was now just coming up on 2 A.M.

By two-twenty, Geena was ready to go. Actually she'd been ready for almost two hours. She just couldn't quite bring herself to hit the road.

Immediately after she'd hung up with Carol, she had packed Amanda's bags. She had carried the bags out to the car and put them in the trunk. Then she'd come back inside, ready to drive Amanda to her 3 A.M. rendezvous at McDonald's—whereupon she'd found to her dismay that it was barely twelve-thirty.

She turned on the television. Stared at it. Then it began to occur to her that the noise of the TV might be drowning out other noises: creeping footsteps behind her for instance, or a terrified scream from the child upstairs.

I think they're close.

She shut off the box, then turned out the lights in the house. She sat on the sofa, jumpy as a hamster. She couldn't think of one good reason to calm down.

So she got up and, for the next hour or so, walked from room to room in the darkness.

It was awful. Waiting, thinking. The confines of her own house began to make her flesh creep. Lighted clocks—the clock on the oven, the clock on the video, the clock on a radio alarm—confronted her from every corner. None of them seemed to be moving. Sometimes she sat on the sofa and dozed but, whenever she did, she jerked awake in moments, thinking: *Did I miss the time? Is someone in the house?*

Once, after falling alseep for only a moment, she dreamed that the door was kicked in by men with machine guns. She opened her eyes with a gasp. The house was dark and silent.

She began to consider getting out early. Putting Amanda in the car, leaving the place, driving around town until it was time to meet Carol at McDonald's. But as much as she wanted to get out, to move, it struck her as somehow more dangerous than staying put. She didn't want to miss it if Carol called again with some change of plan. And even the idea of cruising around the streets of Morburne—empty now that the student hangouts had closed—made her feel exposed, at risk.

Instead, she waited, dozed, paced. And she finally

came to rest upstairs, leaning against the door jamb, looking down through the dark at the shadow of the sleeping child.

It was two-twenty. She was ready to go. She just couldn't quite make the move.

Amanda was lying on her back, her mouth hanging open. She held Elmo close against her with one arm. Geena could see the toy rising and falling with the girl's breath.

She had known this moment would come from the beginning. She had never had any illusions. Marie had warned her about Helix and Executive Decisions right from the outset. "On a scale of one to evil, these guys are eleven," she'd said. "They won't stop till they've got her. You should know that up front."

But by then, Geena had been widowed almost five years. Her husband—a kindly, mild-mannered but witty and quietly subversive historian—had opened his veins like a Roman at the onset of Alzheimer's. Her three sons had all turned out smart and ambitious and had headed South and West to the big cities. They phoned her often but only visited at the holidays.

She considered that she had had a happy and fulfilling life. There simply hadn't been enough of it. She wasn't old yet. She wasn't ready for the rocker. The choice between contemplating her bygone joys and helping a child in trouble was an easy one for her to make. She had agreed to take Amanda in.

And these last four months—they had been like a reprieve. Taking care of a child again, a little girl at last, talking to her, baking cookies with her, bathing her. It had been a sudden splash of color over what she feared was the prematurely gray end of things.

And all along, she had known this day would come. The urgent escape. The men closing. She had prepared herself, braced herself for the fear she would feel.

She just hadn't been ready for the grief.

Because she loved the child. She had come to love her fiercely. So she leaned there in the doorway and watched her sleeping. A few minutes more. And then a few minutes more.

And then suddenly something happened.

She didn't know what it was, at first. She just started. She just straightened, blinking. She had a sudden sense of danger. A deep feeling that something terrible had come to find her. A second more and she became absolutely convinced that they were here—the bad men—that they had just suddenly shown up in front of her house.

She was right, of course. They had.

The Mondeo had pulled up to the curb outside. The four men were getting out. Dewey was checking the magazine of his Walther. Ike Lewis was rolling the wheel of his .38. Ferdinand was scanning the front of the place with the thermal imager. He had found the red heat of two life-forms in the little room upstairs.

Winter, his hands in his overcoat pockets, signaled them forward with a nod.

Geena MacAlary didn't know what had alerted her to this. She hadn't heard the car's engine. She hadn't heard its doors open and close. She wasn't aware of having heard them anyway. She was simply aware all at once of a taut and quivering silence around the place, as if a long, steady noise outside had suddenly ceased.

She stood in Amanda's doorway, ears pricked.

Nothing. She heard nothing.

But she knew they were there.

She rushed forward. Rushed to the child's bed.

"Amanda!" She whispered the word harshly. Pulled the cover off the girl, shook her shoulder. "Amanda, wake up!"

The little body stirred. Geena lifted her head, listened. Was there a footstep on the porch? She wasn't sure. There was no window onto the front, no way to check.

But now she heard a twig snap in the backyard. Her throat went coppery, then dry.

They were surrounding her.

The little girl sat up slowly. Screwing a fist into her eye, moving her mouth silently. Geena put her hands under the child's armpits. She gave a grunt of effort, and hoisted the soft, dead weight off the bed, set her down on her feet, holding her upright.

"Amanda! Sweetheart!" Whispering hard. "You've got to wake up now! You've got to! Listen! They're here!"

Amanda stood there, rubbing her eye, holding Elmo under her other arm. She was wearing red pajamas with a teddy bear on the front of the shirt. The teddy bear grinned at Geena with maddening idiocy.

Amanda gave a sleepy sniff. "I don't feel well."

"I know, I know." Geena knelt in front of her, grasped her shoulders desperately. "But please! Listen to me! Wake up! There are bad men here! The bad men."

Downstairs, the lock to the front door snapped back.

It was quietly, deftly done. But the noise traveled. It was unmistakable. Geena felt it hit her in the gut like a fist. The breath was punched out of her.

She sobbed. "Oh God, please. We've got to hurry."

She stood quickly. The child went on standing there, watched her dully as she moved to the window.

Geena looked out through the dark glass, down into the backyard, into the night. She felt her heart squeeze small: she saw them. There in the moonlight. Two of them, two men, two shadows, just now fiddling with the back door, just now pushing it open. Just now, they were stepping through.

And at the same time Geena heard the front door below clicking open.

They were in the house.

Geena clutched her hair in a second of panic. A thousand urgent thoughts collided with each other in her brain. Her eyes flashed every which way, looking for some avenue of escape.

There was an attic, she thought. And for a second, she pictured it. Rushing into the hall, getting the hook from the closet, pulling the trap down, spiriting Amanda up the ladder . . . Yes, and then what? They'd simply find her there. And there was no time for it anyway. They'd be coming up the stairs in a minute. They'd see her the second she ran into the hall.

The stairs, she thought then. They had to use the stairs. It was the only way up. They'd meet in the living room and then they'd all come up the stairs.

There were no windows on the stairs. They couldn't see outside as they were coming.

She caught her breath. She looked out the window again. Both men were gone from the backyard now. They'd both come inside.

Geena leapt to the bed. Began tearing off the covers.

"Aunt Geena . . ." said Amanda in full voice.

"Ssssht!" Geena shot it at her from between gritted teeth. Pulling at the covers. Yanking off the top sheet, then the bottom. "You have to go to Mr. Roth," she said. "You have to run to Mr. Roth. Just go in through the front door. Don't knock. Just go in. He leaves it open. Tell him he has to take you to McDonald's. Now."

"But I'm not hungry."

A floorboard squeaked in the living room, near the bottom of the stairs. And worse than that, there was the sound of men murmuring. Geena heard this clearly: a murmured voice, a murmured answer.

Clammy sweat broke out on her face as she tied the sheets together with a double knot. "Hurry, God, please . . ."

Done. She knelt in front of Amanda. She tried to get one end of a sheet around the little girl's wrist. Her fingers were shaking so wildly she couldn't do it. Elmo was getting in the way.

She pulled Elmo away from the girl. Tossed him onto the bed.

"I don't want to go to McDonald's." Amanda understood to whisper this time, a child's stage whisper. "I have a tummy ache."

Geena had the sheet around the girl's wrist. She tied it, pulled the knot tight.

"O-ow," Amanda whined softly.

"I know, I know, sweetheart, just hold on, just hold on to this sheet. Hold on to it tight, sweetheart. Your mommy's at McDonald's. She's going to meet you at McDonald's. You'll see your mommy there. Tell Mr. Roth."

"Mommy?" said the child. Her eyes widened. She was awake now more or less. Thank God for that anyway.

Geena doubled the knot, pulled it tight again. "Hold on to the sheet. Don't let go until you get down. Then run to Mr. Roth as fast as you can, sweetheart. As fast, as fast as you can."

There was a footstep on the stairs. They were coming up.

Geena rushed back to the door. Pushed it closed as quietly as she could. There was a keyhole but no key, no way to lock it. She just hoped it would keep them from hearing what she did next.

She went back to the window. Undid the latch. She couldn't hear the footsteps now but she could sense them, feel them, rising, slowly, coming up to the landing step by step.

She opened the window, pressing one palm to the frame to keep it from rumbling. Then she turned.

Amanda was crawling onto the bed. Collecting Elmo again.

"Don't let go of the sheet," said Geena.

And she scooped the child up in her arms and set her on the window ledge.

There was no time for tears, but Geena was crying. There was no time for good-byes, but she kissed the child fiercely in her yellow hair.

"I love you," she said.

Then she yanked Elmo from the girl's arms again and threw him out into the backyard. She wrapped the sheet round Amanda's arm and placed her small hands on it.

"Hold on to it, hold on," she said again. Then she wrapped the other end of the sheet-rope around her own forearm and said, "Dear God. Don't let go."

And she pushed the child out the window.

For those next few seconds, time became a vise, closing on her. The child dangled and spun in the air, gripping the sheet for dear life, her little face puckered in fear, her wide eyes staring up at her. Geena had thought the weight would be terrible, hard to hold, but it was nothing, nothing, and she realized there must've been enough adrenaline coursing through her now to float a ship.

She passed the sheet-rope out the window, hand over hand, letting the child's weight carry her toward the ground.

And in the meantime—the footsteps. She could not hear the damned footsteps. She didn't know where they were. Still rising up the stairs? On the landing? At the door?

And then, a jolt. A sharp tug at the sheet-rope. Staring out the window, down at the twisting figure of the child, Geena saw the little body jerk.

One of the knots around her wrist had slipped. There was only one other left.

Hang on! she thought.

Amanda was halfway to the ground. The fall wouldn't kill her, but she might sprain her ankle, break her leg. She was little—she was still half asleep—even a skinned knee might keep her from running, might make her cry or slow her down until they saw her.

Geena let the sheet-rope slide faster through her hands, let the weight of the child carry her another half of the way down. Another half of that.

And the second knot came undone.

Amanda hung on to the sheet by herself for another second. Geena lowered her, lowered her, but the jolt of the slipping knots had jarred Amanda loose. The child's grip was slipping. She was sliding to the end of the sheet.

And then, with a quick, high-pitched little cry, Amanda fell.

It was all right. Just a few feet. Amanda went down onto one hand but she didn't topple over. Plus she was free of the sheet. It would be easier for her to run. Geena started to pull the sheets up quickly.

And, as she did, she heard a floorboard creak in the hall outside the door. They were out there, maybe three steps away.

Geena pulled the sheet in, tossed it behind her. Kicked it under the bed. She shut the window as swiftly and as quietly as she could. She spared herself one last glance, out into the moonlight, down at the little figure of the child.

She gasped as she saw her.

Amanda wasn't running. She was just standing there. Turning in a circle.

"Amanda." Geena squeezed the word out tearfully.

The child was searching for Elmo in the grass.

Geena stood staring down at her, wishing her, willing her with all her might to forget the goddamned doll and run.

"Go, go, go," she whispered.

Then another floorboard creaked. This one right outside the door.

Geena jumped back, away from the window. Turned to the bed.

The door flew in with a crash, and the men stormed in after it.

The room's light went on, blinding. Geena stumbled back, her arm up, protecting her eyes. There were four of them she saw. Black shadows sweeping toward her. A red-haired man was in the lead.

Geena backed away, backed away. She tried to speak, but couldn't, could only back away. Now she was at the wall, against the wall. And the red-haired man was standing over her. Smiling down at her easily. She could smell his cologne. She could see the absolute confidence in his eyes, the authority, the easygoing expertise. She had no hope and despair made her fear sickening.

"Where is she, Mrs. MacAlary?" the red-haired man said softly.

Geena lowered her arm. She cursed it for shaking so much. She looked as if she were in an earthquake. Her voice came out a squeak.

"Who?"

The red-haired man snorted, gave a little roll of his eyes. He glanced around the room, smiling. Saw the disheveled bed. This made him pause, made him thoughtful.

Then he turned away from her and moved to the window.

Geena stood pinned to the wall, watching him. She felt the fear would pull her to pieces.

Let her be gone, she thought. *Let her have found Elmo and run away and be gone. Please, God—you son of a bitch—do something here for us, at least.*

The red-haired man looked out the window into the moonlit backyard. Then he turned sharply to the other three men.

"She must still be in the house," he said. "Search it."

Relief poured over Geena and made her weak. Her knees buckled. She reached out, took two steps and sat down hard on the bed. She lowered her head. Stared stupidly at her feet.

She saw a pair of shiny black shoes move up to her.

She looked up slowly, up into the smiling, authoritative, pitiless face of the red-haired man. She was vaguely aware that they were alone now in the room together.

"If you don't tell me where she is," he said softly, "what happens to you next will be . . . beyond imagining."

Geena could only nod weakly. She understood. Dazed with fear, she turned to look at the clock with the smiling pony.

It was two-thirty-five. Twenty-five minutes to three.

Twenty-five minutes, Geena thought. In a vague, distant sort of way she knew they were going to be the worst, and the last, minutes of her life. She was so afraid of what would happen next that she felt as if her bowels had turned to water. She wished to God that she had died at birth rather than lived to see this day.

She lifted her face to the red-haired man. She couldn't see him through her tears. She tried to speak but could only snuffle loudly.

"Who are you?" she managed to say. "Have you no mercy?"

"I'm just a businessman trying to make a dollar," he answered. "And no."

Geena nodded again, sick with despair.

"Really, ma'am," the man said. "Save yourself the trouble. Believe me, you can't hold out forever."

Geena laughed at that, at the very idea. Hold out forever. She hated pain. And when it came to the sight of her own blood, she was a baby. She gasped out of her tears. She wiped first one eye with her hand and then the other.

"Not forever," she managed to say finally. "But maybe a little while."

Twenty-five minutes, she thought. Maybe.

Then Roth woke up and Amanda was standing over him. Clutching Elmo. Sucking her thumb. Her face was still pale, but her gaze was steady. The bear on her red pajama top grinned like a vaudeville comedian on drugs.

Roth's first thought was that he was dreaming. His second thought was that the end of the world was nigh and Amanda had come to judge the living and the dead.

"You're supposed to take me to McDonald's," Amanda told him.

Thus saith the Lord, Roth thought.

Running a hand down over his face, he sat up. "Amanda? Is that you? Are you asleep? Are you sleepwalking?"

"I don't think so," said Amanda. "Aunt Geena said you had to take me to McDonald's to see Mommy. She says the bad men are here."

Roth was out of bed instantly. Pulling his pants off the back of a chair, pulling them on over his underwear. His mind was still thick, his thoughts blurry. But it was funny, he thought—he wasn't afraid. As he frantically wriggled his pants over his legs, he wondered: why not? He should've been afraid. Plenty. The bad men were here. And they sounded really bad. And he—Roth— had never been in a violent situation before; not since childhood anyway when he'd been beaten up by bullies once or twice or a dozen times. And he'd never thought of himself as a particularly brave person; the opposite if anything. But then, how would you know whether you were brave or not unless you were put to the test? Maybe—he thought with a certain distant academic interest—maybe it would turn out that he was brave. Who could say? He felt cool enough just now anyway. And as his mind began to clear, he felt he understood what was in front of him, what he was going to have to do.

"McDonald's, huh," he said, figuring he ought to say something to keep the child calm.

She clutched her doll, sucked her thumb, watched him solemnly. Nodded.

Roth buttoned his pants, zipped them. He was already wearing a T-shirt. That would have to be enough. He sat on the bed to pull sneakers on over his bare feet.

Then Geena occurred to him. As his mind woke, as a picture of events came into focus. He thought of Geena and the thought twisted in him like a knife.

He began to understand what must have happened. She'd gotten the kid out somehow, probably by the skin of her teeth. The bad guys must be there, next door, in her house with her right this minute. The familiar acid of rage spread through him as he thought of what they'd do to her to make her talk.

But still he was unafraid, cool, his mind working.

One thing was certain, he figured: she'd talk all right. Eventually, they would make her tell where the kid had gone. In fact, it wouldn't take them more than a couple of minutes.

Which meant there was no time to waste. Roth had to get the kid out of here. He had to get down to the garage. He had to pray that his old Citroën, which he hadn't used in over a week, would start in one try. He had to hope he could open the garage door quietly enough to avoid detection. He had to drive at least to the corner without headlights and endure the suspense of waiting for the gunfire to start. Not until he got to McDonald's—if he actually did get to McDonald's— would there be time to call the police. The fire department. The army. Everyone. Anyone who could get to Geena's house and get her out of there.

But first, he had to get to McDonald's.

He went over all this as he laced his sneakers

quickly. And all the while, some observant part of his brain wondered at the fact that none of it made him feel panicked or helpless. He was an old academic with no experience of such things as this. He insisted to himself that he ought to be terrified to the point of dithering.

But he simply wasn't. He felt fine. Clear, angry, coolly determined to get the girl to her rendezvous, to call the cops to rescue Geena.

So it turned out he was Superman. Go figure.

He jumped to his feet.

"You ready?" he said.

Amanda nodded solemnly.

"All right," said Roth. "The Happy Meal's on you."

"So what's really the story with your daughter?" Lonnie asked.

He was lying on the backseat, his hands behind his head, his head against the door. He gazed over his raised knees at the night racing past the other window.

Carol guided the old Chevy up the interstate. She was smoking feverishly as she drove, her cigarette hand working like a piston, mouth to ashtray, ashtray to mouth. She had not spoken for half an hour.

"What about her?" she said.

"Chubb was telling me all this crazy stuff. How she brought him back to life and shit."

"Yeah. Something, isn't it? I just wish I could get her to knock it off."

Lonnie laughed. Then his laughter died. He turned his head. Studied the back of Carol's head, her curls, the pistoning cigarette hand, the smoke trailing out through a thin gap at the top of her window.

"You're not gonna tell me this too, are you?" he said.

She gave a rough snort. "What the hell do you think all the shouting's about? I mean, I don't know if Chubb was actually *dead*—I mean, maybe he just thinks he was *dead*, you know, but . . ."

"But what? You mean, she . . . ?"

"Oh yeah." She sucked hard on her cigarette, blew out hard. "She's, like, abracadabra, you're well, man. I saw her do it to a kid with chicken pox once. I'm telling you. It's some kind of genetic thing. They gave her father some medicine or something. I don't understand it. And I don't care either. All I know is it's supposed to go away when she reaches puberty. So I figure if I can just keep her alive that long, maybe everyone'll just leave us alone."

Lonnie went on gazing at the back of her head. Crazy, he thought. Crazy. And yet . . . She seemed so sure. Chubb seemed so sure. Lonnie thought about it for a long moment.

"So what do they want?" he said then. "This Winter guy. What does he want with her?"

Carol shrugged. She jettisoned the last of her cigarette out the window. "They'll sell her. That's what I heard. First they do experiments on her. Then they sell her, make her heal people, rich people, you know. And see, the thing is: it'll kill her. Whenever she does it, it makes her sick, and then if she does it enough she stays sick and dies. No one knows how many times it takes. It's like Russian roulette. Just one day she steps over the line—and that's it."

Lonnie was about to answer—then he just let out a whiffle of air, shook his head. What the hell was he supposed to say?

He heard the *kachink* of the cigarette lighter being pushed in. Carol fit another white reed to her lips.

"So if this stuff is true . . ." he said.

"Oh, it's true, believe me," she said bitterly.

"Well, then, shouldn't you talk to someone or something? I mean, if she can do this, maybe someone ought to know."

"Like who? Enough people know already."

"Well, I mean . . . scientists or something. Experts. I mean, maybe this could help mankind, something like that."

"What's so helpful about it?" The lighter popped. She grabbed it. Even over the rush of wind at the window, Lonnie could hear the tobacco crackle as she set it ablaze. She jammed the lighter back into the dash and her hand started working like a piston again. "I mean, people get sick, right? People die. If it's not today, it's tomorrow, that's the way things are. Buncha scientists are gonna take my baby, cut her up, punch her full of holes, study her—kill her probably—you know they would—they wouldn't be able to stop—it'd be, like, oops, sorry, we killed her—and for what? Cause she can give people another day or year or whatever. Who cares? You know? Everybody's gotta die in the end anyway. They gotta learn to live with it, that's all."

"Yeah, but . . . I mean . . . Man!" Lonnie thought about it. Made a face in the dark. "I mean, Jesus did stuff like this and, lookit, they appointed him God."

"Yeah, that's the second thing they did," said Carol. "First they fucking crucified him. Not my little girl, you hear me? Not Amanda."

Lonnie fell silent after that. Watched the skeletal trees speeding past in the dark, the fields beyond them moving slowly past, the stars seemingly motionless. The moon. Another day of life, he thought. A year. Whatever. A little more time, even with the end still certain. What would he have given? If the child could've saved Suzanne? If the child could've healed her, even brought her back to life. Given him another hour of her smile, of her fingertips against his face, of the sound of her voice . . .

Man, if he thought she could bring her back now, he would be hunting down Amanda himself.

His body swayed as the car handled a curve. Then:

"There it is," said Carol.

Lonnie sat up on the backseat.

The McDonald's arches. Shining yellow against the gray-black sky. The half-moon, in its low autumn crest, just moving over them.

There was an exit, then a cloverleaf, then a short stretch of service road to the restaurant's driveway.

"God, God, God," he heard Carol murmur.

Lonnie glanced at his watch. Quarter to three. He drew a breath. Put his hand in his pocket, wrapped his fingers round the butt of his gun.

No one in the place 'cept you and me, he thought.

"Just let her be there," said Carol. "Just let her be there. Okay?"

She was there. Roth had her. She was sitting in the passenger seat of his Citroën. She had the box of an uneaten Happy Meal beside her. She was holding Elmo and playing dully with the toy that had come in the box, a hamburger on wheels. The Citroën's engine was running and the heater was on. Even clad only in her pajamas, she felt warm and sleepy. She was fighting to keep her eyes open.

Roth was standing outside, just at the passenger door. Fiddling with an unlit cigarette. Watching the ramp where the interstate cloverleaf emptied onto the service road. His stare was intense. His nerves were stretched thin. But he felt ready for anything. He was nodding to himself: so far, he had done what he had to do.

He had hustled the child to the car in his garage. Started the Citroën in the dark. Cruised out quietly onto the street, braced for a barrage of gunfire. He had driven away from the house, past the dark Mondeo parked outside Geena's. Calm—he had kept himself calm—though the thought of what was happening to Geena made him physically ill. He had kept himself calm and driven on to the restaurant. Called the cops and the fire department from there, told them he'd heard Geena screaming. Just now their sirens had sounded in the distance. They were on their way. There was nothing to do but wait.

He had done what he had to do.

And still, to his surprise, he was unafraid. He smiled a little, mirthlessly. Nauseated, yes. Strangling on his own suspense, waiting here helpless. But afraid? No. There was no fear at all. If anything, he felt a pervasive sense of floating unreality. As in: excuse me, but what the hell am I doing here? As in: how has a classics professor gotten himself into a situation like this?

As in: it's almost three o'clock in the morning, booby, have you any idea where the flying fuck you are?

He shuddered. He had his coat on over his T-shirt, but he was still plenty cold in the Vermont November. Blowing plumes of frost, he raised his tired eyes to the sky.

A clear night. The lights from the restaurant and from the interstate exit blotted out the stars. But he could see the half-moon, like a great white idiotic grin, arching into the crevice of the restaurant's double arches, which rose to meet it like . . . like . . .

Well, like enormous golden buttocks.

And Roth, still smiling grimly, thought: there's the anwer to the question, right there. Where was he? Where else could he be? In the parking lot of a fast-food joint at 3 A.M. With men running around all over carrying guns and women running off God knows where without their kids and kids sitting all alone and frightened in the night—while in the sky above, an idiot grin stoops to kiss the ass of gold. Where was he? Western Civilization. He was in Western Civilization, that's where he was.

He laughed. Then he stopped laughing. Then he stiffened. He felt his whole body thrum. A car had just rolled off the interstate, out of the cloverleaf. It was coming up the service road. He could not make out its shape beyond the headlights.

But now it pulled closer to the parking lot. Roth saw that it was not the dark Mondeo. It was an old red-rusted Chevy. A woman driving.

Mommy, he thought.

Roth turned quickly back to the car, to the child. Saw her in there, sitting sleepy with her Elmo and her hamburger toy and her red pajamas with the stoned comedian of a bear. Her eyes were falling shut and her mouth was falling open. She was adorable. And, for a second, deep waters of emotion welled in Roth. He was surprised how deep. He had known the child for only a few days and yet here he was willing to risk everything for her. Hell, he would've been willing to *give* everything for her if that's what he'd had to do. Why? Who knew? Because she made his cancer go away. Because she looked at him with her big solemn brown eyes and said *That's a good story*, which was what he'd needed to hear. Because he'd been right about her: she was the messiah. She was his messiah anyway. Or maybe she was just a child, and children were God's answer to history—and that was also something he needed to hear.

He pulled the car door open. "Come on, sweetheart," he said. "Your mother's here."

"Mommy?"

The child bolted awake. Tried to open her door. Couldn't. Started crawling across the bucket seat, knocking her Coke over on the floor as she came.

"Come on." Roth reached in to help her. Caught her under the arms. Lifted her out. Planted a kiss on the side of her head as he swung her round, and then placed her down on the parking lot pavement.

At the same moment the old Chevy—barely slowing as it fired past the high curb bordering the lot—reached the entry ramp and spun into it, burning rubber. Even as the car jerked to a stop, even as its chassis shook, the door creaked open. The driver spilled out of it, ran toward them.

"Amanda."

"Mommy!"

The child dropped Elmo to the pavement and ran into her mother's arms.

Roth felt the impact as they came together, saw the look of relief and pleasure and love on the woman's face, and his eyes misted. Irritated, he blinked the mist away. The mother rocked the child back and forth as she held her. The child buried herself in her mother, vanishing into the embrace. Roth sniffed, tossed his unlit cigarette to the pavement.

Another person, meanwhile, emerged from the Chevy's backseat. A tall black man with sharp, feline features. He came out of the car and stood with his hands in his overcoat pockets. He looked down at the mother and child and smiled with one corner of his mouth.

Roth bent over, scooped Amanda's discarded monster up by its arm. He carried it over to the black man.

It was strange but, as their eyes met, Roth thought— would have sworn—that he knew the guy from somewhere. He couldn't place him, though, and he let it pass. He handed him the toy.

"Elmo," he said.

The black man took his left hand from his pocket and received the furry creature. He nodded. "Elmo. Right."

And then, with a shriek of tires, the Mondeo shot onto the service road, and roared toward them.

8

Roth pointed, his face blank with fear. "That's them."

Lonnie, Elmo in one hand, pulled the gun from his pocket with the other. He waved to the backseat's open door. "Get in, get in!"

There was an interminable half second in which Carol didn't understand. In which she looked up reluctantly from the feel and scent and flavor of her child, in which she looked over her shoulder at the onrushing car, saw it, took it in.

"Come on!" Lonnie was screaming. Even the words seemed to come out of him slowly, as in an awful dream.

Only the car, the Mondeo, seemed to be traveling at full speed.

Now, though, now, Carol was on her feet. She had the little girl by the hand and was pulling her after. She ran for the car.

Lonnie jumped into the driver's seat. Pulled the door shut. Glanced back over his shoulder. Saw the Mondeo's headlights in his rearview. Saw Carol tumbling into the back, saw her draw the child in after her, reach across her for the door.

He hit the gas. The tires screamed under him as he wrenched the wheel over.

Carol screamed too. "The door!" But Lonnie couldn't look back.

The Chevy turned sharply, faced the service road. The Mondeo was now cutting across it toward the lot.

Lonnie heard Carol shut the door behind him. He floored the pedal.

The Mondeo fired over the high curb into the lot just as the Chevy fired over the curb and out. The cars passed each other in midair and hit the macadam with sprays of sparks.

Both were turning in the next second, half circling each other in a steel and rubber ballet. Lonnie's Chevy smeared the lighted street with smoke as it gripped the road and then leapt forward, racing for the interstate. The Mondeo, at the same moment, wrenched around and charged the ramp, bounced out through it and swerved, its chassis leaning with the force of the motion.

The Chevy was still in sight ahead, still motoring toward the overpass that would take it back onto the big road. It would be nothing, the business of a minute, for the Mondeo to catch it, to run it onto the shoulder.

Shrieking out of its sharp turn, the Mondeo sped forward.

And Roth's Citroën flew over the curb and landed in front of it.

Roth had seen the necessity at once, had started running the second he spotted the oncoming car. He was in his Citroën as the two other cars leapt the curb. The Citroën's engine was already running, the nose was already forward. Roth only needed to throw it into gear. Already, he saw through the windshield, the other two cars were turning, the Chevy was racing off, the Mondeo was spinning round and about to go after it.

He only wished he had time to fasten his seat belt. But he didn't. He stepped on the gas.

Roth felt his butt lift off the seat as the Citroën hit the curb and flew into the air. In the next moment, he was thrown forward, his forehead smacking the wheel as the car touched down. An endless instant of expectation followed and Roth observed with mild surprise that he still felt absolutely no fear at all.

Then the Mondeo hit him broadside, hard.

The scream of tires, the crump of metal, the tinkle of glass. The Citroën caved in. The Mondeo's headlights shattered. Its air bag exploded outward smashing Ike Lewis, its driver, in the face. The impact broke his nose.

As for Roth, he was sent flying against the door. The window smashed and his head went through it. The door sprung open and he tumbled out onto the pavement, landed with a jolt that left him drained of all his strength.

Then it was quiet but for the sharp hissing noise of the Mondeo's burst radiator. A geyser of steam rose over the momentary tableau.

Roth lay on the street, only half conscious, unaware of the pool of blood fanning out around his head. He knew that he was floating on an island of shock in an ocean of pain. He understood that the moment he moved or spoke or even thought too much about it, he would be awash in such agony as he had never before known.

So he didn't move—even as a pair of legs came into his field of vision. He barely shifted his eyes as a red-haired man squatted down in front of him.

The red-haired man looked down at Roth, pursed his lips with disgust and shook his head. Roth tried to smile. *Do I look as bad as that?* he wanted to say. But he didn't have the strength for it. He found that he was fading away into a place of great darkness and serenity. He had read about this somewhere and he realized that this was what it felt like to be dying. Already, he could no longer muster the simple worldliness required to detest the red-haired man. And yet, at the same time, he understood that if the bad guys had found him here, the police had not been in time: the red-haired man and his friends must have made Geena talk and then killed her. At least, thought Roth, it hadn't taken very long.

After a moment, Roth found that he had said something. "Geena," he had said.

The red-haired man gave an angry sniff. "Yeah, she died screaming, you old fuck," he told him.

In the serene darkness to which Roth was fading this seemed a matter of no importance at all. And yet he was still alive, still within sight of the frenzied light of life.

So he did manage a smile at the red-haired man. And he whispered, "Kiss my ass."

And that was his valedictory.

Winter stood up from the corpse, still shaking his head. For a moment, his anger choked him and he almost indulged in something like self-pity. What the hell was it with this goddamned operation? Women ready to be tortured to delay him, men ready to die to get in his way.

What was it all about? What was wrong with everyone? For Christ's sake, wasn't it better for one child to die instead of all these people? It was simple arithmetic. If they'd just let him take the kid and go it would all be over. Why did they want to cause themselves so much pain?

He cast his eyes over the scene, his face impassive, his gut seething. He felt as if poison were coursing through him. As his car had leapt the curb, as the Chevy had passed him in midair, he had looked out, past Ike Lewis, and seen the Chevy's driver. He had recognized Lonnie Blake. The thought that Mortimer and Hughes had been somehow right, that Blake and Carol Dodson were in this together, that Blake and Carol might actually *be* together, his fingers on her white skin . . . It was like poison in him. Like fire in his veins.

The fucking saxophone player, he thought.

Oh, he would kill the man out of hand, that was nothing. And the little girl he would sell for money. But this woman—this woman he was going to keep for himself. He would make her forget her black lover. He would make her forget everything, even her child. He wanted to be inside her when she cried out that he was the man, that he was *God* to her, that she would do anything, anything if he would only grant her death.

This was central to the operation now as far as Winter was concerned.

Hissing out a breath, he returned to the steaming Mondeo. He looked in through the window at where Ike Lewis swayed drunkenly, blood streaming into his mouth from his shattered nose. The air bag had already deflated to a white blob on his lap.

"Shit," Winter said aloud.

He tried to open the door but it was locked. He hammered on the window with his fist. The bleeding Lewis looked up at him stupidly.

"Open the damned door," Winter said to him through the glass.

Ike Lewis looked stupidly at the door. Then he shifted to find its handle.

The workers from McDonald's were coming out of the restaurant now. Two sticklike boys and one spherical girl. They stared at Winter openmouthed.

"Are you okay, sir?" one of the boys shouted to him. "We called the police."

Winter briefly considered shooting him.

But now Ike Lewis had managed to open the door. Winter shoved him to get him to move over. He slid in behind the wheel. Tore the air bag out of his way and threw it into the backseat.

Ferdinand, the skull-faced man, caught it, stowed it on the floor.

Winter turned the key. The engine whined. He tried again. It started, rumbled unsteadily. The hood steamed and wobbled.

"We won't get far in this," said Ferdinand.

Winter threw the car into reverse. Looked over his shoulder. One of the car's hubcaps fell off and rattled over the pavement as he began to back up.

"Let's just get out of here before the cops come," he muttered angrily. "I'll call in for a replacement. We'll have it in half an hour."

"Gives them a lot of time to get away," said Ferdinand.

Winter faced forward, eyes bright. Threw the car into drive. "They're not getting away," he said. "They must be going to Meridian. We'll meet them there."

He stepped on the gas.

The boys and girl from McDonald's watched as the Mondeo started rattling forward. It pulled around the Citroën, and skirted Roth's body where it lay.

Then it headed off, past the arches, under the moon, into the night.

He stepped on the gas.

The boys said-light from Michael Donnelly watched as the Mondeo started rolling forward. He pulled ahead, then braked, and started rolling when it hit.

The call had led off, past the gate to under the moon, into the night.

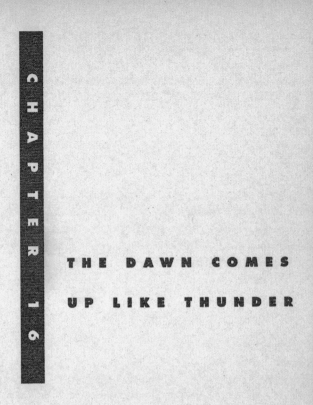

CHAPTER 16

THE DAWN COMES
UP LIKE THUNDER

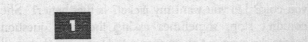

1

The last hundred miles seemed to stretch out forever. Lonnie began to feel that they would never reach the mountain. Everything seemed to conspire to slow him down. He had had to leave the interstate soon after Morburne. He'd had to wander meandering two-lanes and spend hours chugging up forested mountains or idling at traffic lights in snoring towns. He'd wanted to speed—he'd wanted to metal the pedal. His whole body felt like a spring coiled and ready to thrust his foot to the floor. But there were the cops to think about. Anything that drew attention could be fatal. It cost him sweat and a twisting tightness in his chest, but he kept the car steady and endured the slow miles rolling to his fender, slipping under him, slipping away.

So that was tough. And the rearview mirror didn't help much either. Every time he saw the glare of head-lights following him, his spirit seemed to seize up on him. And even when it was only the night back there, he imagined Winter hiding in it, his headlights off, his car steadily gaining ground. That also made the distance seem long.

And then there was the quiet too. At first—after they saw that they'd escaped from the McDonald's—he had Carol and the child to keep him company. It felt good to see them in the backseat, the little girl tucked under

Carol's arm, her face upturned to Carol's and Carol's eyes drinking in the sight of her. The murmur of their voices felt good, they soothed him. "Are you all right?" Carol kept asking. "Have you been eating all right? Aunt Geena said you were sick, are you feeling better? Are you cold? Do you want my jacket? Is that better?" She couldn't stop, sometimes asking the next question before she even got an answer to the last—which was all right because the little girl seemed only to answer, "Fi-ine. Fi-ine. Fi-ine," again and again in the same slow voice, pressing her body deeply into Carol's—"Fi-ine. Fi-ine"—gazing up at her all the while.

In time, though, their voices slowed, faded, ceased. Looking in the rearview, Lonnie saw that the child was sleeping. Carol was humming her a lullaby. Lonnie could hear the tune of it: "Stardust."

A few minutes later, Carol was sleeping too.

After that, he drove through the night in silence. The time dragged and he felt alone.

But then, when he judged he was maybe half an hour outside Meridian, he heard a noise beside him. He looked over and saw the little girl, Amanda, crawling into the front passenger seat. She slid down and bounced into place. Sat there and gazed at him. Her face looked small and serious in the dashboard light.

"Hey," Lonnie said after a minute.

"Hello," she said. "My name's Amanda."

"Yeah. Yeah, I know that. My name's Lonnie. Here, put your seat belt on."

He reached over and pulled the belt out for her.

"I can do it," she said, and mightily snapped it home herself.

"I thought you guys were asleep back there."

"I woke up," she said. "My tummy was hurting."

"Yeah?" said Lonnie. He had no idea what the hell else to say; he didn't hang with children much.

No problem. Turned out this one was a font of conversation.

"You're brown," she said after a moment or two.

Lonnie laughed. "Yes, I am."

"My daddy was brown. I saw a picture."

"That right?" Lonnie glanced at her through the shadows. "Where'd you get all that pretty yellow hair then?"

He saw her shrug. "I don't know. I just got it. My daddy was a sailor. Only he died."

"Oh yeah? That's bad luck. I'm sorry about that."

"I wasn't there," she said. "If I was there? I would've sparkled him and brought him back."

Again Lonnie didn't know what to say. He turned away from her, looked out to the next bend in the night road, the place where his headlights faded into the darkness.

If I was there I would've sparkled him, he thought. *Yeah, well, I know the name of that tune.*

"But I've sparkled other people," the child went on. "Howard. And the man from the plane. I made them feel better."

For some reason he didn't quite understand, Lonnie found this a very poignant thing for her to say. As if by healing those other people, she was really trying to bring back her father. It made his throat feel tight. It made him ache at the impossibility of the enterprise.

"I hear you're not supposed to go around sparkling people," he said. "I hear it makes you sick. Could make you very sick. Could kill you."

"Oh, that's all right," said Amanda.

Lonnie looked over at her. Funny kid. Giving him that solemn stare. "What do you mean, 'Oh, that's all right'? It's all right if it kills you?"

"Yes. Because I'd just go to heaven cause I'm so small."

Lonnie rolled his eyes. "Yeah, well, you're so small, you're not supposed to be in heaven yet," he said. "Heaven might not be ready for you yet. You know what I'm saying?"

She didn't answer. She just went on gazing at him. When he turned to the windshield again, he felt her eyes on the side of his face.

"Anyway, your mother would miss you," he added.

And Amanda said, "Are you my mother's friend?"

"Sure I am," he told her. "I'm your friend too. I'm gonna help you get away from the bad men coming after you."

"That's good," she said.

Again, without knowing why, Lonnie found this poignant. He smiled crookedly at her in the dark.

She unsnapped her seat belt. "I think I'm going to go back to sleep now," she said.

"Okay."

She crawled over the seat into the back, humming to herself: la la la. She was humming "Stardust."

When Lonnie checked the rearview, she was curled up again against her mother, wrapped in her overcoat, her eyes closed. As if she'd never woken up at all. As if he'd imagined the whole thing.

Weird, Lonnie thought. And as he drove on through the night he was aware of a weird feeling inside him, a feeling half oppressive and half sweet. It felt as if his conversation with the child had effected some kind of change in him, though he couldn't have said exactly what it was. He tried to think about it but his mind only slipped off into its usual bittersweet daydreams and he was with his wife again and she was turning to smile at him . . .

The impossibility of the enterprise.

And his heart was leaden with yearning.

That's how the last of the time went by.

Then he was passing through Meridian, the small town on the state border. The Chevy slipped past outlying motels and grand old houses. Paused at the light on Main Street by the stone courthouse and the clapboard town hall. Cruised past the darkened storefronts, all empty and silent in the night. And then, another minute or two and the town was behind him. Lonnie straightened at the wheel—drew in a sharp breath—as he saw the small green sign with the white arrow: "Meridian Mountain."

Another slow minute; another. There was the mountain's base. He turned the wheel and the old car started climbing.

The lodge at the top must not have been closed very long. There was still a small white sign just after the mountain road began: MERIDIAN LODGE. A strip with the word CLOSED had been plastered diagonally across it. Lonnie drove past this and began a steep, twisting climb. The old Chevy groaned under him as it ascended.

The road went up a long distance. Thick evergreen forest clustered close. A strip of stars shone bright before him, but the moon was low now, near enough to the horizon to be hidden by the conifers. The way was dark. There were sudden edges, sudden drop-offs into a deep nothing. And the grade was growing sharper. Gray patches of snow began to appear along the shoulder and through the woods. The Chevy had to strain for speed. Lonnie had to fight to keep it going, keep it under control.

Carol stirred behind him now. "Lonnie?"

"Yeah," he said tensely, leaning toward the windshield.

"Are we there?" she asked him.

And then they were. Another sharp curve, and they passed the tree line. The sky broadened and the road went flat. The pavement spread out in front of them into a small parking lot.

Lonnie released a breath. He felt he had been holding it for two hours and more.

They'd made it. They were on top of the mountain.

He figured they had maybe forty-five minutes to wait until the break of day.

From the woods just below the crest, Winter and his men watched them passing. His long years of professional work notwithstanding, the red-haired killer could not deny he felt a welling thrill of triumph. For four months, his operatives had been chasing this woman. For four months, they had been right behind her, always one step behind. Now he had taken over, and in three days, the thing was accomplished. With anticipation, coordination and leadership, he had gotten ahead of her, and was lying in wait for her arrival.

This was how a new bureau chief set a standard of excellence.

He could not see the others in the trees. Ferdinand and Dewey with their night goggles and their Walthers. Ike Lewis at the wheel of their new black Cadillac, hidden away off the road. They were all there. They were all ready to move at his signal.

Winter drew in a deep breath of the cold night air and waited while the Chevy rolled up the hillside to the lodge.

The lodge stood dark on a last little rise. It was a broad, square two-story structure, modern, wooden, functional, with wide windows to take in the views.

Those views must have been spectacular during the day, because here above the trees the world spread out on every side for miles. As Lonnie pulled the Chevy across the lot, he could see the wide sky and the spiny Milky Way and the black outlines of distant mountains rolling against the stars.

He stopped the car, killed the lights and then the engine. He sat staring at the silhouetted shapes beyond the windshield. He could sense the cold out there and the almost uncanny stillness. In that sudden silence, it was impossible to believe that rescue was on its way.

"Let's see if we can get inside," he said.

"Oh. She's sleeping," said Carol. Lonnie had not heard her voice sound so plaintive before, so gentle. "Can't we just sit here, run the engine? That way we could keep the heat on until the chopper gets here."

Until the chopper gets here. He restrained his little noise of contempt. He turned to look over his shoulder at her. He imagined her hopeful expression in the dark. He imagined what she was thinking: it's over. We've made it now. Chubb's chopper will come for us. It'll take us away. They'll never find us. We'll be free.

Yeah. Well, she was entitled to her hope. She'd fought a good fight and come a long way. But Lonnie didn't buy it. The chopper might never come. Winter might get to them first. He wanted to preserve their gas in case they needed to make a run for it. He wanted to be inside in case they needed to make a stand.

"I think we oughta see if we can go in," he repeated quietly.

And from the shadowy backseat, he heard Carol sigh. But she said, "Okay. Okay, you're right. I get you. Let's go." She handed him her flashlight.

There was a flight of stone steps to the lodge door. Lonnie climbed it while Carol tried to wake her daughter, tried to coax her out of the car. The door was stuck, but it wasn't locked. The lock, in fact, seemed to have been broken away. Lonnie pulled the handle—pulled it harder, grunting, and got the door open. As he stepped across the threshold, he heard animals scrambling for cover.

Lonnie flicked on the flashlight, passed the beam

over the interior. He was in what had been a restaurant, it seemed, a broad open space with picture windows on three sides. Cobwebs hung from every corner lazily rising and falling in every current of air. Leaves and trash and old plastic bags littered the floor. In one corner was a broad table with two broken chairs piled on top of it.

As Lonnie turned, the flash picked out the line of the bar and the shelves behind it. There was still a single stool there as if a ghost were sitting, waiting for his drink.

Lonnie moved deeper into the room, following the pale light. On the far wall, there was a door. Lonnie tried it, opened it. Saw a hall of webs and shadows, of doorways opened and closed: the rest of the lodge, the guest rooms. He shut the door. Turned away.

He moved to an eastern window. Brushed handfuls of cobwebs aside, spitting dust from his lips as he did. Then he used his sleeve to rub the grime from the glass. Clicked the flash off, pressed his face to the pane.

There was a stand of low thin stunted trees. Lonnie could see the stars beyond them and the mountainous horizon. And between the trees and the stars he made out a small field, a stretch of flat ground dotted here and there with conifers. It ran to the edge of a rocky cliff. Lonnie saw patches of snow glinting on the rocks in the last of the moonlight.

He moved from window to window then, scoping as much of the territory as he could make out. There was a sheer drop close to the southern side of the lodge. More parking lot and a telescope viewpoint to the southwest. There were also some hulking shapes hugging the building on that side. He pressed the flash to the glass and shone the light down on them. A Dumpster, a large propane tank, a metal door. He picked them out of the dark one by one.

Carol came in with Amanda.

Lonnie glanced over his shoulder at them. Carol had her daughter in her arms, was holding her against her front. Bundled in her mother's brown overcoat, the child had her legs wrapped around Carol's waist, her arms around her neck. When Carol turned to examine the place, Lonnie saw Elmo clutched in one of the child's hands. Held by the paw, the red monster dangled down Carol's back.

"Jesus, it's cold in here," Carol said. She'd given up her coat to the child and had on only jeans and a blouse.

But Lonnie in his overcoat was beginning to shiver too. "I see a gas tank outside," he said. "Maybe if we find the kitchen we can get the stove going."

"I don't feel well, Mommy," Amanda murmured sleepily.

"I know, sweetheart, I know. You'll be better soon."

Lonnie switched on the flash, played its beam off the walls. He spotted the kitchen door behind the bar.

The bar's wooden flap creaked as he lifted it. He passed through, went to the door. Pushed it open.

"Yeah," he called over his shoulder. "Stove's still here."

Lonnie went to it. Carol came in behind him.

"I'm gonna put you down now, sweetheart," she said. "You're such a big girl, Mommy can't hold you anymore."

She stooped to set the child on the kitchen floor. Amanda leaned against her leg, sucking her thumb. Carol rubbed the little girl's back.

At the oven, Lonnie was twisting knobs. He opened one of the range's doors. Leaned his head down to listen.

"Nothing," he told her. "Gas must be off. The lines seem to run into the cellar, maybe I can find a stopcock down there."

Shivering, Carol nodded. Lonnie could hear her teeth beginning to chatter. He took his gun out of his overcoat, stuck it into his waistband. Then he stripped the overcoat off and draped it across her shoulders. Their eyes met.

"I'll be right back," he said.

She nodded. He lingered there, his eyes on her, about to turn away.

"Hey," she said. Her voice trembled with the cold.

Lonnie lifted his chin at her. "Yeah."

"Thanks," she said. "For everything. I mean it."

"My pleasure."

"Yeah. I'm sorry. You know?"

"Nah. You told me to blow. It was me who came after you."

"Yeah." She stood with the child against her leg, looking up at him. "Only I mean I'm sorry I can't be her."

He felt the words go into him, twist in him. "Hey . . ." he said. "Hey, no . . ."

Carol gave a sour smile. Rubbed her daughter's back as she spoke. "I bet she was really sweet, huh."

Lonnie looked away. "Suzanne."

"Suzanne. She was, like . . . sweet, the sweet type."

"The sweet type," said Lonnie. "Yeah."

"I guess you loved her pretty big-time."

"I guess. Yeah. That's right."

"Yeah," said Carol. "Well, that's what I mean. I'm sorry I can't be her."

Lonnie gave a small, unhappy laugh. "Hey, listen . . ." he said. Then he took her gently by the shoulders and kissed her. Just pressed his lips against hers, long, slow, warm. When he drew away, she followed after, tilting toward him. He kissed her again, softly.

"I'll go see if I can get the heat on," he said.

"Yeah," she said.

Lonnie went to the door.

"I'm tired, Mommy," he heard Amanda say behind him.

"I know, sweetheart," Carol answered. "So am I."

Lonnie stepped outside. Paused a moment at the top of the stairs. He looked out over the parking lot to where the road sank back into the woods. He listened hard for the sound of a car, for anything. But the stillness hung there. He felt the emptiness of the night. He felt the dawn aching to rise. He thought: *Hey. There's a chance, right? The chopper might come. There's still a chance we make it out of here.*

The cold was eating through his sweater and into his skin. He started moving fast now. Down the steps, around the building. He found the door between the propane tank and the Dumpster. There was no knob, just a hole where the lock had been. Lonnie worked his fingers into the hole and pulled. The door came open.

There was a short flight of wooden steps leading into

the cellar. He started down it—and walked into a curtain of cobwebs. Cursing, he swiped the stuff away, pulling it from his lips.

"Yech," he said.

He went down the rest of the way.

The cellar was little more than a concrete bunker, only partially underground. He heard the animals skittering as he came into it, but by the time he played the flashlight over the place, all he saw was junk. There were piles of it. It covered the cellar's dirt floor. It climbed up the walls. Suitcases, furniture, even some tires and car parts. An old washing machine lying on its side. An old lawn mower. Two stuffed armchairs were sitting on top of each other and, above these, Lonnie's flashlight picked out cobwebs drifting over the solitary window. The window was just a long thin rectangle at ground level, its glass gone. Lonnie shuddered as the cobwebs lifted with a movement of the cold night air.

He turned to the wall beside him, to the gas line running indoors from the tank outside. Using the light, he traced the copper tube along the wall. It ran into a pile of tin and plastic—old garbage bags torn open and picked clean by rodents and raccoons. He kicked the trash away. There was the stopcock. Lonnie crouched down and tried to turn it. It was stuck fast.

Crouched there, rubbing one shoulder against the cold, he cast his flashlight beam over the floor until he spied a tire iron. He went and fetched the thing, carried it back to the pipe.

At first, he tried hammering at the stopcock, but the old line threatened to buckle. Instead, he wedged the iron's sharp end into the dirt floor, braced the bar behind one wing of the cock, made a lever of it. That did it. He drew the bar toward him and the stopcock turned. If there was any gas left in the tank, he thought, that ought to get it flowing.

By this time, he was kneeling there. Kneeling on the cold floor, working the stopcock, all his attention engaged.

He didn't hear the footsteps on the stairs, the whisper of an approach behind him.

Then, as he knelt there, he felt something brush against his leg.

Lonnie gasped. Released the tire iron so that it fell against the wall. He spun round, reaching clumsily for the gun in his belt.

The mouse was already dashing for cover, was already disappearing into a jumble of broken furniture against the opposite wall.

Lonnie laughed. Shook his head. "Damn," he said.

And then he froze as he felt the muzzle of a pistol, cold against his neck.

"I don't feel well," Amanda said again.

"I know, sweetheart," Carol said, rubbing her back. "We'll go very soon and then you can sleep and you'll feel better. We're going to take a ride in a big helicopter."

"We are?"

"I sure hope so," Carol said, half to herself.

The child still leaned exhausted against her legs. Carol still had one hand between her daughter's shoulder blades. With her other hand, she began to work a cigarette and her lighter out of her purse.

"Is that man Lonnie going to live with us?" Amanda asked.

She had the cigarette between her lips now. It dangled there, unlit. "Oh . . . I doubt it, sweetheart. He's just our friend."

"He's nice, though. He's not like your other friends."

She nodded. "I know."

"He could live with us if he wanted."

"Yes, he could. But I think he lives with someone else already."

Carol lifted the lighter, paused. It was very still. There was a narrow window beside the oven and she could see through it to a strip of night beyond. She wished the sun would rise. Even now she thought that maybe the ink-blue of the sky was beginning to lighten a little. Or maybe it was her imagination. It was just so quiet. Why did it have to be so quiet? What if the chopper didn't come?

She pushed the thought away quickly. Snapped a flame from the lighter. Torched her cigarette.

She drew the smoke in deeply with a cool sense of relief. She dropped the lighter back in her purse. Back with the envelope that held her passports and her cash.

"Mommy?" said Amanda.

"Yes, sweetheart." She released the smoke on a long sigh.

"Who's that man over there?"

Carol was lifting her cigarette to her lips again, but stopped the movement midway. She felt as if her insides had turned to acid, as if the world had turned sickly green. "Man?"

She spun to see the shadowy figure in the doorway. The cigarette fell from her shaking hand.

"Lonnie?" she whispered hoarsely, but she already knew.

"Hello, Carol," the shadow said. "My name is Winter. I've been looking for you a long time."

Carol held her daughter tightly against her legs. The fear pumped through her like blood. The shadow-figure stepped out of the doorway, came toward her. There was another man right behind him. A very big man, a solid slab of flesh.

"Who is it?" Amanda said.

Carol could barely answer her. "Ssh, sweetheart. Ssh."

"Are they the bad men?" Amanda asked.

"Yes," said Carol. "They're the bad men."

"Oh, now don't scare her," said the one called Winter. He had paused, halfway between the door and Carol. She could just make out his eyes. There was just enough light to flash in them. "We're not that bad. We just have a job to do, that's all. We're just making a living, doing the job we're paid for."

"You think that's an excuse?" Carol said. She cursed herself as her voice broke. She pushed on tearfully. "You think that's, like, an excuse for what you guys do? It's no excuse, man. You hear me?"

She saw Winter lift his shoulders in a shrug. "Take the kid to the car," he said to the slab.

The big man behind him started forward. Carol held her daughter tighter. Amanda clung to her mother's legs.

"Mommy."

Carol stared hatred at the silhouette called Winter. She saw his eyes glint back at her dispassionately.

"We don't want this to be ugly for her," he said.

"Oh, you bastard. You bastard."

Carol trembled with rage and terror, holding on to her daughter. The second shadow came toward her. Carol could see just how big he was. He had huge thick muscular arms. A block of a head that seemed attached directly to his shoulders. At first she thought he was wearing a mask, but they were some kind of goggles. They made his thick face look inhuman and terrifying.

Amanda clung to her harder. "Mommy," she said.

"It's all right, sweetheart," said Carol. There was no way out of this. They'd kill her where she stood, right here, right now. She had to stay alive. Think. Survive. "It's gonna be all right. I'll come and get you. Okay? Just like before. Mommy will come and get you just like she did before."

All the same, when the hulking giant took hold of the child, Carol held on to her fiercely. Amanda wrapped herself around Carol's legs.

"I don't want to," she cried.

Carol was crying too, crying hard. "I'll come for you,

sweetheart. I swear it to God. Mommy will come and get you just like before and we'll go away. We'll ride on a big helicopter . . ."

The monster yanked Amanda's arms free. Lonnie's overcoat fell from Carol's shoulders. Her purse fell on top of it.

"Mommy!"

"Don't hurt her," Carol screamed.

The slab picked the struggling child up.

"Mommy!"

"I'll come for you!" Carol tried to say. She was crying too hard.

The slab carried the screaming Amanda to the door.

The shadow called Winter glanced at him as he passed. "Put her in the car with Lewis. Then go tell Ferdinand he can get rid of Mr. Saxophone. Just do him and toss him in the woods," Winter said. His voice sounded thick with disdain.

"Hokey-dokey," said the giant slab.

"I don't want to," Amanda screamed. She struggled uselessly as the slab carried her out of the room.

Winter turned back to Carol. She stood in front of the big range, bent over with crying, choking on her sobs.

"Now," Winter said to her quietly. "Let's talk about you and me."

Then, from the cellar dark behind Lonnie, came the voice of the gunman: "Okay, nigger-boy, this is all over."

Down on one knee on the dirt floor, Lonnie lifted his hands into the air. The hard gun barrel dug painfully into his neck. The sound of his own heartbeat nearly deafened him.

"You try to do anything interesting and I'll blow your fucking head off," the gunman said. He had a rasp of a voice, faintly Hispanic.

"Okay. Okay," Lonnie said quickly. "What're you, man, a cop?"

"Yeah, that's me. I'm a cop. I'm a cop all over."

Not a cop, thought Lonnie. Good. He fought to keep his voice steady. "Okay," he said. "My hands are up, right? I'm not moving."

"Now gimme your gun. I saw you had one. Just give it to me."

"Okay. I'm going for it."

"Left hand, thumb and middle finger."

"I'm going for it now," said Lonnie. "Real slow." He lowered his left hand slowly toward his belt.

"Just hand it back to me," said the gunman.

"Just stay easy," said Lonnie.

"Oh, I'm easy, nigger-boy. I'm real fucking easy."

Lonnie's hand was unsteady as he lowered it. His

heartbeat was loud. He pinched the butt of his gun between his thumb and his middle finger, just like the man said. He tugged at it. It resisted, stuck in his belt.

"Come on," said the gunman.

"Okay," said Lonnie.

He tugged harder. The gun came free. He worked it out from under his belt. He turned, holding the gun gingerly, bringing his left hand back to deliver the weapon to the man.

The gunman reached to grab the Cougar. He was close. For one instant, even in the dark, Lonnie could see his face. A scary sight. The eyes—the night vision goggles—bugging out at him like insects' eyes beneath the skull-like dome of the head.

The gunman grabbed Lonnie's Cougar.

At the same moment, Lonnie grabbed the tire iron.

It was still half upright, stuck in the floor, leaning where it had fallen against the wall. As Lonnie turned with the gun, as skull-face reached for it, Lonnie's right hand dropped and found it blind.

It was all the same motion, handing back the gun, grabbing the iron, continuing around with the iron in his other hand. Even on one knee, Lonnie had the leverage for a full, whiplike blow.

The iron made an awful noise as it connected with the big dome of the gunman's head. A squelching thud: a melon falling to the sidewalk. Lonnie saw one side of the gunman's head cave in. The goggled eyes seemed to bulge out even further.

Then the gunman was lurching backward. Lonnie leapt up. He raised the tire iron for a second strike.

But the gunman dropped to the floor: a marionette

with cut strings. He lay jerking and twitching at Lonnie's feet. Lonnie watched him, fascinated, horrified, until the body lay still.

Then he let his breath out. He stooped, picked up his gun, his Cougar. Scooped up the other gun—Skull-face's—and shoved it in his belt. Above his panting breath, above his heartbeat, he heard voices.

He heard Amanda wailing: "Mommy! Mommy! I don't want to! Please!"

Jesus, he thought. They already had the girl. How had they come so quietly, so fast?

Or had they already been here, waiting for them?

He listened to the child's screaming. She was just upstairs, just outside. He heard a door—a car door— thunking shut. Amanda's screams diminished. They had put her in their car.

The Cougar in his hand, Lonnie hurried to the stairs. He went up quietly but quickly, three steps at a time. In two strides, he was at the open door. He was about to charge through.

But then a giant slablike figure stepped into the opening, framed against the night.

Lonnie and the slab confronted each other. For a second, both men were still, frozen in surprise. The big man's goggles peered at Lonnie.

Then Lonnie reacted, leveling his gun.

But the big man was faster. With a clubbing blow of his right forearm, he knocked Lonnie's arm aside, drove it into the wall. The Cougar dropped out of Lonnie's grip. The next blow—the back of the giant slab's right fist lashing out like a snake—hit him square in the face. Bright lights exploded in front of him as he went tumbling backward down the stairs. His arms pinwheeled as he fell and he hit the floor hard, the breath rushing out of him.

In the next second, the giant came storming down after him.

And Winter, meanwhile, advanced toward Carol slowly.

She backed away from him, crying. *You and me?* she thought. *Let's talk about you and me?* What the hell did that mean? She backed away.

She came up against the range. Her eyes moved everywhere, looking for a way out.

There was no way out.

He advanced on her. She knew she was going to die.

And she thought crazily: *Poor baby. She has no coat.* In the frantic confusion of her thoughts, this seemed a fact of terrible importance. She saw her coat and Lonnie's coat through the shadows. They were lying on the floor in front of the oven door beside her, the door Lonnie had left open. Her purse lay on top of the pile. They had all fallen during the same struggle while Carol and Amanda fought to hold on to each other. Somehow this underscored Carol's sense of grief. It made her feel how cold her daughter would be, how unprotected.

Then the sight—of the coats, of the purse—was

blocked by Winter's body as he pressed in close. Carol looked up at him. Through the dark, through her tears, she made out the contours of his face, the predatory ease of his smile.

And she breathed his cologne. His cologne and his hot breath pouring down on her. He was going to kill her and she trembled with fear and hatred. She could feel the white heat of her hatred pouring off her in waves.

"Ooh, look at you," he said. "You're mad, aren't you? You are one angry lady. You'd like to rip my eyes out, wouldn't you?"

"Your eyes first," she said roughly. "I'd start with your eyes."

She knew at once she had said the wrong thing. She heard the way his breathing changed. She knew that sound full well. Her anger excited him.

"Mm." It was a hoarse sound deep in his throat. "You're a tiger, a mama tiger, aren't you?" he said. "All that rage. But what can you do? You're helpless, aren't you? If you try anything, I'll kill you. And then what becomes of poor, poor Amanda?"

He pressed in even closer. The warmth of his breath and the thickness of his cologne and the heat of her hatred made Carol's stomach churn. She gritted her teeth. "You're a sick son of a bitch" was all she could say.

Again, she could hear how her anger turned him on. Her anger and her helplessness. *Is that what he wants?* she found herself thinking. *Is that what he wants from me?*

"You say that now," Winter was murmuring. "But you're going to change your mind about me, Carol. You're going to come to think of me in a whole new way." He reached up and touched her cheek with the back of his hand. Carol couldn't help herself. She gasped at the touch; turned away as if it burned her. He caressed her cheek as his hand sunk to her throat. "You're gonna come to understand that I make the sun rise in the morning. I make the oceans roll. I make the wind blow. You'll see. By the time I'm done with you, I'll be your whole world, everything."

A groan broke from Carol as the man's cold fingers stroked her neck. She closed her eyes. Licked her dry lips. Tried to think. Had to think. She worked the streets. She knew men. The way they formed pictures in their minds and how they wanted women to be like those pictures. That's what they paid her for. To be like the pictures in their minds. They were in a relationship with you before they even met you.

Winter's lips came closer to her ear. "Oh, I've thought a lot about you, Carol," he said.

That's right, she thought. *He's thought a lot about me.* She opened her eyes. Maybe that was the way out.

She glanced down at the range.

Sniffing back her tears, she cleared her throat. "Oh yeah?" she said. Still harsh. Believable. But just a little bit interested. Just starting to come around to him. Like the picture of her in his head. "Like, what've you been thinking?"

That was it. That was what he wanted. She felt the hitch in his breathing. She felt his lips burn against her cheek. She had his number. He nuzzled her and her hand began to move out slowly from her side, to slide slowly along the range, over the knobs.

"Oh, I've been thinking about how smart you are," Winter murmured. Pressed against her, close against her. She could feel the hard bulge in his pants rubbing lightly against her jeans. "How smart and cool and tough. I don't think you're going to be smart and cool and tough with me, Carol."

That's it, she thought. *I'm tough and angry but I'm at his mercy.* She let out a whimper. "Look, you're not going to hurt me, are you?" she said.

Oh yeah, that stirred his sauce, she could feel it. He moaned and burrowed his face into her curls.

She slid her hand further along the stove.

His tongue snaked over the top of her ear. "I have a place we're gonna go, Carol. A place where we can be alone. It's going to be your Bible school. That's right. I'm going to teach you who's the master of creation."

Carol wasn't paying attention. Her hand closed around the oven's knob.

But at the same moment, Winter grunted angrily. His hand tightened on her throat, choking her. He drove his crotch up against hers. Somehow she'd pissed him off.

"Are you listening to me?" he snarled. "Do you hear me?"

Carol was lifted onto her toes, her hand came off the oven knob. She felt Winter's fingers closing off her breath.

"I'm talking to you," he said. "I'm talking to you, do you understand?"

"I'm listening," she squeaked. Her submissive tone was well rehearsed. She'd used it dozens of times. "I'm listening, I swear to God. I didn't mean to do anything bad."

Winter kissed her, hard. Pressing his lips into hers until it hurt. Pushing his tongue through her teeth, lashing it back and forth inside her mouth.

Then he pushed her roughly back against the stove. Straightened away from her. Turned away with a growl.

Carol grabbed the range's knob quickly. Gave it a half turn, not enough to make it hiss too loudly.

If it hissed at all. If Lonnie had turned on the gas.

When Winter faced her again, she was rubbing her throat. Her head sunk down, her eyes lifted, as if she hardly dared look into the searing light of his face.

He grinned at her, breathing hard. Trying to recover his control. "All right, Carol, we're gonna go now," he said. "We're gonna go to Bible school."

Carol swallowed hard. "Can I . . . ?" she said meekly. And meekly, she reached down for her purse.

Winter stepped forward swiftly. Swooped down and scooped up the purse. He held it in one hand, kneaded it with his fingers, feeling for a weapon.

"I only wanted a cigarette," Carol said, giving him her frightened look.

He tossed the purse to her. She reached inside, brought out a cigarette and her lighter. Lit the cigarette and drew in deeply.

"Thank you," she said. "I appreciate it."

Winter surveyed her as if from a great height, as if she were a piece of conquered territory. He was smiling to himself, smiling distantly.

"That's better," he said. "Come on now."

Carol shivered. Sniffed. Brushed tears from her cheeks. In the same meek voice she said, "Can I take my coat . . . please?"

Winter heaved a large sigh. His excitement was ebbing for now. He looked around and saw the coats on the floor.

Had Lonnie turned on the gas?

Winter bent over, reached for the coat. His head came level with the oven door. He stopped. He looked at the door. His eyes narrowed.

He smelled something. Carol could see it. He smelled gas.

She shot her cigarette into the oven, a perfect bogart. Winter's expression changed as the burning reed flew through the open door.

And nothing happened. Winter turned. He watched the cigarette's arc. Watched it disappear into the oven. Nothing.

Then the gas exploded.

There was a hoarse cough and the blue flame billowed out. The force of it knocked Winter sideways, sent him rolling, his hands thrown up instinctively to protect his face.

But Carol didn't hang around to watch. Clutching her purse to her side, she was already running for the kitchen door. An instant more, and she was out, behind the bar. At the bar. Leaping over it.

There was no time to look through the windows, to see where the others were. She knew they were outside. If she went out there they'd have her.

She headed to the right instead. To the door into the hallway. If she could get there, get to a room, get out a window, maybe she could slip away.

She threw the door open. She plunged headlong into the shadowy hall. And at the same time, she heard footsteps. A loud roar of rage.

"Goddammit!"

Winter was right behind her.

9

And Lonnie now, flat on his back on the cellar floor, looked dazed through swirling stars to see the giant slab thundering down on top of him.

The slab was reaching into his overcoat. He was drawing out a gun that seemed a toy in his great paw. But it was not a toy. He was bringing it round to point it at Lonnie as Lonnie lay staring.

Lonnie pulled Skull-face's gun from his belt and fired.

The roar of the pistol was deafening. And the giant slab answered with a deafening roar of his own:

"Hey! Shit!"

He kicked out angrily. Pain shot up Lonnie's arm as his second gun went flying.

The giant drew a bead again, ready to blow Lonnie away.

Lonnie twisted to the side, shot his feet out, one behind the big man's ankle, the other kicking him hard in the shin.

There was another explosion as the slab's gun went off. A high whine as the bullet ricocheted off the concrete walls. Then it was like a tower toppling. The big man fell through the dark to the cellar floor.

Lonnie let out a war cry and leapt on him. Found his gun hand. Grabbed it.

The big man twisted, trying to get at him. Trying to get his gun hand free.

Lonnie grabbed something—he didn't know what—a broken chair leg it felt like. He lifted it. Hammered the giant's head with it again and again.

This annoyed the giant. He roared and flung Lonnie across the room.

Lonnie could not believe the strength of the man. Shot, beaten—and still, with one arm, he sent Lonnie flying. Lonnie slammed into a mountain of debris and sprawled in it, feeling sharp edges cut his hands, jam into his back.

He struggled to get on his feet again, but it was too late. The big man was already standing. Already bringing his gun up. He pointed the barrel directly at Lonnie's chest.

"You shot me, you son of a bitch," he said.

And then he keeled over, dead.

At almost the same moment, Carol was careening down the lodge's dark hall. The cobwebs clutched at her face. The walls seemed to bend and weave around her. She could barely see through the clustered shadows.

Black doorways seemed to open to the left of her. A pool of blackness gathered straight ahead. But she was too afraid to slow down, to look. She was too afraid to stop and find her way. Winter must be crossing the bar now, she thought. He must be coming to the door. In a second he'd step into the hallway and see her.

In a panic beyond thought, she glanced back over her shoulder. All the dark was jouncing, weaving, as she ran. But she thought there was another movement back there. The door opening. Winter charging forward.

There was an open doorway to her left. She dodged through it.

This was a mistake.

She was in an all-but-empty room. A small square with a picture window nearly filling one wall. By the rising light through that window and the light of the fading stars, she could make out closets to her left, an old mattress lying in the corner to her right, a broken chair on top of it.

She stood there panting, her heart pounding. She could see the picture window didn't open. There were small vents to either side of it, but she'd never fit through them. She couldn't get out. She was trapped in here.

She turned to head for the hall again.

It was too late. She heard Winter's steady tread approaching.

"Uh-oh," she heard him growl in the hallway. "I'm coming for you, Carol. I'm coming for you—and I'm really, really pissed off." He laughed. "Tough little bitch."

Carol stood there frozen like the hunted creature she was. Her eyes darted back and forth, but there was nothing to see, nothing to do. The boards in the dark corridor creaked as Winter approached the room. His footsteps sounded closer and closer.

She tried to think. Some means of escape, some strategy. There was nothing. Nothing at all. There wasn't even a door she could shut. It had been taken off.

Swallowing tears of panic, she moved quickly to the mattress, seized what was left of the chair. It was just the seat and the back, but it was metal, heavy enough. She carried it to the spot beside the doorway. Pressed herself there against the wall. When Winter came through, she would launch herself at him. She might get one swing at his head. It was doubtful. She wasn't strong. And he'd be careful. He'd be quick. It was long odds he'd kill her dead before she even took a step.

But there was nothing else to do. Not a single thing. She had to try it.

So she stayed pinned there against the wall, her hands sweating on the chair back. And she listened to the footsteps nearing, listened to the old boards creaking closer and closer. Listened to Winter's voice, just yards away now.

"Carol, Carol, Carol. You've made this more fun for me than you can possibly imagine."

She tensed herself, lifted the chair, ready to attack. He was right outside.

And then she heard something new. A different sound. A short, high chirping.

The footsteps in the hallway stopped. There was silence. Pressed against the wall—pressed into the wall—Carol held her breath.

Winter spoke again. "What," he said.

He was talking into a radio or a phone or something. Someone had called him. Carol swallowed a sob of fear. Pressed there, she listened.

"Christ," she heard Winter say. "Don't move."

And then his footsteps began again.

But now they were hurrying away.

Ike Lewis had only barely heard the gunshots. He was sitting behind the wheel of the Cadillac. All the doors were locked, and the car's windows were shut. The heater fan was going.

And the kid—the kid was in the backseat, shrieking like a banshee.

"I want my mommy! Mommy! Mommy! Mommy!"

"Aw, shut up already," Ike Lewis muttered.

She threw herself against the rear door. She scrabbled at the door, pulled at it, tugged at it, making squeaky noises. Even Lewis found her a pathetic little figure in her red pajamas with the smiling bear, with her stuffed red monster doll clutched under one arm. But the pathos of it just made him angrier. He couldn't wait till Winter came back and drugged the little bitch.

"I don't want to! I don't want to!" she screamed.

Lewis raised his voice. "Would you shut up! And quit that. It's locked. The door's locked. Only I can unlock them. You're stuck. You're not going anywhere. Little twit," he added under his breath.

His head was throbbing. His nose—broken by the Mondeo's air bag—was also throbbing. His whole body, in fact, was one big pulse of pain. It would have given him an enormous sense of relief to just haul off and crack the kid a good one—the way he did one of his own kids when they were acting up in the backseat.

But this one was little Miss Precious. He wasn't allowed to clock her unless Winter said so. So she just went on screaming. Ike Lewis shook his throbbing head and sighed.

And so the sound of the first gunshot in the lodge's cellar—thunderous as it was—reached him only faintly. And it didn't bother him at all. He figured it was just Ferdinand taking care of the black guy.

Ike Lewis looked through the windshield to the right, toward the cellar. He expected to see Ferdinand and Dewey returning to the car. Instead, he heard another shot. Clearer this time, because he was paying attention.

"Now what the hell was that?" he said quietly.

"Mommy! Mommy! Mommy!"

"Wait a minute. Would you shut up a second?"

The kid didn't shut up. Concerned, Lewis opened the door and stepped out into the parking lot.

He stood in the cold beside the open door, listening. The child went on screaming in the car behind him. He really let her have it this time.

"*Shut up*," he shouted at her, loud.

That had some effect at least. The girl fell into a quiet sobbing.

In that quiet, Lewis stepped toward the hood of the car, toward the lodge. He listened. There was nothing now. He heard nothing at all.

He went into his pocket for his radio. He beeped Ferdinand. Listened. Nothing. He beeped Dewey. Nothing, no answer.

Lewis lowered the radio. Stood there, staring into the dark. He wished his head would stop aching so he could think more clearly.

"Hey, Ferdinand? You okay?" he shouted. "Dewey?"

Nothing. The night was quiet.

"Shit," said Ike Lewis. He pressed the button for Winter.

In a moment, he heard the red-haired man's voice on the box. "What."

"Yeah, Winter, I think we got a problem out here," Ike Lewis said. "Gunfire from the cellar. I can't raise Ferdinand or Dewey."

"Christ," Winter said. "Don't move. You hear me? Stay with the kid and watch out for Blake. The kid is the only one who matters. We can forget the rest of them and just take her out of here. Just don't move and stay with the kid, you copy?"

"Yeah, yeah, copy, roger. Stay with the kid."

"I'm on my way," Winter said.

"Right," said Ike Lewis.

With another sigh, he slipped the radio back into his pocket. He cast his eyes once more over the night. The blue of the far horizon was growing lighter now. It was nearing dawn. The features of the lodge, its doors, windows, clapboards, were starting to be more clearly visible.

But Lewis saw nothing moving there. No one.

He stepped back around the door. Lowered himself behind the steering wheel. Pulled the door shut.

He looked over his shoulder into the backseat. "All right, listen up, kid, here's the deal," he said.

But he never did get to explain the deal to her.

Because the kid was gone.

12

Amanda hurled herself through the darkness, blind with tears. She headed for the lodge. She headed for her mother. She didn't think about the bad man in there. She didn't think about the cold on her bare feet. She didn't think about anything. The man in the car had opened the door. She had thrown herself over the front seat, Elmo clutched under her arm like a football. She had scrambled through the opening, shot straight past the man's legs and shot away. She wasn't trying to escape or anything. She was just trying to get back to her mother. Her mother would help her. Her mother would take her someplace safe. They would ride in a big helicopter.

She ran for the lodge.

Spurred on by her terror of the man behind her, sure he was running after her, sure he was about to reach out any minute and grab her from behind, she ran without stopping, without daring to look back, until she reached the steps that led up to the lodge door.

She was about to scramble up those as well. But then the bad man with red hair stepped out above her.

Amanda gasped. She felt as if her heart had stopped. The bad man with red hair loomed gigantically against the stars, blocking her way. She stood petrified at the foot of the steps, staring up at him.

But he didn't see her. She was too small. He was

looking out above her, looking toward the parking lot, toward his car.

So Amanda turned and scrambled for the corner of the lodge. Running to get around the side of the building, the side opposite the cellar door. She heard the deep shouts of the bad men behind her. She knew they were calling to each other. And she knew they would come after her. She could almost feel them already, running after her, reaching for her. Any second, she thought they were going to grab her. She was too terrified to look back and see.

Then she was around the corner of the building. Running past the concrete base that was the upper section of the cellar. Running, waiting for the hand to reach out behind her. Waiting for the hand to grab her.

And then it did.

Amanda let out a little scream as the arm snaked around her waist, as she was jerked backward off her feet.

Then her scream was cut short as a hot palm clamped hard over her mouth.

"Don't scream, sweetheart. It's me, it's Lonnie. Don't be afraid. Just keep quiet. It's me."

Lonnie held the child close against him. He felt her body fluttering in his hand like a bird. For a moment, he closed his eyes in relief.

He had climbed out through the cellar's narrow window only moments before, right after the enormous thug had fallen dead. He had recovered his Cougar again and snatched up the slab's gun too, a Walther P99. He had stuck both guns in his belt and then he had climbed out. He had crept under the windows of the lodge to the corner of the building. From there, he could peek around at the parking lot. He could just make out Winter's car down at the end of the road, right where the lot began.

Lonnie watched. He could see the tall, thin thug standing by the car's open door. He could see him talking into his radio. He could even hear the murmur of his voice.

But he never saw the child. She had already run past his line of vision. She was already around the corner, already at the stairs.

Lonnie was absolutely shocked when she shot around the building and went motoring past him. He grabbed her without thinking, pulled her to him, his left hand cutting off her scream. He hugged her, closing his eyes in relief.

Then he turned her around so he could look at her.

"You okay?" he said softly.

The child nodded, frowning, fighting tears. "Where's Mommy?"

Yeah, thought Lonnie, *that's the question.* The odds seemed to him about a hundred to one that Winter had gotten to her. In which case, she was either dead or wished she was. Which didn't seem like a very comforting thing to tell the kid.

So as soothingly as he could he said, "Well, the important thing right now is that you're here with me and we're safe, right?"

And then the window above his head exploded.

Lonnie threw his body over Amanda's as the big picture pane blasted out into the night. Kneeling there, bent over her, he felt the fragments raining down onto his back, felt the cold prickle of glass on his neck, heard the shards pattering into the earth all around him.

There was a clanging thud to his side. Lonnie chanced a look. He saw a portion of a metal chair settle onto the ground.

He looked up. A mattress came through the broken window. Carol crawled out on top of the mattress. She dropped down onto the earth beside him, gasping for breath.

She had busted out of the little room.

Silently, the child broke from Lonnie's arms and rushed into hers. Openmouthed with shock, still unsteady on her feet, Carol staggered as the little girl flew into her. Then she wrapped herself around her daughter, knelt beside her, murmured through her tears.

After a moment, she looked over Amanda's head at Lonnie. "Can we go now?" she said.

Lonnie laughed. "Sounds like a good idea to me."

Crouching low, he crept back to the edge of the building. He drew the Cougar out of his belt. He peeked around again at the parking lot. The air was growing lighter now. Lonnie had a clear view of the figures moving by the car.

Behind him, Carol said softly, "What's that?"

Lonnie didn't answer. He watched Winter and the driver moving to the Cadillac's trunk. They popped the trunk open.

"Listen," said Carol. "Listen."

"What?" Lonnie lifted his head. He listened.

"You hear it?" said Carol.

And in a moment, he did.

A soft dawn breeze was rising. And within the whisper of the breeze was another whisper, a stuttering breath, an almost silent rhythm of the air.

Lonnie's lips parted. He glanced up at the brightening sky.

"It's the chopper," Carol said, her voice cracking. "Oh God, it's the chopper. It's on its way."

As the sky grew brighter, they could see it. A Black Hawk coming in fast and low toward the cliff, sailing for the flat patch of ground beyond the rocks at the end of the little field. The dark dot of the chopper against the blue sky took slow shape as it approached and descended. Its stuttering whisper became a low thunder.

For a moment, Lonnie's spirits lifted.

Then he turned and looked down the drive. Fear squatted on his heart like a toad.

From where he was, crouched at the corner of the lodge, he could see the two men, Winter and the driver. They were starting to move away from the car. They were moving back toward the building.

They were both wearing night goggles now to pierce the predawn shadows. And they were both carrying weapons. Winter had some kind of sniper machine—a genuine M24 maybe. The driver's piece looked mighty like an AK.

Lonnie gripped the Cougar harder in his sweating hand. The men were too far for a shot in the dark. He'd only draw their fire. And they stayed far, moving toward the opposite side of the building. The driver led the way around the edge of the wall. Winter trailed behind. Lonnie saw the red-haired man's head moving as he took in the lie of the land.

"It's coming, Lonnie," Carol said behind him. She was breathless with hope and excitement now. "It's coming down. We gotta run for it. He's not gonna wait for us. We gotta go."

Lonnie glanced back over his shoulder. No, no, no. It was no good. In order to get to the helicopter, they would have to break through the scraggly stand of trees and then cross the open field to get to the landing site. It was a run of about a hundred yards, a touchdown run.

Winter and his man had it covered.

From the opposite side of the building, from a post by the cellar door, Winter and the driver would have a clear shot at them every step of the way. They would pick off Carol first to stop Amanda. Then they'd get him. Then they'd come for the child.

"Come on, Lonnie, come on," said Carol.

She had to raise her voice as the chopper thundered louder. Its insectile shape was clear now as it clawed the blue air above the cliff.

Lonnie drew a deep breath. He could feel his heartbeat rising into his throat, almost gagging him.

"We can't go yet," he said.

"What're you . . . ?"

The chop of the Black Hawk grew louder and louder.

"You gotta wait here," he said above the noise. He shifted the pistol in his hand, the Cougar. He drew the Walther from his belt. "You hear what I'm saying? You keep Amanda here until I give you the signal. Then you run across that field and get in that chopper and don't look back."

"What're you . . . ? We gotta go, Lonnie," Carol said. "We gotta go now."

"You hear what I'm telling you?" Lonnie shouted at her fiercely. "Wait for the signal, then run like hell."

She stared at him, holding her daughter close. The chopper beat the air. Then she nodded once quickly. "Okay. What's the signal?"

"Either I get killed or they do," Lonnie said—and he ran for the stand of trees.

There were maybe ten yards between the end of the lodge wall and the line of small conifers. The minute he broke cover and headed for them, the rifles opened fire.

To the thunder of the chopper and the thunder of his heart came the thunder of the weapons as they spat bullets into the rocky turf. The mountain, so quiet just moments before, now drummed with noise as, head down, Lonnie hurtled wildly over the open ground. He fired back blindly, thrusting his arms out, pulling the triggers of both pistols at once. Large chunks of dirt kicked up to the right of him. Sparks flew as rifle slugs glanced off stone. For three seconds that ticked at their own dismal pace he felt his whole body exposed to the sweeping barrage. He pulled the triggers of both pistols once, twice, again.

Then he was in the trees, on the ground. Twisting around with the pistols in his hand. Panting. Unhurt.

The Black Hawk was settling down now, dropping the last distance from the sky to the ground. The sound of its blades seemed to swell up and fill the dawn air. Cutting through it, the sound of the rifles coughing bullets came in bursts. Branches snapped off and chips of wood flew over Lonnie's head.

He pressed low to the ground. Looked out through the trees. He could make out one man, the driver, stretched prone behind a rock beside the lodge wall. He had the AK out in front of him. He was panning it over the trees, letting off fire at intervals. Lonnie had no shot at him, no chance of hitting him at all.

But that was all right. He had a better idea.

Rolling onto his side on the cold earth, he stuffed the Cougar back in his belt. Then he rolled onto his belly. He raised the Walther in one hand. Steadied his wrist with the other.

He aimed for the propane tank beside the Dumpster.

He had no idea whether it would work. He figured he had four or five shots left in the Walther, another one or two maybe in the Cougar. If he aimed close to the building, if he got off enough rounds, maybe he'd hit the line, maybe he'd cause a spark. He just didn't know.

He ducked down a moment as the AK fire crashed through the branches above him. The chopper drummed the air behind him. He held the gun steady.

Then he pulled the trigger twice and the lodge exploded.

The chopper noise, the gunfire, his own heartbeat—all were swallowed as the tank went up with a single echoless roar. The stars went out, the trees came clear, a corner of the dawn turned morning-bright. The whole left side of the building was swallowed in a rising billow of flame.

Lonnie didn't see the two riflemen die, but he saw the blue-orange storm of light lift the man on the ground behind the rock and engulf him completely.

Then he was on his feet. He was waving his gun hand wildly.

"That's the signal!" he screamed through the noise. "That's the goddamned signal!"

But Carol already had the idea. She was running for the trees with Amanda in her arms.

She tore through the brush, she shot past Lonnie as the flame-light settled. He had a quick glimpse of her illumined face contorted with effort and with fear. The child clinging to her. Elmo bouncing against her back.

Then they were gone, past him, running across the field. Lonnie took one more glance back at the building. It was burning on one side and by the glow he saw debris and empty ground. There was no one left moving.

He turned his back on the place and went after Carol, running for the chopper.

15

The dirt and pebbles flew in waves. Chunks of snow lifted from the dead grass and rolled away. They were blown by the wind from the chopper's blades as the Black Hawk slowly lowered itself to the earth.

Carol was almost halfway across the field, still carrying Amanda, clumsily dodging the big rocks that littered the ground and the small trees that grew up here and there on the sere plateau.

Lonnie caught up with her quickly. He ran beside her, one hand on her arm, one still clutching the Walther.

The stars were gone. The sky was light blue now, but the sun was still behind the distant mountains. The big helicopter drifted down and down, coming out of silhouette, showing its red and white sidelines. Lonnie could see the outline of the pilot through the windshield.

Then the aircraft landed. Its noise encompassed them until it almost wasn't noise at all, just a great throaty throbbing of air.

Carol and Lonnie took another few stumbling steps toward it. They were just approaching a slender pine. There, by its roots, Carol hit a patch of snow and slipped. She let out a cry as she lost her balance.

Lonnie was there. He had her by the arm. He held her upright. She paused a moment and then set Amanda down on the ground.

In that moment, Lonnie glanced back toward the lodge.

And he saw Winter coming for them.

He was driving the black Cadillac. The big car spit dirt, whining, as it skirted the little stand of trees and shot toward them over the field. Its tires shuddered on the rocks but it was coming so fast that it seemed almost to fly above the uneven ground.

Carol looked back and saw it too. Another few seconds and it would run them down. They'd never make it the rest of the way.

She turned to him. He saw her lips move, her voice drowned by the chopper. He thought she had whispered, "Jesus."

"Go!" he shouted at her. "Go!"

He shoved her. She grabbed Amanda's hand and ran.

Lonnie stood where he was, in front of the pine tree. The Cadillac sped toward him. Its grill seemed to grin at him as it bore down.

Lonnie lifted the Walther in both hands. He aimed for the Cadillac's windshield. He figured he had three seconds before it hit him. He figured he had one shot a second. He squeezed the trigger.

A hole appeared in the windshield. A web of cracks flew out around it. The car never slowed. Lonnie squeezed the trigger again and the windshield shattered.

But the car sped on. It just kept coming. Lonnie had to dodge to the side now if he was going to get out of the way.

He stood where he was. He squeezed the trigger.

Then he jumped to the side. But it was too late.

The fender caught him in the hip and he flew over the hood, tumbled and somersaulted across the hard metal, flew through the air and came down hard. He was alert through all of it, aware of the impact and the long tumbling fall. He felt himself tearing and breaking inside. He felt himself lofting across what seemed a terrible distance to a certain crash. He knew he was about to hit.

And then he did hit and he felt his insides shattering.

The Cadillac went straight on and flew into the pine tree. It lifted onto its side. Rolled over onto its hood. Its windows blew out, the glass twinkling in the dawn. It slid several yards across the hard earth, the rocks sending up sparks beneath it. Then it came to rest a little way from where Lonnie had fallen.

Lonnie lay still. He was conscious. He could feel the life force draining out of him. He could feel the blackness swimming in to take its place. The noise of the chopper seemed far away now. Everything seemed far away.

With a great effort, he raised his head. He saw the Caddy as it came to rest. He saw it catch fire. The flames snickered up from the engine for a second. And then the gas tank blew with a whump that shook the earth beneath him.

The car lay black and dead in the heart of the burgeoning flames. Lonnie saw only darkness and stillness within the broken windows.

That was done then, he thought. And grunting with pain, he tried to turn, tried to look out over the field. Carol and Amanda must almost be at the chopper now. Maybe he would see them reach it. Maybe he'd live long enough to see them lifted safely into the air.

But when he finally managed to bring his head around, he felt a sadness close to heartbreak.

They had not reached the chopper at all. They weren't even trying.

Amanda had broken loose from her mother. She had pulled her hand from her mother's hand and she had turned around.

She was running back across the field toward Lonnie.

16

The girl's movement had taken Carol by surprise. It was a long moment before she could pull up, before she could turn, before she could start back after her daughter. By then, Amanda was already halfway between her and Lonnie. She had almost reached the burning car and was running with all her might to where Lonnie lay.

Lonnie was watching. He saw Carol turn. He saw her trying to shout over the noise of the chopper. He saw her throw out her arms and start running back after Amanda. She was shaking her head. He could see her shouting, "No!"

Lonnie wanted to stop the child, shout at her to go back. But he couldn't shout. He could barely move. He lay where he was, his strength failing. He watched the child running toward him.

The child ran on, coming abreast now of the burning Cadillac. Carol was far behind, coming after her, reaching out. She would never stop the little girl in time. Amanda was already passing the blazing car.

And then Winter leapt out of the flames and grabbed her.

His clothes were on fire. His flesh was smoking. His face was a streaked mask of blood and pain and rage. He had crawled out of the far window, the one Lonnie couldn't see. He had crawled around the front of the car. As the little girl passed he flew, burning, bleeding, across the distance, reached out and wrapped a hand around her ankle.

Amanda screamed and fell. She hit the ground hard. Blazing, Winter climbed to his knees, still gripping her ankle. Even with the chopper's thunder, Lonnie could hear him screaming down at her.

"Touch me! Touch me! Touch me!"

Lonnie closed his right hand. The Walther was gone. With an enormous effort, he lifted his left hand. He moved it to his waist. Found the Cougar still in his belt. He drew the gun out.

Winter clutched at Amanda, dragged her over the ground to him. She shrieked and shrieked, struggling against him, clawing at the ground, but he drew her, all the while screaming:

"Touch me!"

Carol ran toward them, reaching out.

Lonnie leveled the gun.

"Judgment Day, motherfucker," he whispered.

He pulled the trigger and blew Winter's head off.

What was left of Winter's body flopped to the earth, burning.

Amanda was free. She jumped to her feet. She began running toward Lonnie again.

But now Carol had caught up with her. She had caught hold of the child's shoulder. The child struggled and reached out, reached out and down for Lonnie, for his right hand stretched out on the ground.

She twisted and Carol's grip slipped. She had her daughter by the wrist now. But Amanda, straining, was leaning far forward, was stretching down, was almost able to touch Lonnie's hand.

She reached for him, reached for him, pulling hard, crying. And now she almost touched his fingertips.

Lonnie summoned the last of his strength. He drew his hand away from the child. He laid it wearily on his chest.

A moment later, Carol pulled her daughter up into her arms.

She held the child close. She stood there holding her, looking down at Lonnie. Lonnie could see she was crying. She was crying hard, sobbing. She was clinging to her child and crying and shaking her head at him. Shaking her head to tell him she couldn't, she couldn't. She couldn't risk her daughter's life. Not for him. Not for anyone.

Lonnie nodded to her. He understood. It was all right. Letting out a breath, he lay back against the earth.

When he turned his head, he could see them. Carol was backing away from him now. Still crying, still shaking her head at Lonnie. Then, reluctantly, she turned away.

She hurried across the field to the chopper. All the way, the child was looking back at him over her mother's shoulder. Looking back and reaching for him as she was carried farther and farther away.

Sayonara, baby, he thought. *Stay alive.*

Now they were at the end of the field, nearing the shadow of the chopper's whirling blades. A man was standing in the chopper door. Carol reached him. She lifted her child off her shoulders. Handed her up to the man in the machine.

Lonnie watched her. He saw her look back at him one last time. He could see she was still crying. She climbed up into the chopper.

You wander down the lane and far away . . .

The helicopter rocked and roared. Slowly, it lifted into the air.

. . . leaving me a song that will not die . . .

Then it was rising, gradually at first, then swiftly. Lonnie turned his head to watch it go. It shimmered upward, then lanced into the sky. The sky was growing brighter. The chopper rose higher and higher. The sky grew brighter still. Lonnie lay on his back and saw the craft receding, fading and fading away into the dazzling brightness of dawn.

The chopper grew smaller and smaller in a sky gone almost blindingly white. Then it was gone completely. There was nothing above him but the vast bright sky. Everything had become the vast bright sky.

E pluribus unum, Lonnie thought.

He closed his eyes. He could just make out Suzanne. Turning to him. Smiling.

The vast bright sky.

ACKNOWLEDGMENTS

I would like to thank my research assistant, Astrid Oviedo de Miano, for her work on this book; Donald Harrison for taking time to talk to me about his music and his life; Dr. Scott R. Anagnoste for medical information; my agent, Barney Karpfinger, for his tireless support; and, as always, my wife, Ellen, who contributes more than I can say.

ALSO AVAILABLE FROM

ANDREW KLAVAN

Animal Hour

POCKET BOOKS

3003

Visit
❖ Pocket Books ❖
online at

---

www.SimonSays.com

Keep up on the latest new
releases from your favorite
authors, as well as author
appearances, news, chats,
special offers and more.

SIMON & SCHUSTER
A VIACOM COMPANY
www.SimonSays.com

Pocket
Books

2381-01